W9-BMO-942

"A success from top to bottom . . . with a level of sophistication and humanity that's rare for any story of this kind."
—ROB CLOUGH, *THE COMICS JOURNAL*, ON LIFE ON EARTH BOOK 1: *LOSING THE GIRL*

LIFE ON EARTH • BOOK 2

# GRAVITY'S PULL

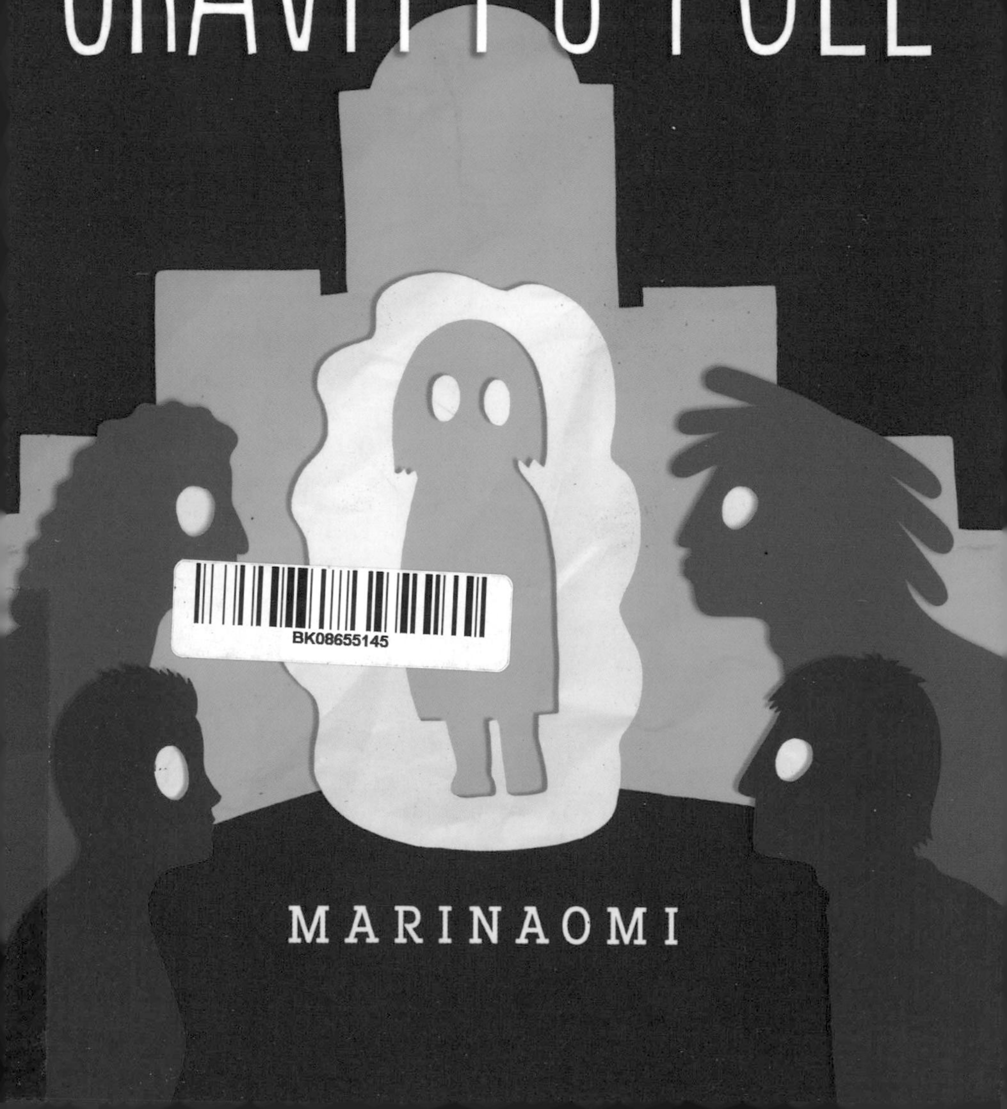



MARINAOMI

What happened in

# LIFE ON EARTH · BOOK 1
## LOSING THE GIRL

Claudia Jones, one of Blithedale High's brightest students, has gone missing, and rumors are swirling.

Emily Hiroko Baker has terminated an unplanned pregnancy and started to realize that her hookup, Brett Hathaway, isn't letting her into his life.

Brett is struggling with his own unrequited crush, on his lifelong friend Johanna, and with family problems he'd rather keep to himself.

Nigel Jones is growing up—slowly—after getting dumped and figuring out how to be a friend to a girl without pressuring her for something more.

Paula Navarro has told Emily their friendship is over. Maybe Emily was too self-absorbed. Maybe Paula was just jealous. Even Paula's not sure.

But things are only going to get weirder. Paula and Nigel have seen signs of Claudia around town—at least it *might* have been Claudia—and felt some strange effects . . .

Content warning: Sexual assault

Graphic Universe™
A division of Lerner Publishing Group, Inc.
241 First Avenue North
Minneapolis, MN 55401 USA

For reading levels and more information, look up this title at
www.lernerbooks.com.

**Library of Congress Cataloging-in-Publication Data**

Names: MariNaomi, author, illustrator.
Title: Gravity's pull / MariNaomi.
Description: Minneapolis : Graphic Universe, [2018] | Series: Life on Earth ; [2] |
    Summary: Claudia Jones has returned to Blithedale High School, but rumors
    about her possible alien abduction persist as everyone begins to feel the
    strange effects of her presence.
Identifiers: LCCN 2018014446 (print) | LCCN 2018020403 (ebook) |
    ISBN 9781541542693 (eb pdf) | ISBN 9781512449112 (lb : alk. paper) |
    ISBN 9781541545267 (pb : alk. paper)
Subjects: LCSH: Graphic novels. | CYAC: Graphic novels. | Alien abduction—
    Fiction. | Missing children—Fiction. | High schools—Fiction. | Schools—Fiction.
Classification: LCC PZ7.7.M339 (ebook) | LCC PZ7.7.M339 Gr 2018 (print) | DDC
    741.5/973—dc23

LC record available at https://lccn.loc.gov/2018014446

Manufactured in the United States of America
1-42843-26507-8/24/2018

LIFE ON EARTH · BOOK 2

# GRAVITY'S PULL

## MARINAOMI

Graphic Universe™ · Minneapolis

FOR MYRIAM GURBA, WHOSE GRAVITATIONAL
PULL I CAN NEVER RESIST

# PART ONE

## Nigel Q. Jones

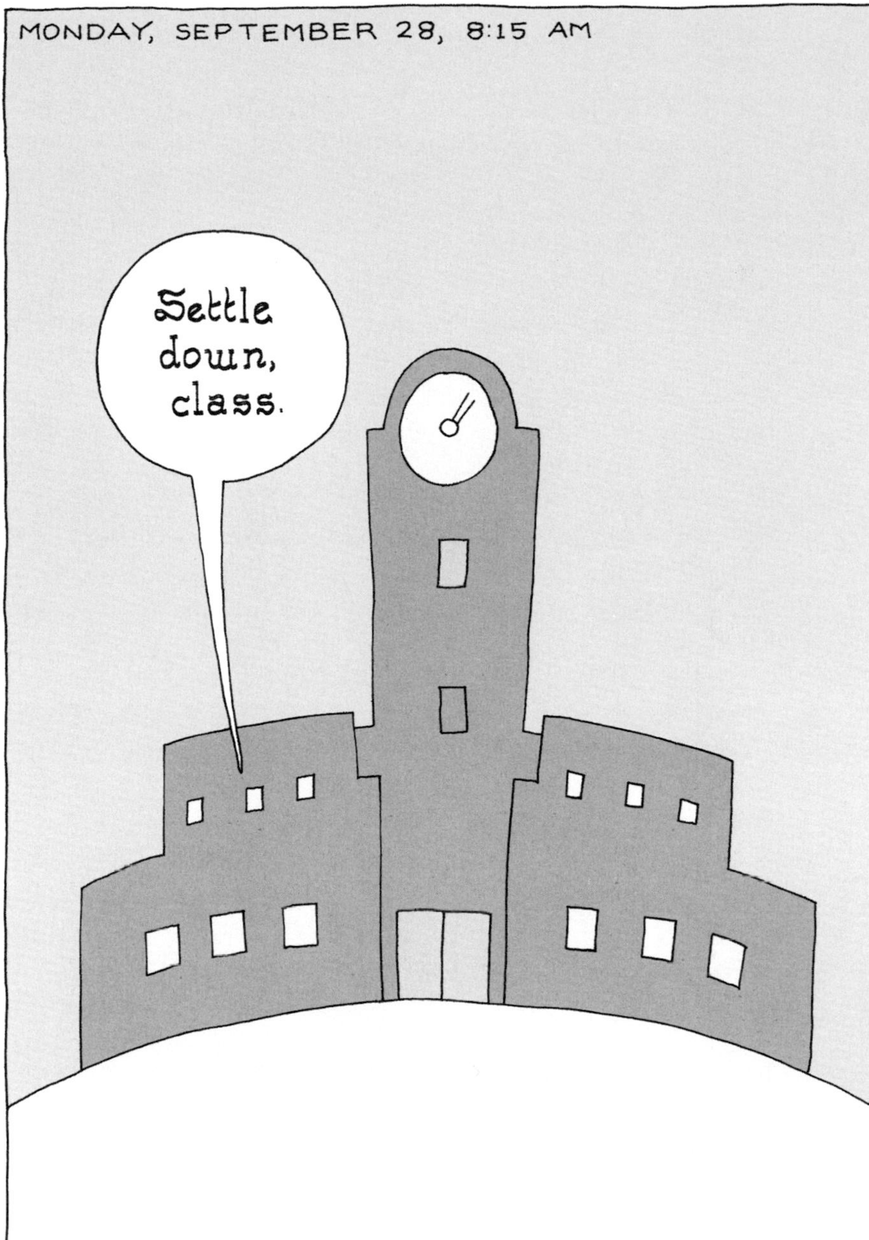
MONDAY, SEPTEMBER 28, 8:15 AM
Settle down, class.
BLITHEDALE HIGH SCHOOL - JUNIOR HOMEROOM

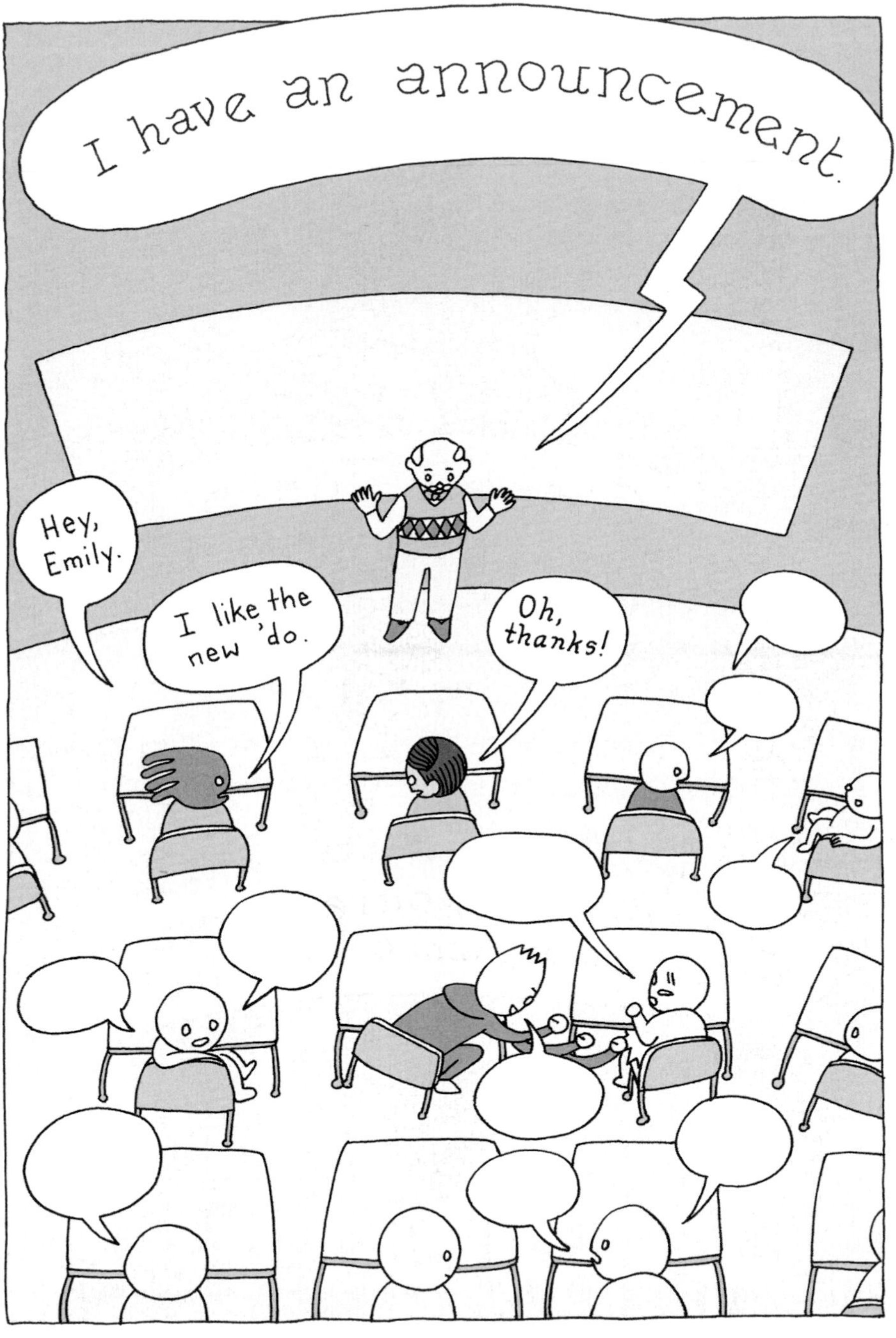
I have an announcement.
Hey, Emily.
I like the new 'do.
Oh, thanks!

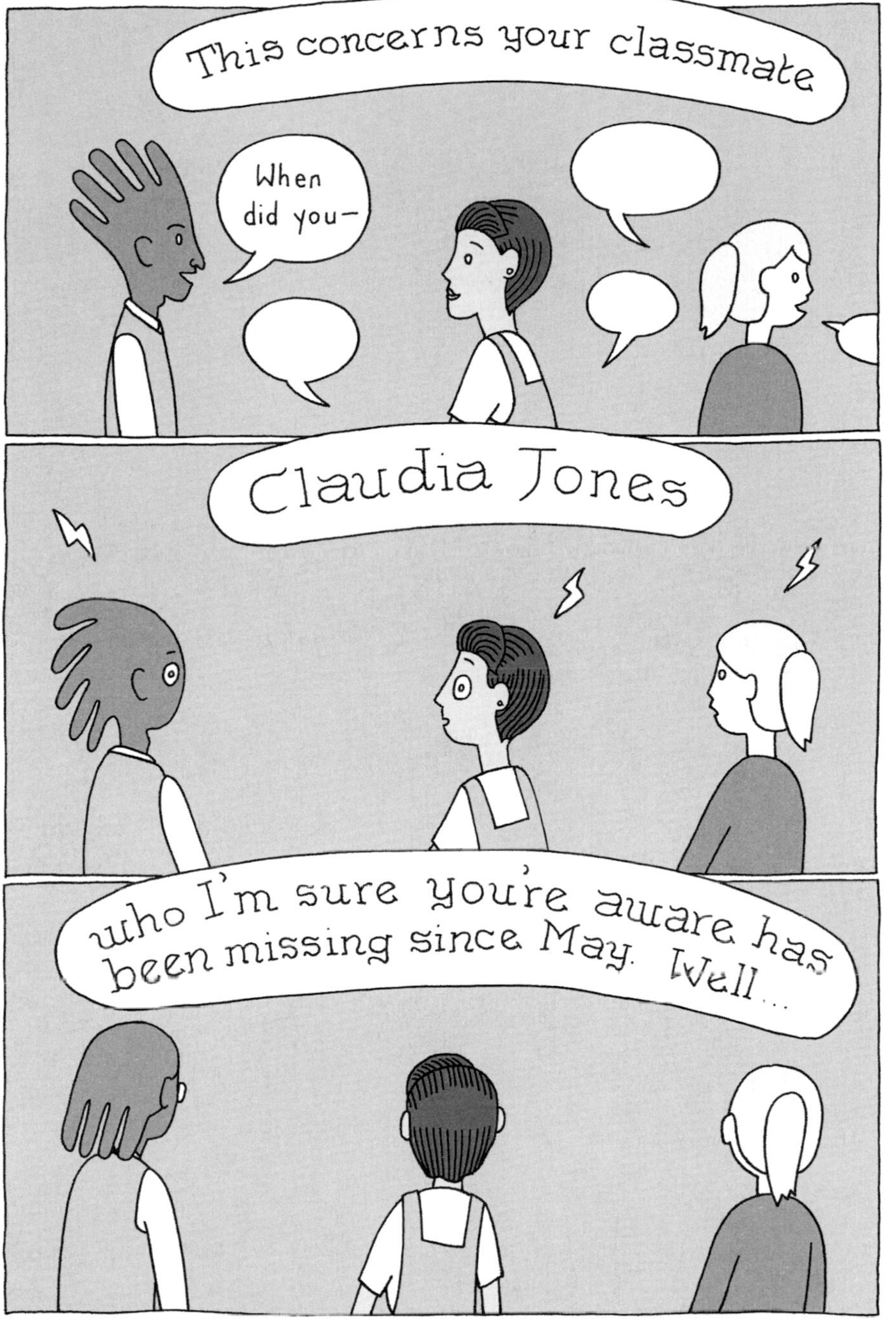
This concerns your classmate
When did you-
Claudia Jones
who I'm sure you're aware has been missing since May. Well...

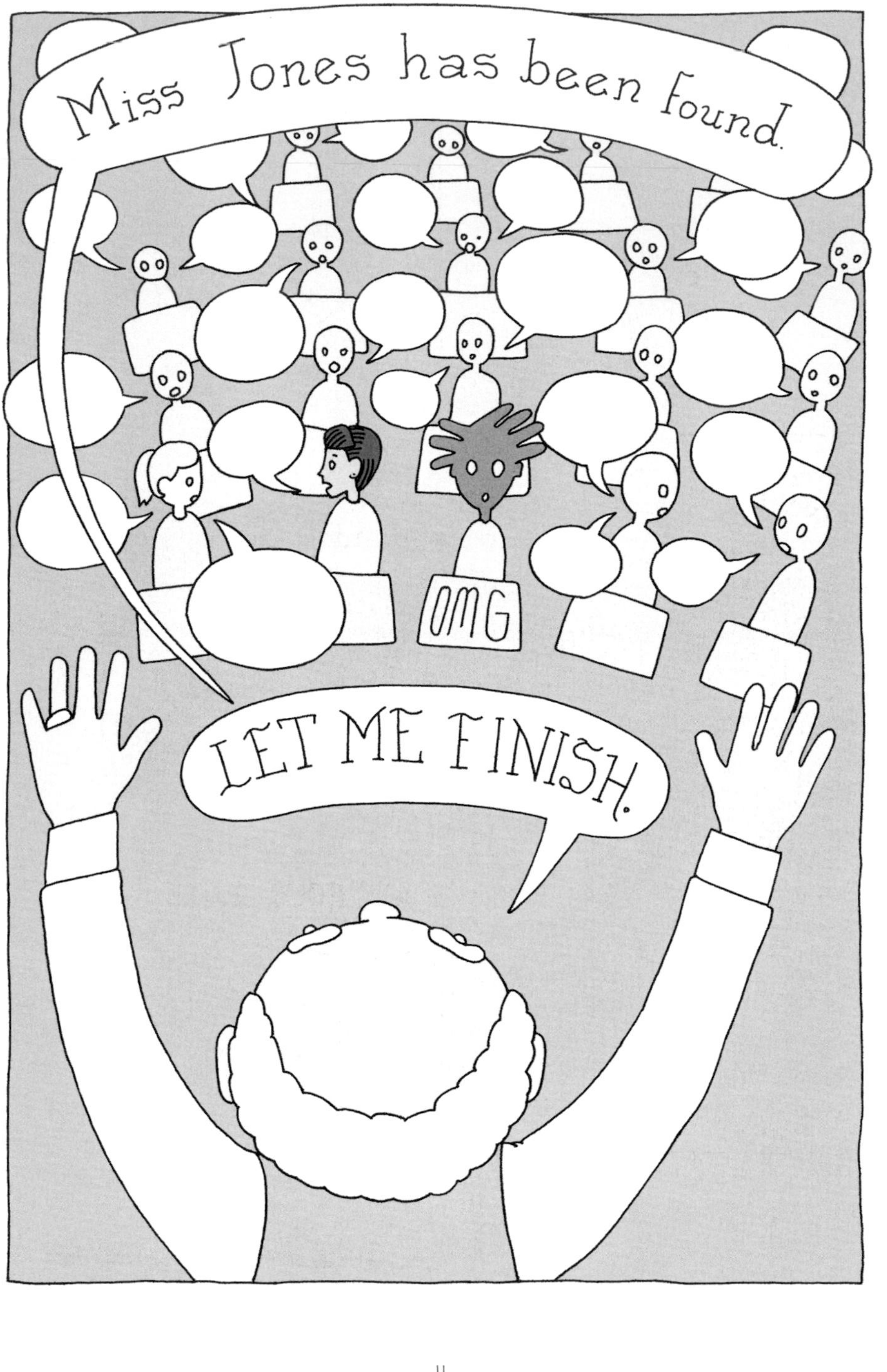
Miss Jones has been found.
OMG
LET ME FINISH.

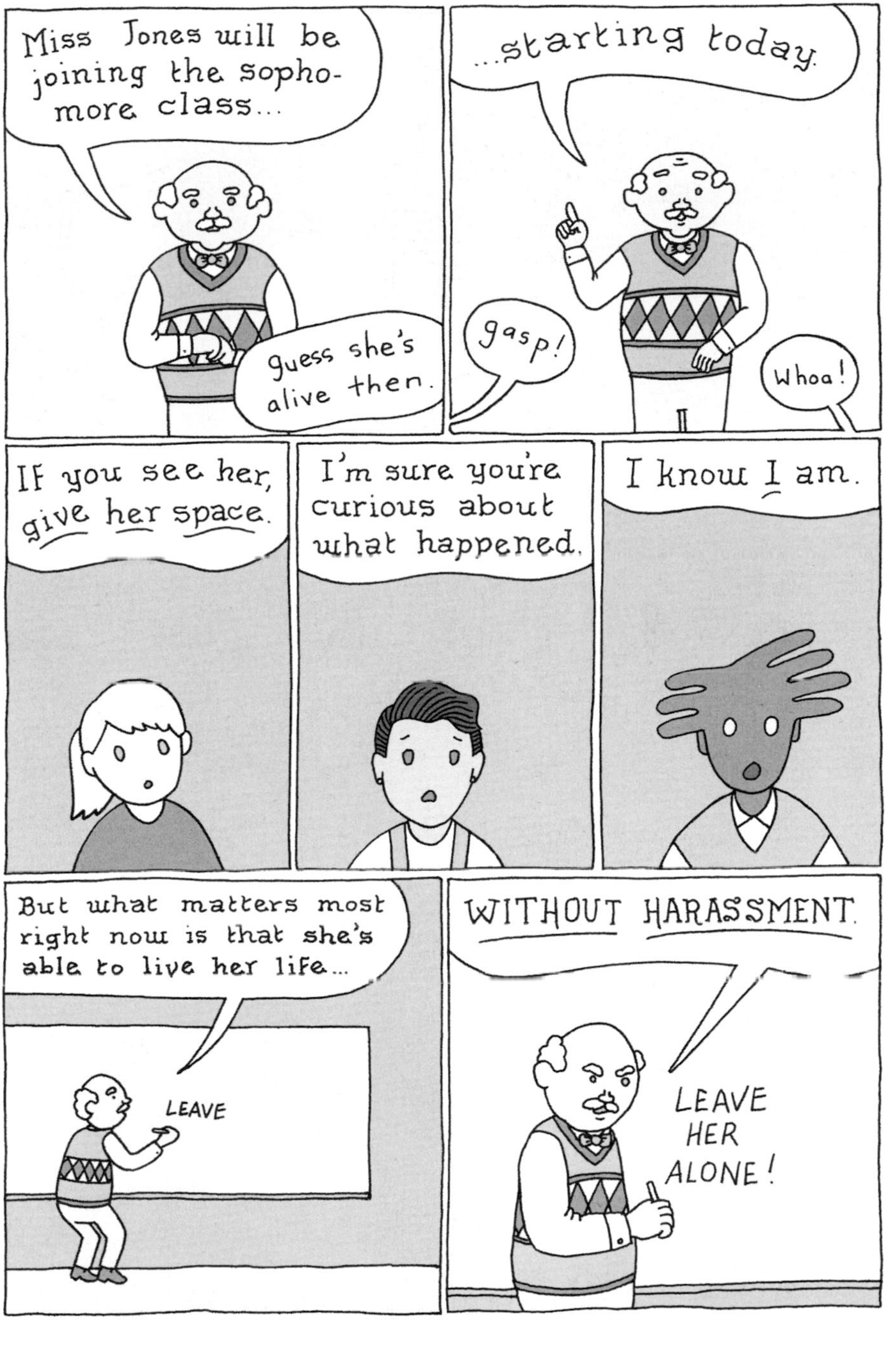
Miss Jones will be joining the sophomore class...
Guess she's alive then.
...starting today.
gasp!
Whoa!
If you see her, give her space.
I'm sure you're curious about what happened.
I know I am.
But what matters most right now is that she's able to live her life...
LEAVE
WITHOUT HARASSMENT.
LEAVE HER ALONE!

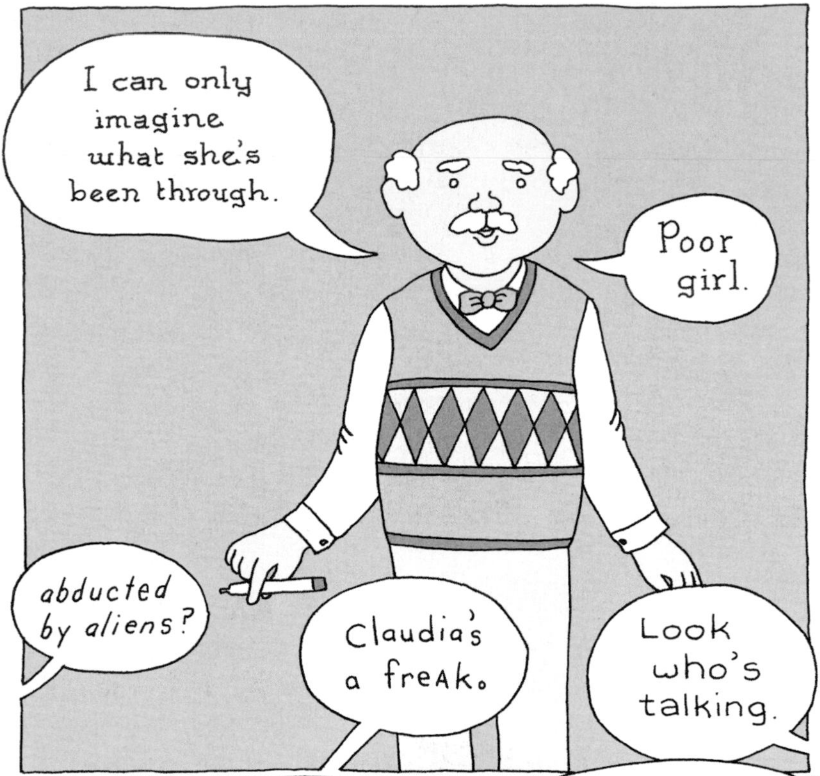
I can only imagine what she's been through.
Poor girl.
abducted by aliens?
Claudia's a freak.
Look who's talking.

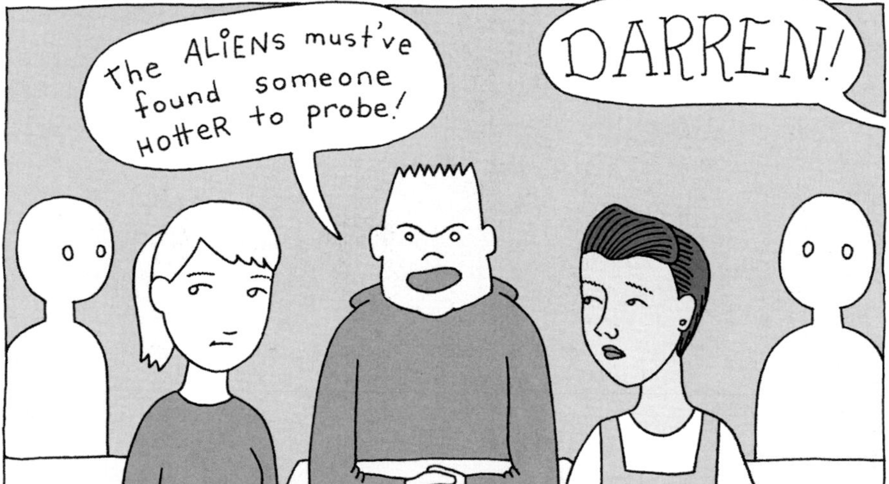
The ALIENS must've found someone HOTTER to probe!
DARREN!

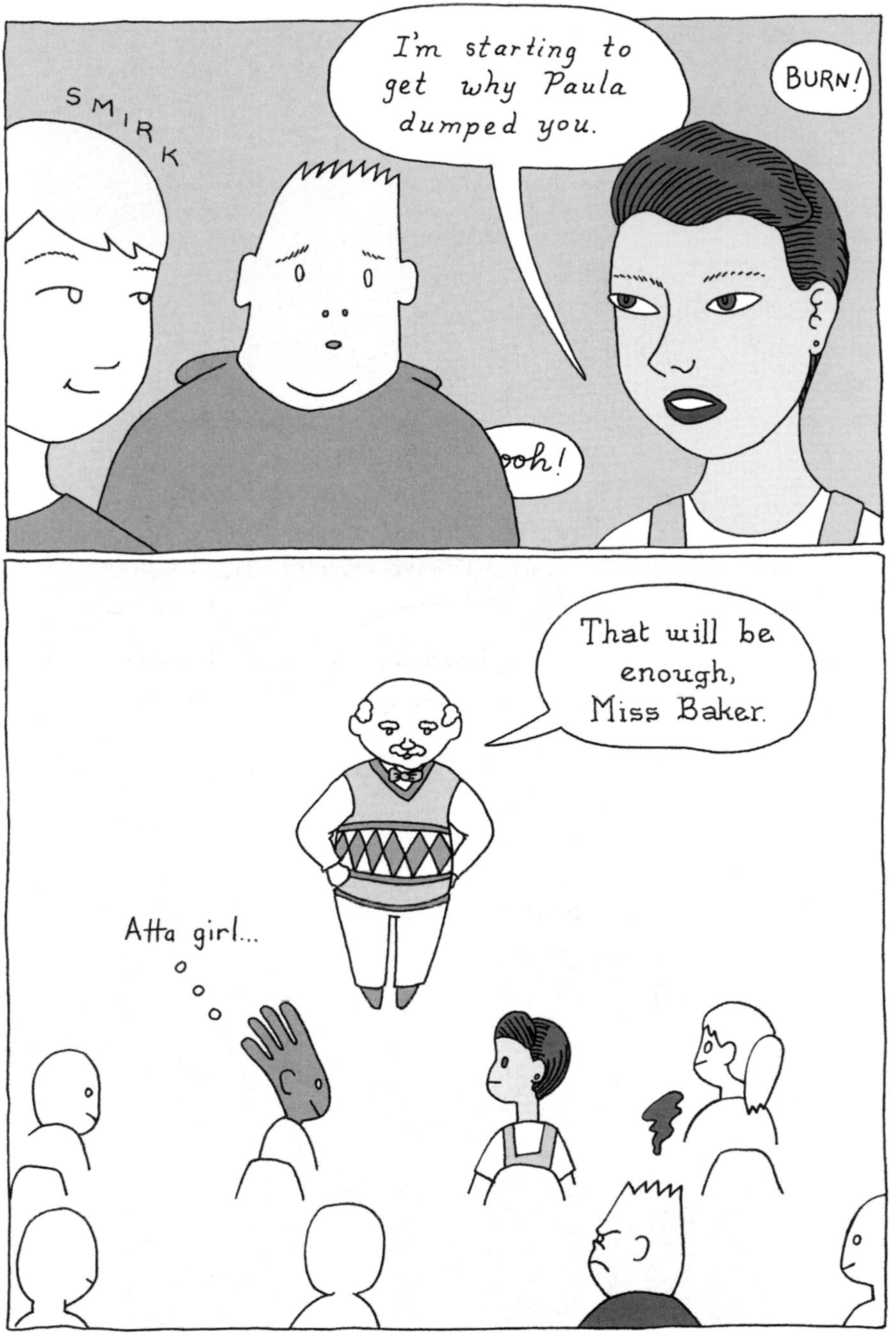
SMIRK
I'm starting to get why Paula dumped you.
BURN!
ooh!
That will be enough, Miss Baker.
Atta girl...

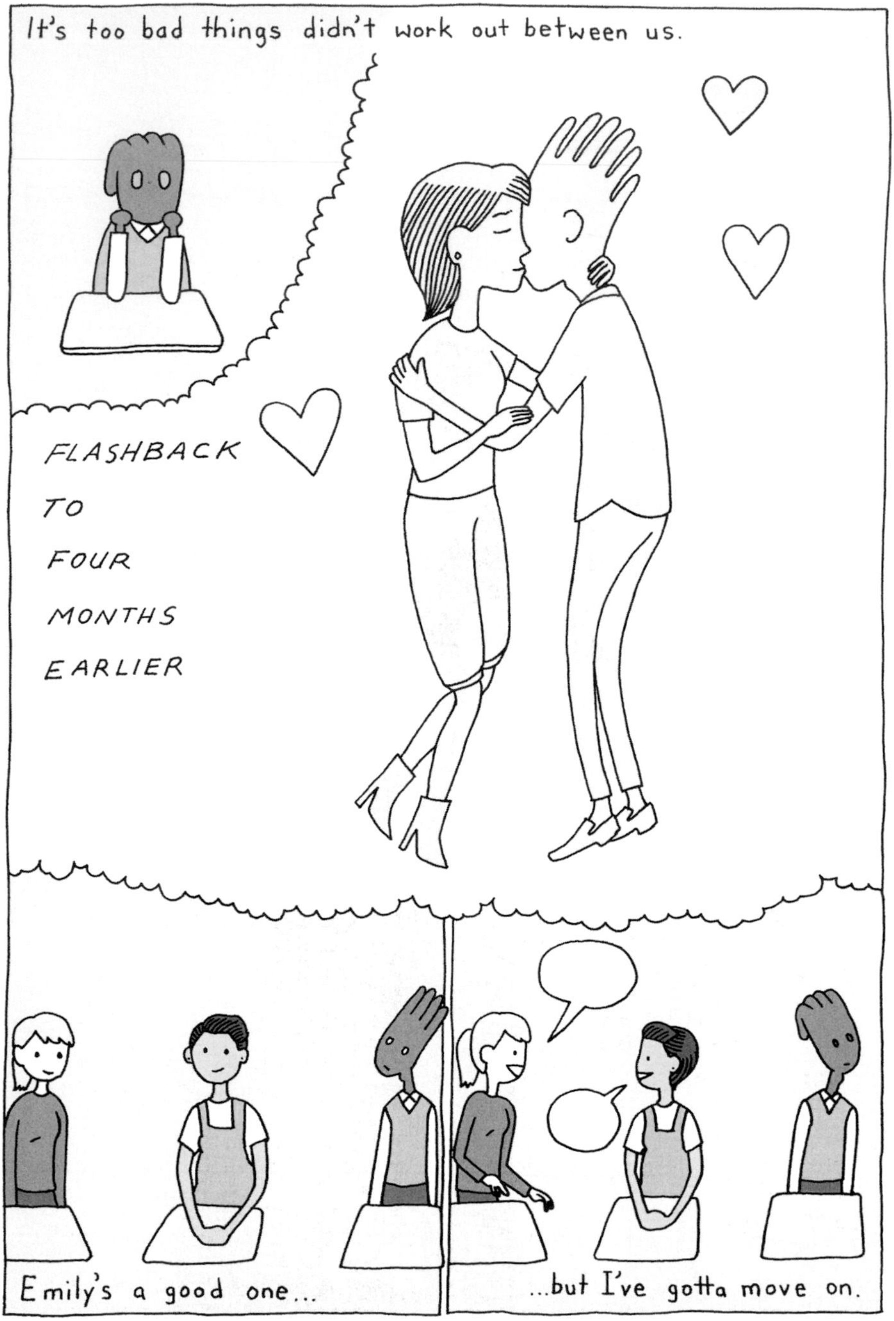
It's too bad things didn't work out between us.
FLASHBACK TO FOUR MONTHS EARLIER
Emily's a good one...
...but I've gotta move on.

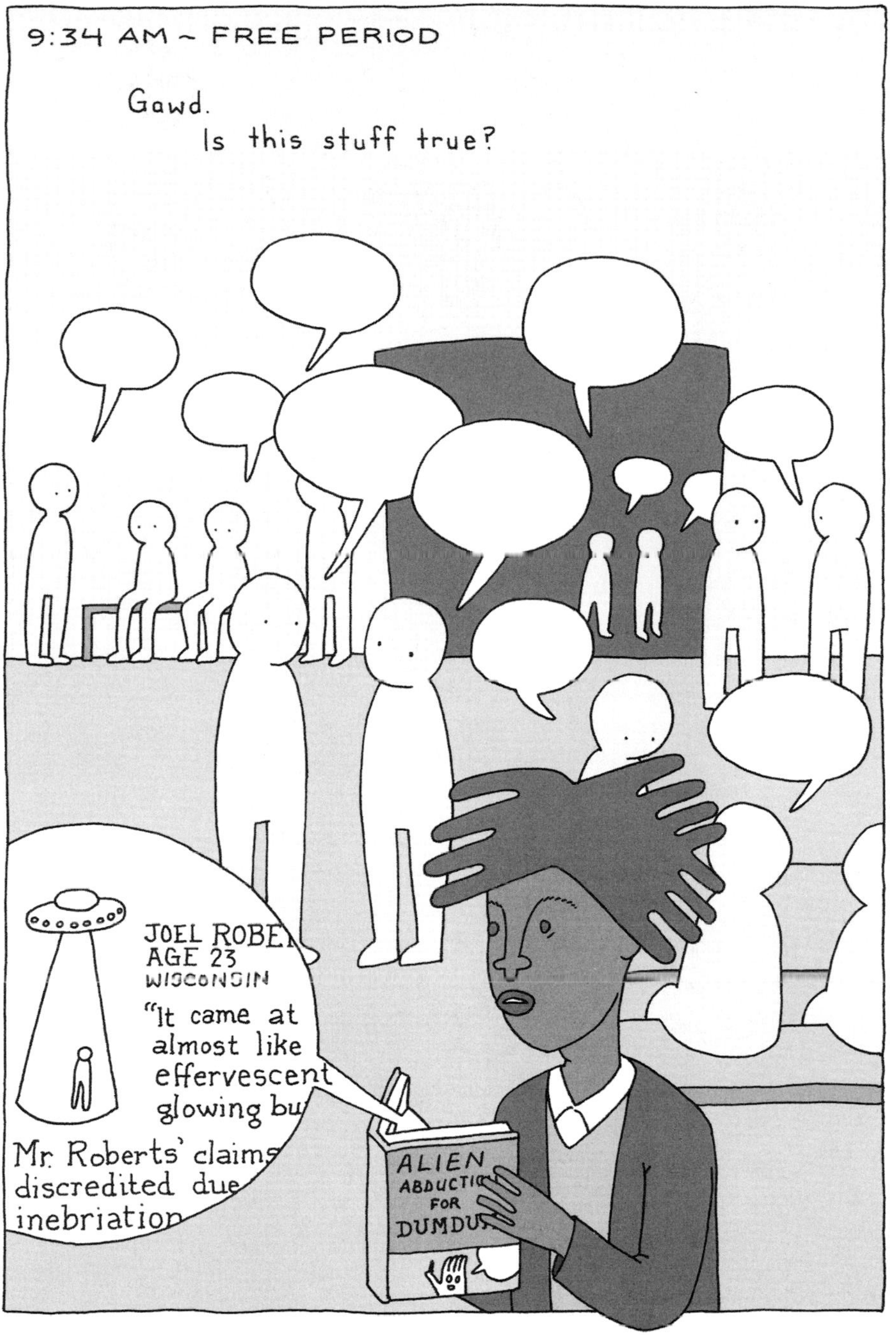
9:34 AM ~ FREE PERIOD
Gawd.
Is this stuff true?
JOEL ROBE
AGE 23
WISCONSIN
"It came at
almost like
effervescent
glowing bu
Mr. Roberts' claims
discredited due
inebriation
ALIEN
ABDUCTI
FOR
DUMDU

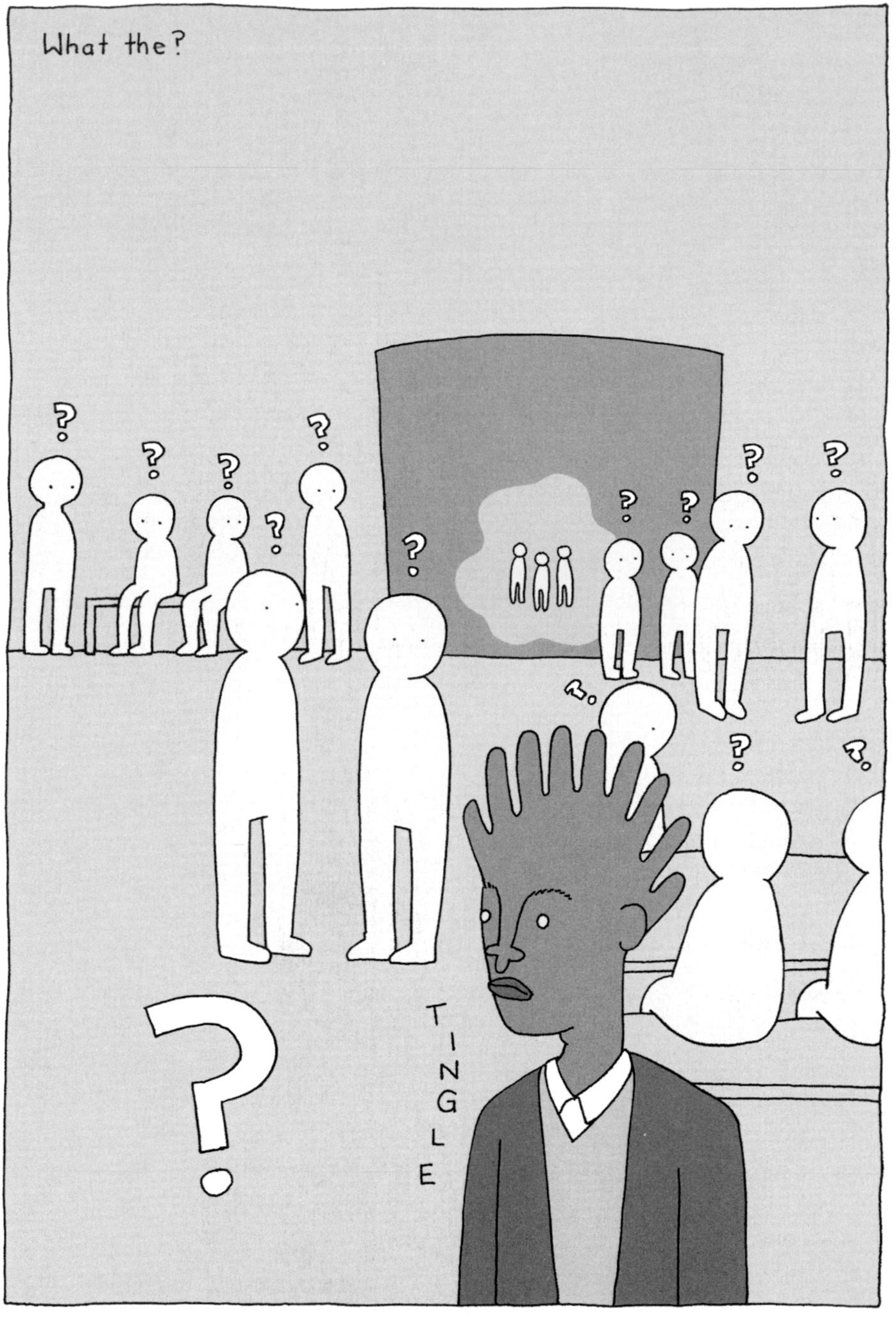
What the?
TINGLE

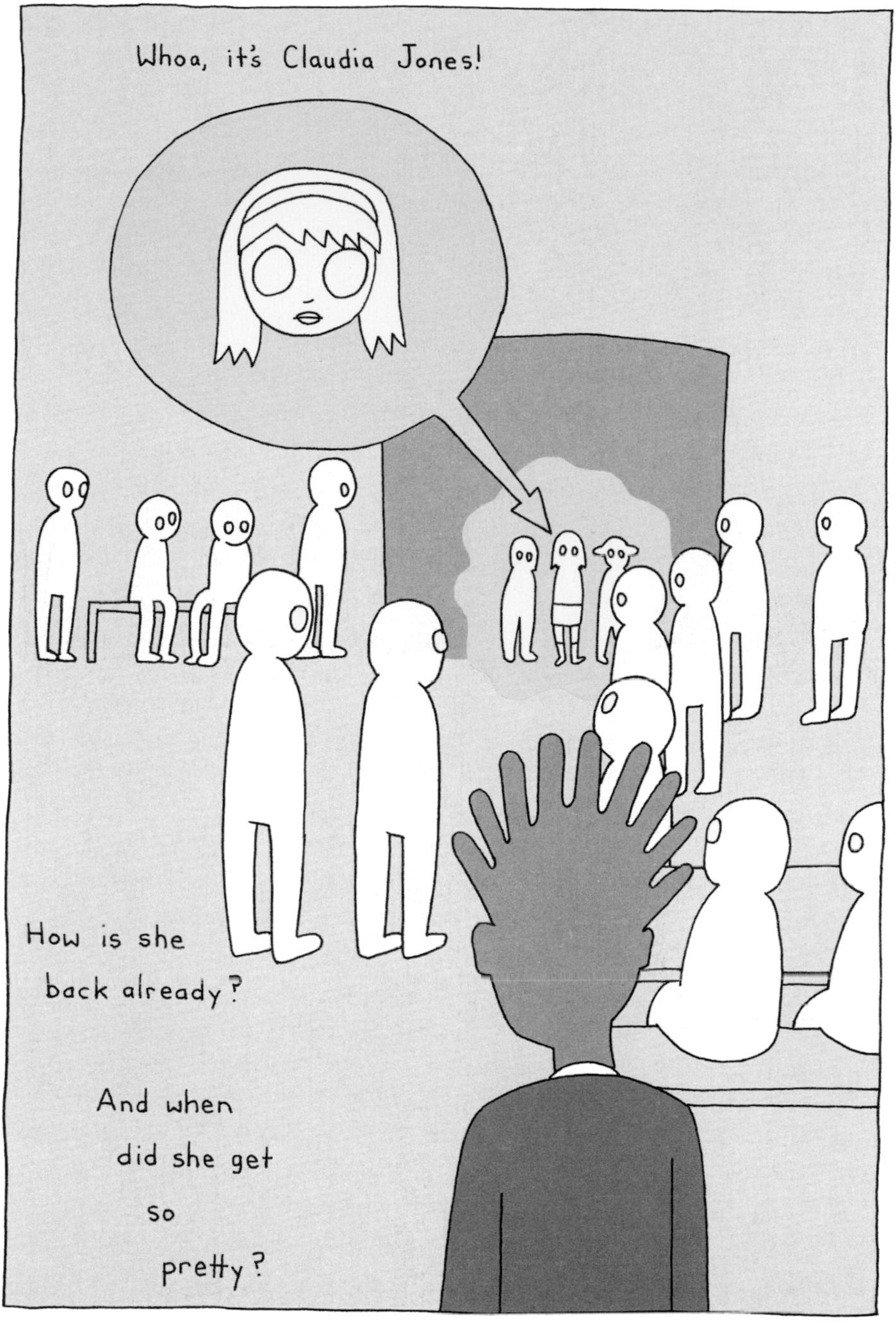
Whoa, it's Claudia Jones!
How is she back already?
And when did she get so pretty?

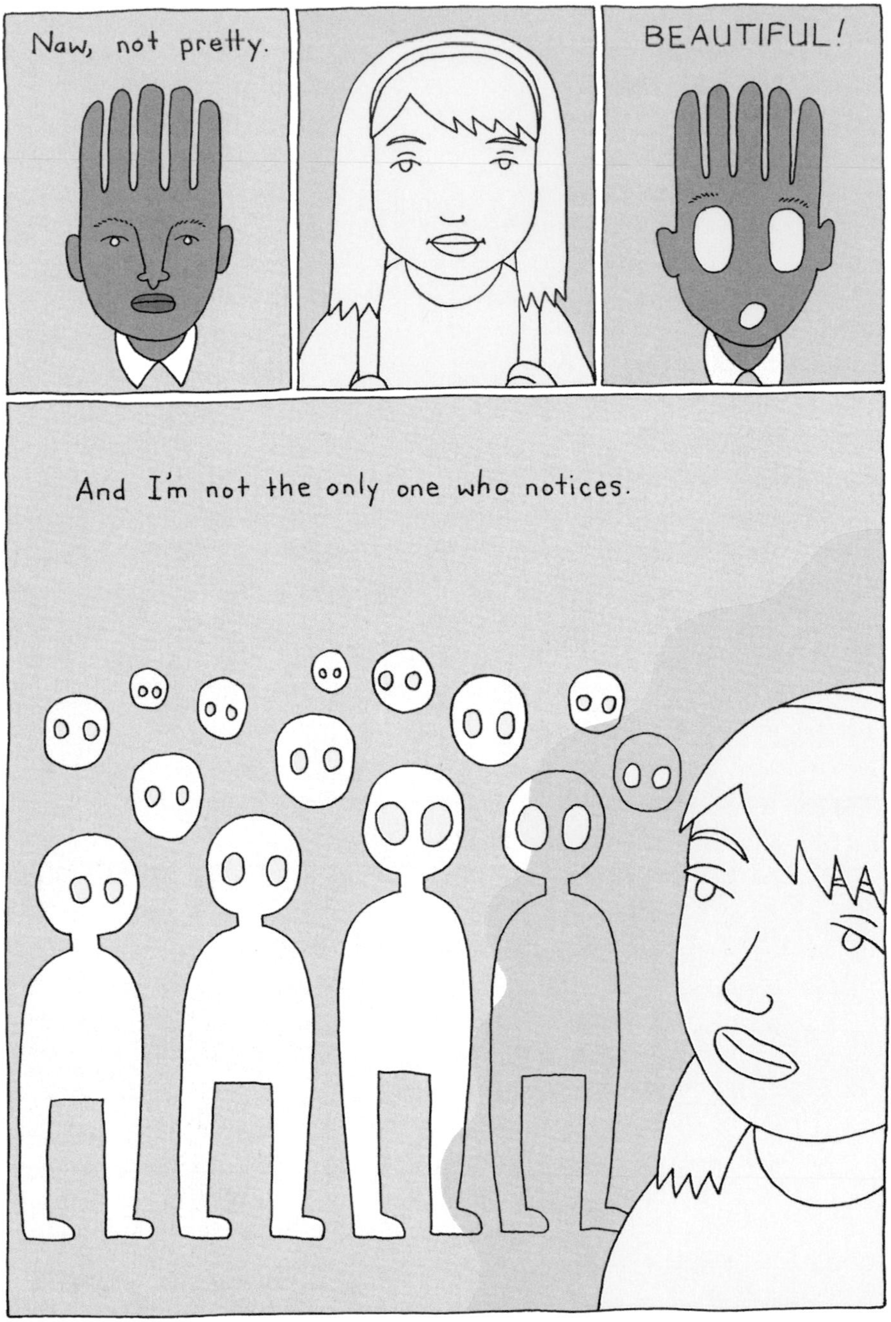
Naw, not pretty.
BEAUTIFUL!
And I'm not the only one who notices.

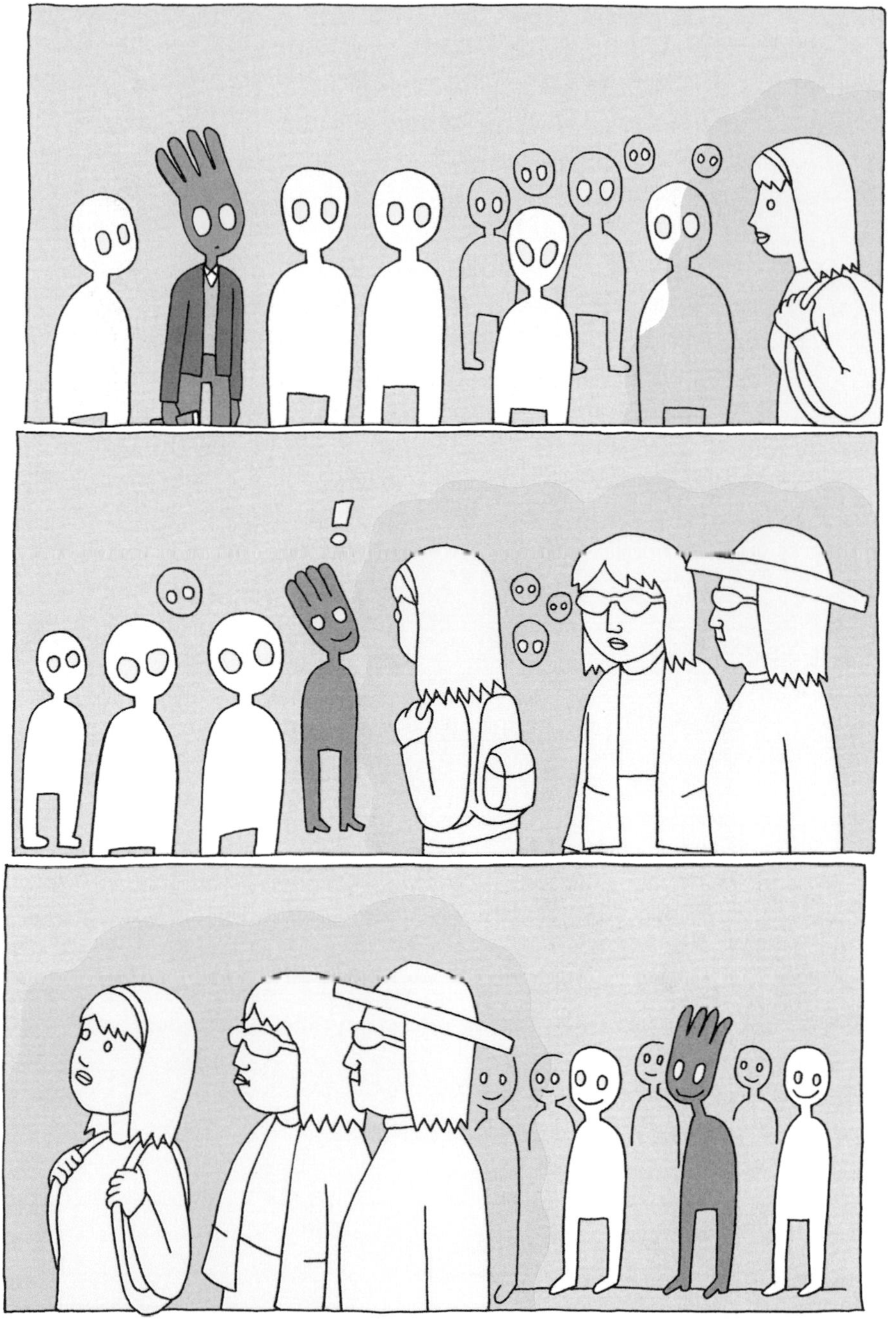
!

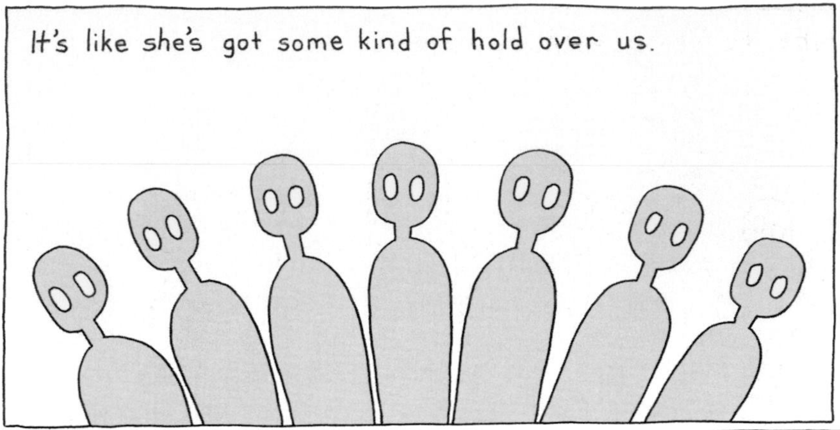
It's like she's got some kind of hold over us.

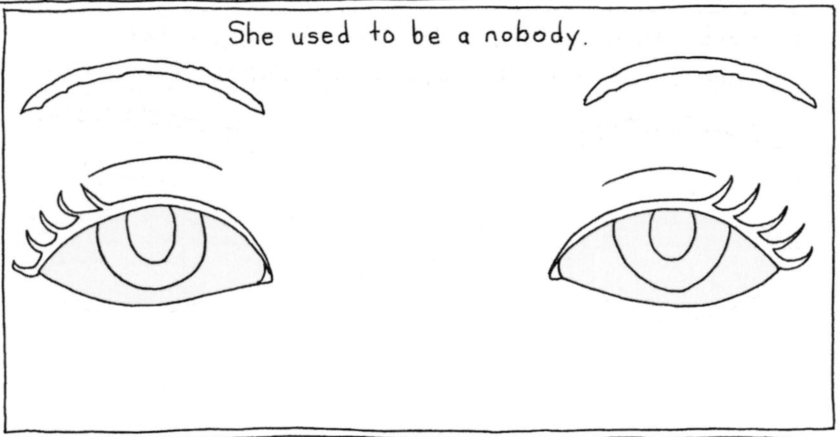
She used to be a nobody.

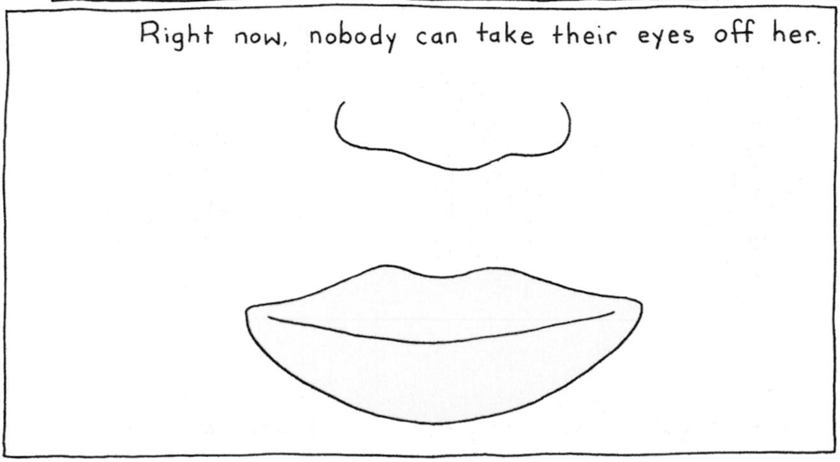
Right now, nobody can take their eyes off her.

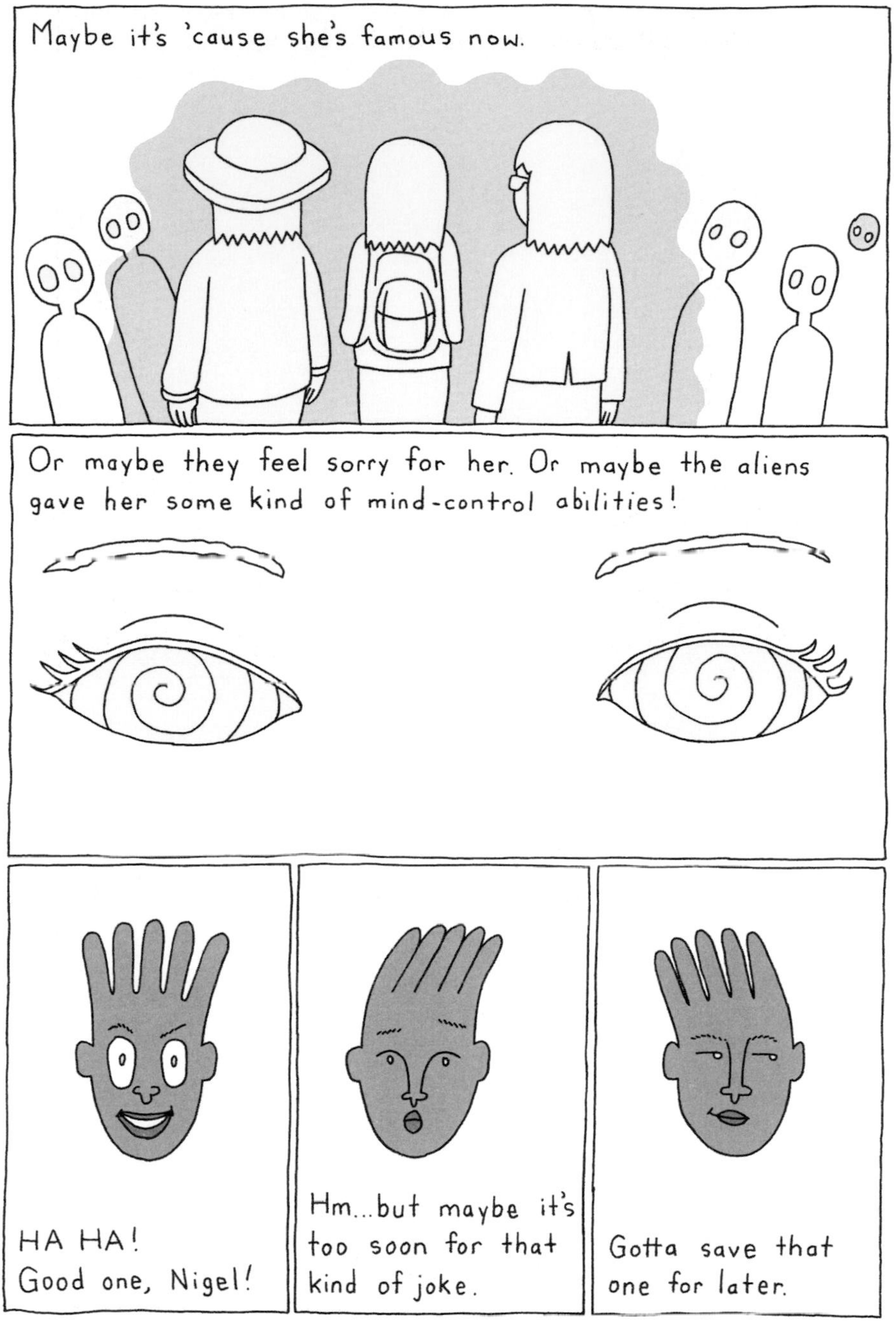
Maybe it's 'cause she's famous now.
Or maybe they feel sorry for her. Or maybe the aliens gave her some kind of mind-control abilities!
HA HA! Good one, Nigel!
Hm...but maybe it's too soon for that kind of joke.
Gotta save that one for later.

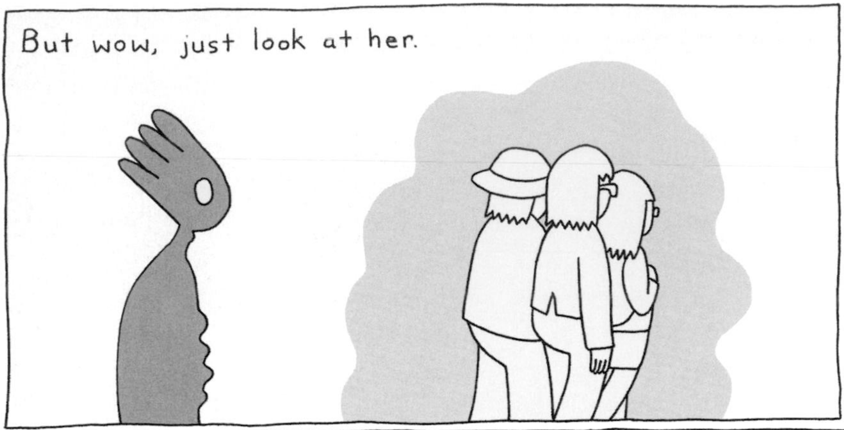
But wow, just look at her.

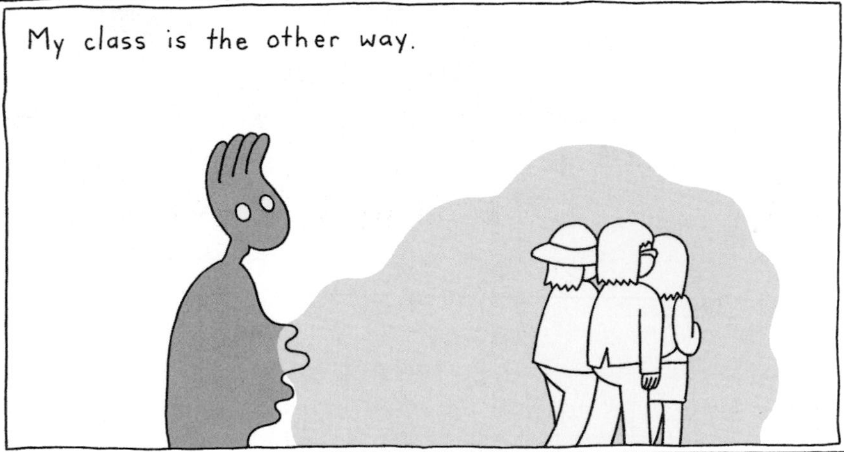
My class is the other way.

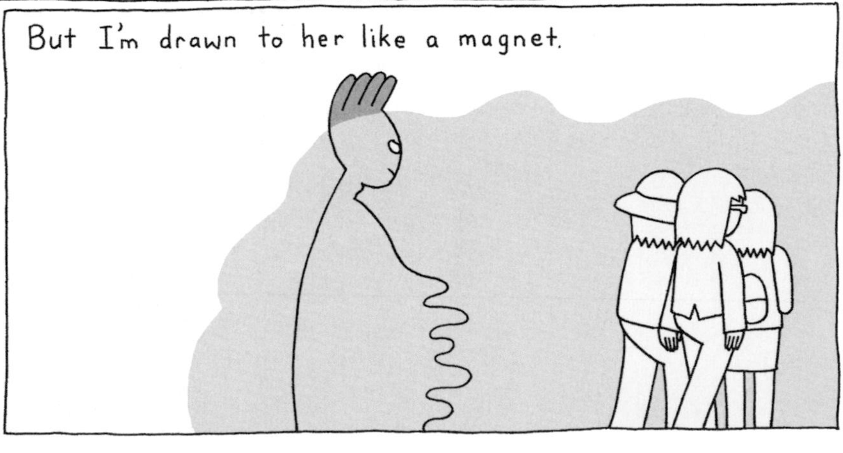
But I'm drawn to her like a magnet.

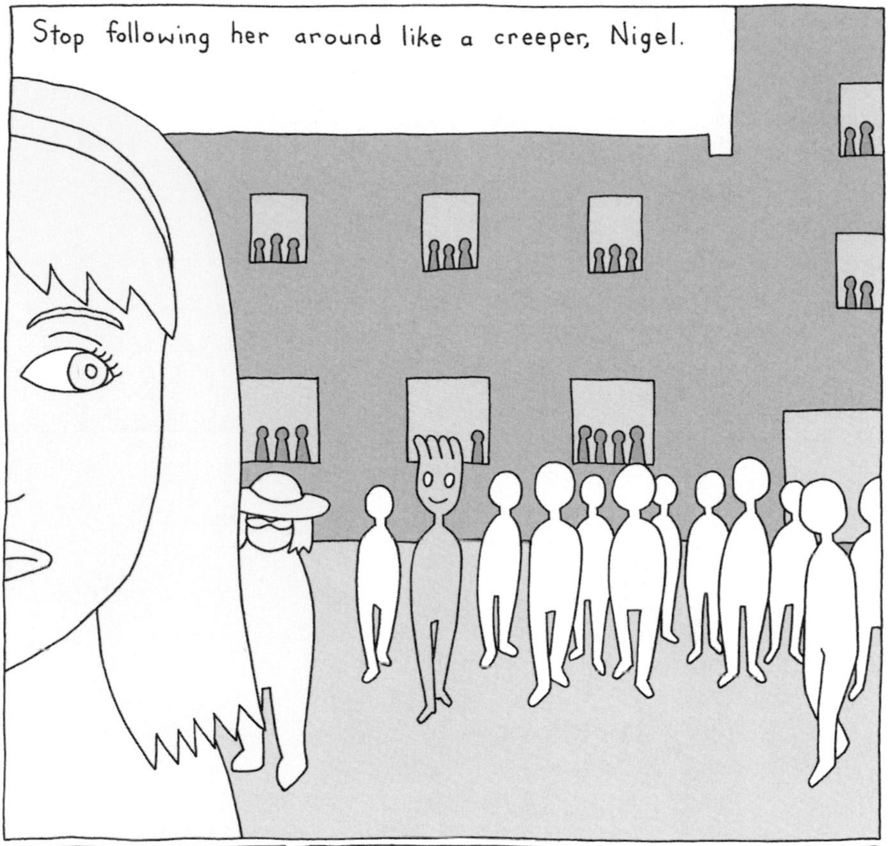
Stop following her around like a creeper, Nigel.

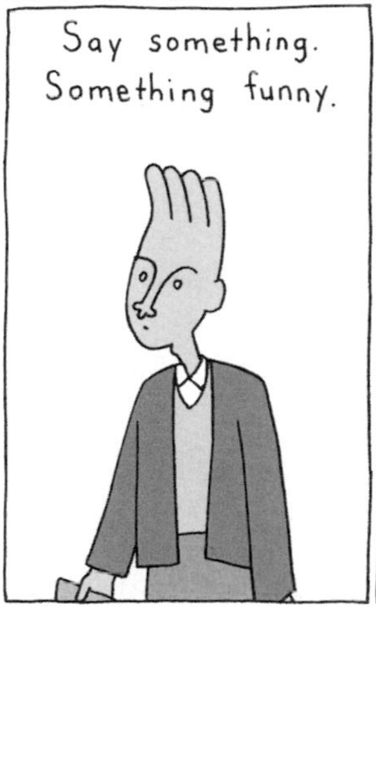
Say something.
Something funny.

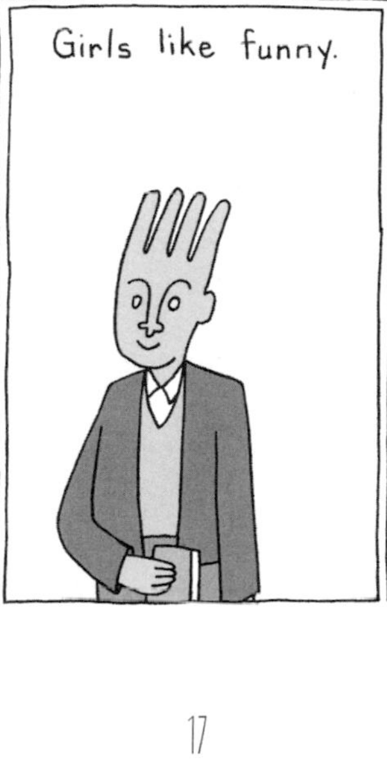
Girls like funny.

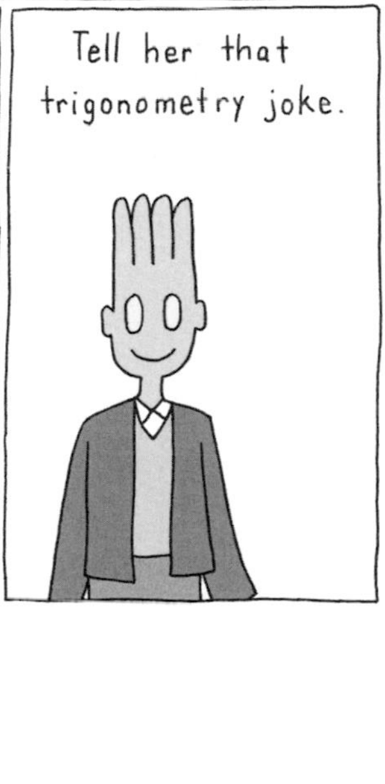
Tell her that
trigonometry joke.

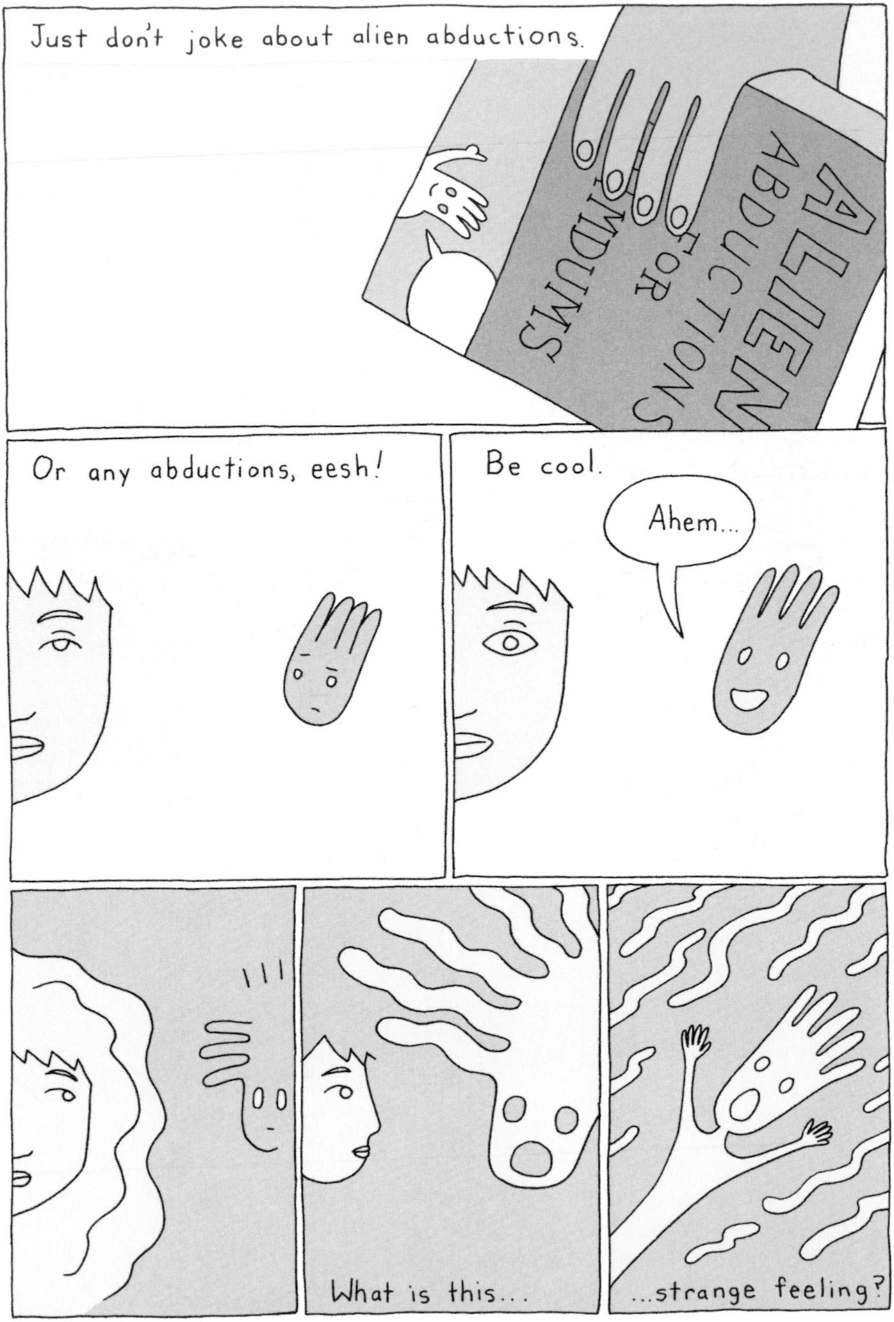
Just don't joke about alien abductions.
ALIEN ABDUCTIONS FOR DUMDUMS
Or any abductions, eesh!
Be cool.
Ahem...
What is this...
...strange feeling?

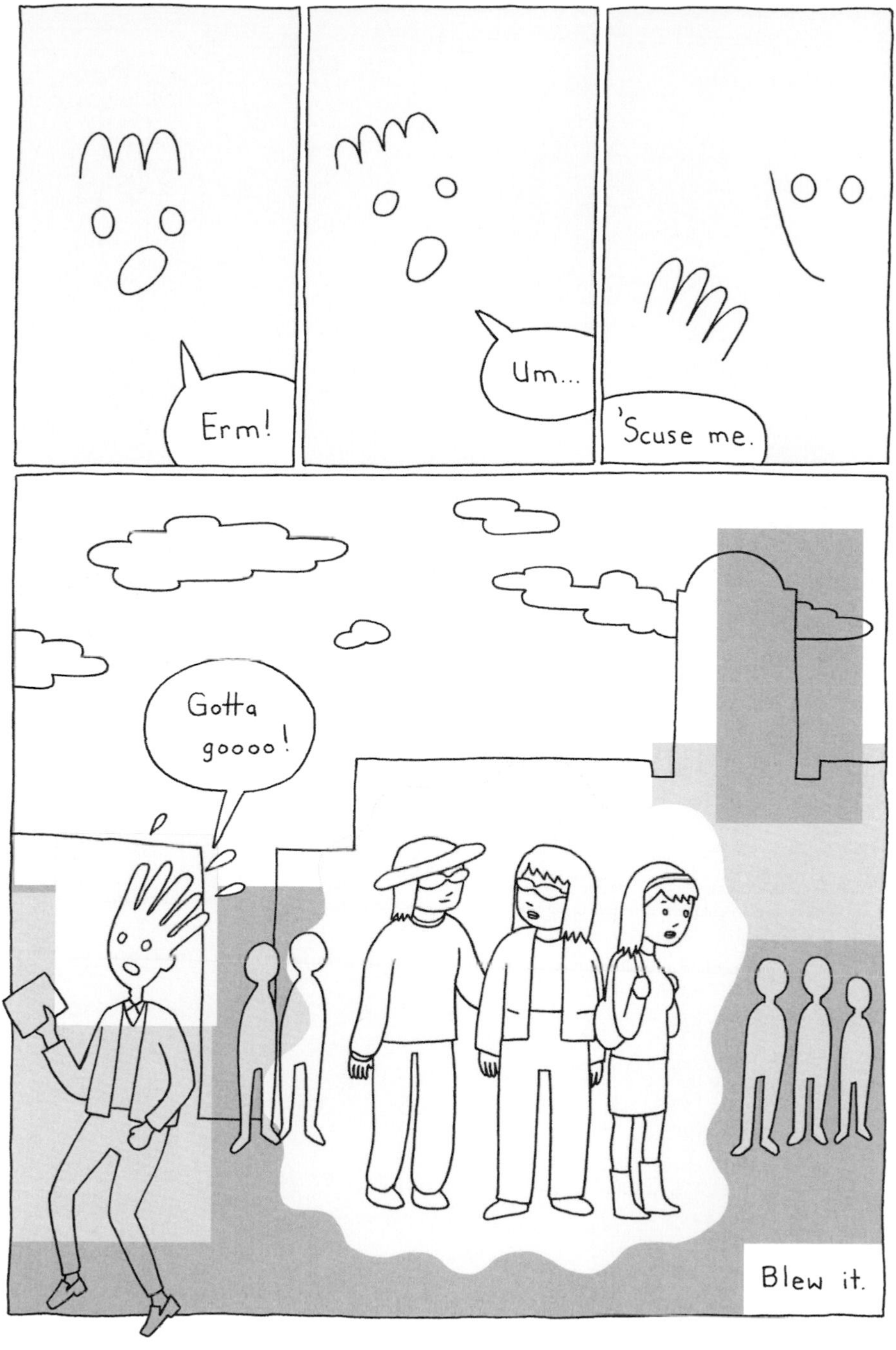
Erm!
Um...
'Scuse me.
Gotta goooo!
Blew it.

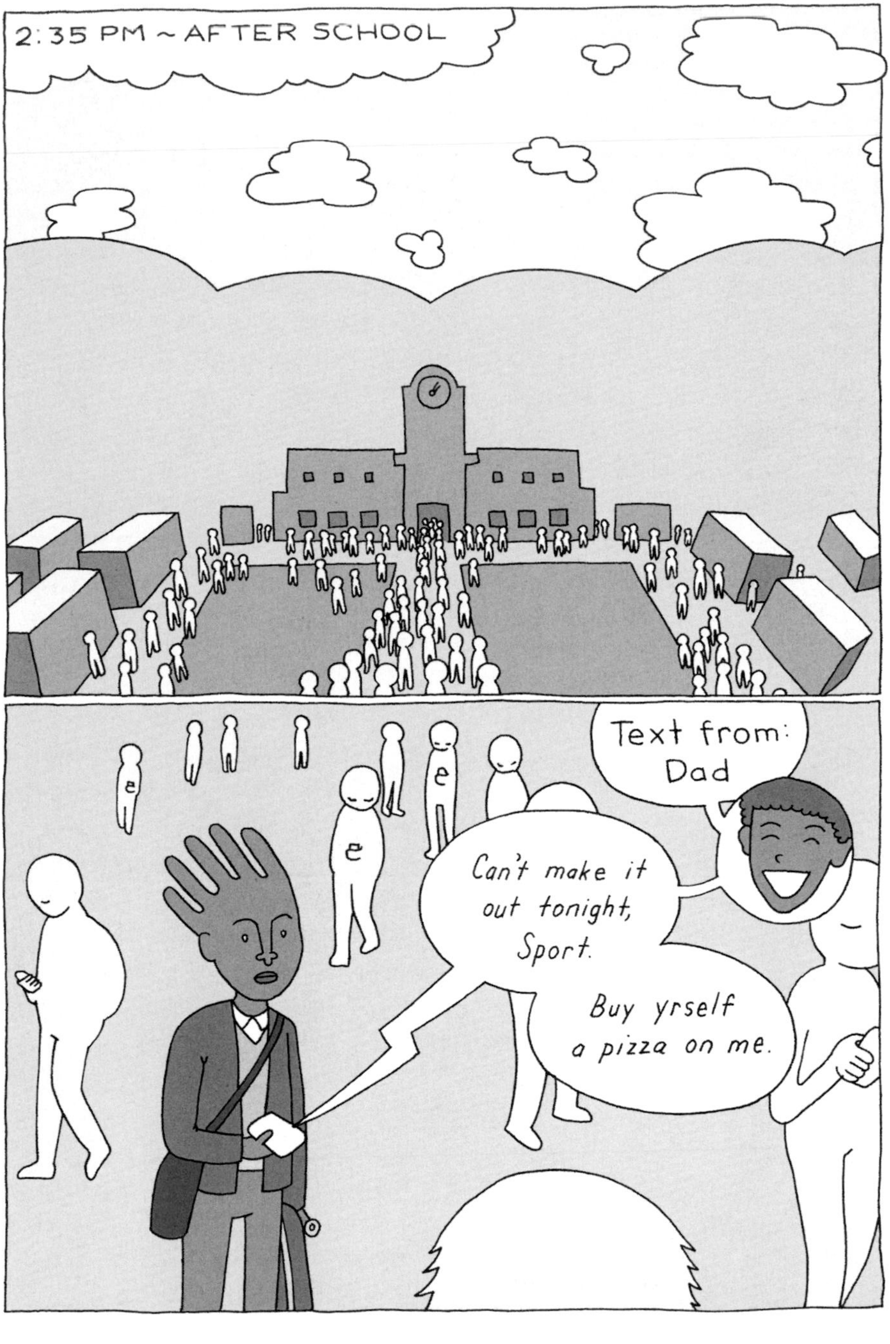
2:35 PM ~ AFTER SCHOOL
Text from: Dad
Can't make it out tonight, Sport.
Buy yrself a pizza on me.

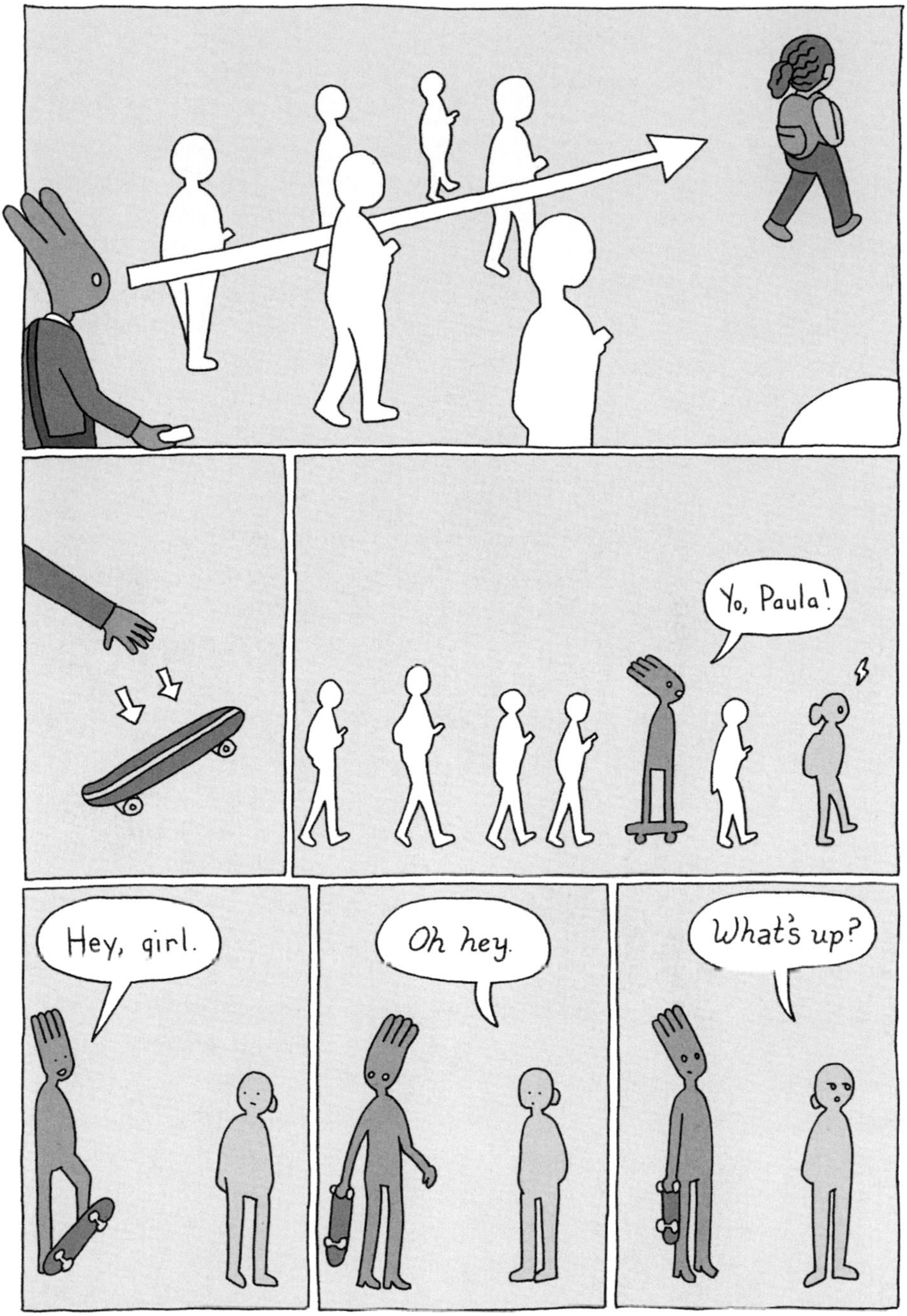
Yo, Paula!
Hey, girl.
Oh hey.
What's up?

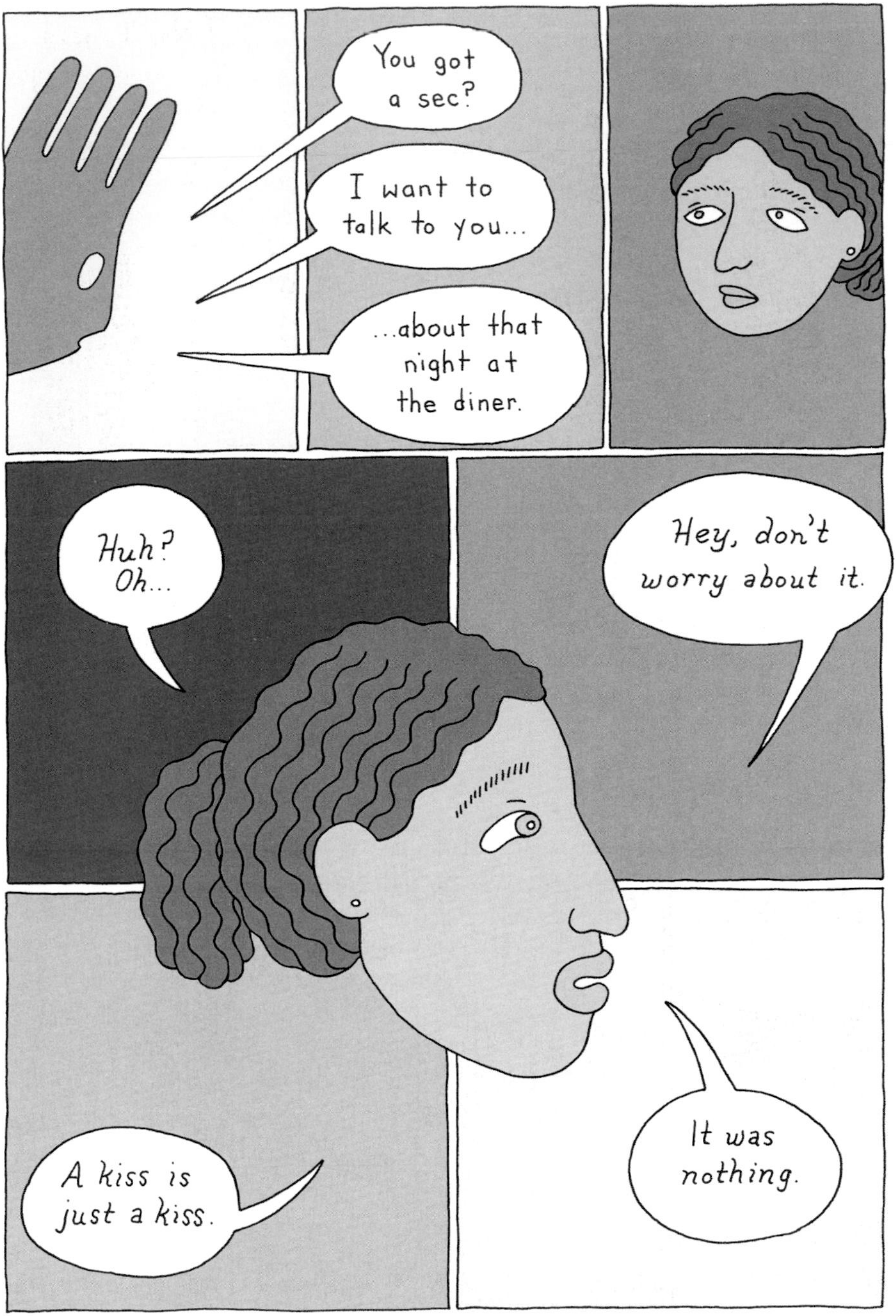
You got a sec?
I want to talk to you...
...about that night at the diner.
Huh? Oh...
Hey, don't worry about it.
It was nothing.
A kiss is just a kiss.

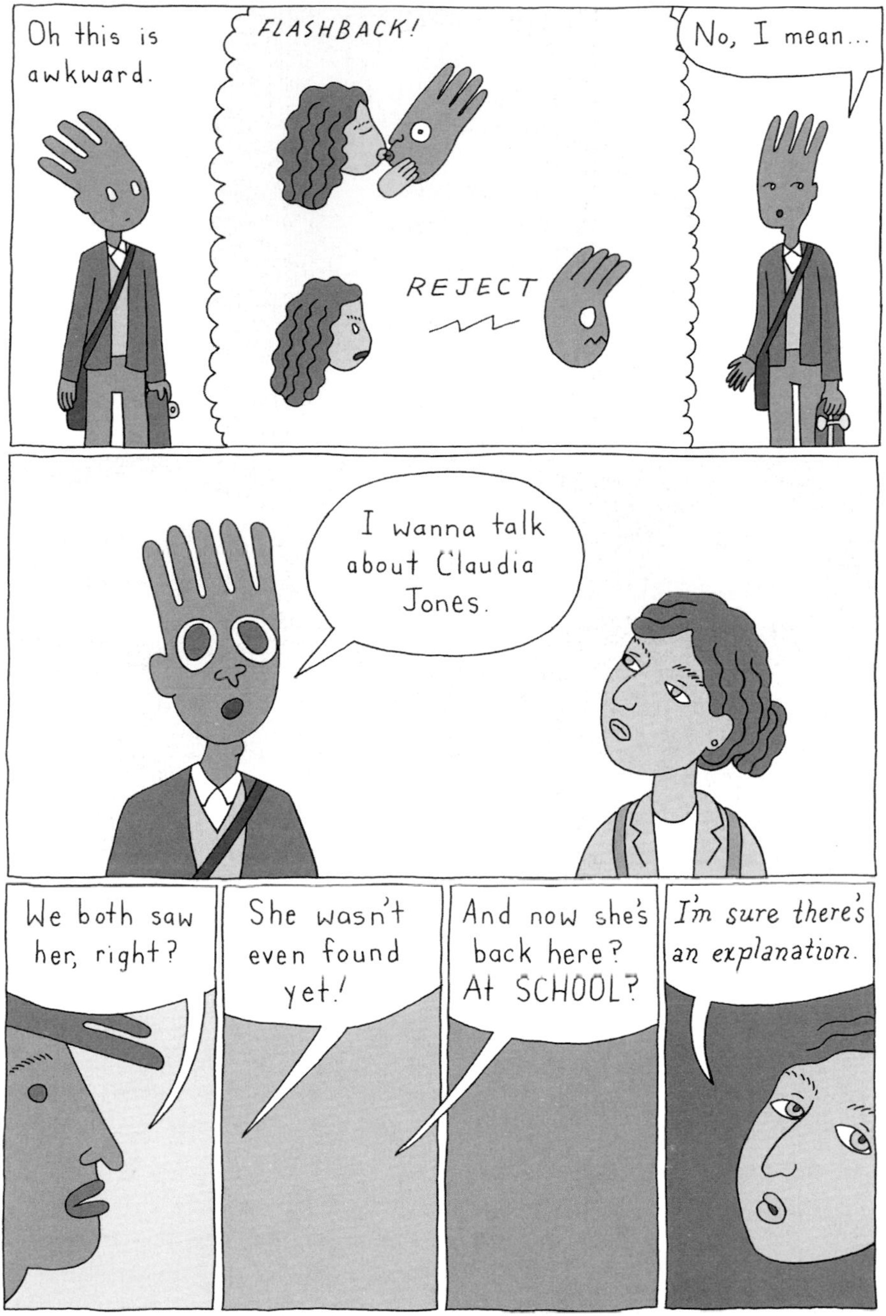
Oh this is awkward.
FLASHBACK!
REJECT
No, I mean...
I wanna talk about Claudia Jones.
We both saw her, right?
She wasn't even found yet!
And now she's back here? At SCHOOL?
I'm sure there's an explanation.

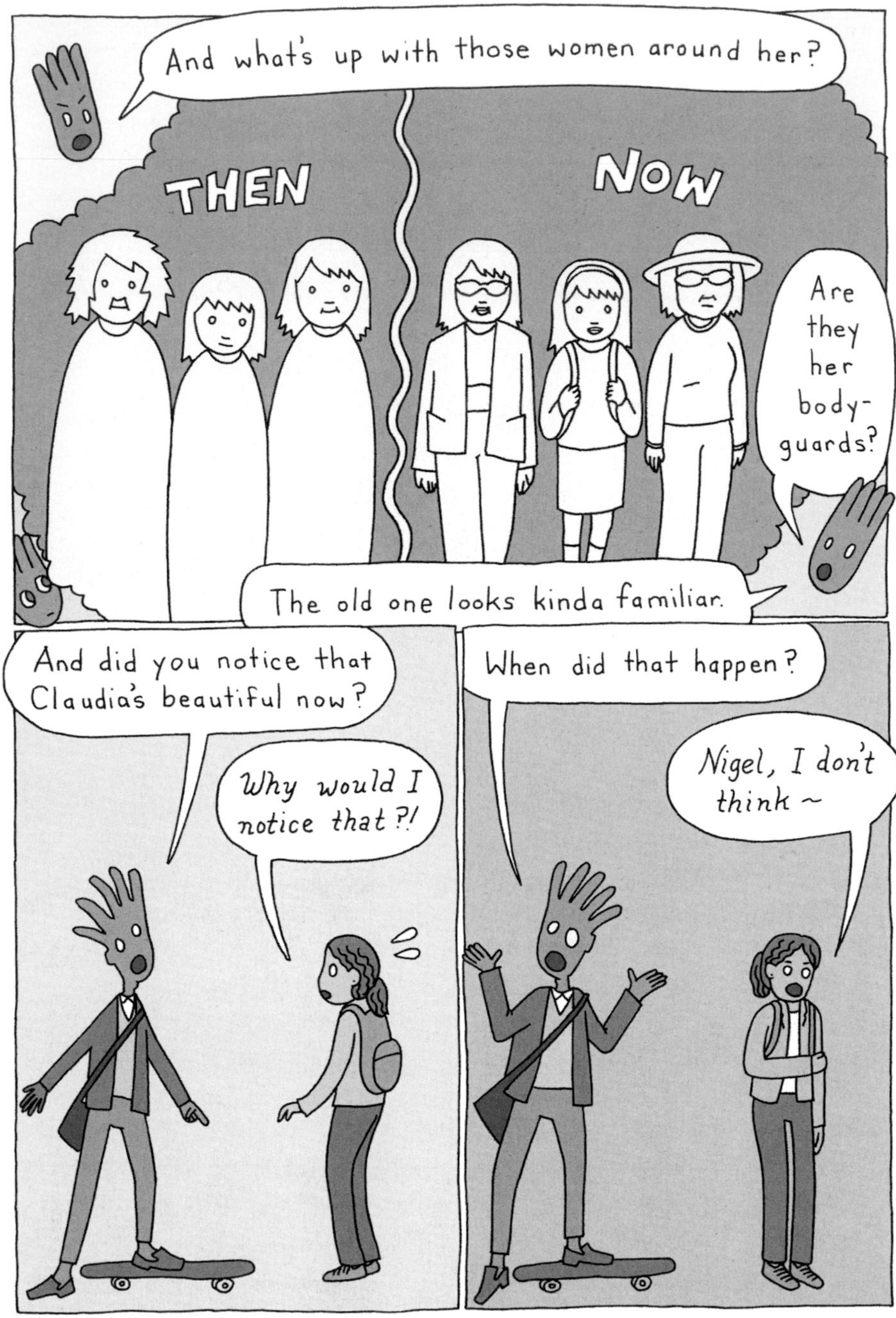

And what's up with those women around her?
THEN
NOW
Are they her body-guards?
The old one looks kinda familiar.
And did you notice that Claudia's beautiful now?
Why would I notice that?!
When did that happen?
Nigel, I don't think ~

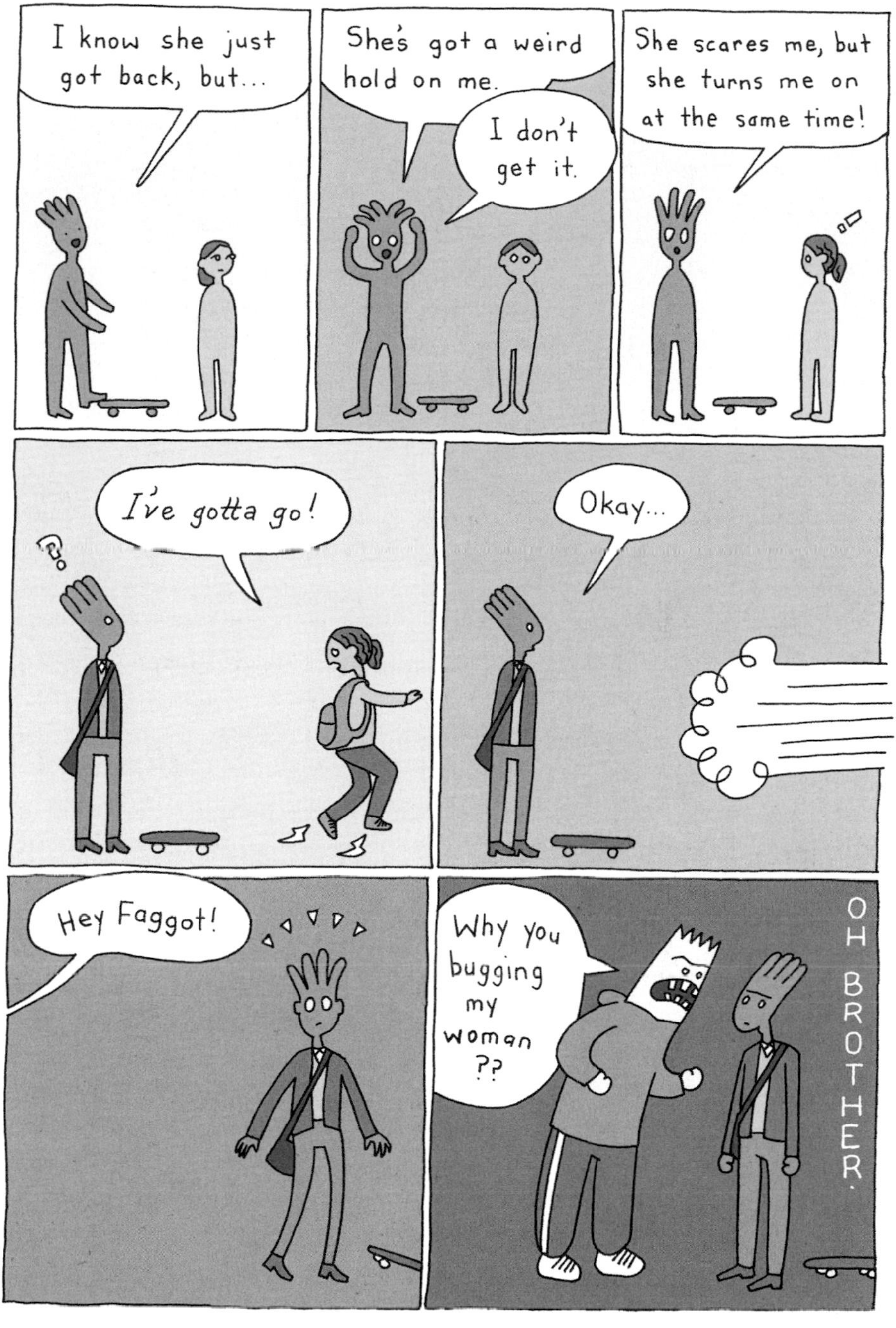
I know she just got back, but...
She's got a weird hold on me.
I don't get it.
She scares me, but she turns me on at the same time!
I've gotta go!
Okay...
Hey Faggot!
Why you bugging my woman ??
OH BROTHER.

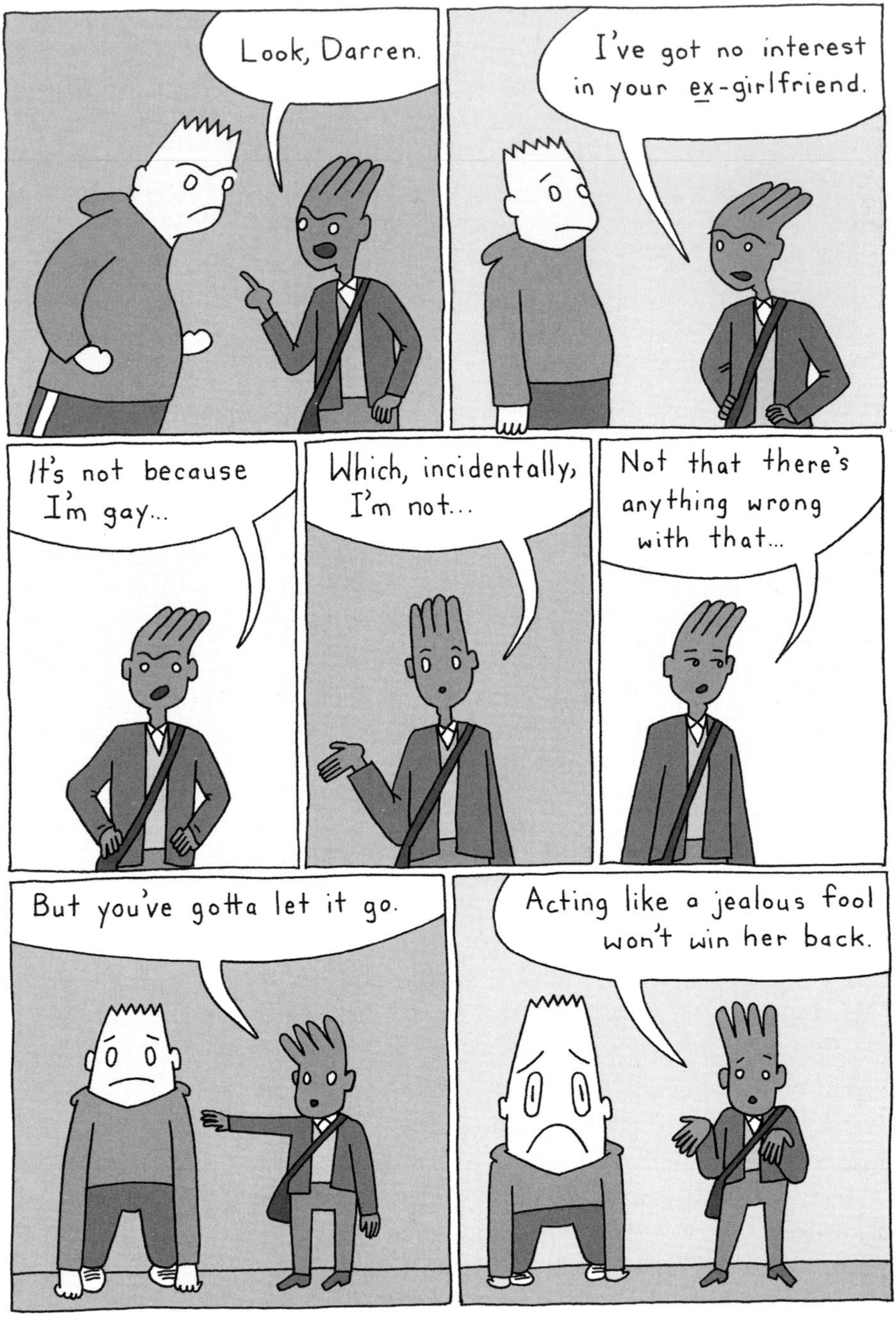
Look, Darren.
I've got no interest in your ex-girlfriend.
It's not because I'm gay...
Which, incidentally, I'm not...
Not that there's anything wrong with that...
But you've gotta let it go.
Acting like a jealous fool won't win her back.

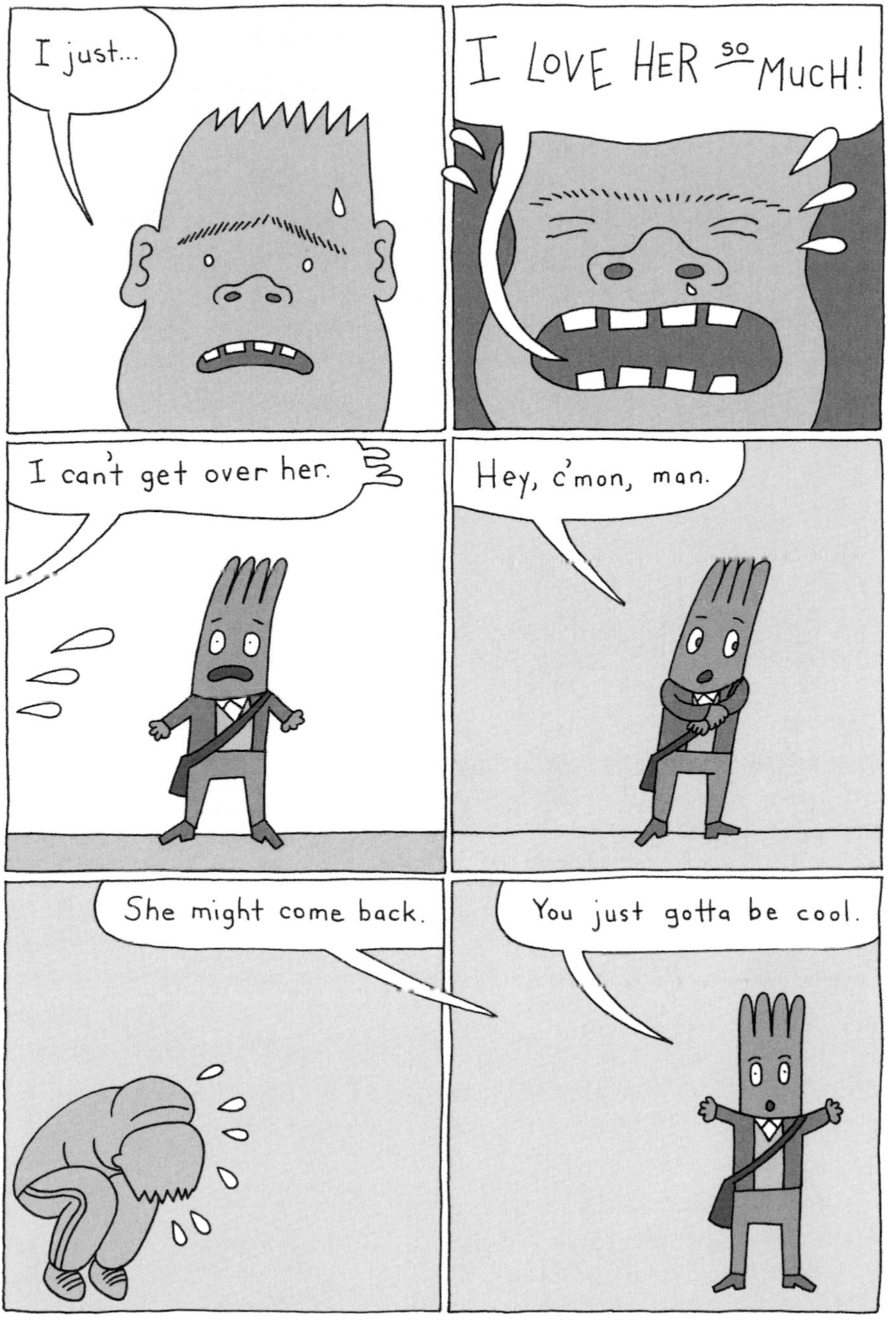
I just...
I LOVE HER SO MUCH!
I can't get over her.
Hey, c'mon, man.
She might come back.
You just gotta be cool.

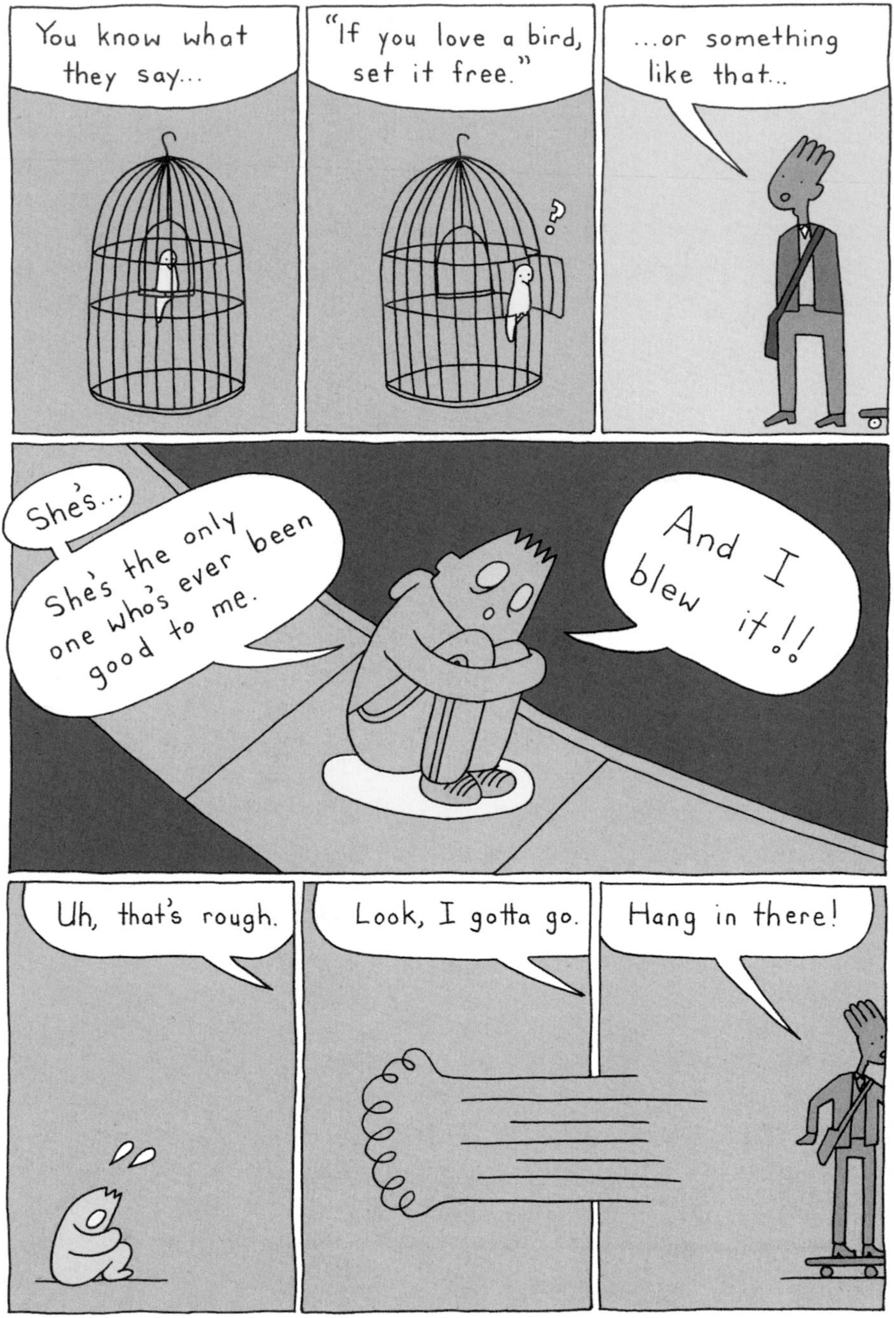
You know what they say...
"If you love a bird, set it free."
...or something like that...
She's...
She's the only one who's ever been good to me.
And I blew it!!
Uh, that's rough.
Look, I gotta go.
Hang in there!

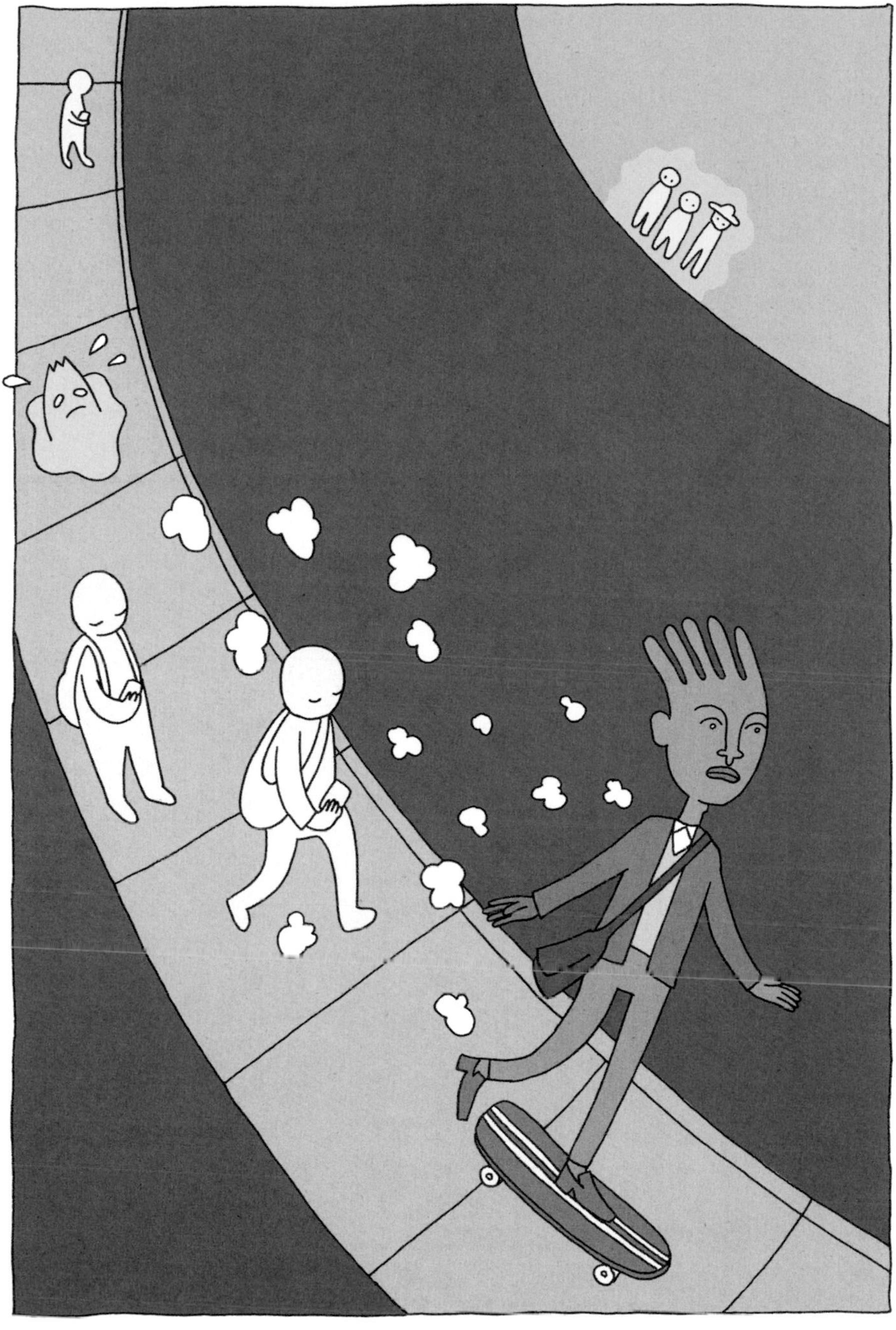

# PART TWO

Paula Navarro

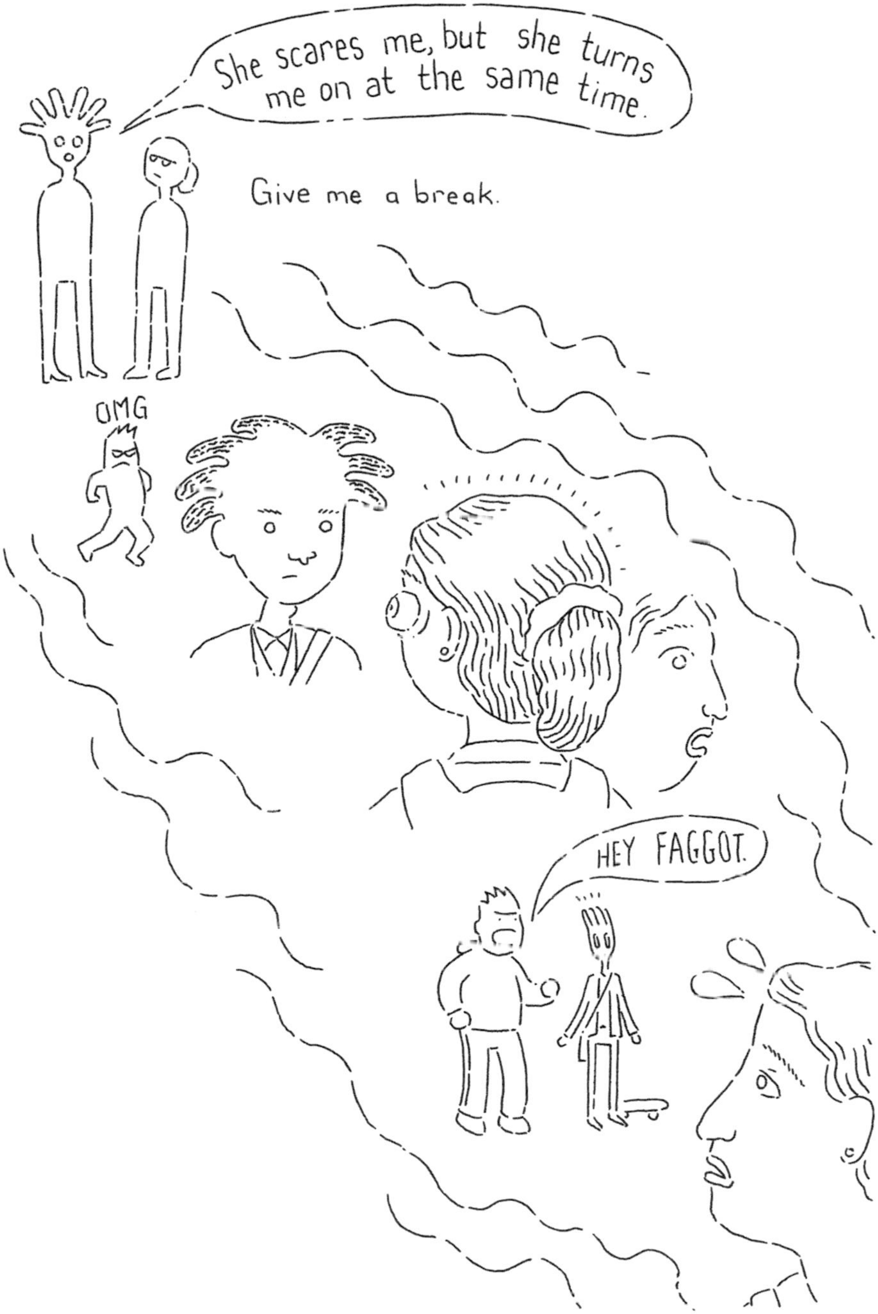
She scares me, but she turns me on at the same time.
Give me a break.
OMG
HEY FAGGOT.

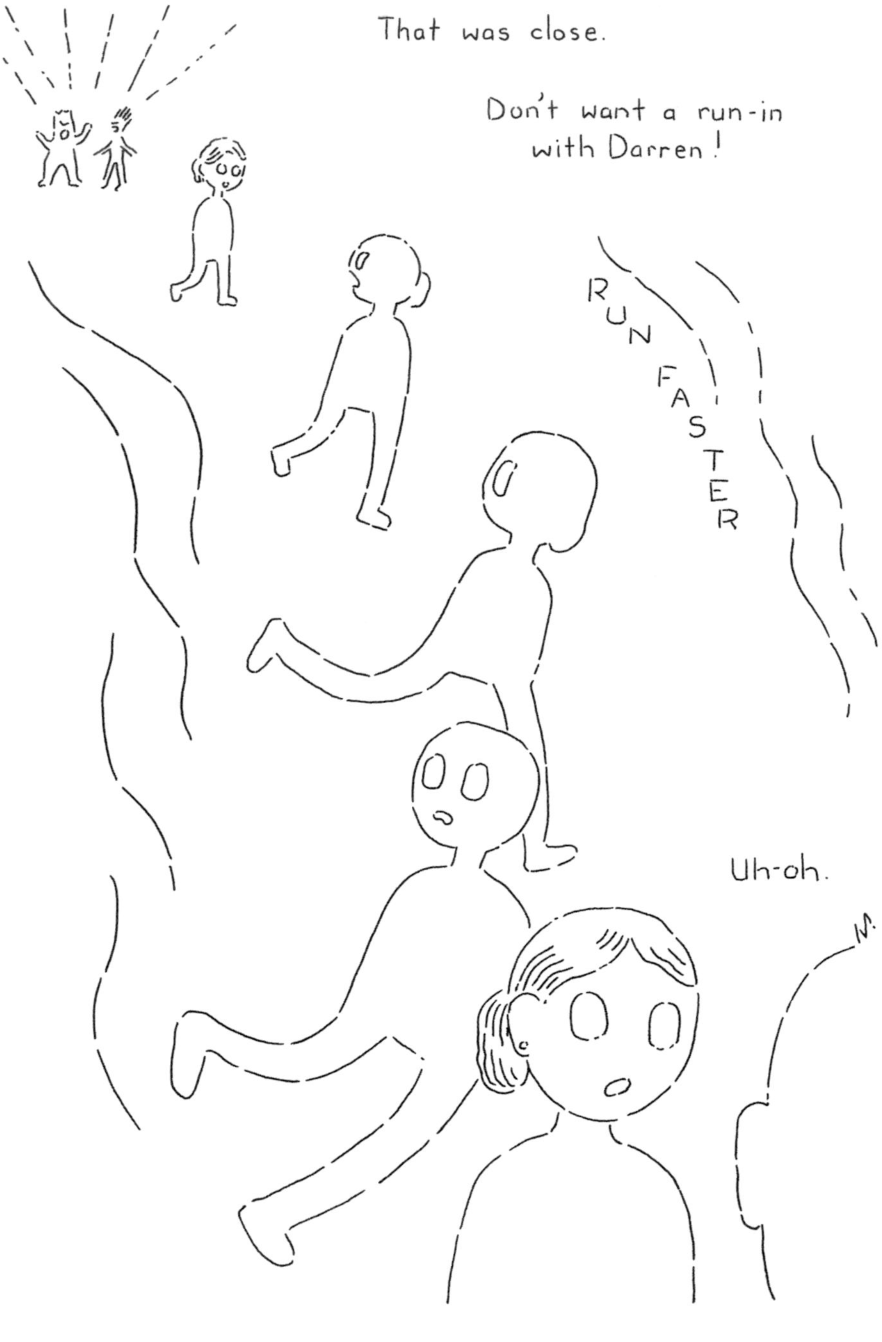
That was close.
Don't want a run-in with Darren!
RUN FASTER
Uh-oh.

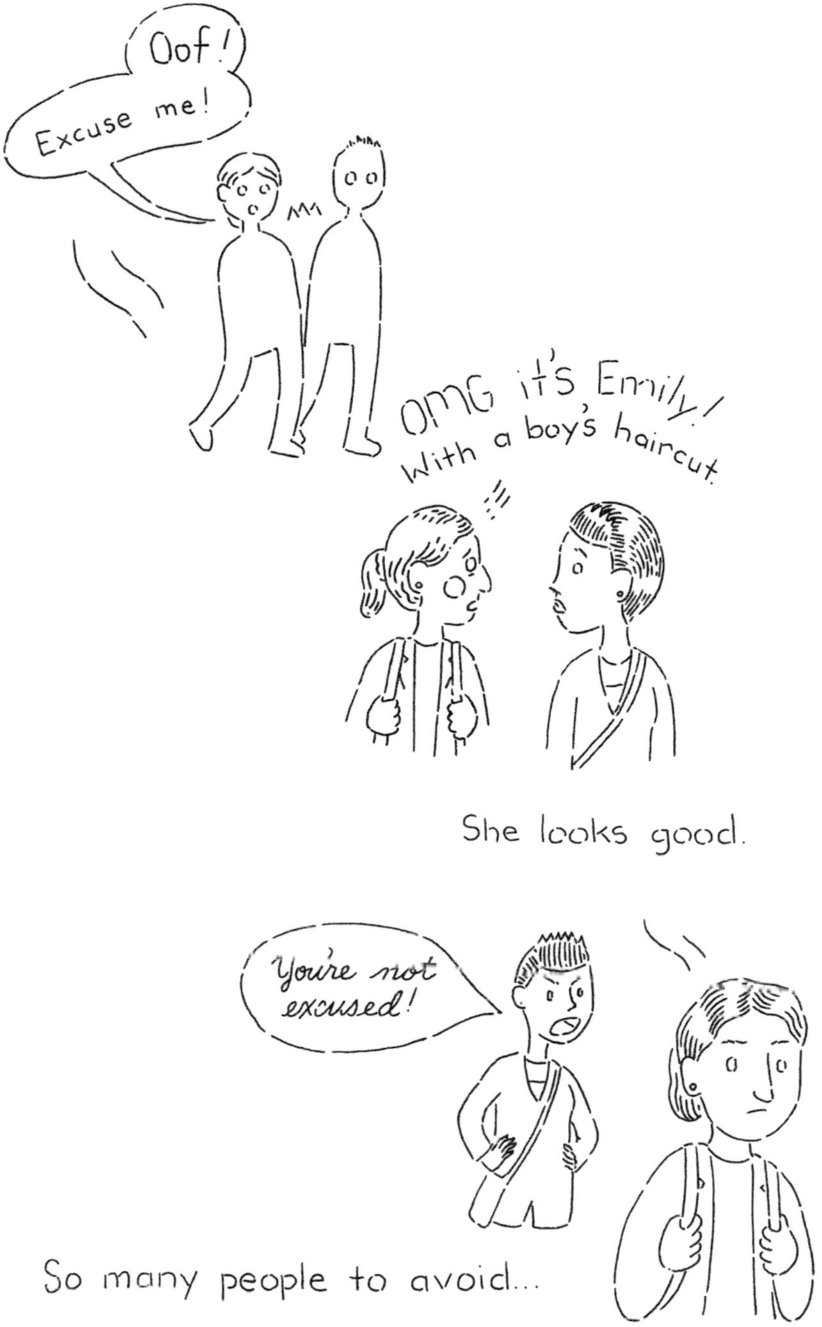
Oof!
Excuse me!
OMG it's Emily!
With a boy's haircut.
She looks good.
You're not excused!
So many people to avoid...

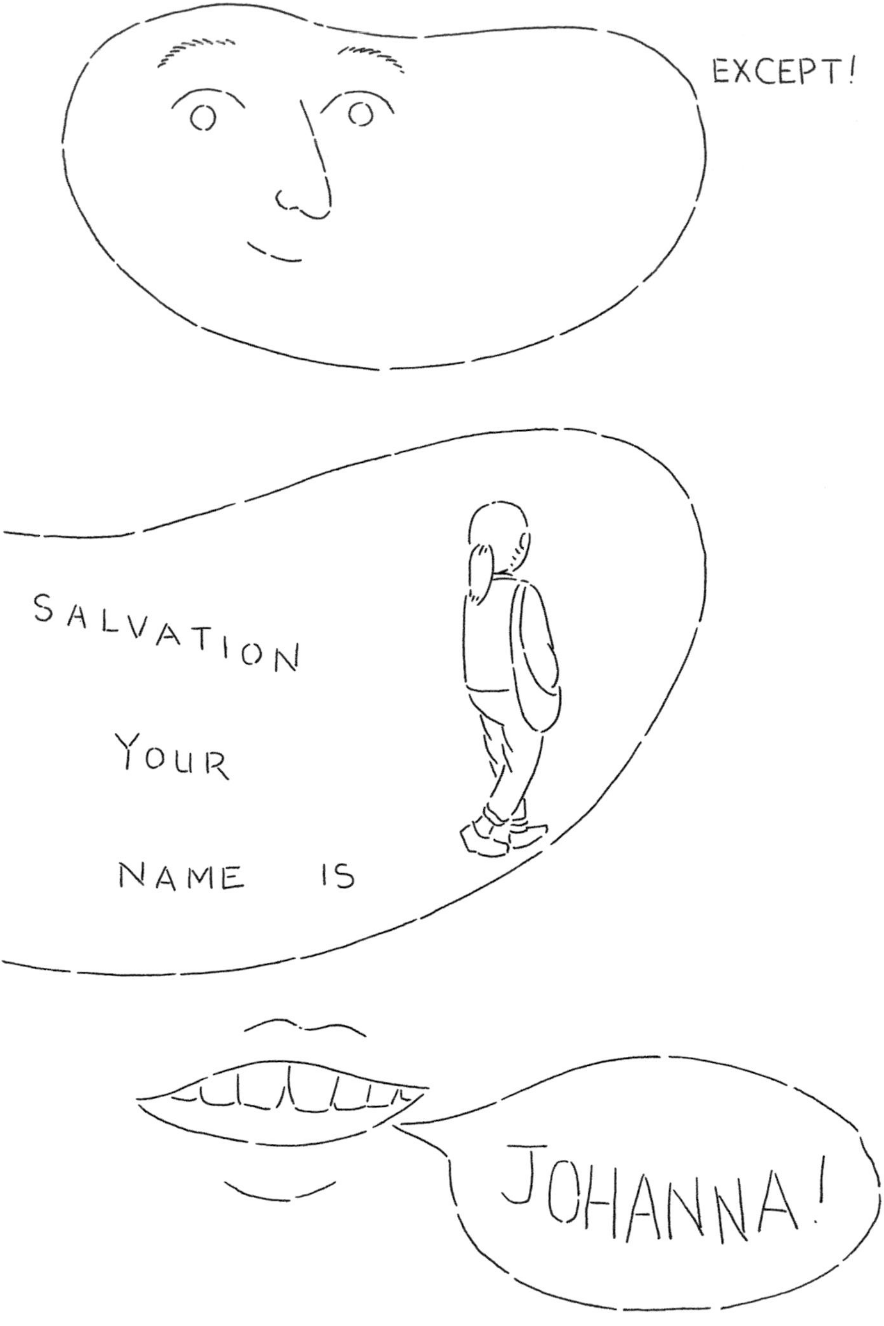
EXCEPT!
SALVATION
YOUR
NAME IS
JOHANNA!

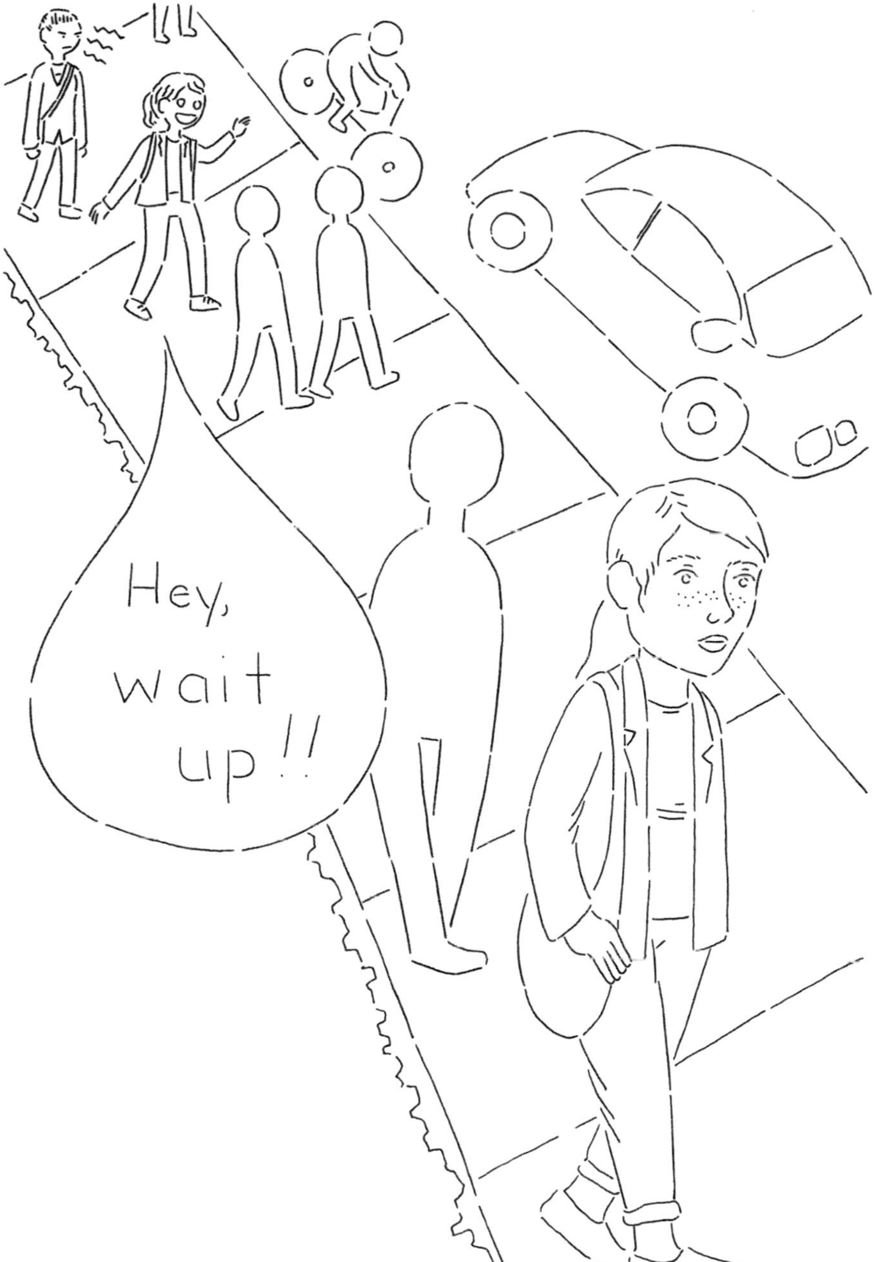
Hey, wait up!!

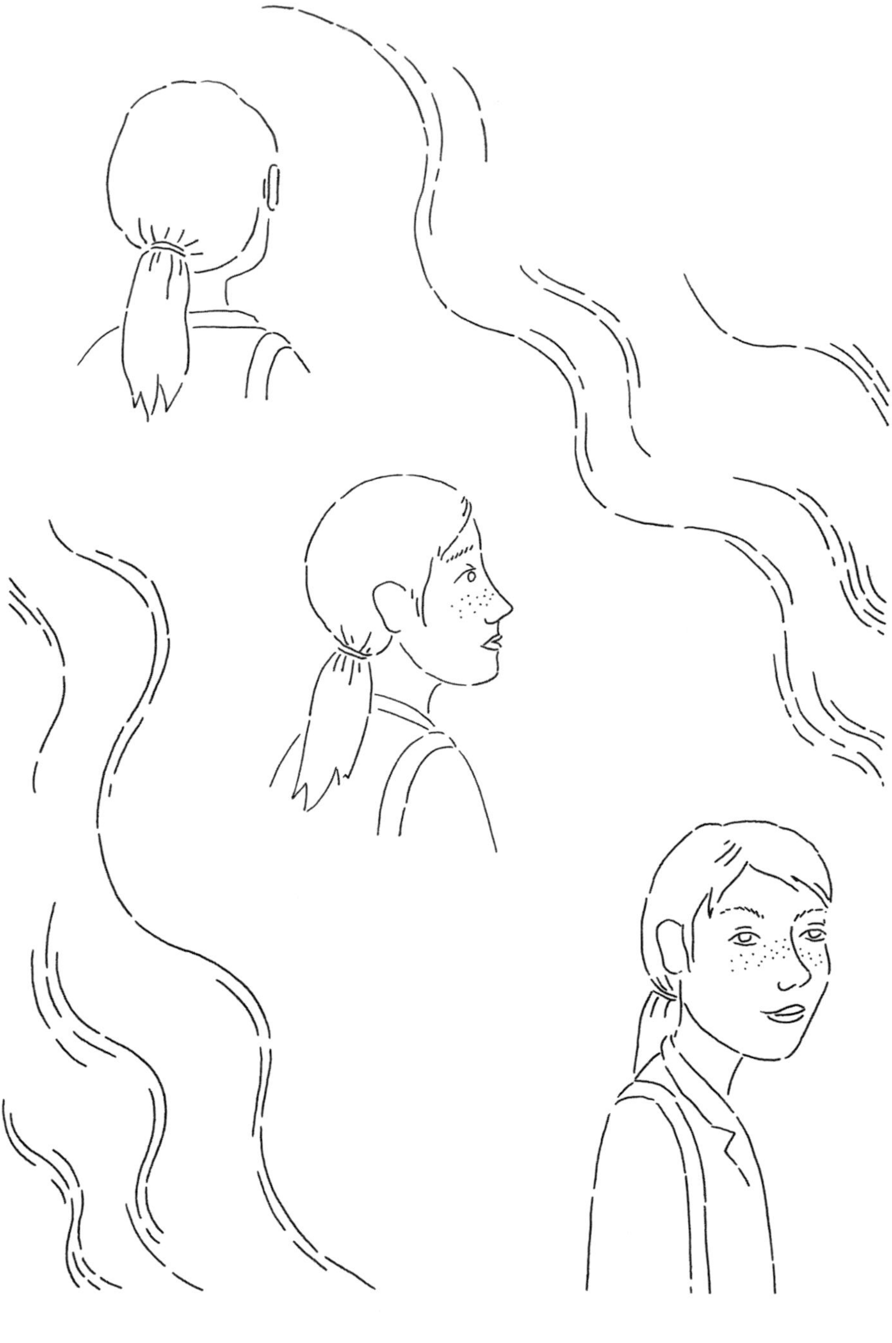

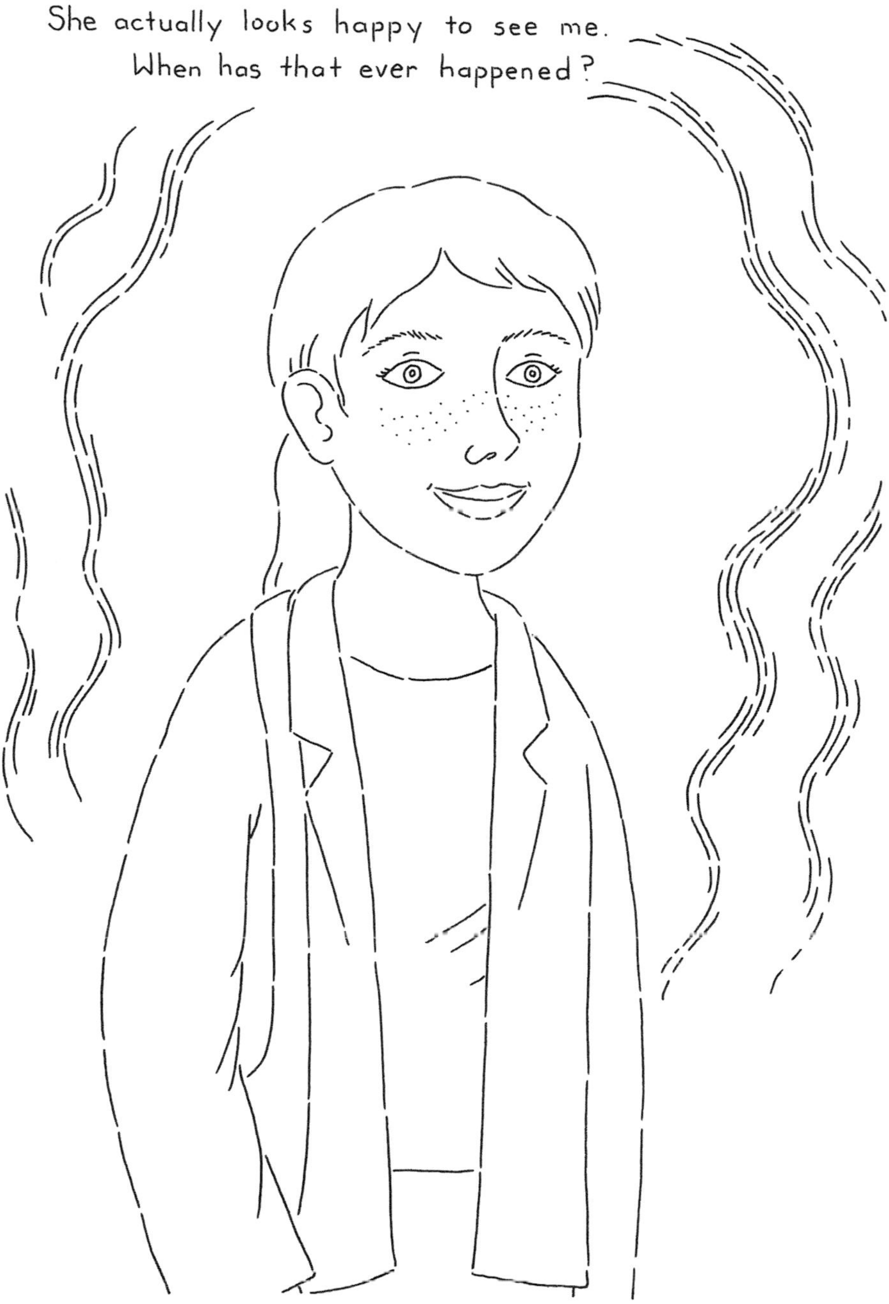
She actually looks happy to see me.
When has that ever happened?

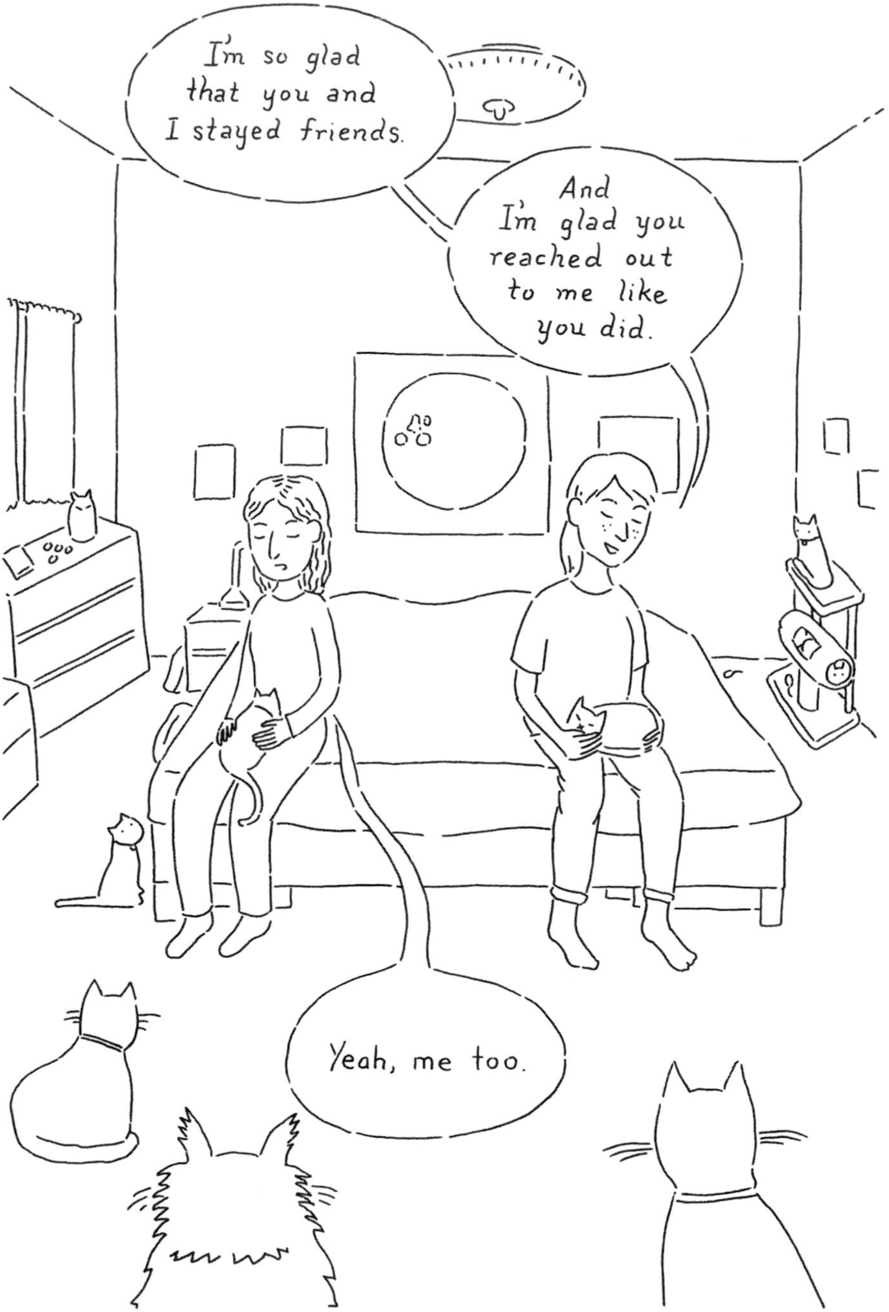
I'm so glad that you and I stayed friends.
And I'm glad you reached out to me like you did.
Yeah, me too.

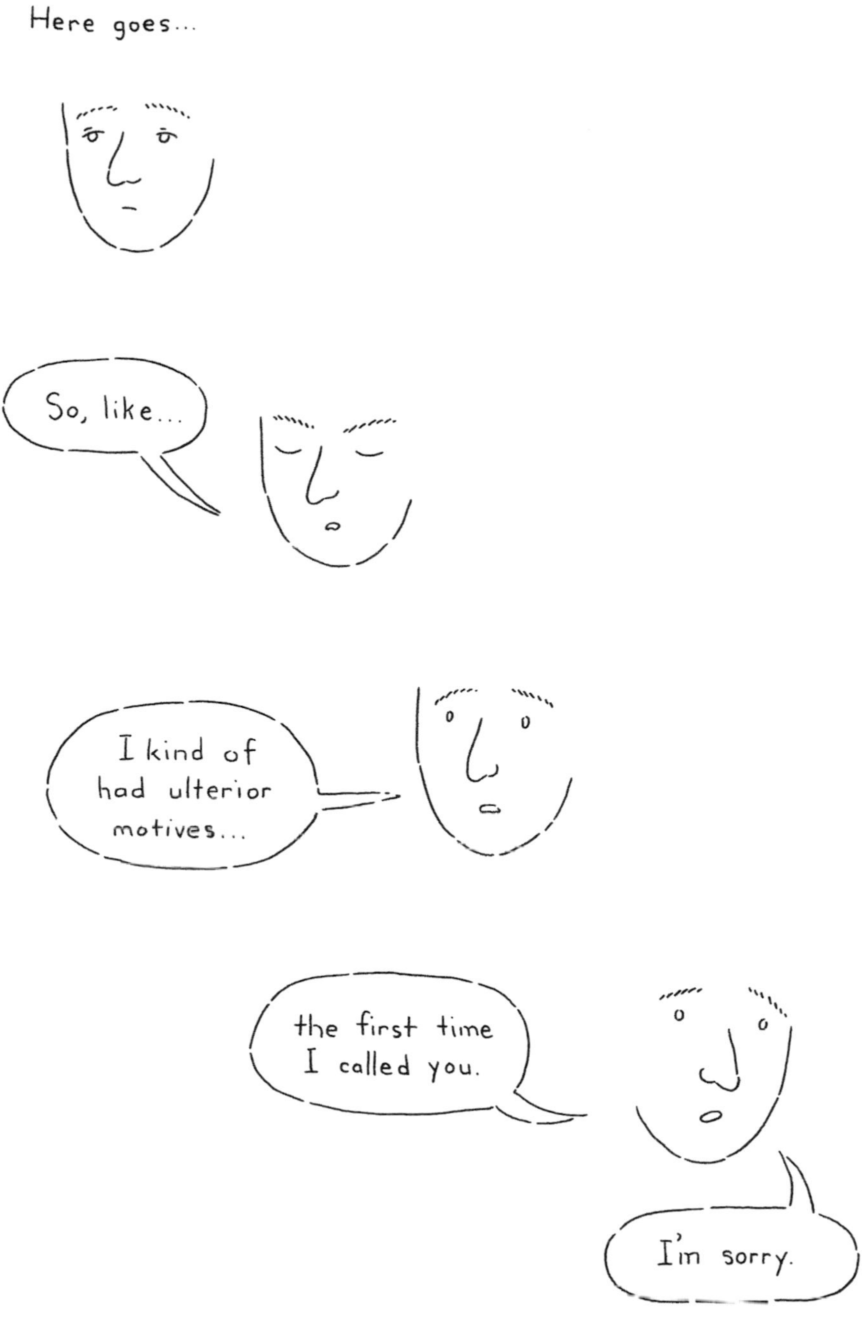
Here goes...
So, like...
I kind of had ulterior motives...
the first time I called you.
I'm sorry.

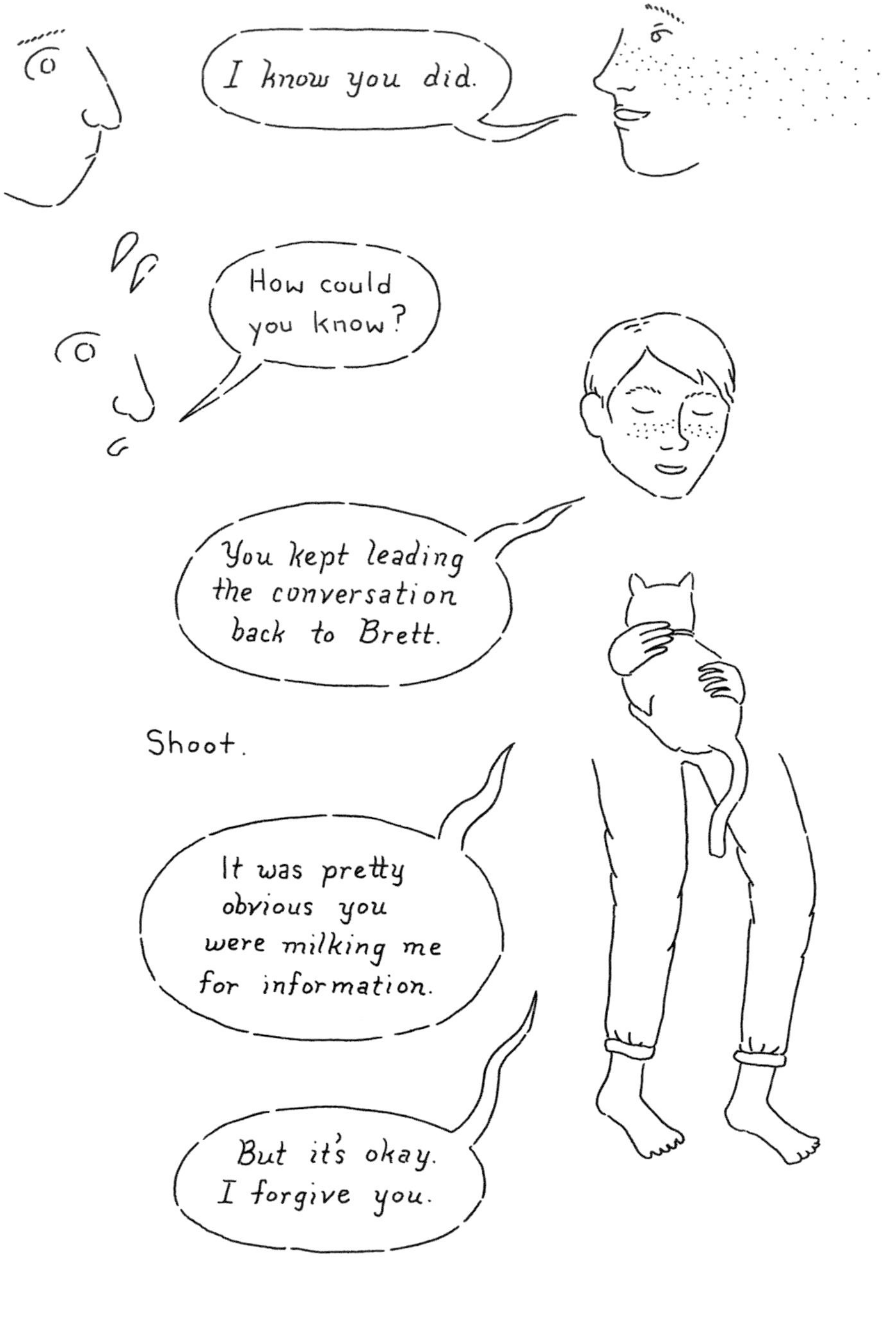

I know you did.
How could you know?
You kept leading the conversation back to Brett.
Shoot.
It was pretty obvious you were milking me for information.
But it's okay. I forgive you.

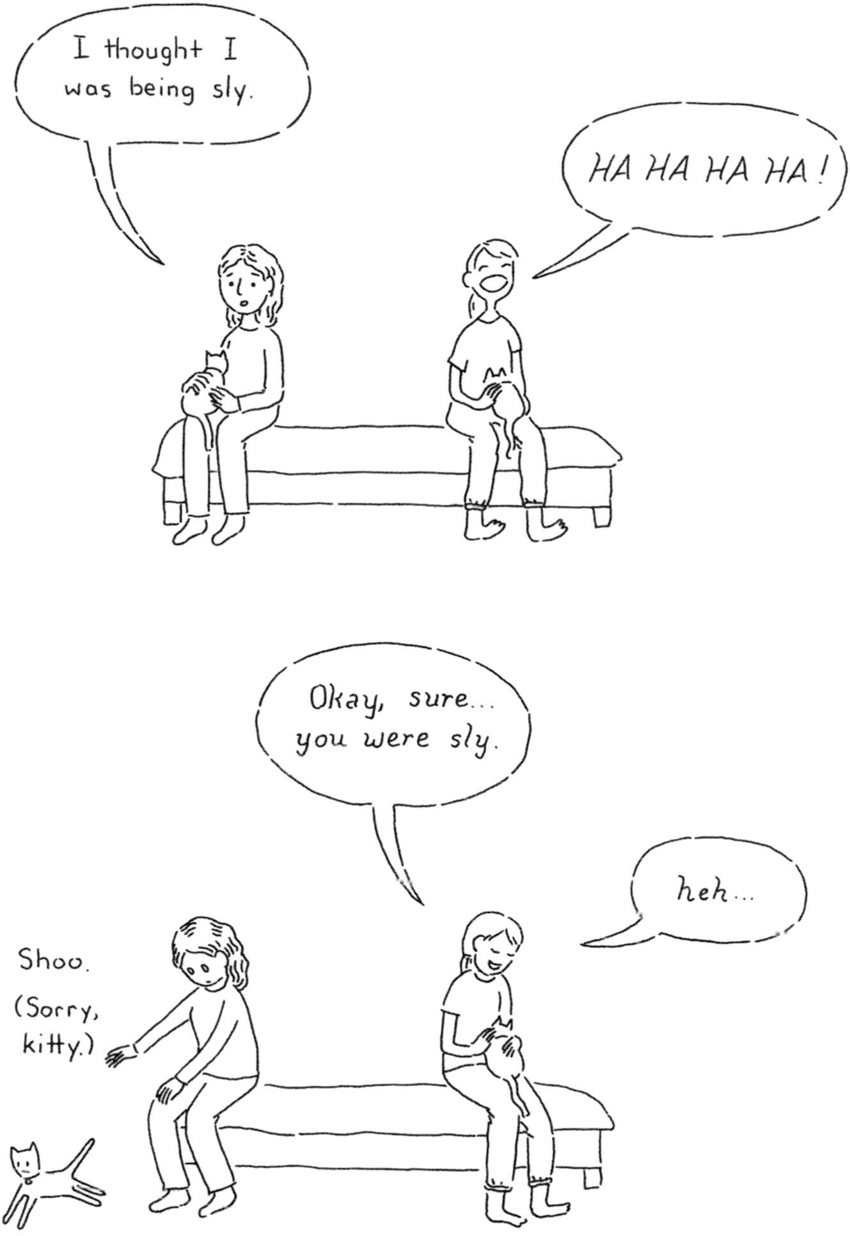
I thought I was being sly.
HA HA HA HA!
Okay, sure... you were sly.
heh...
Shoo.
(Sorry, kitty.)

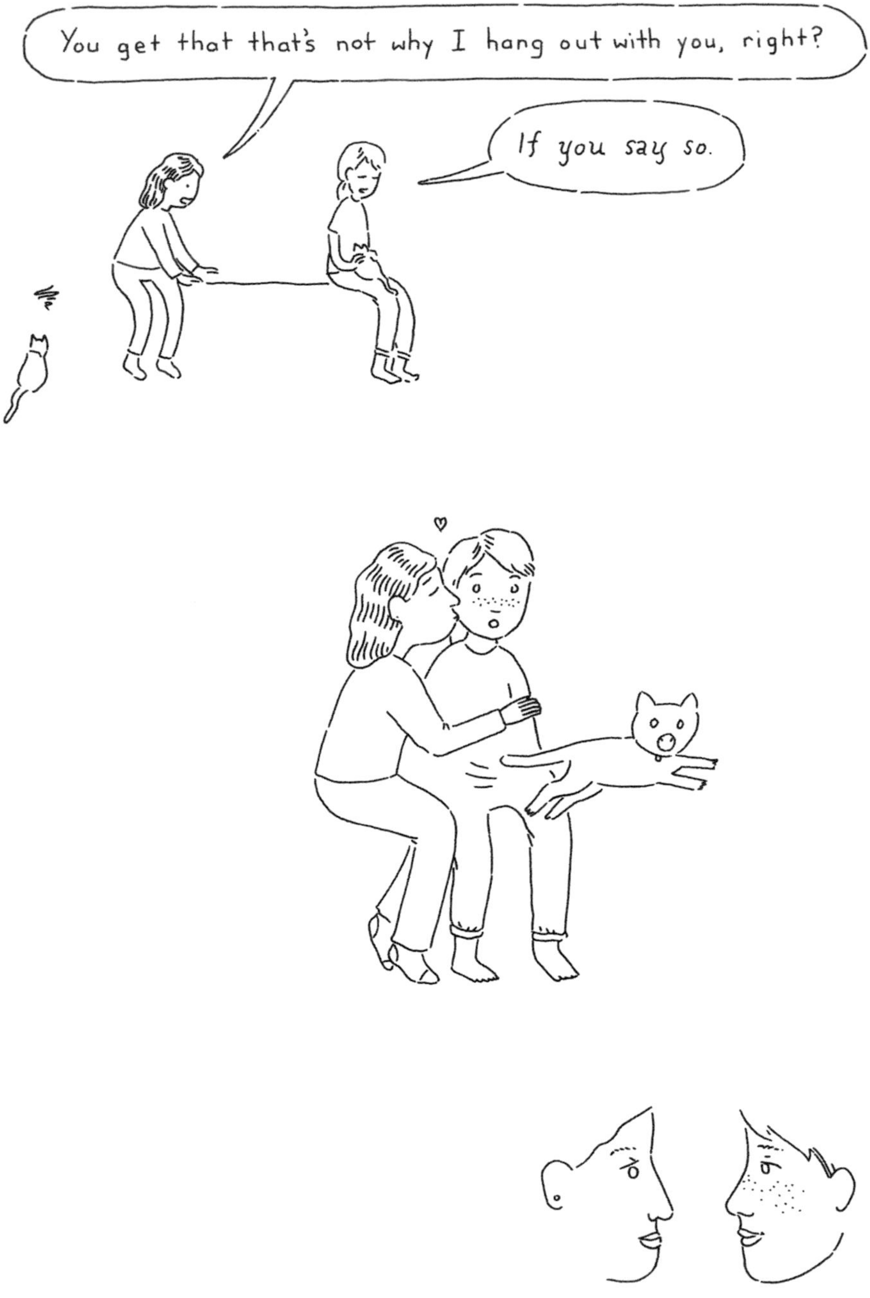
You get that that's not why I hang out with you, right?
If you say so.

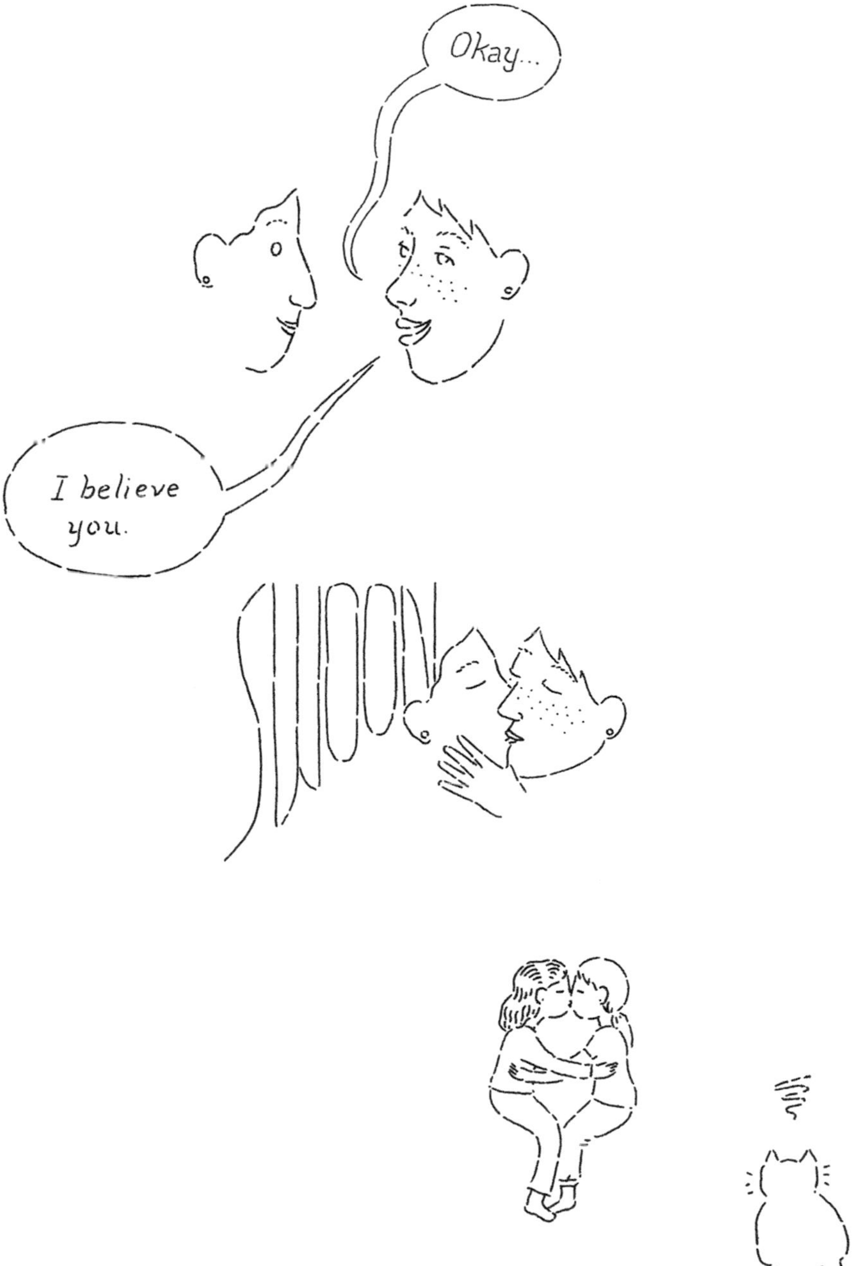
Okay...
I believe you.

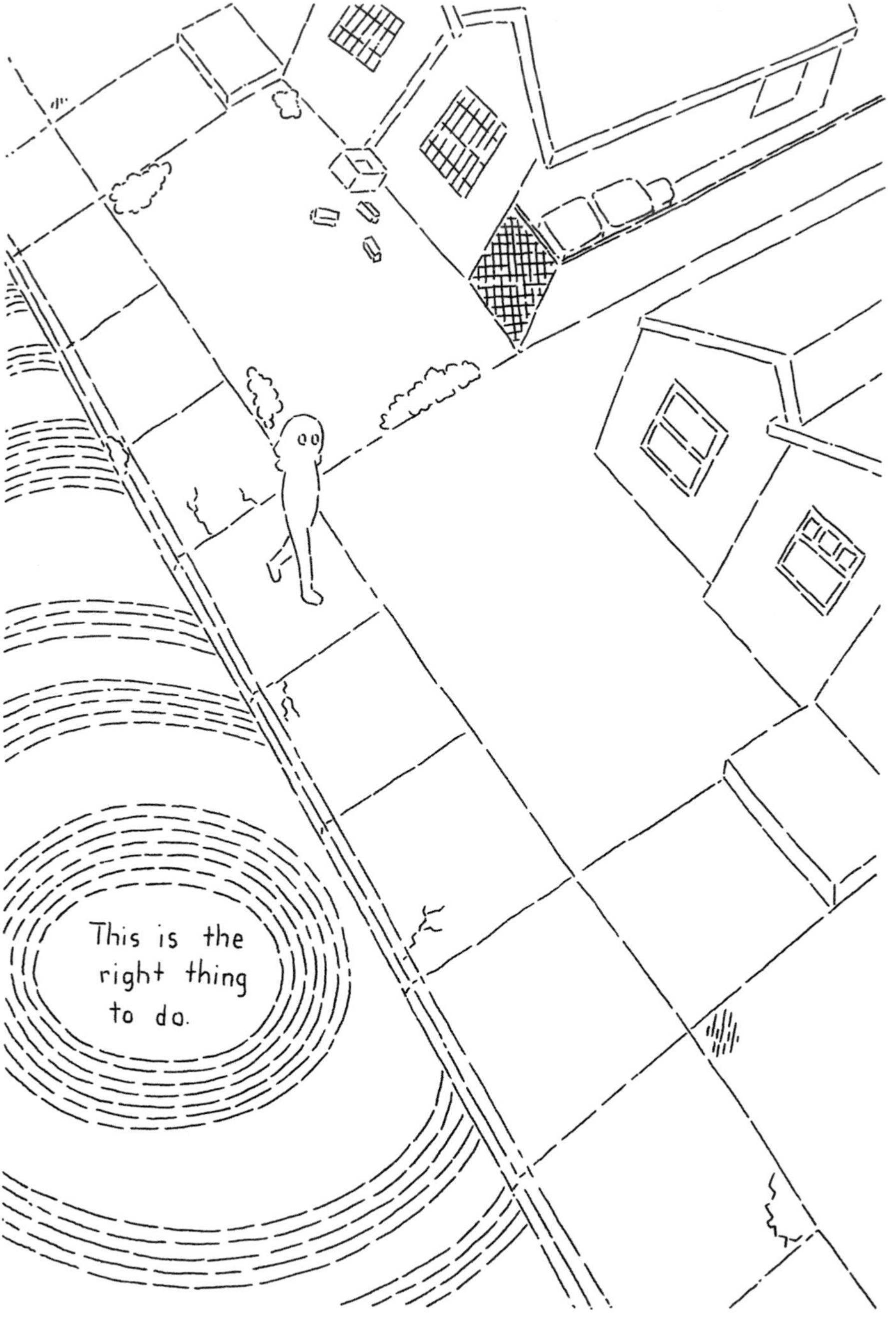
This is the right thing to do.

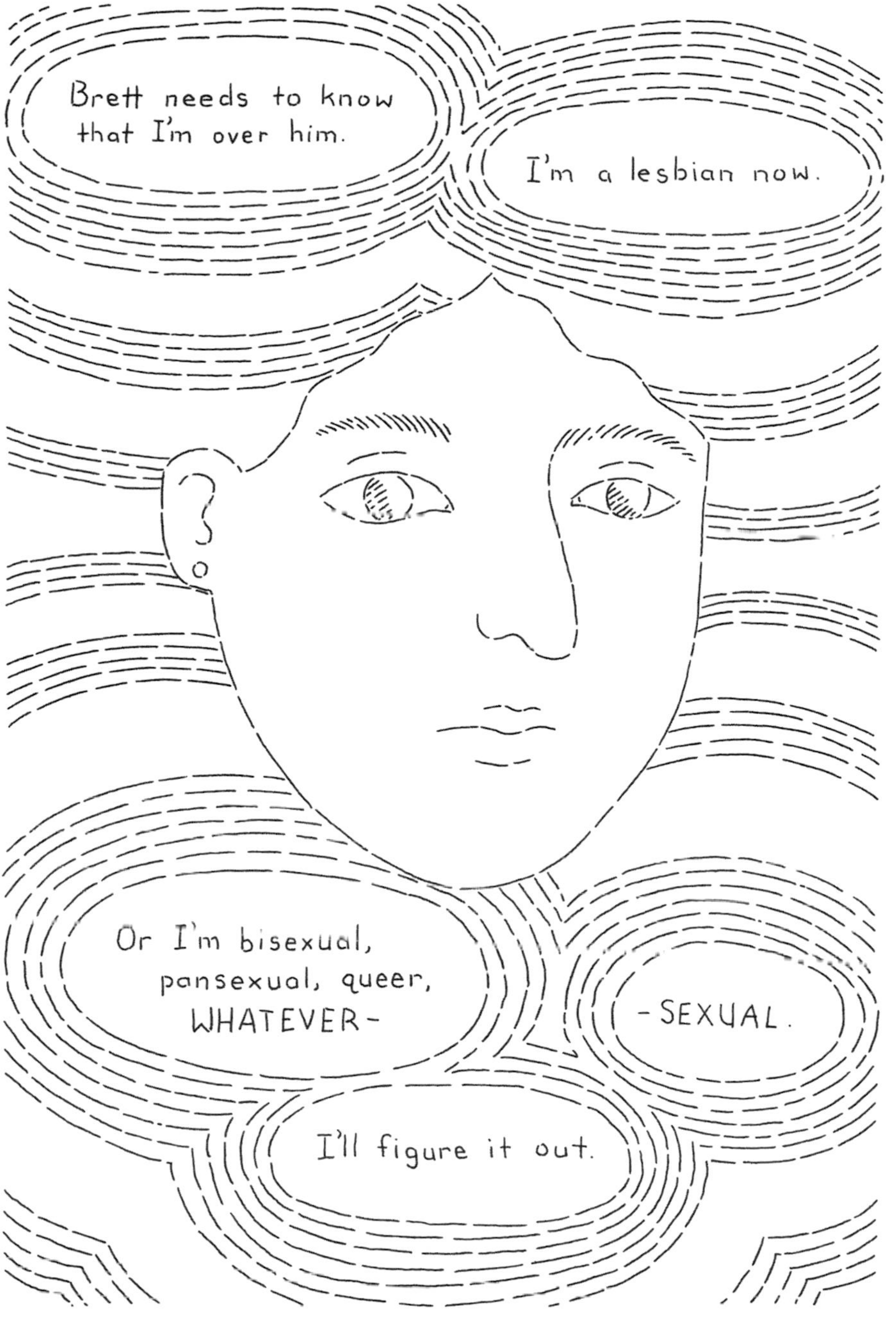
Brett needs to know that I'm over him.
I'm a lesbian now.
Or I'm bisexual, pansexual, queer, WHATEVER-
-SEXUAL.
I'll figure it out.

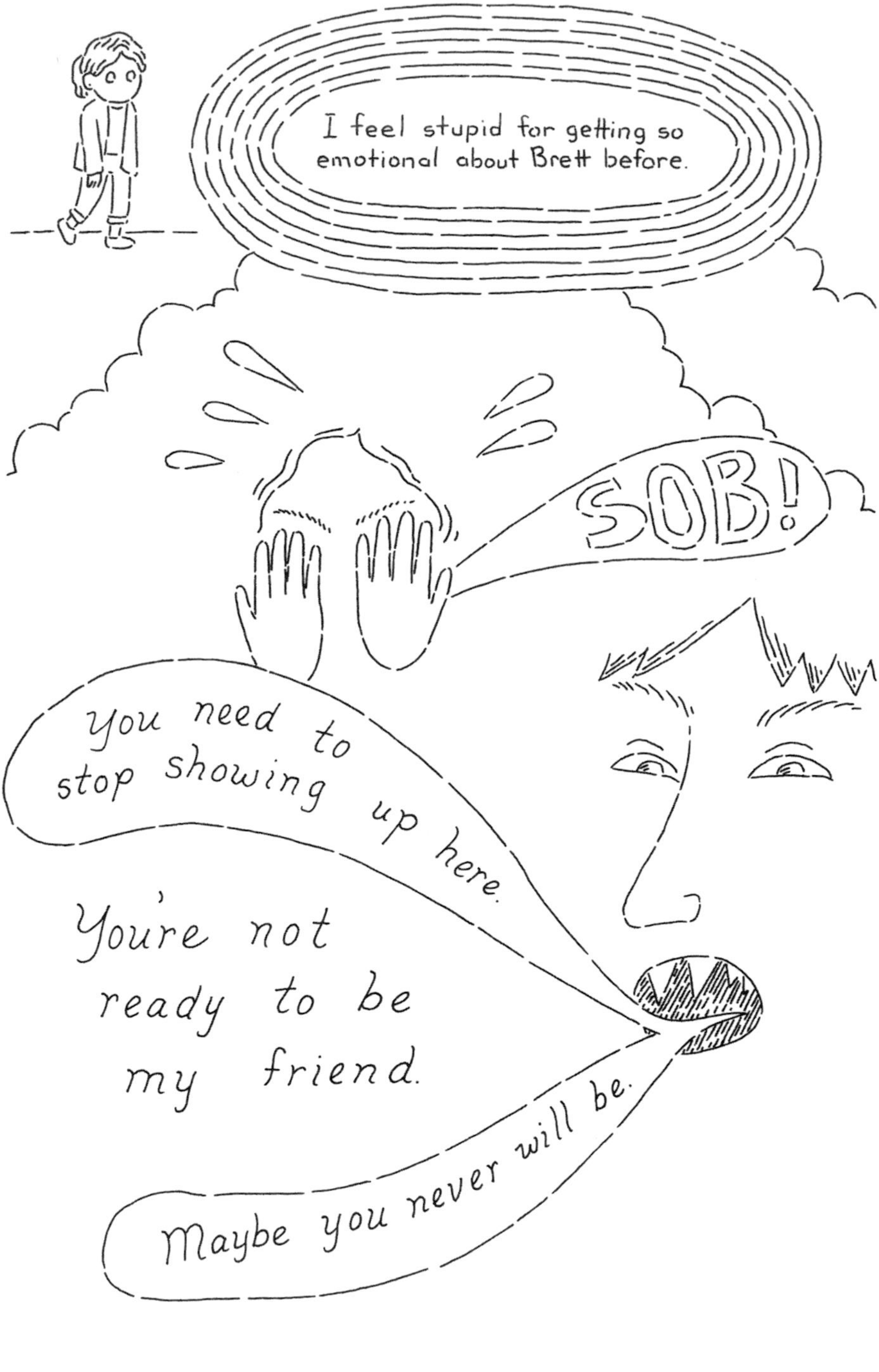
I feel stupid for getting so emotional about Brett before.
SOB!
you need to stop showing up here.
You're not ready to be my friend.
Maybe you never will be.

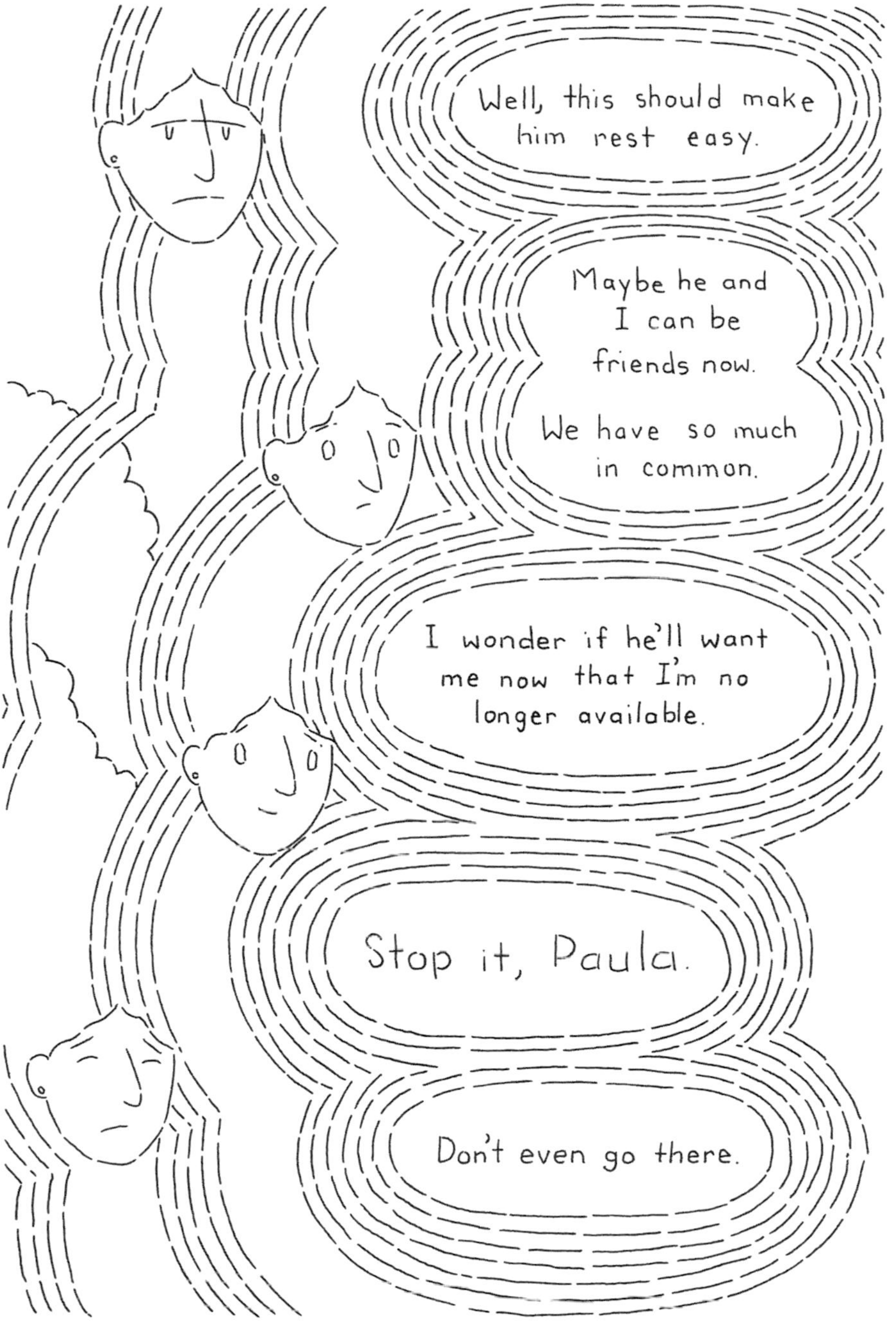
Well, this should make him rest easy.
Maybe he and I can be friends now.
We have so much in common.
I wonder if he'll want me now that I'm no longer available.
Stop it, Paula.
Don't even go there.

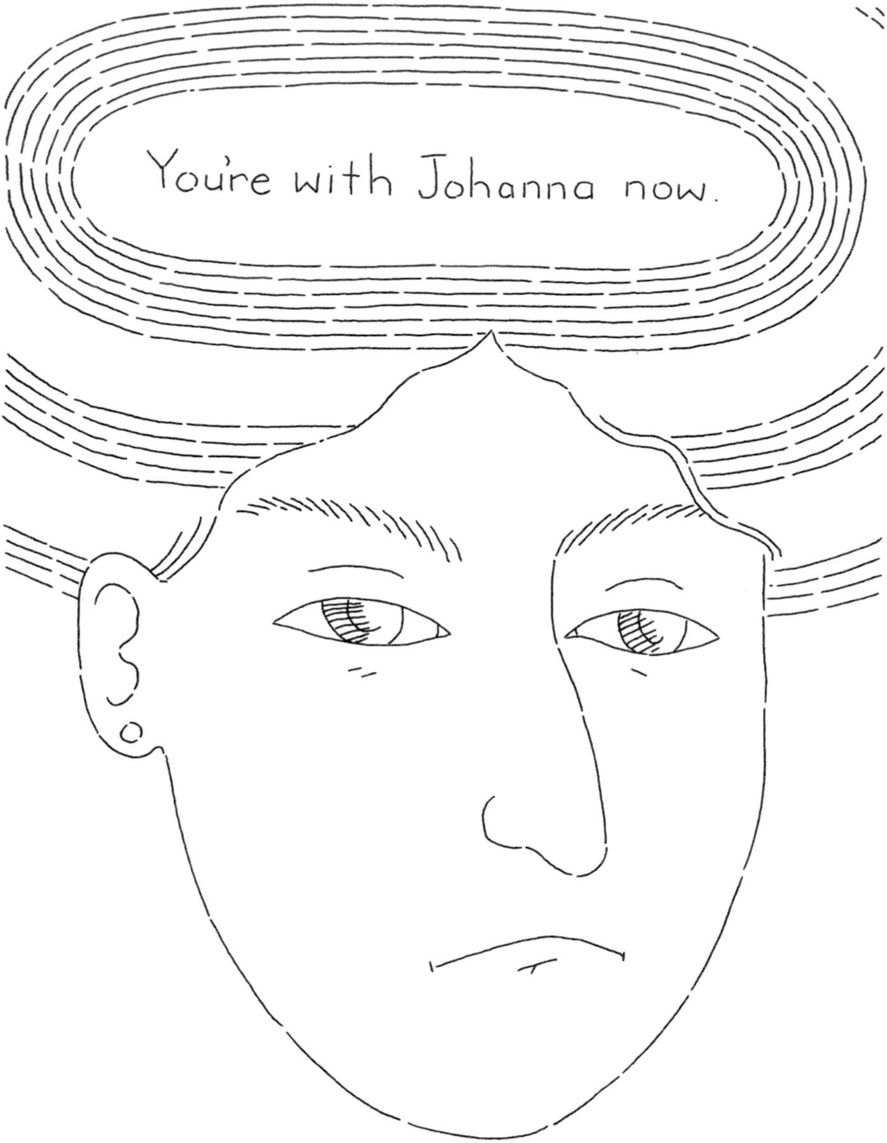
You're with Johanna now.

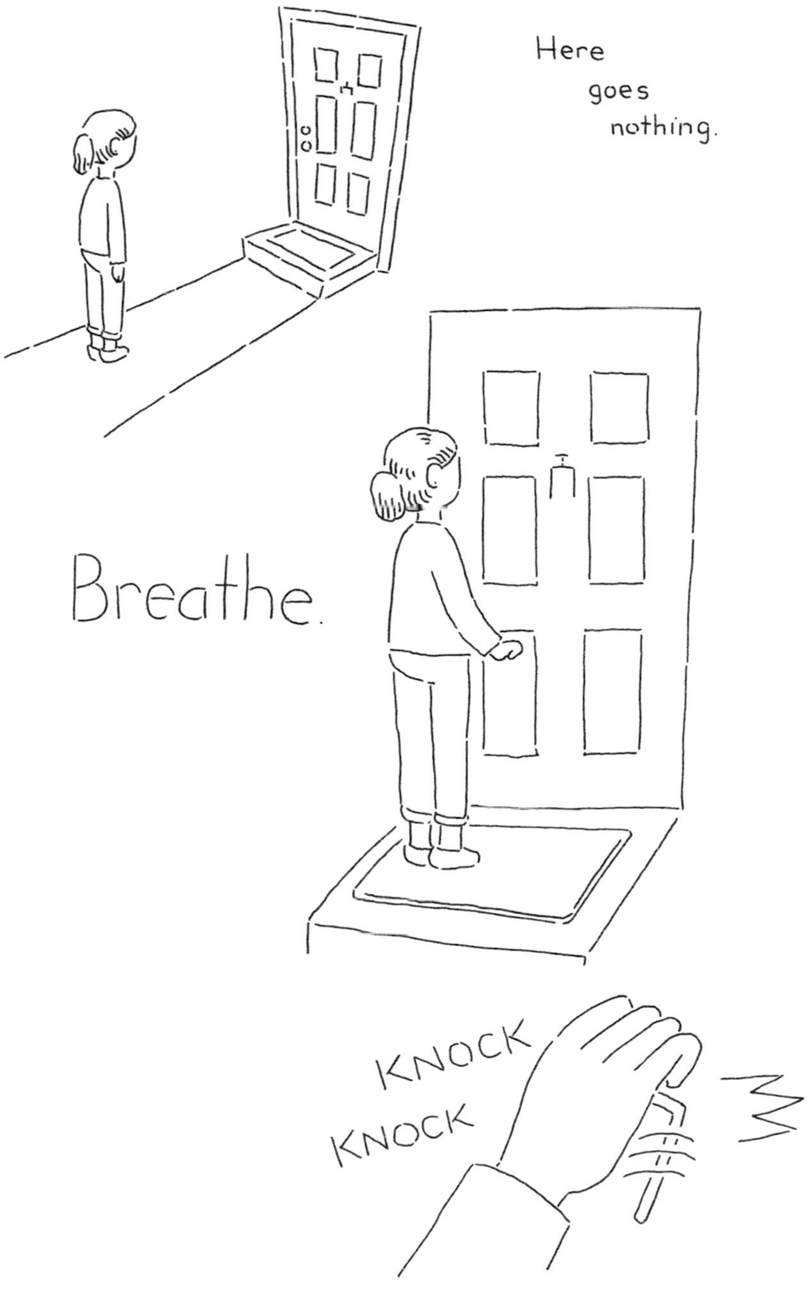
Here goes nothing.
Breathe.
KNOCK
KNOCK

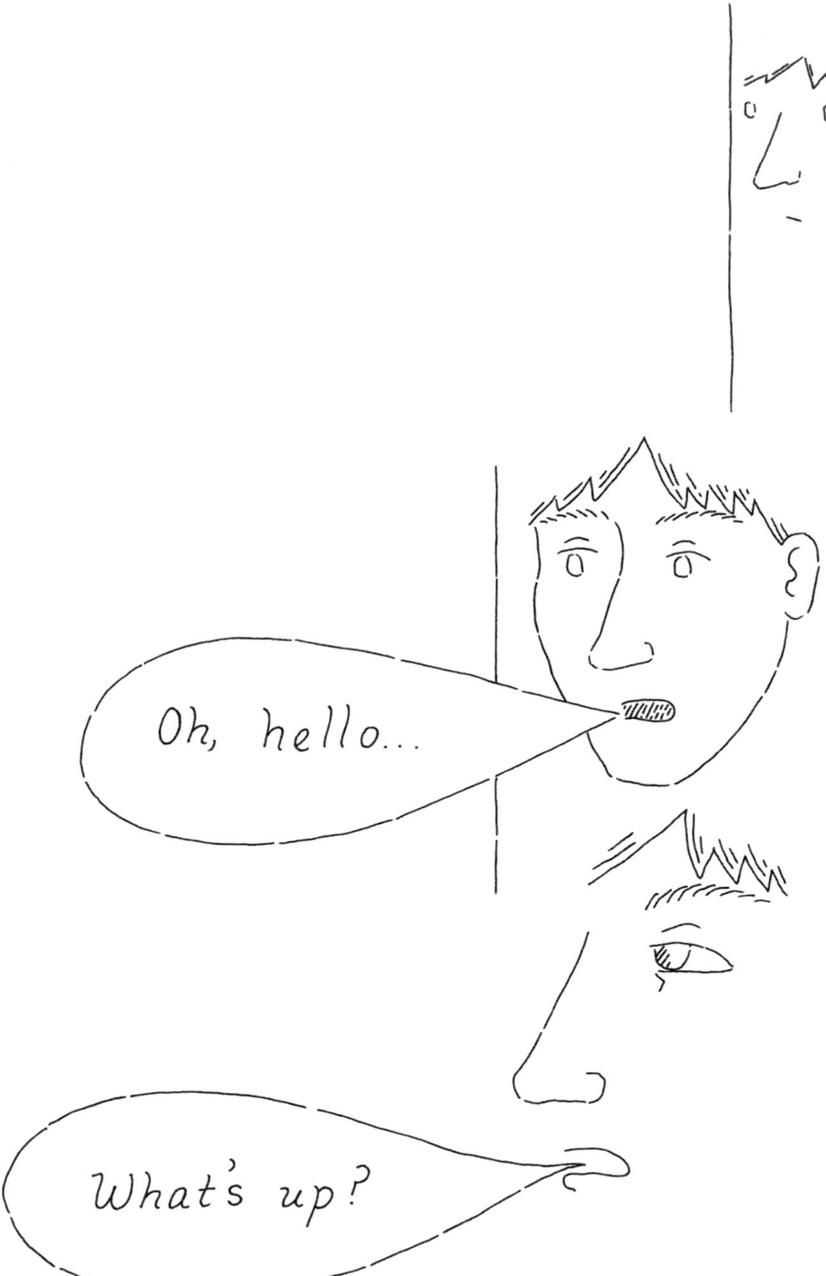
Oh, hello...
What's up?

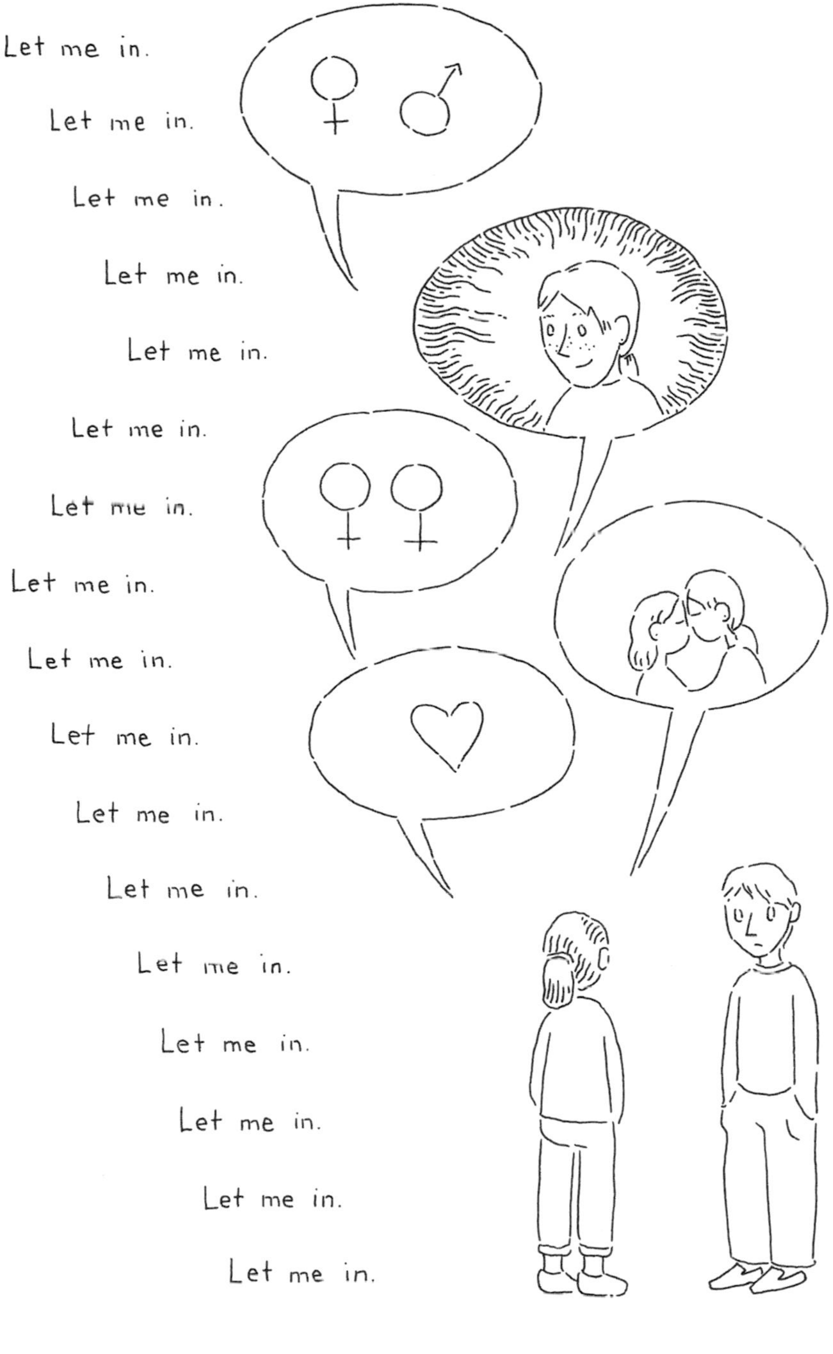
Let me in.
Let me in.
Let me in.
Let me in.
Let me in.
Let me in.
Let me in.
Let me in.
Let me in.
Let me in.
Let me in.
Let me in.
Let me in.
Let me in.
Let me in.
Let me in.
Let me in.

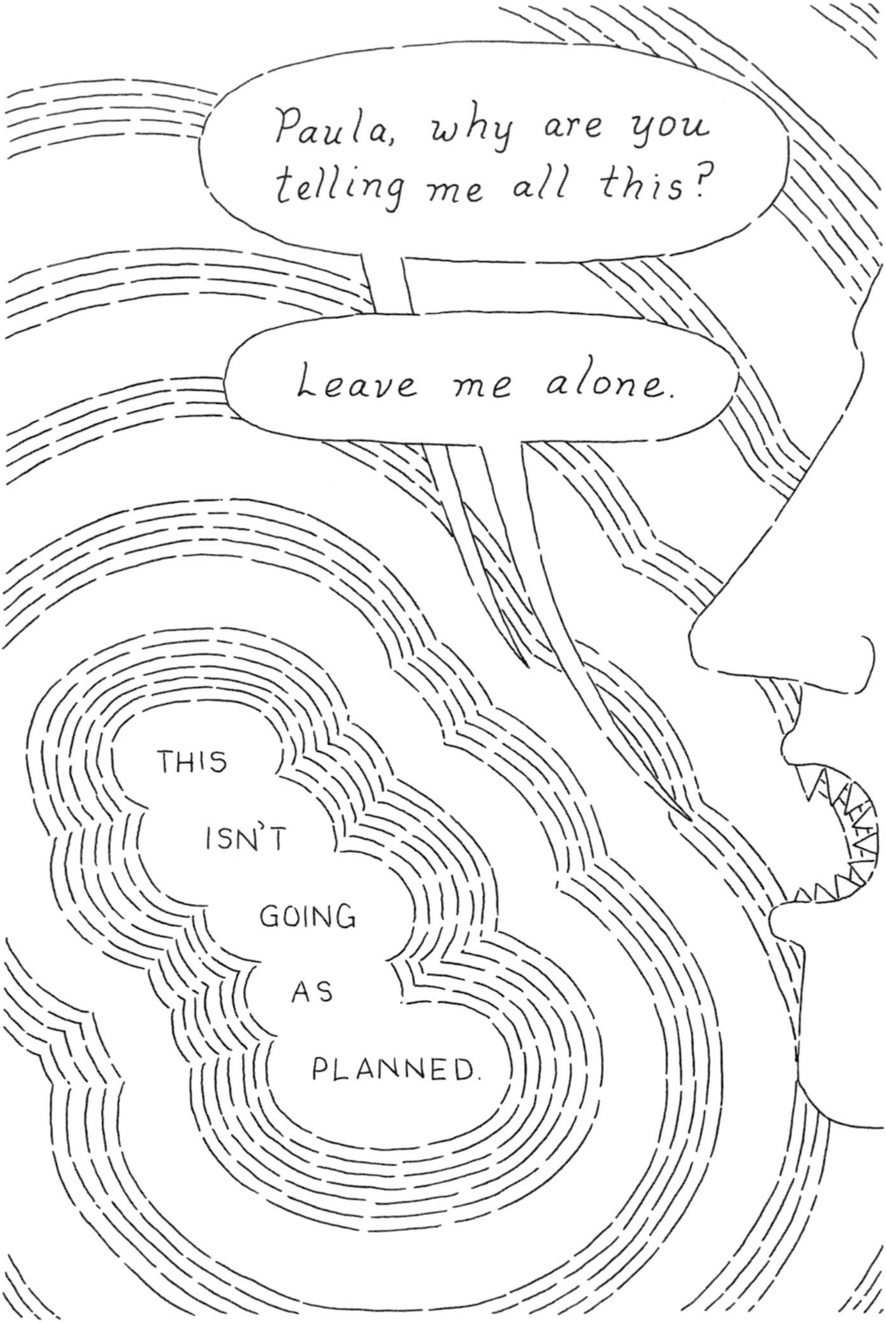
Paula, why are you telling me all this?
Leave me alone.
THIS ISN'T GOING AS PLANNED.

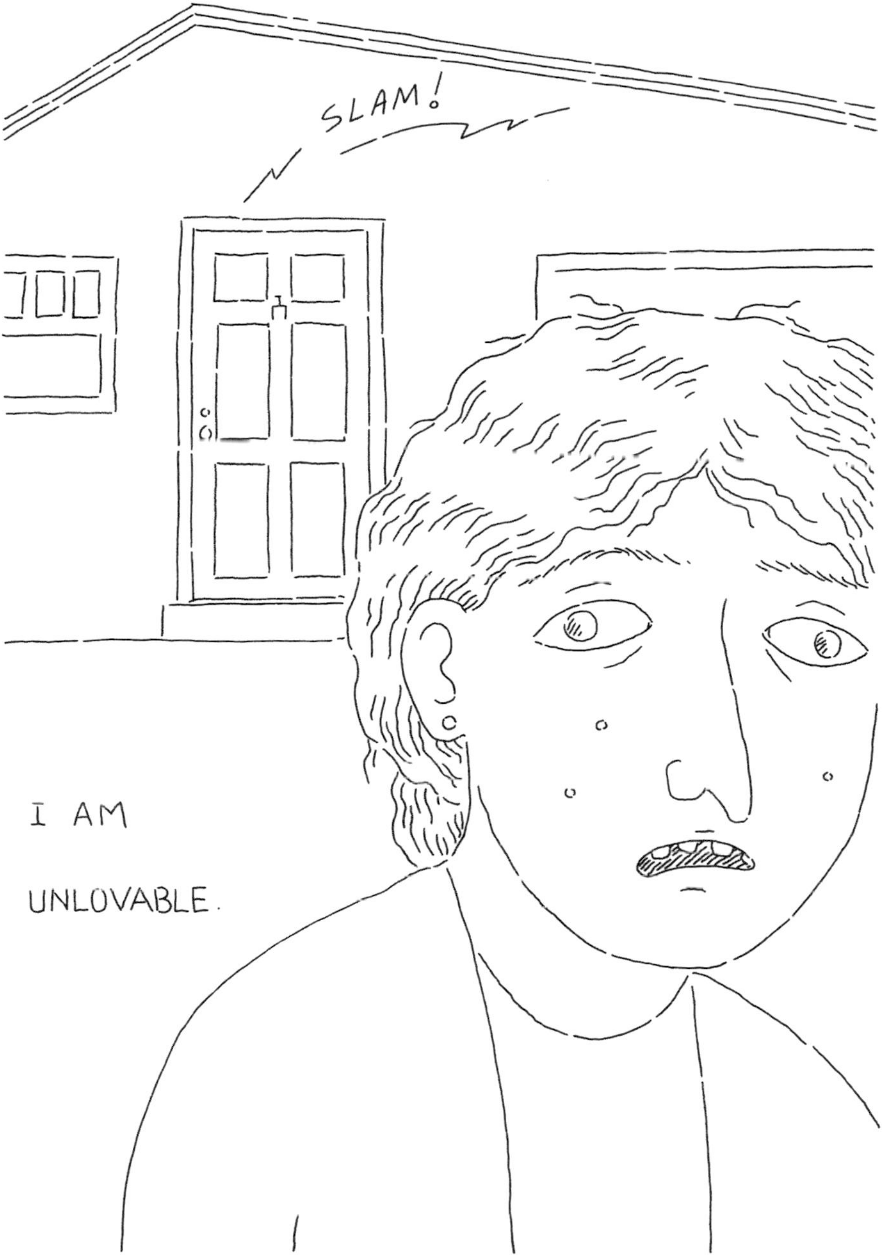
SLAM!
I AM
UNLOVABLE.

## PART THREE

NOT
PICTURED

# Brett Hathaway

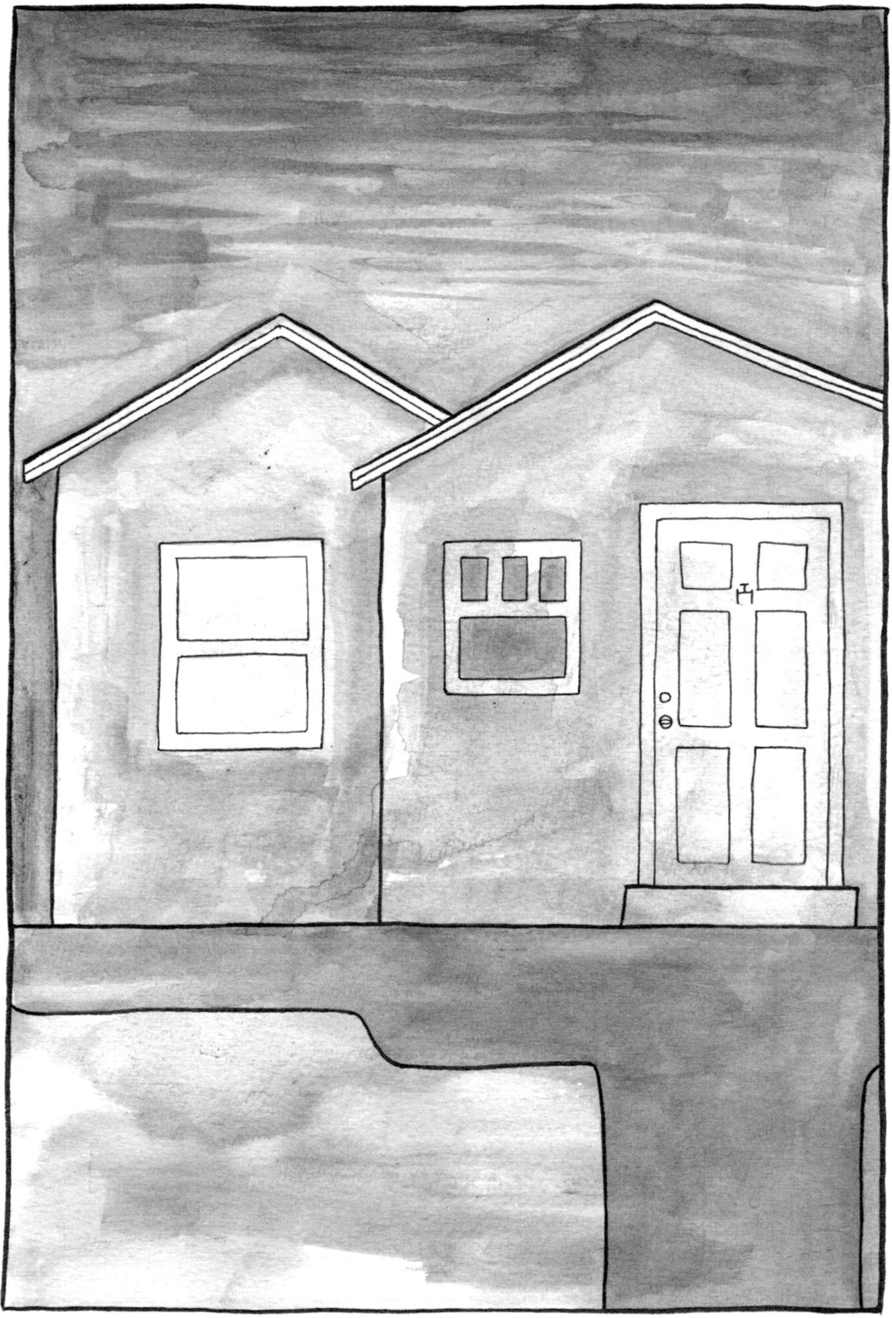

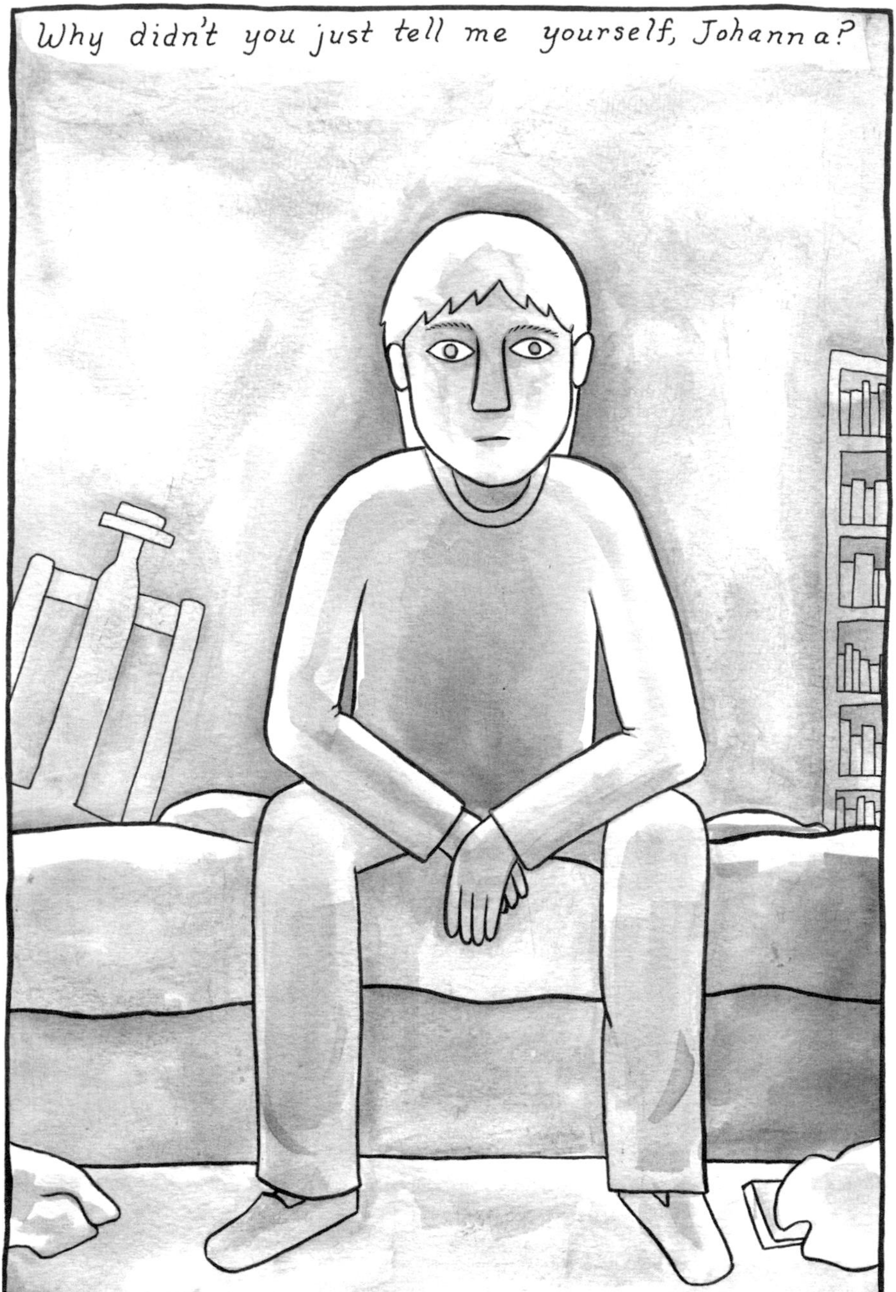
Why didn't you just tell me yourself, Johanna?

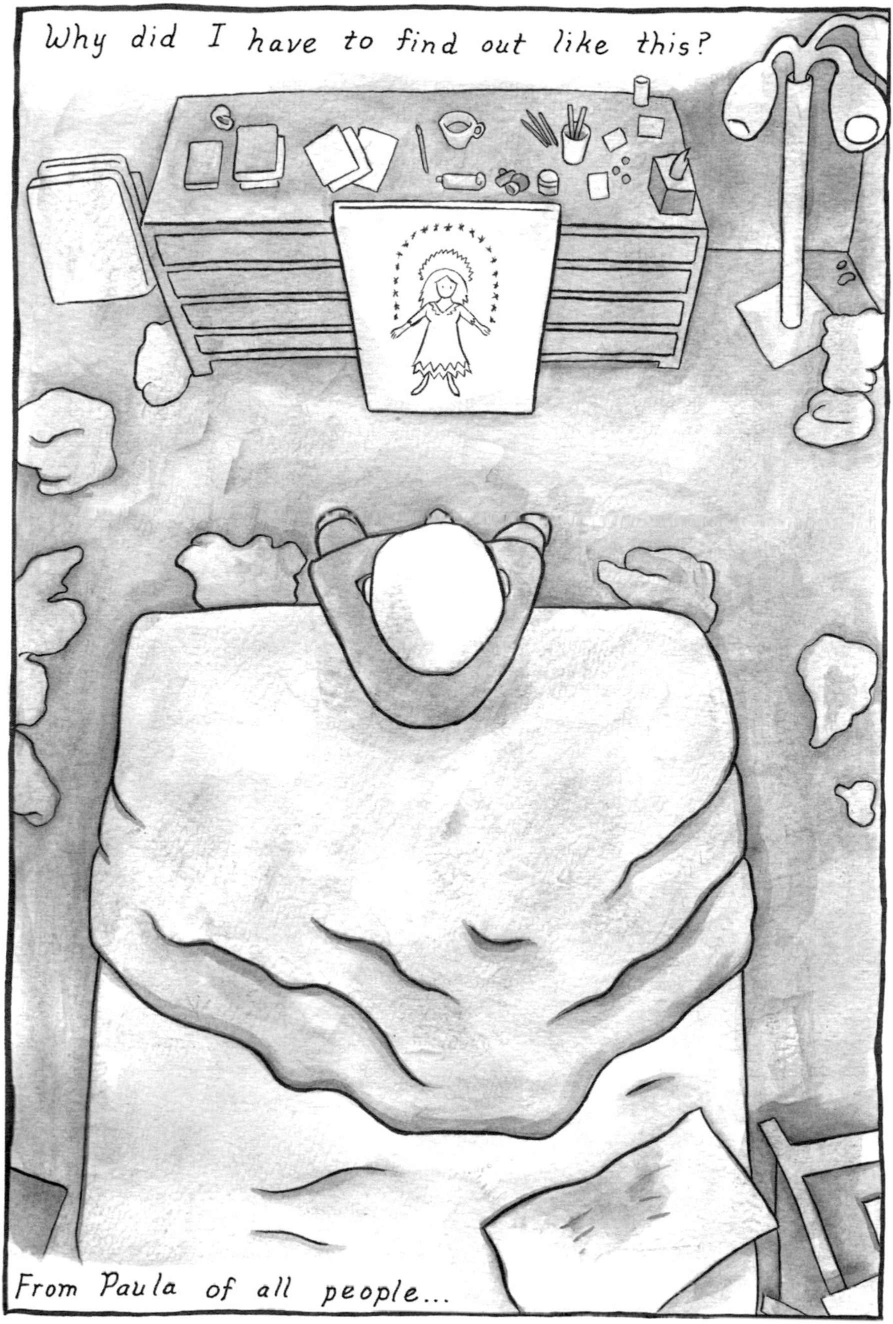
Why did I have to find out like this?
From Paula of all people...

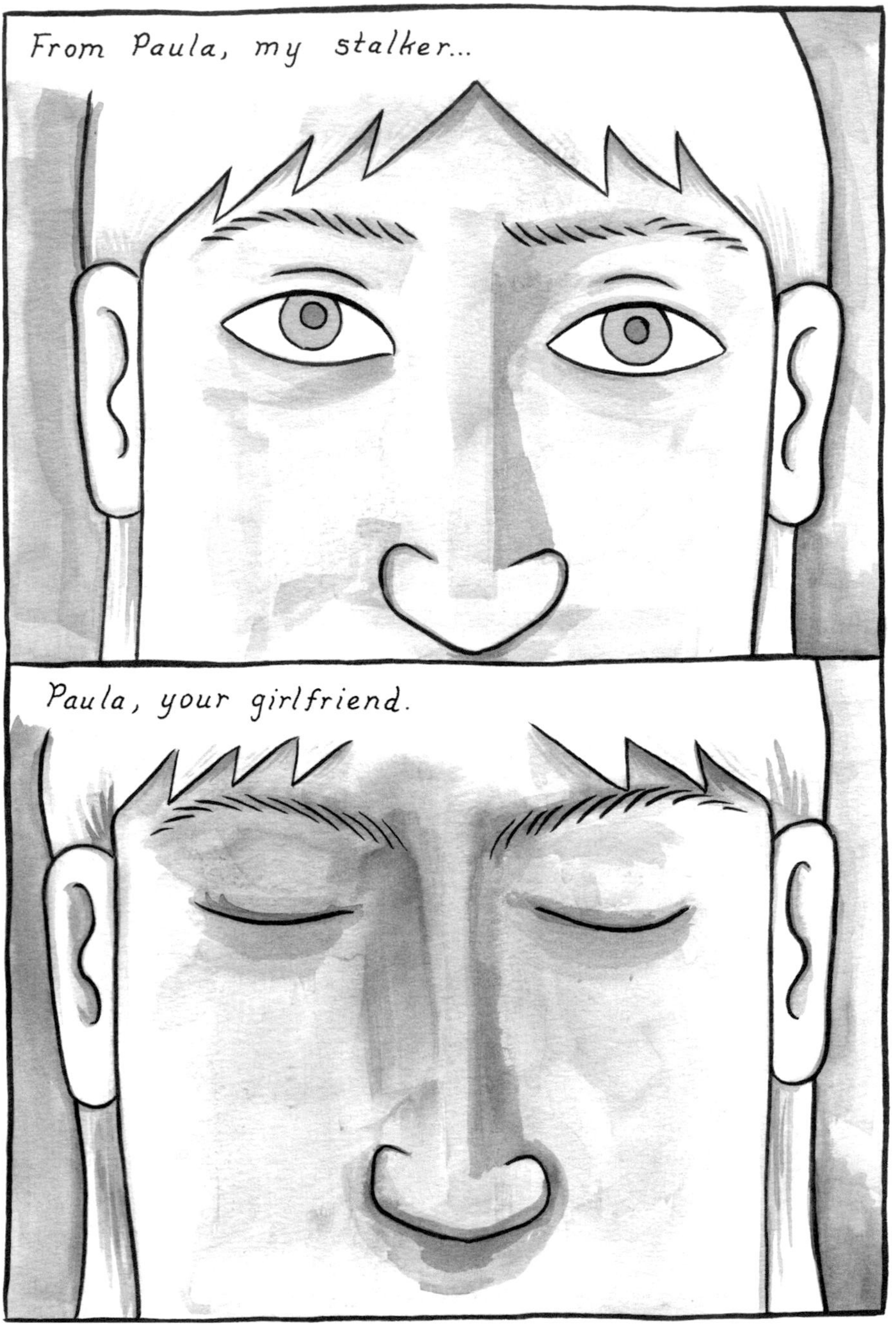
From Paula, my stalker...
Paula, your girlfriend.

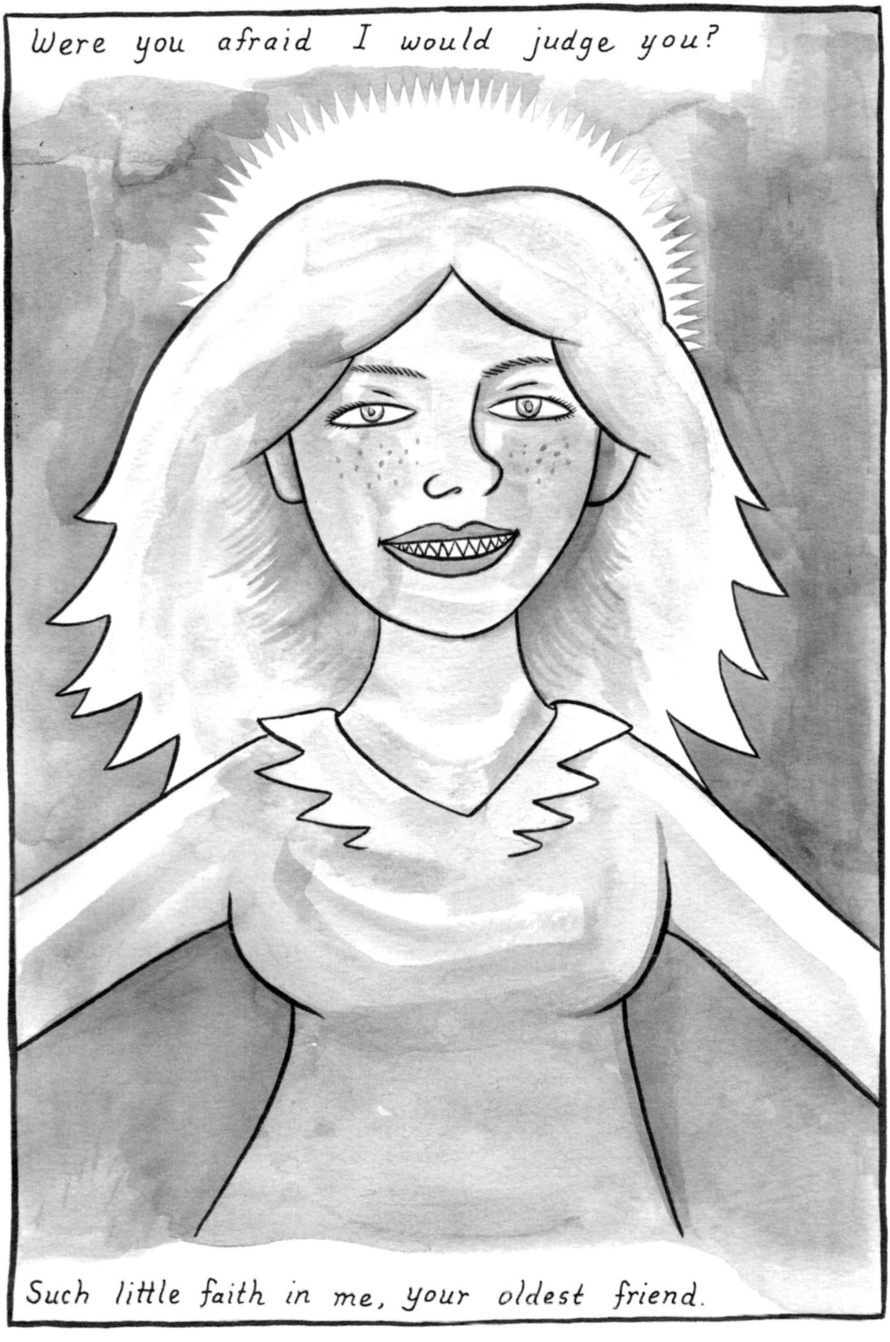
Were you afraid I would judge you?
Such little faith in me, your oldest friend.

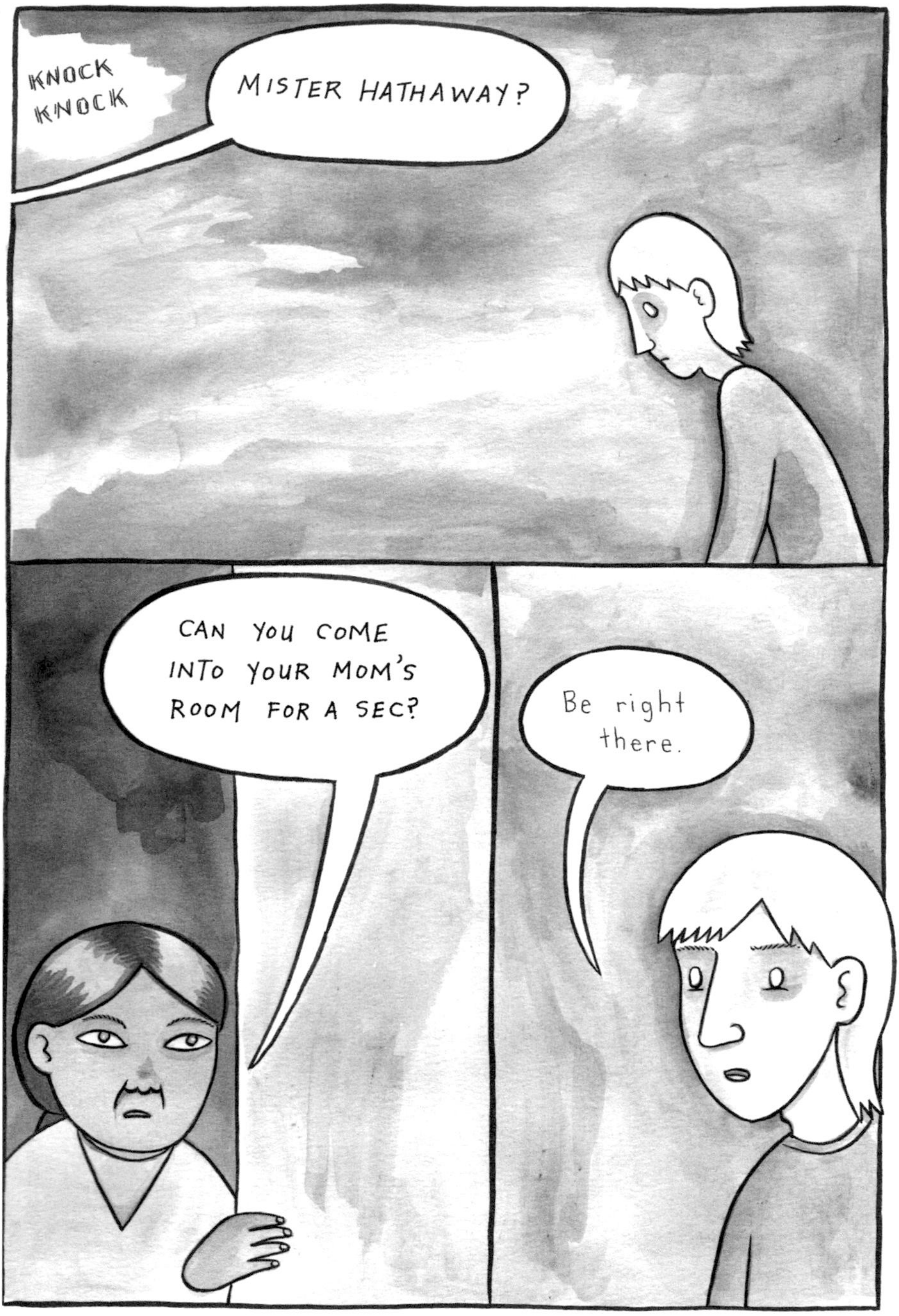
KNOCK KNOCK
MISTER HATHAWAY?
CAN YOU COME INTO YOUR MOM'S ROOM FOR A SEC?
Be right there.

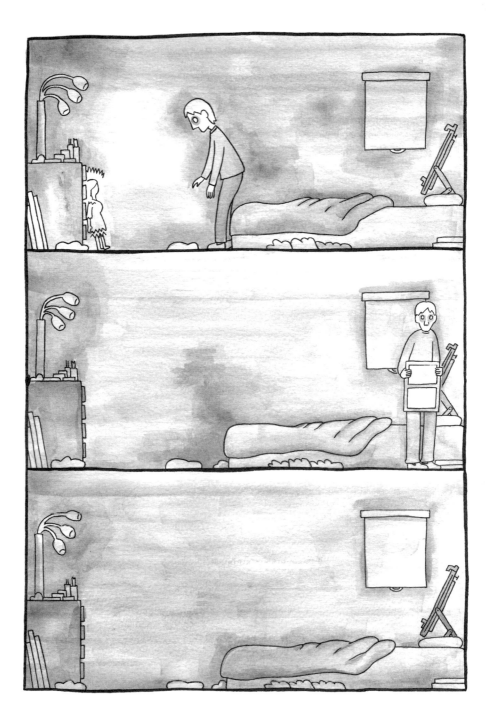

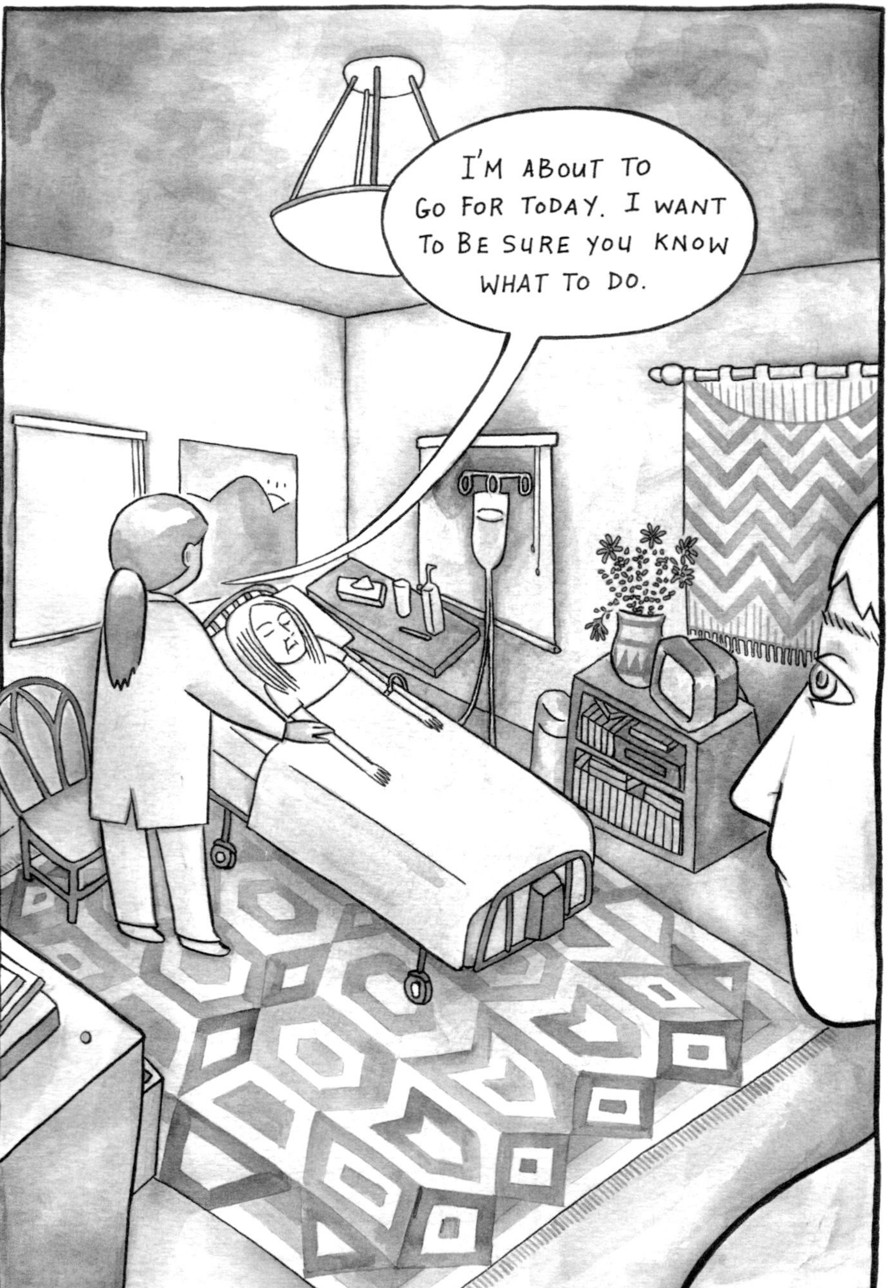
I'M ABOUT TO GO FOR TODAY. I WANT TO BE SURE YOU KNOW WHAT TO DO.

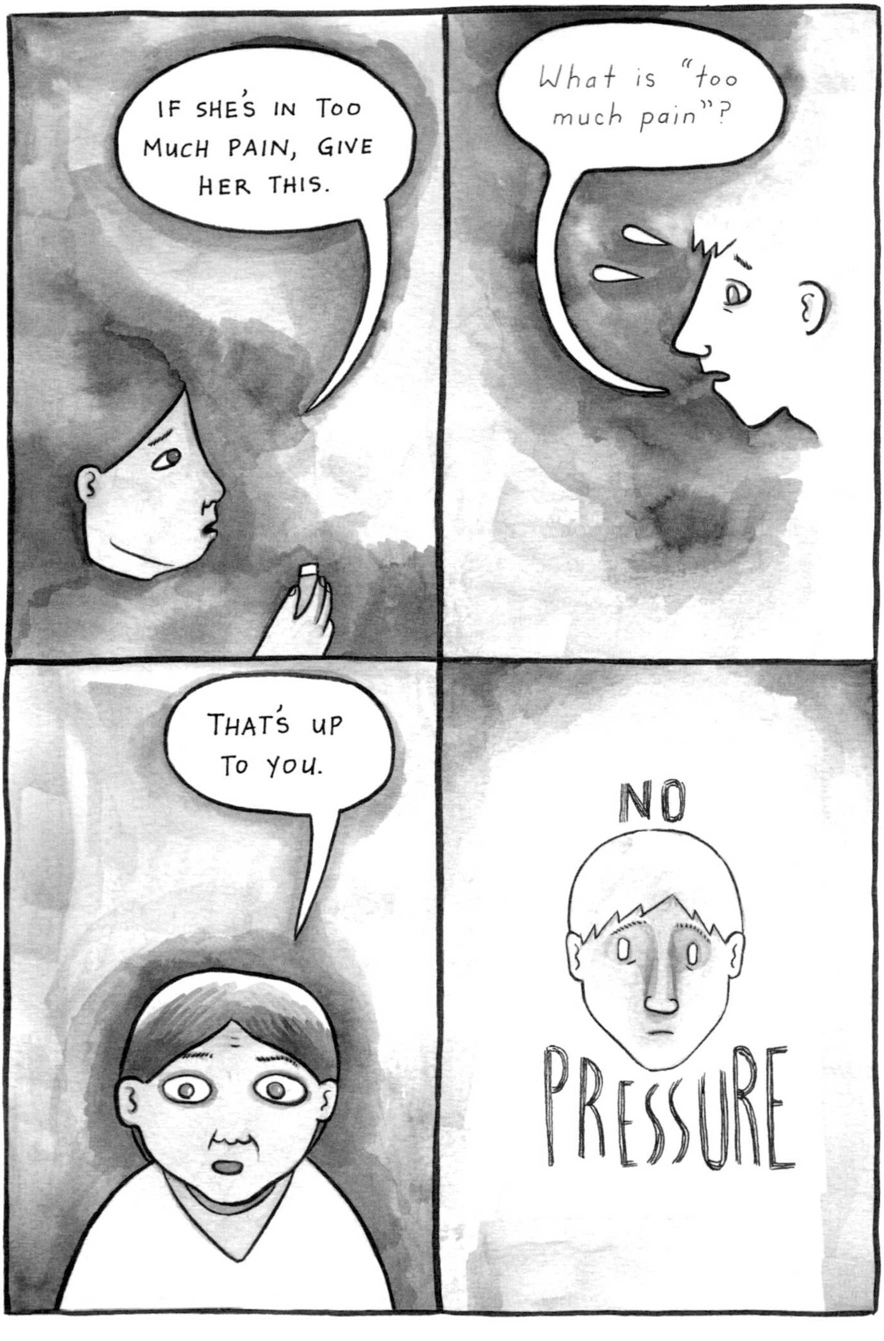
IF SHE'S IN TOO MUCH PAIN, GIVE HER THIS.
What is "too much pain"?
THAT'S UP TO YOU.
NO
PRESSURE

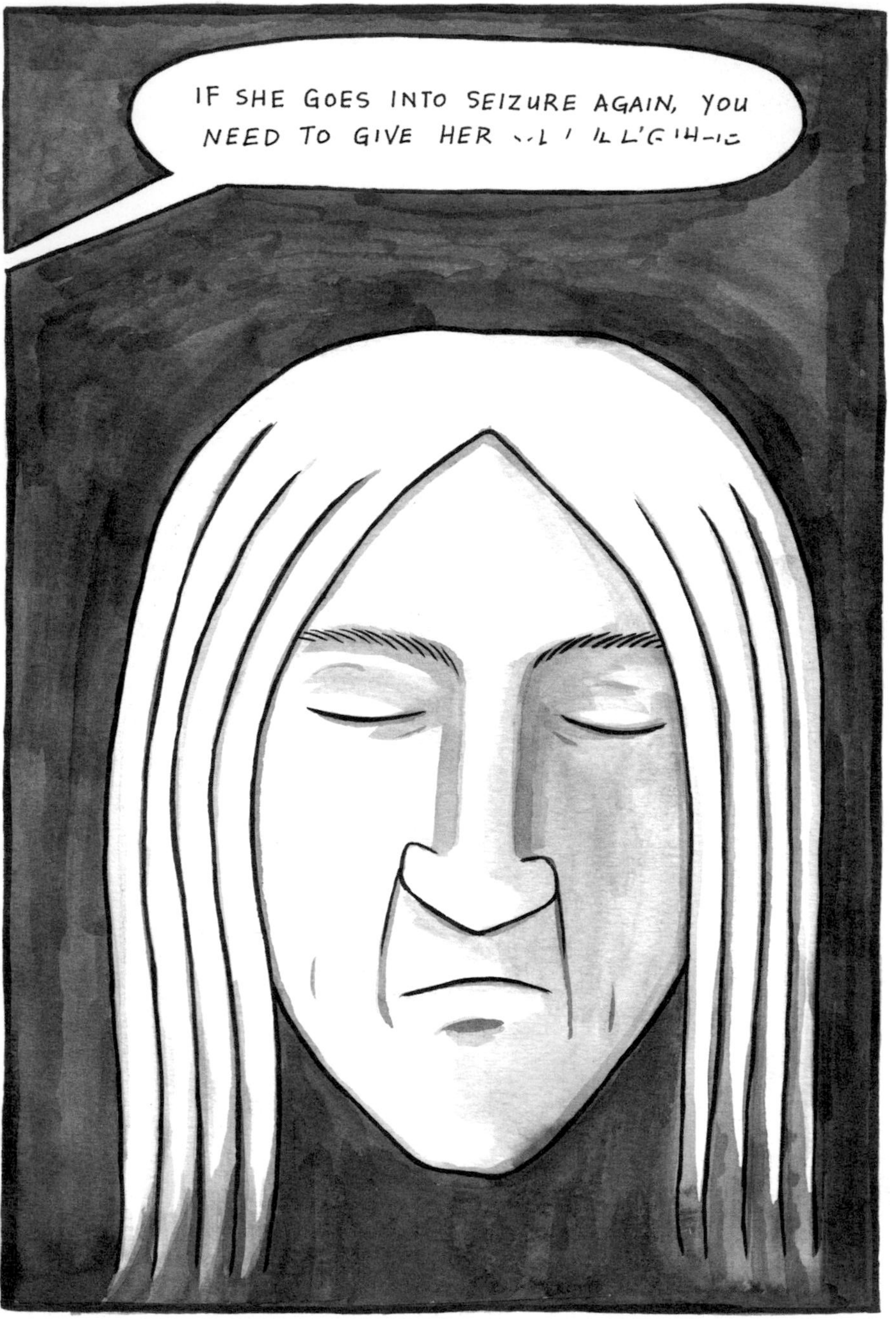
IF SHE GOES INTO SEIZURE AGAIN, YOU NEED TO GIVE HER

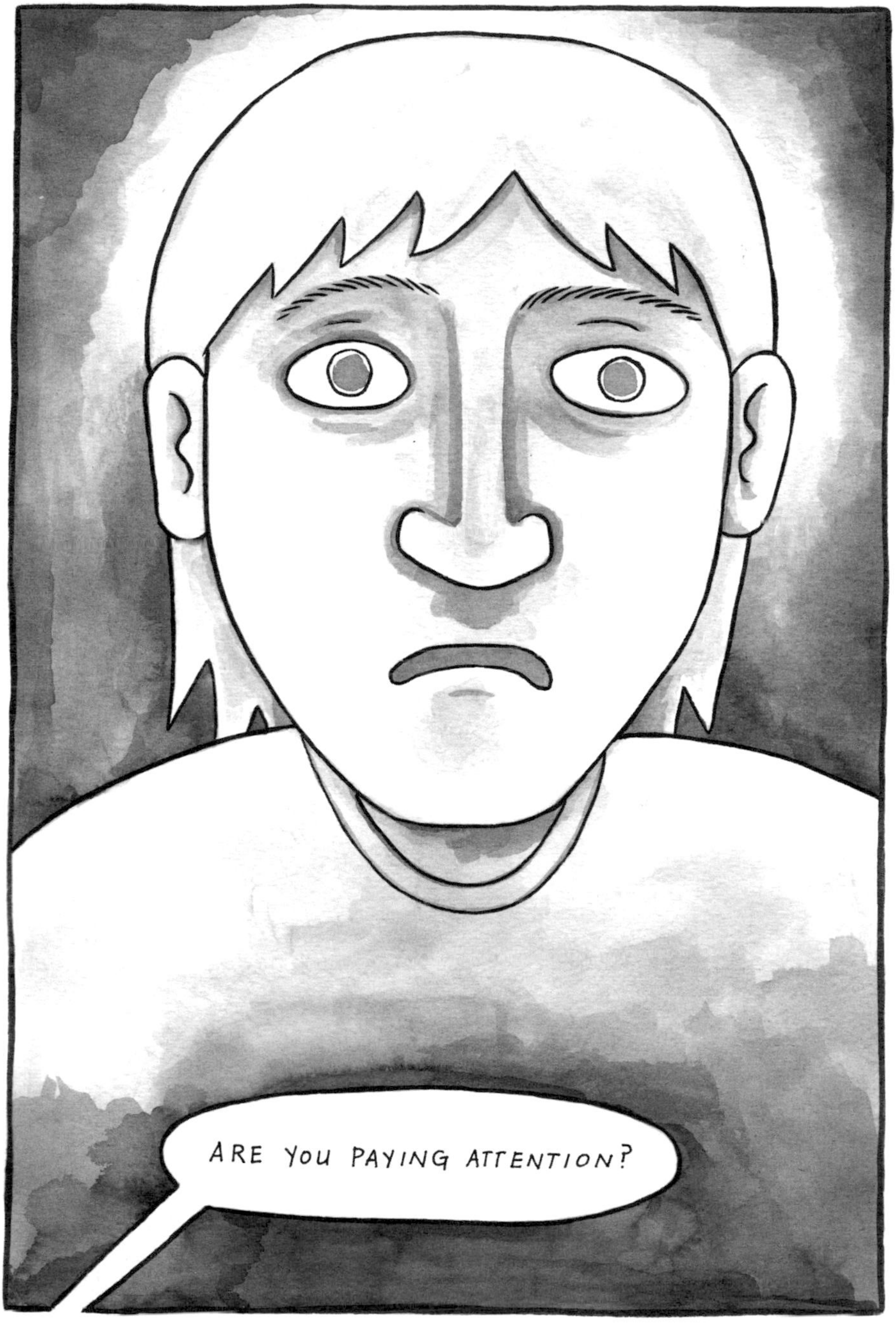
ARE YOU PAYING ATTENTION?

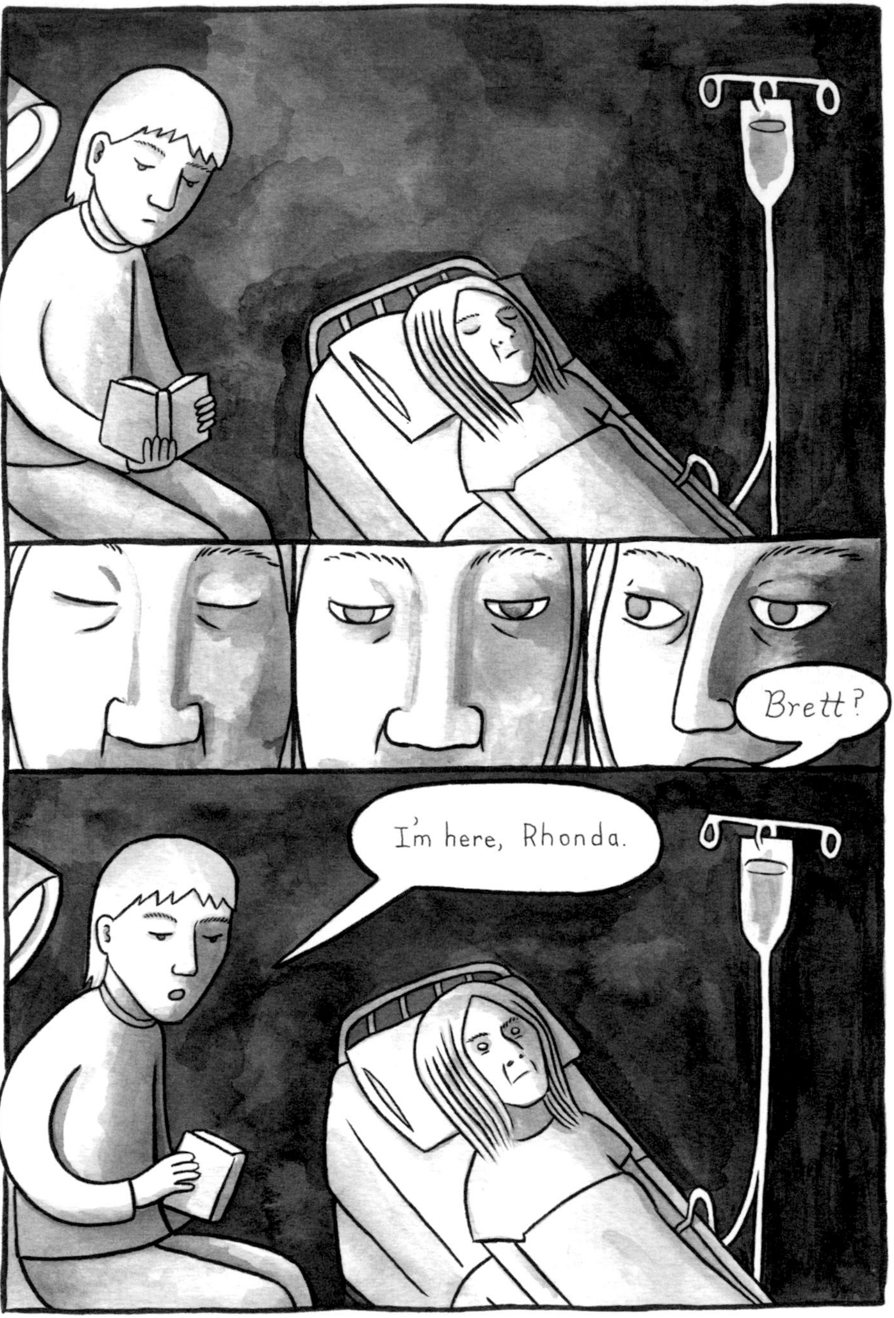
Brett?
I'm here, Rhonda.

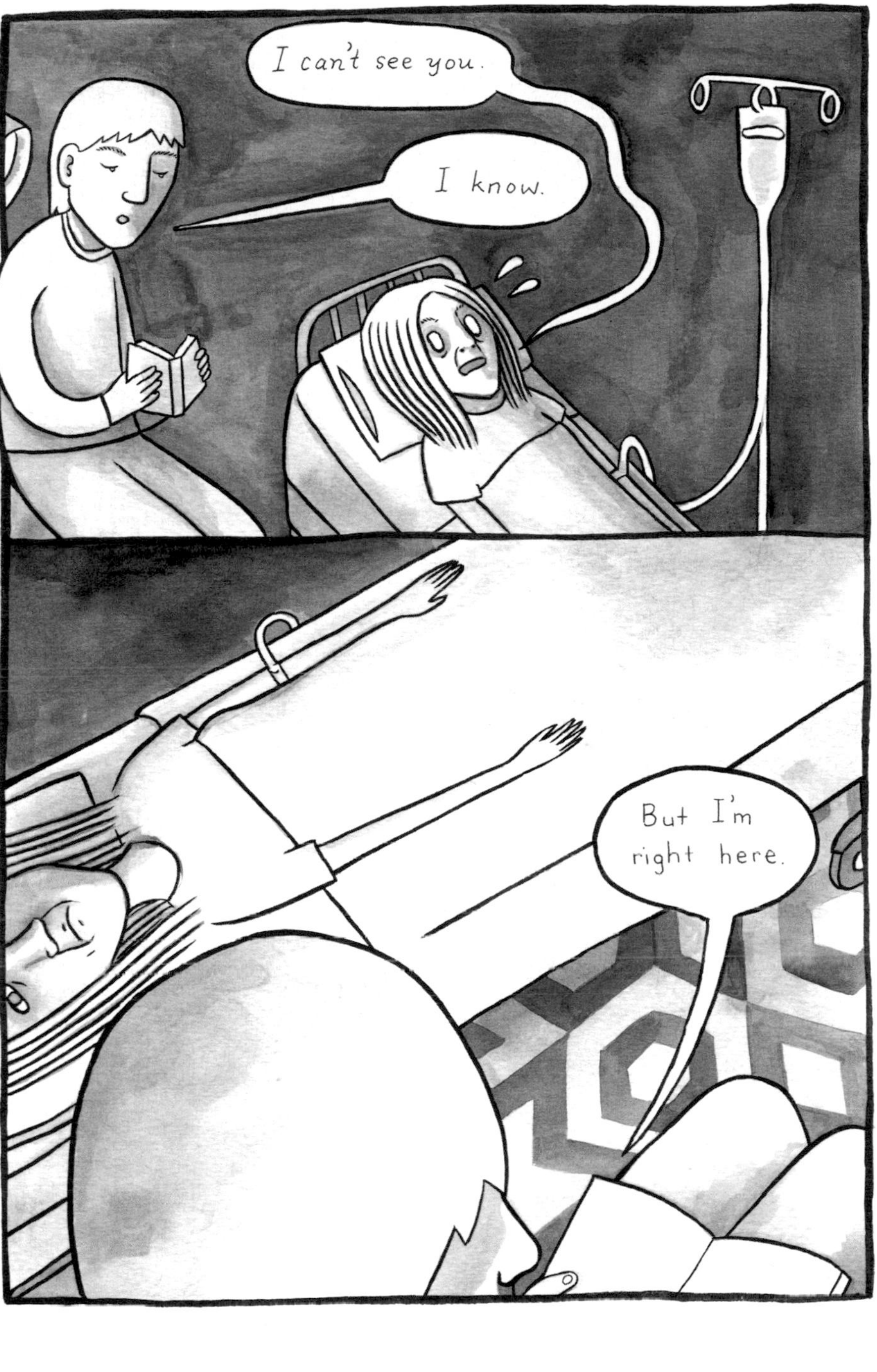
I can't see you.
I know.
But I'm right here.

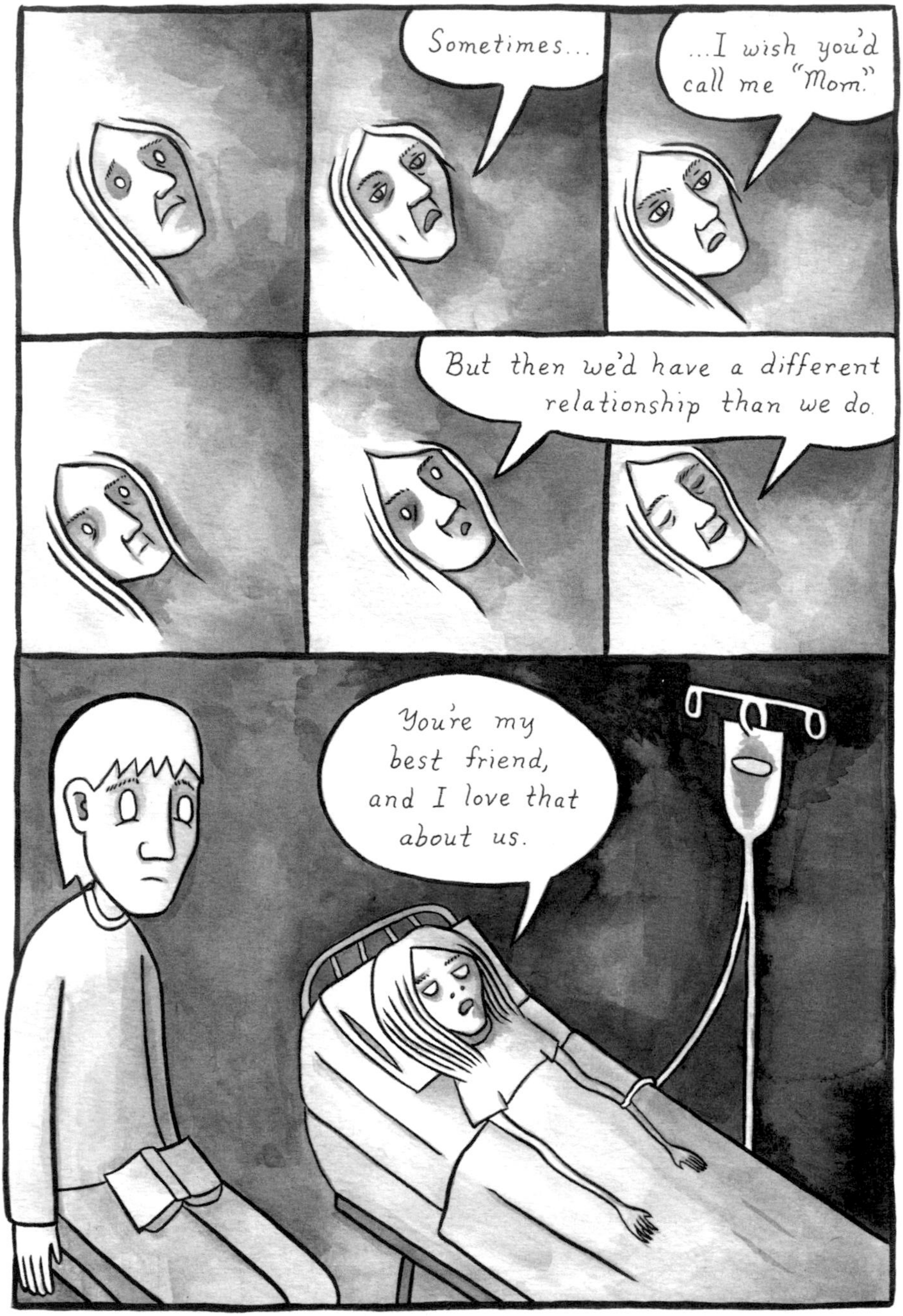
Sometimes...
...I wish you'd call me "Mom."
But then we'd have a different relationship than we do.
You're my best friend, and I love that about us.

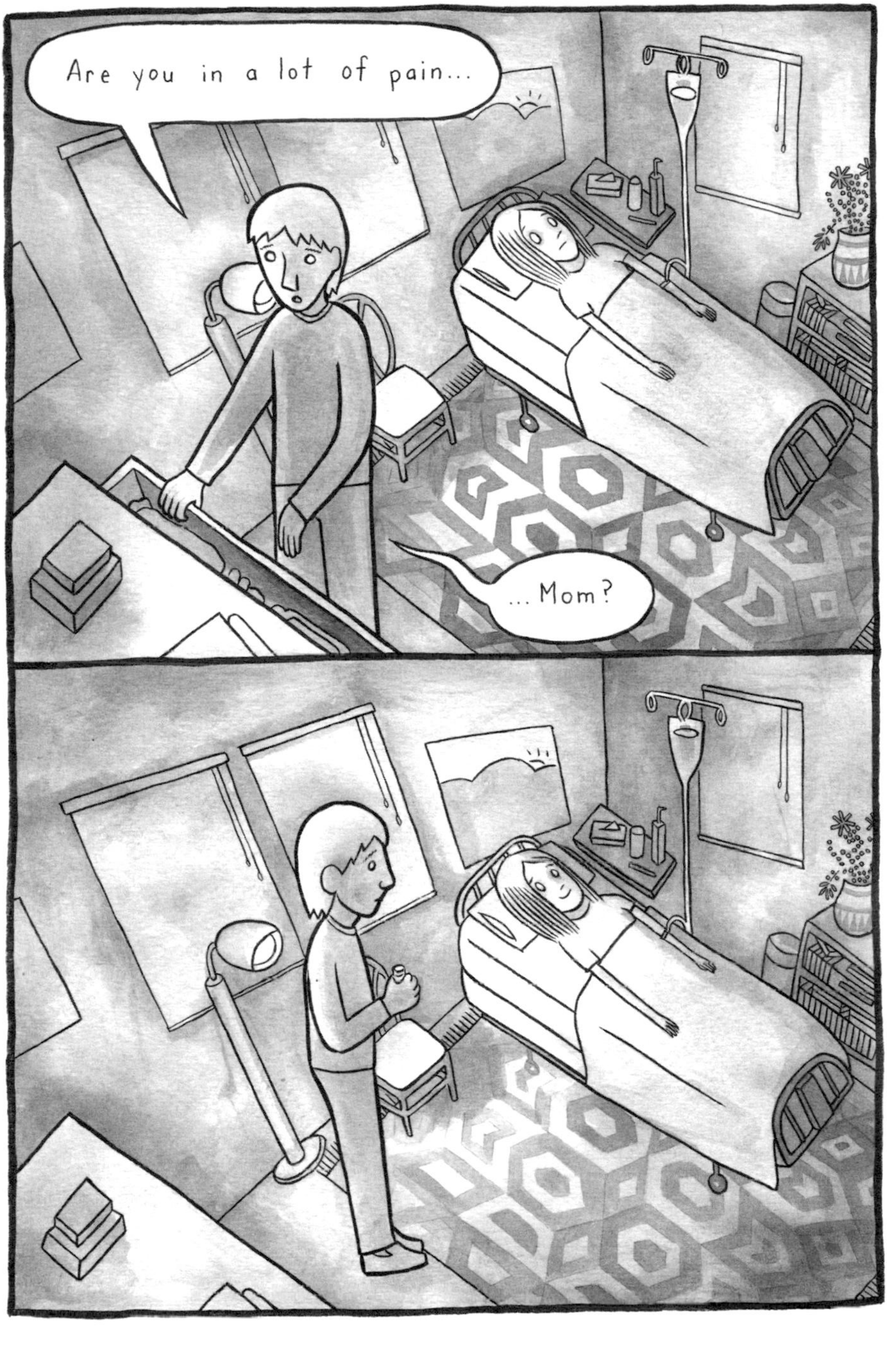
Are you in a lot of pain...
...Mom?

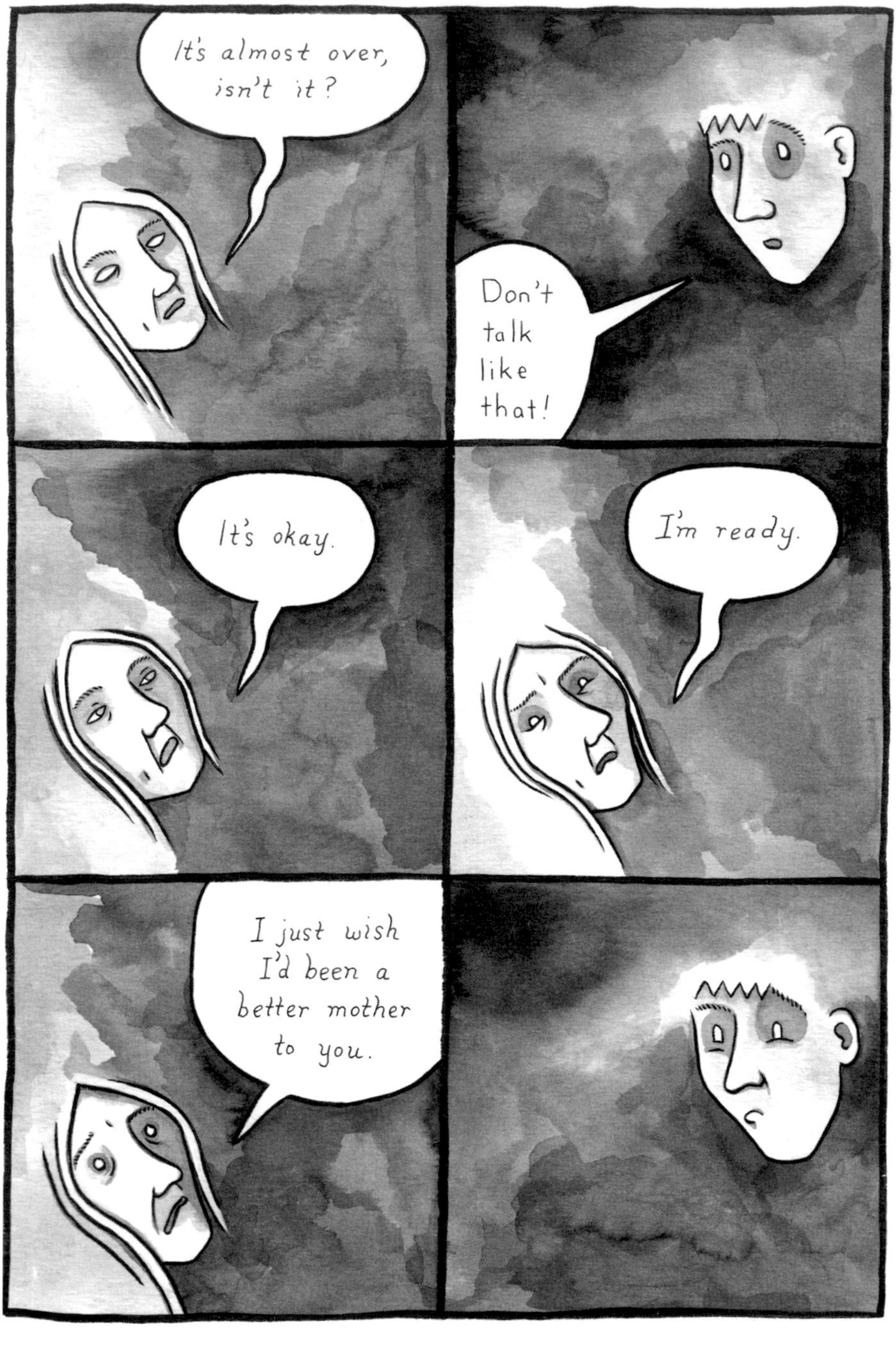
It's almost over, isn't it?
Don't talk like that!
It's okay.
I'm ready.
I just wish I'd been a better mother to you.

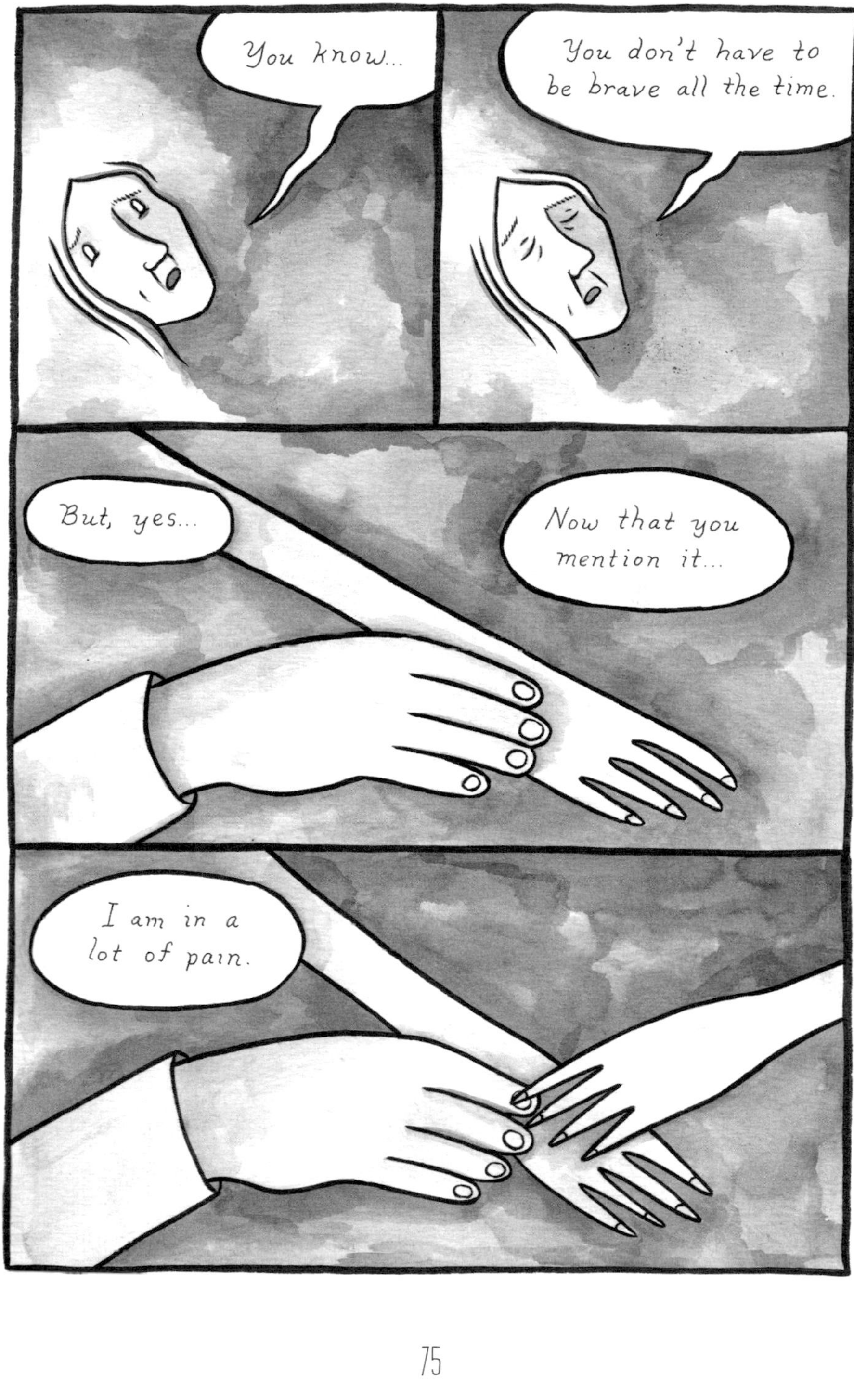
You know...
You don't have to be brave all the time.
But, yes...
Now that you mention it...
I am in a lot of pain.

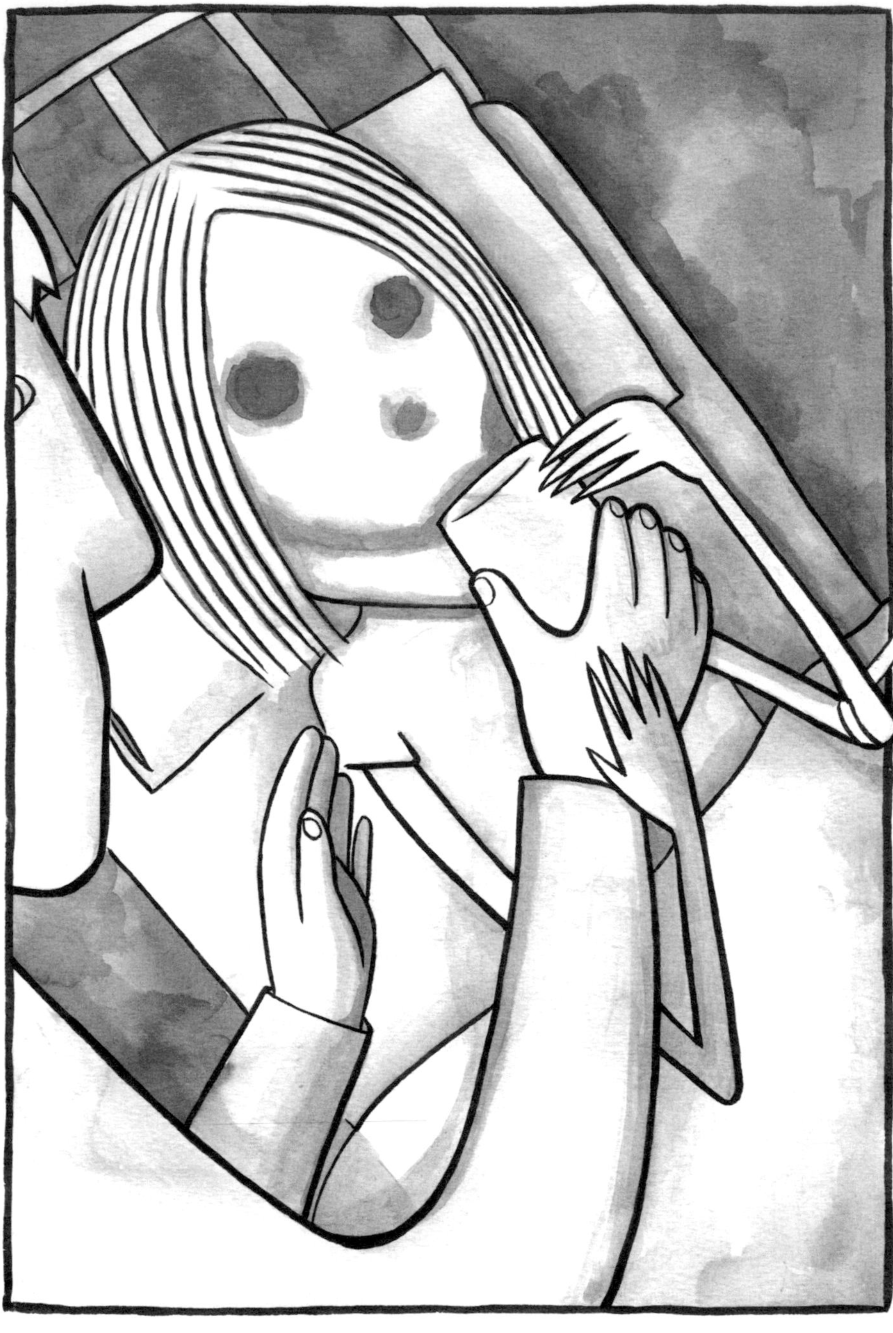

Soon I will have nobody.

PART FOUR

Emily H. Baker

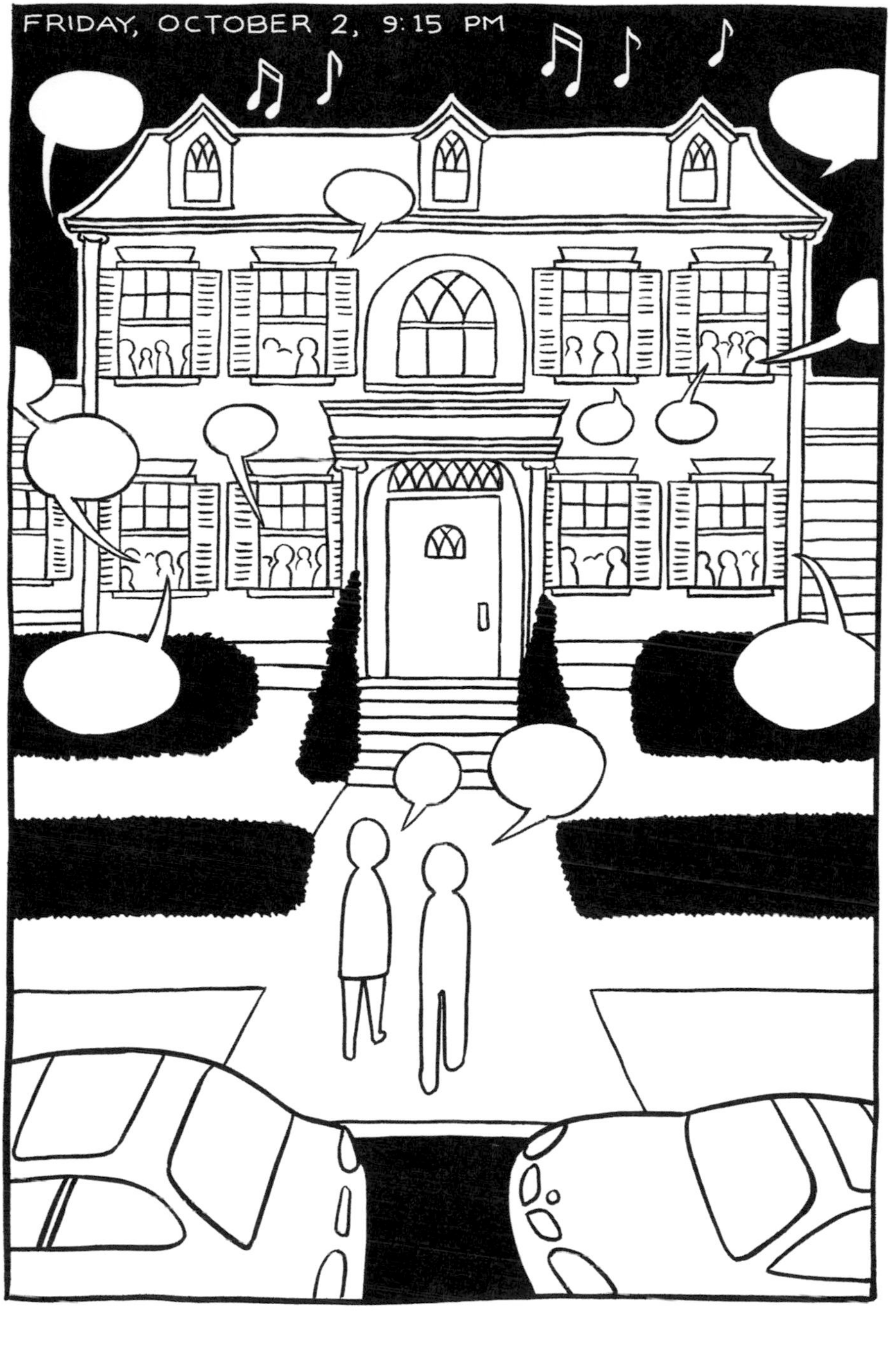
FRIDAY, OCTOBER 2, 9:15 PM

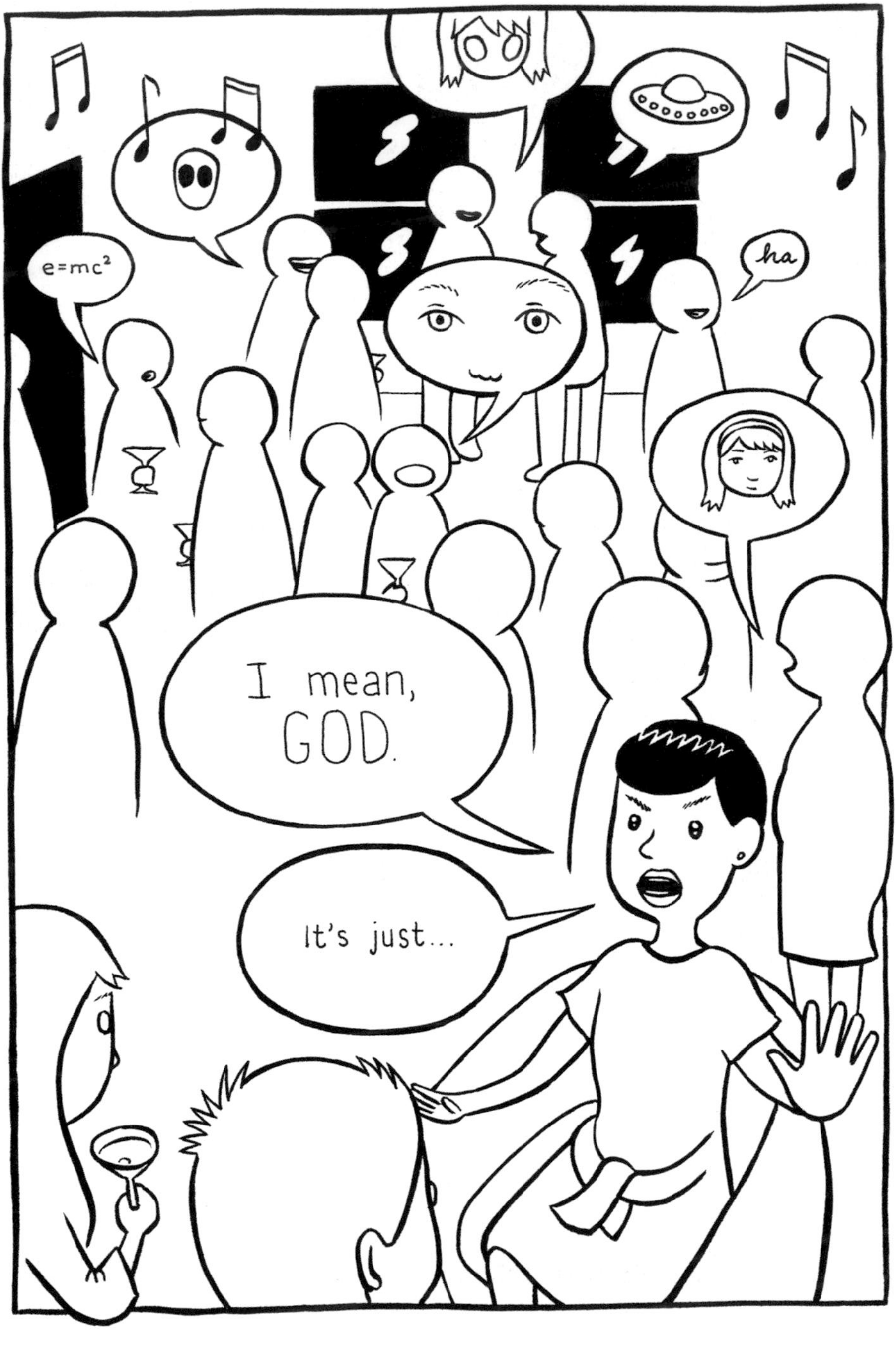
e=mc²
ha
I mean, GOD.
It's just...

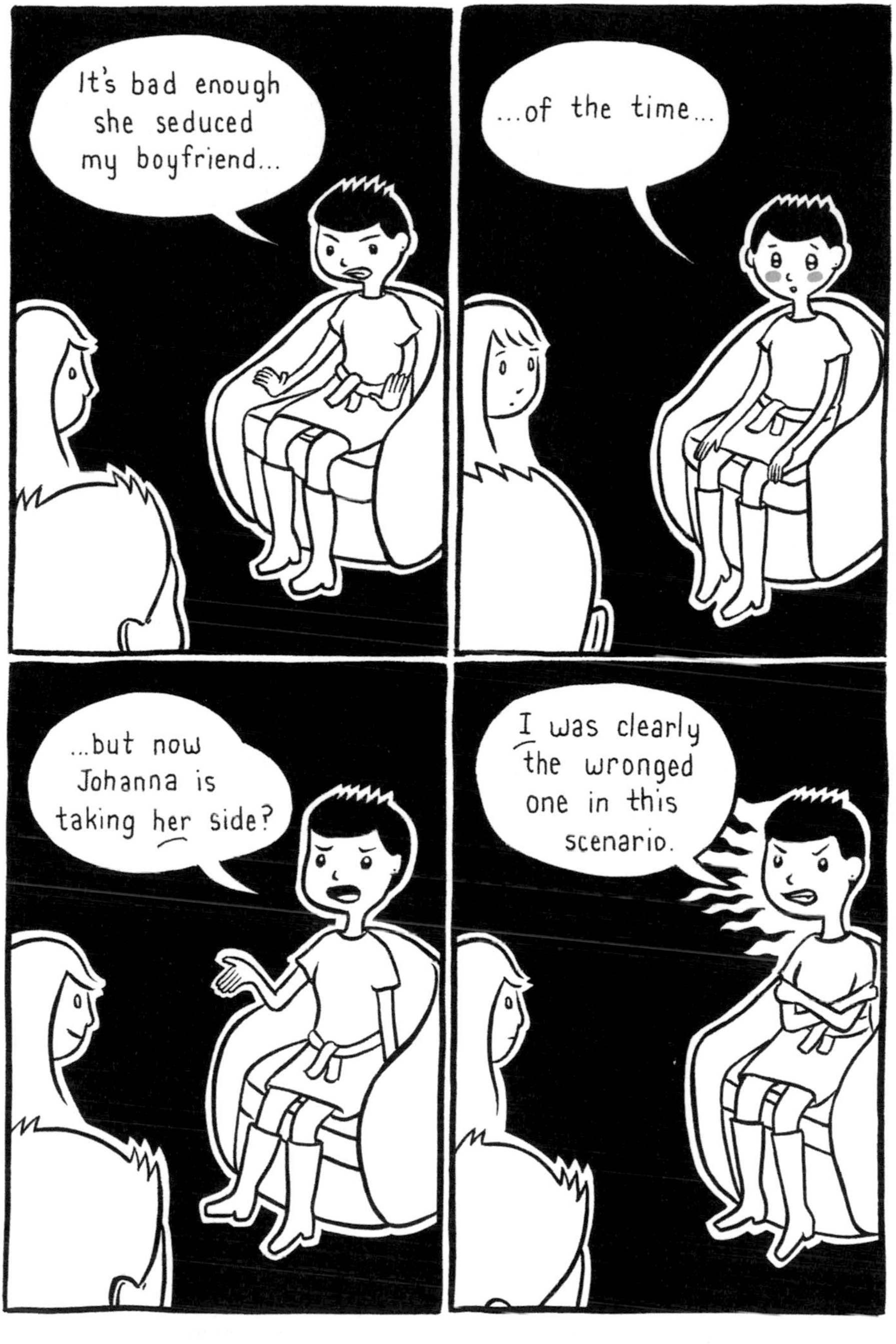
It's bad enough she seduced my boyfriend...
...of the time...
...but now Johanna is taking her side?
I was clearly the wronged one in this scenario.

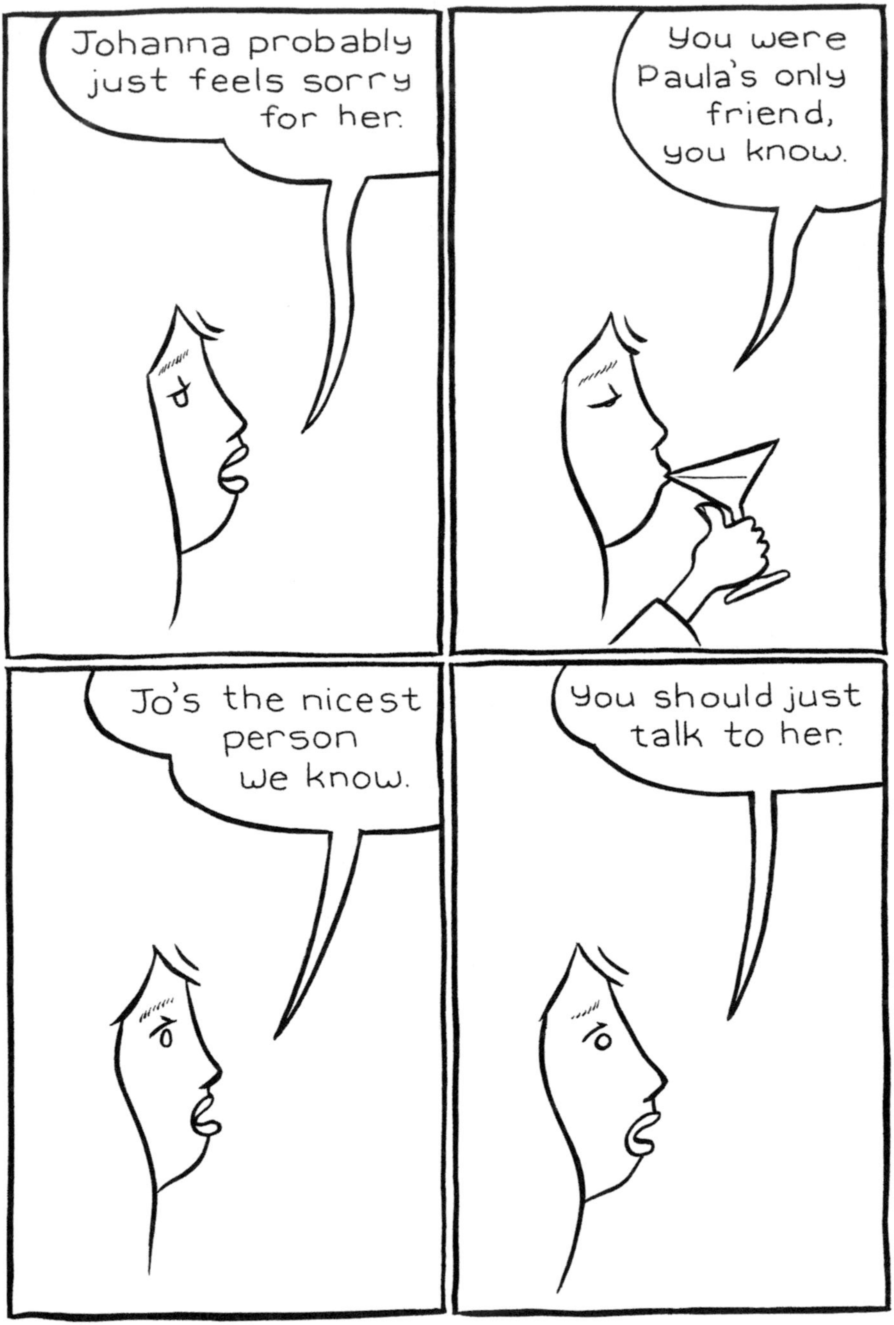
Johanna probably just feels sorry for her.
You were Paula's only friend, you know.
Jo's the nicest person we know.
You should just talk to her.

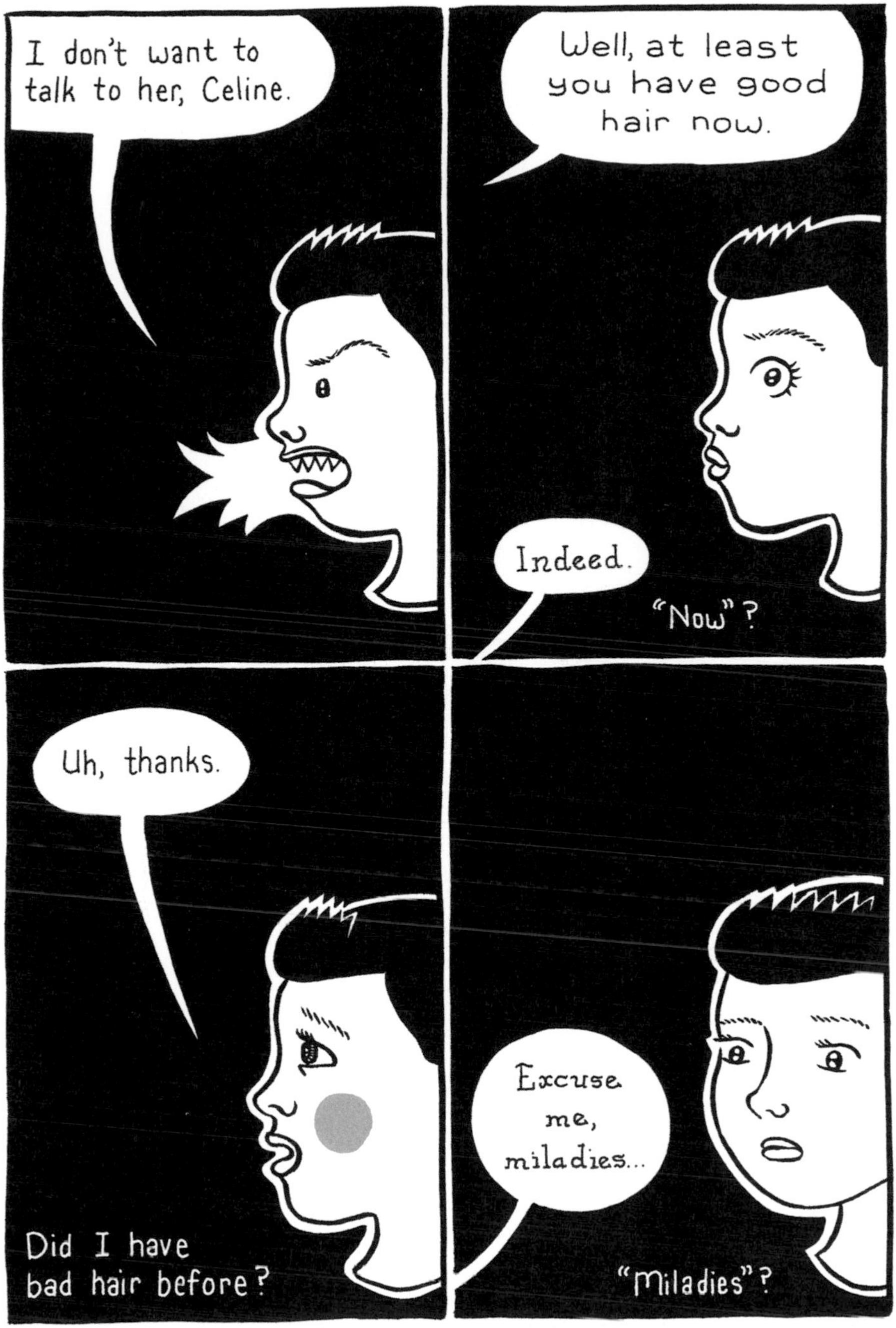
I don't want to talk to her, Celine.
Well, at least you have good hair now.
Indeed.
"Now"?
Uh, thanks.
Did I have bad hair before?
Excuse me, miladies...
"Miladies"?

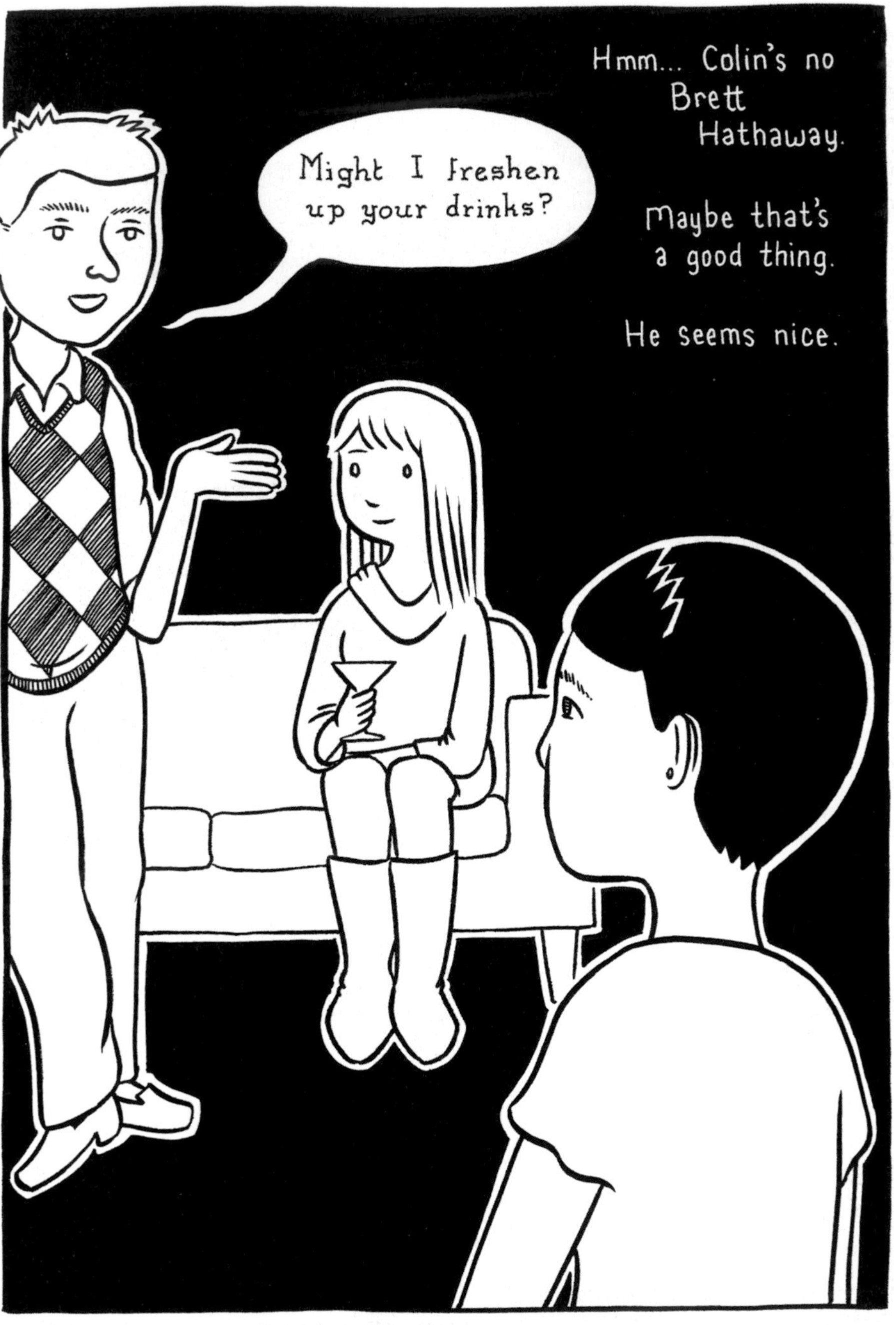
Hmm... Colin's no Brett Hathaway.
Might I freshen up your drinks?
Maybe that's a good thing.
He seems nice.

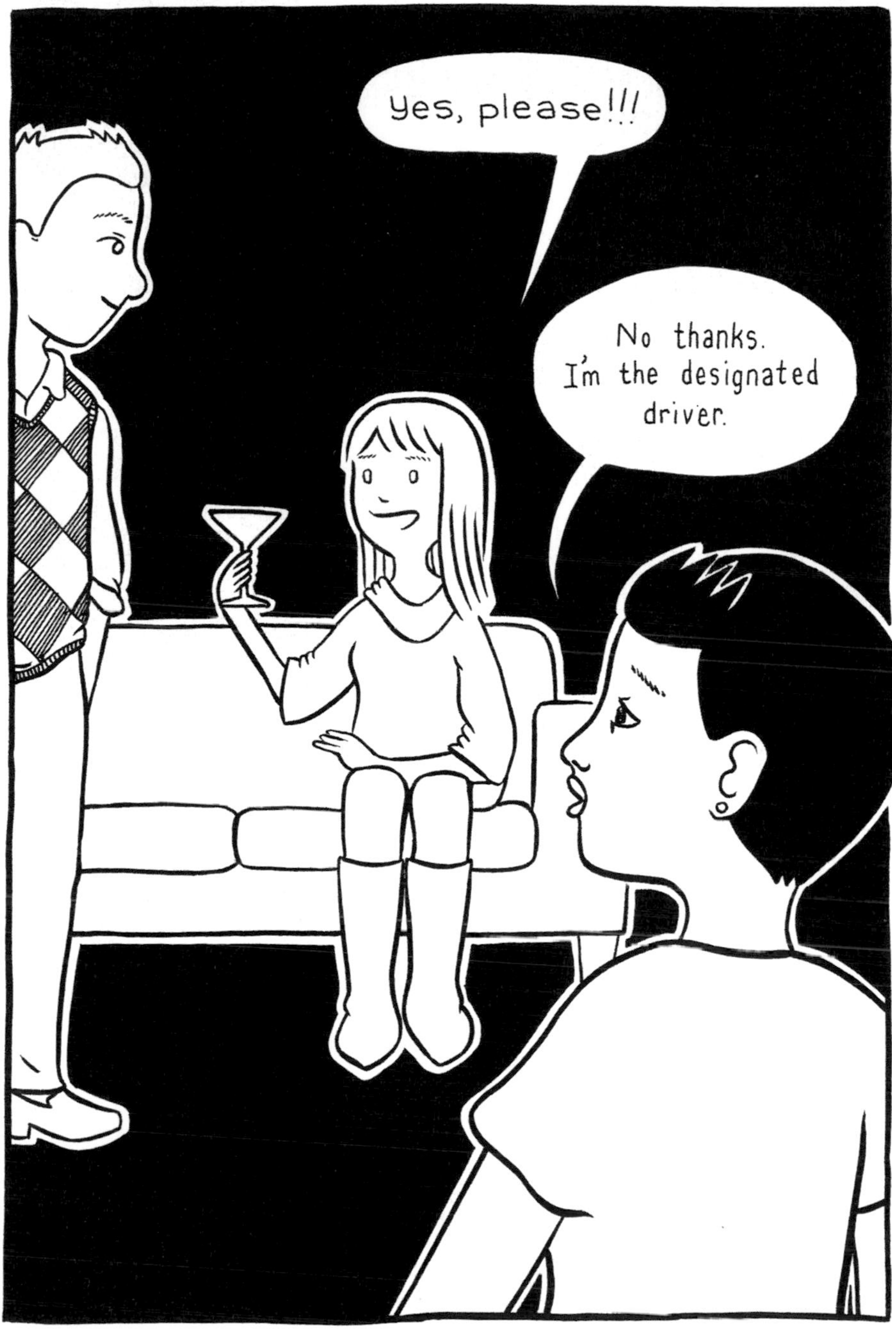
Yes, please!!!
No thanks. I'm the designated driver.

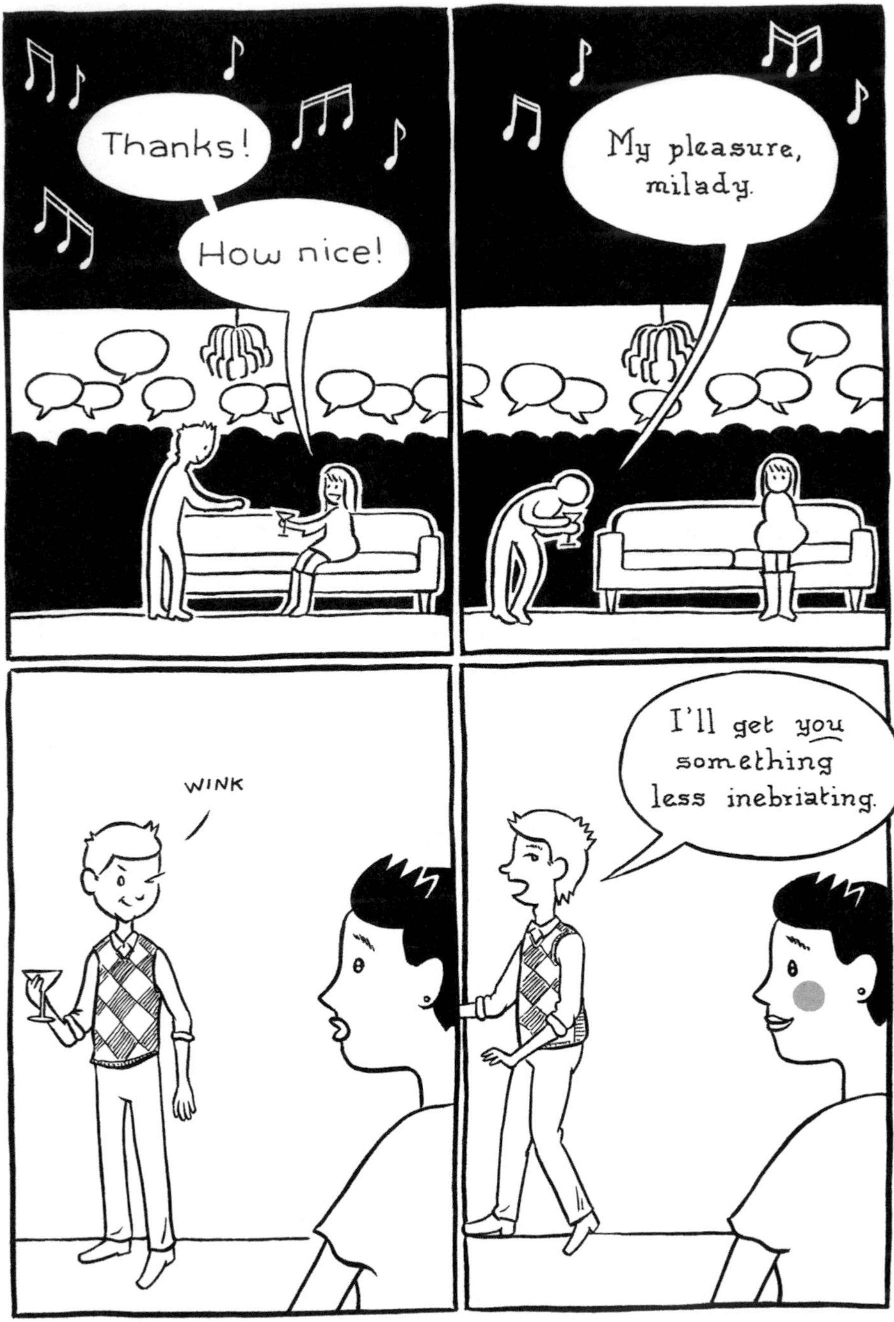
Thanks!
How nice!
My pleasure, milady.
WINK
I'll get you something less inebriating.

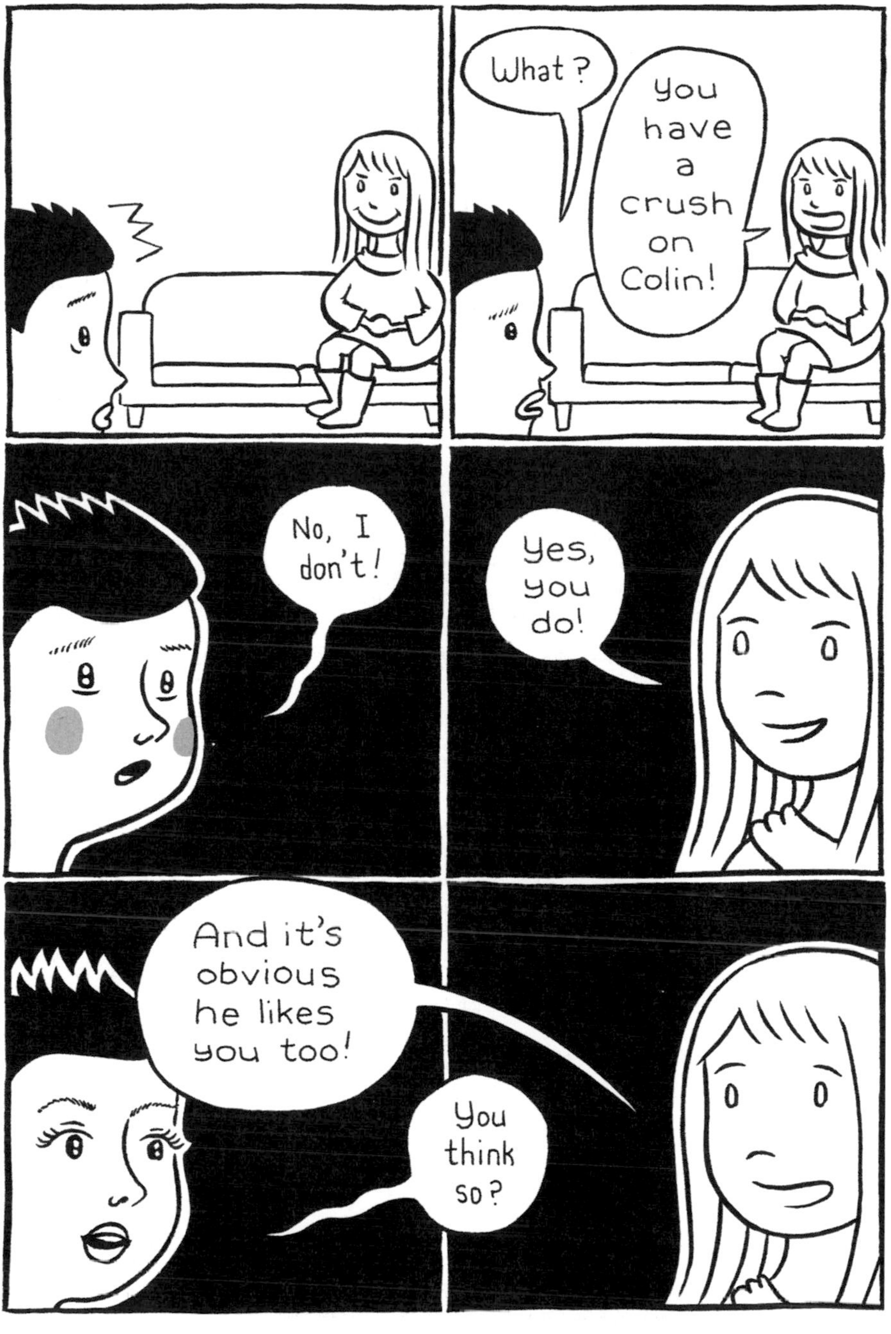
What?
You have a crush on Colin!
No, I don't!
Yes, you do!
And it's obvious he likes you too!
You think so?

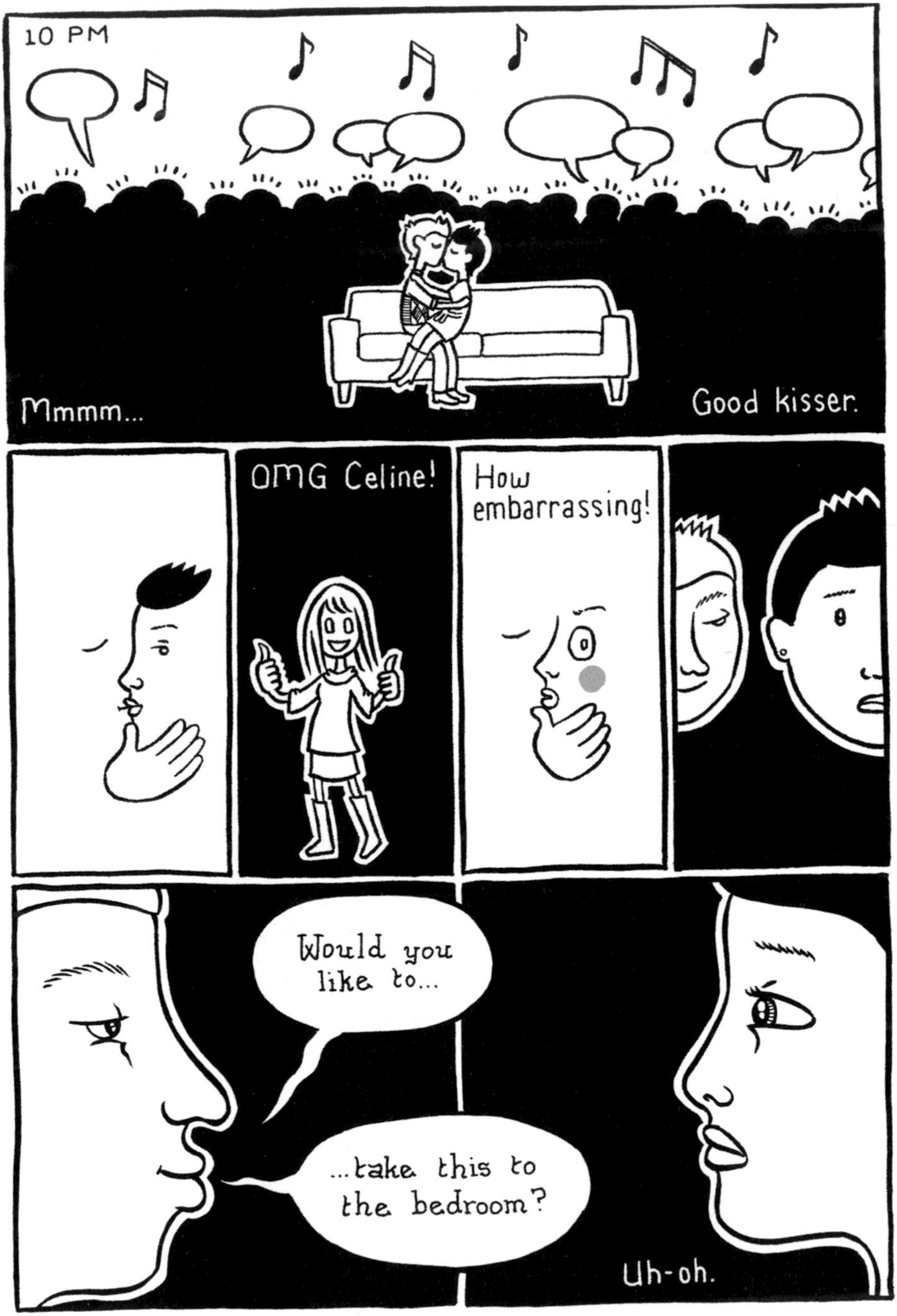
10 PM
Mmmm...
Good kisser.
OMG Celine!
How embarrassing!
Would you like to...
...take this to the bedroom?
Uh-oh.

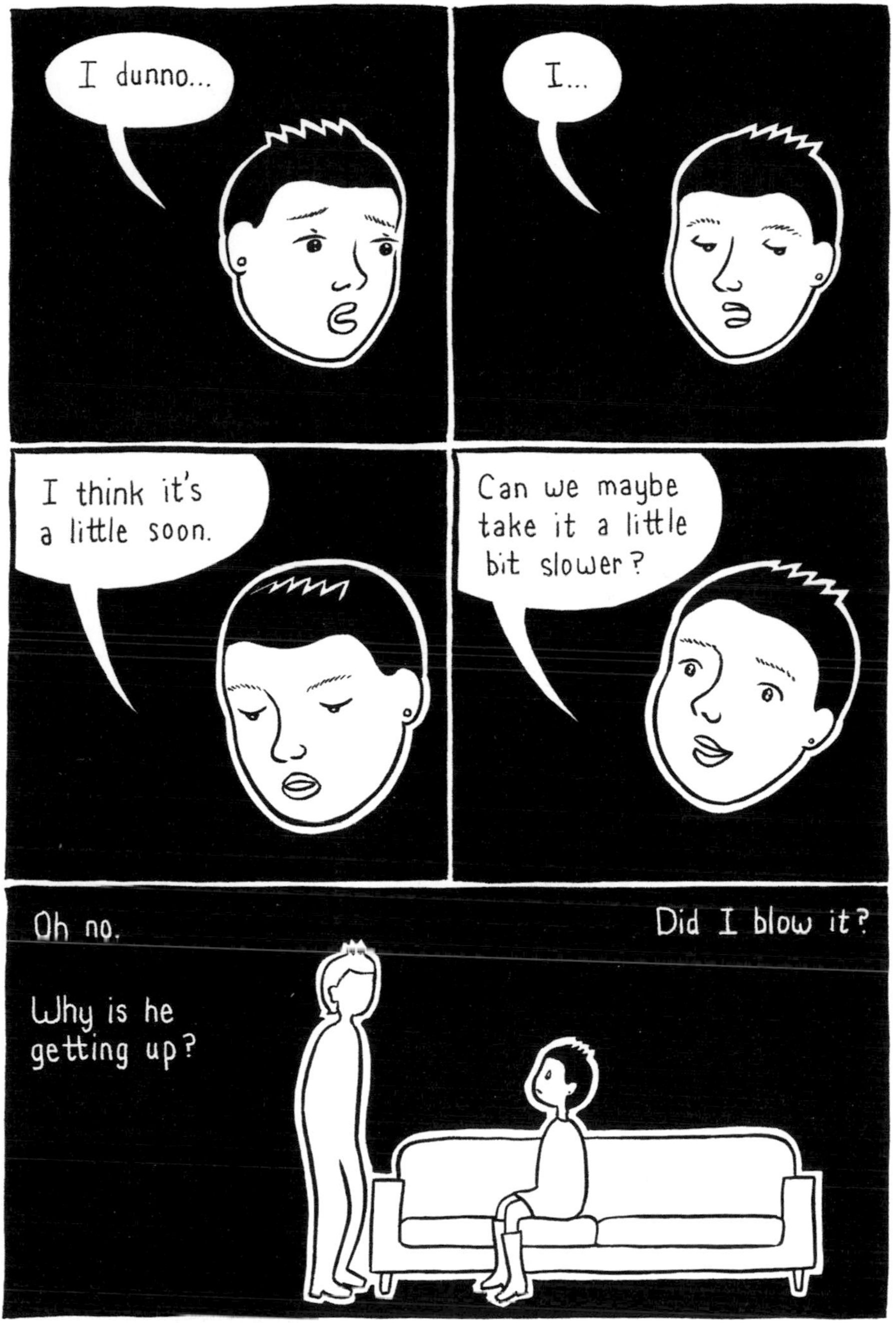
I dunno...
I...
I think it's a little soon.
Can we maybe take it a little bit slower?
Oh no.
Did I blow it?
Why is he getting up?

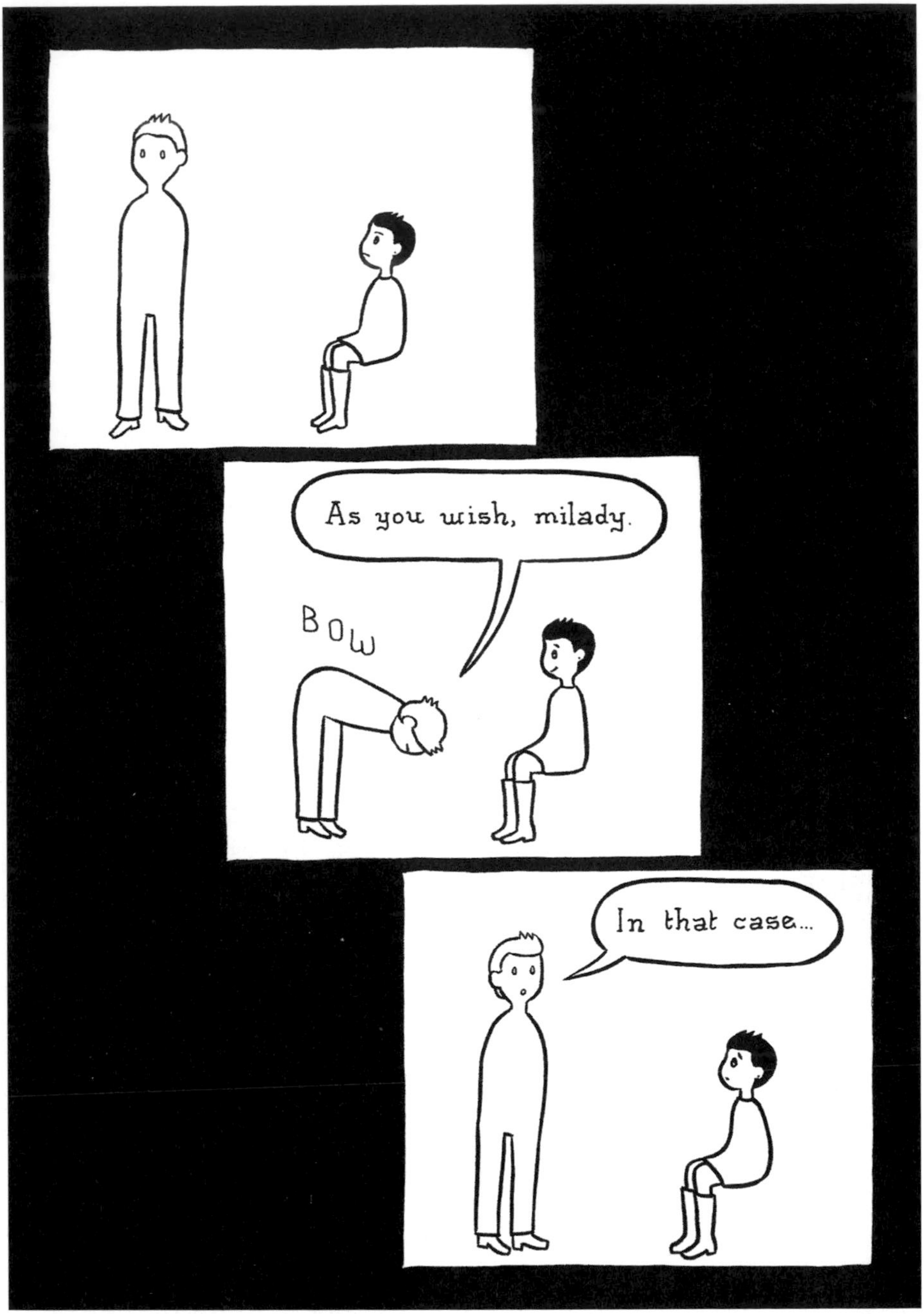
As you wish, milady.
BOW
In that case...

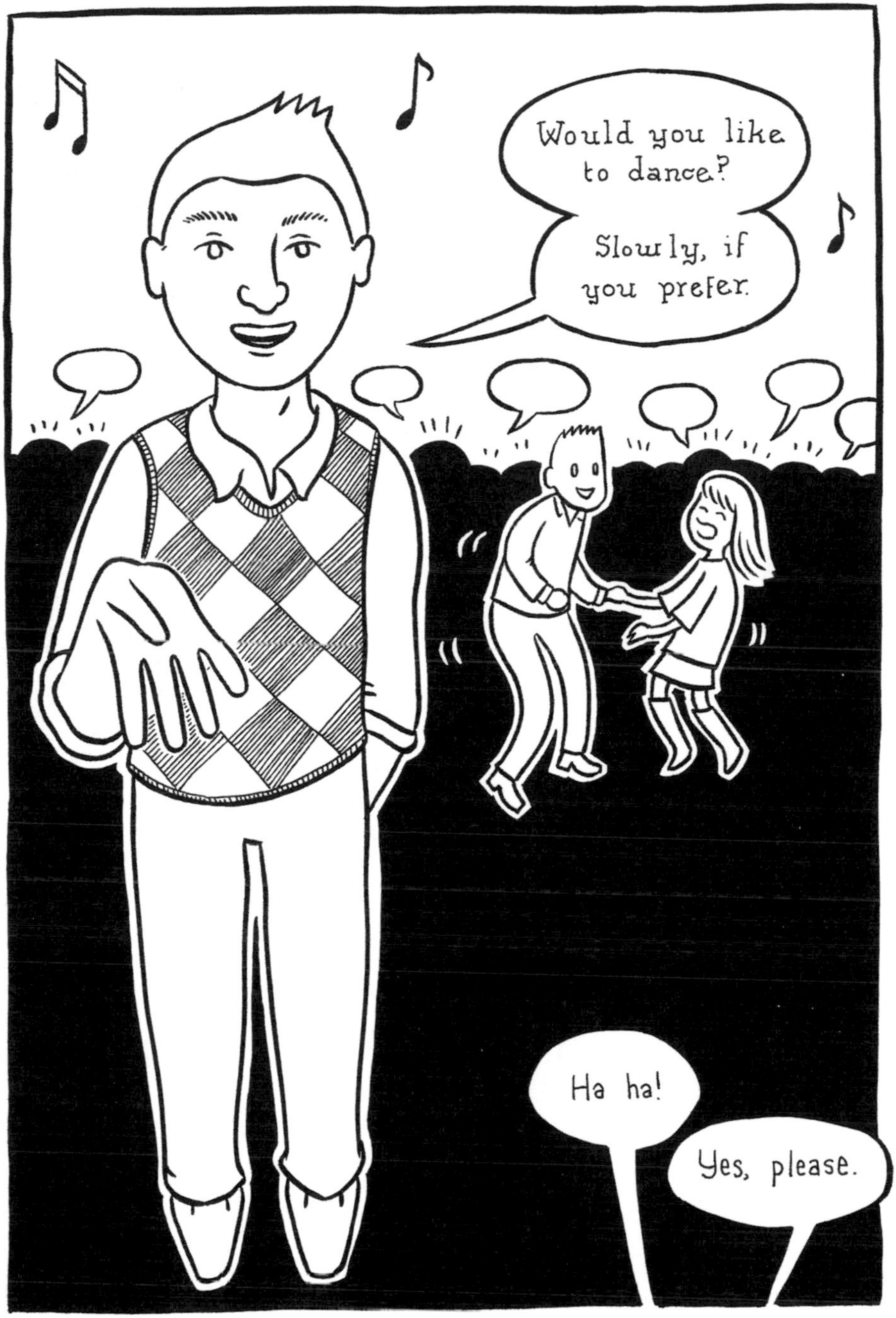
Would you like to dance?
Slowly, if you prefer.
Ha ha!
Yes, please.

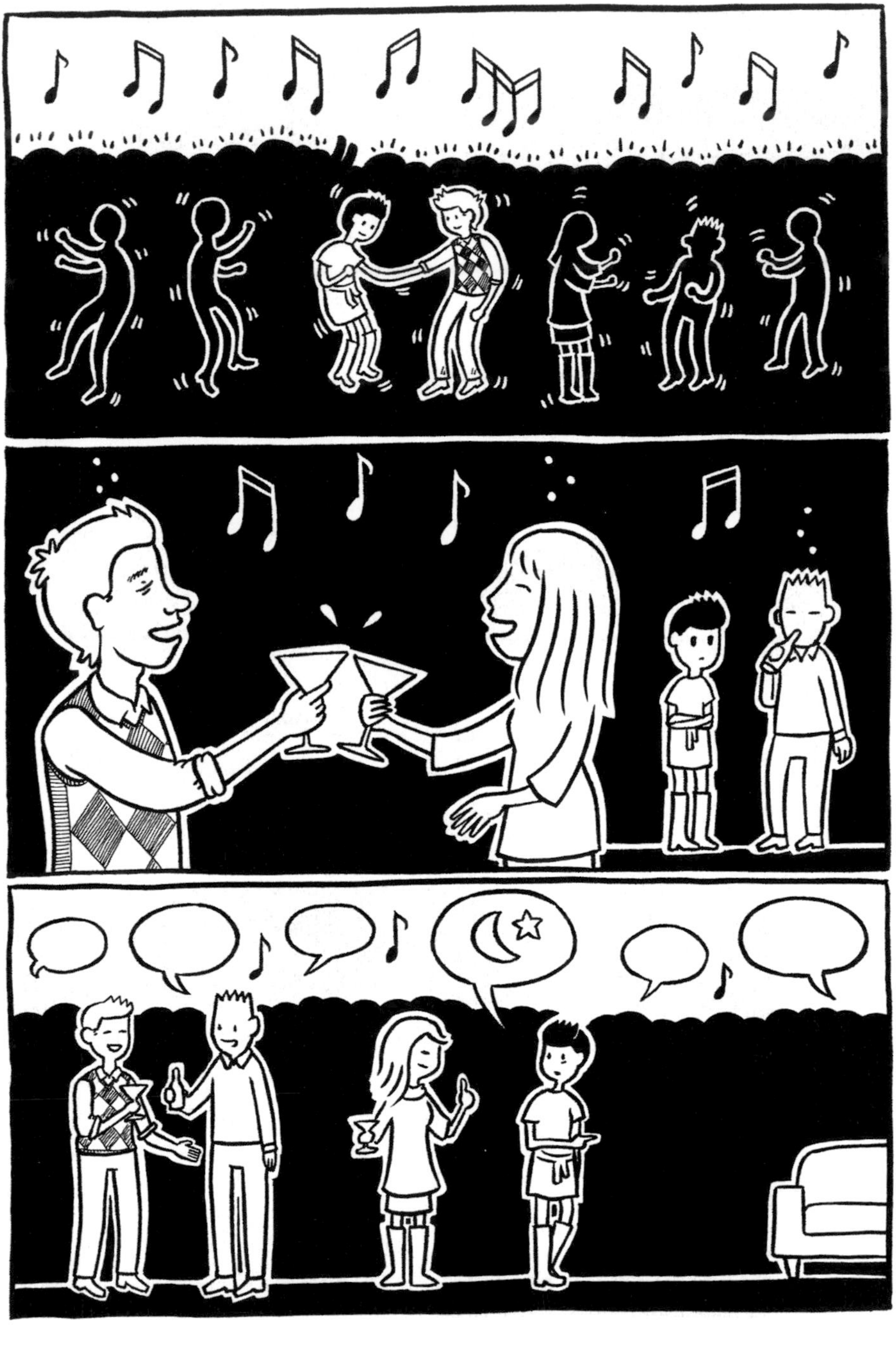

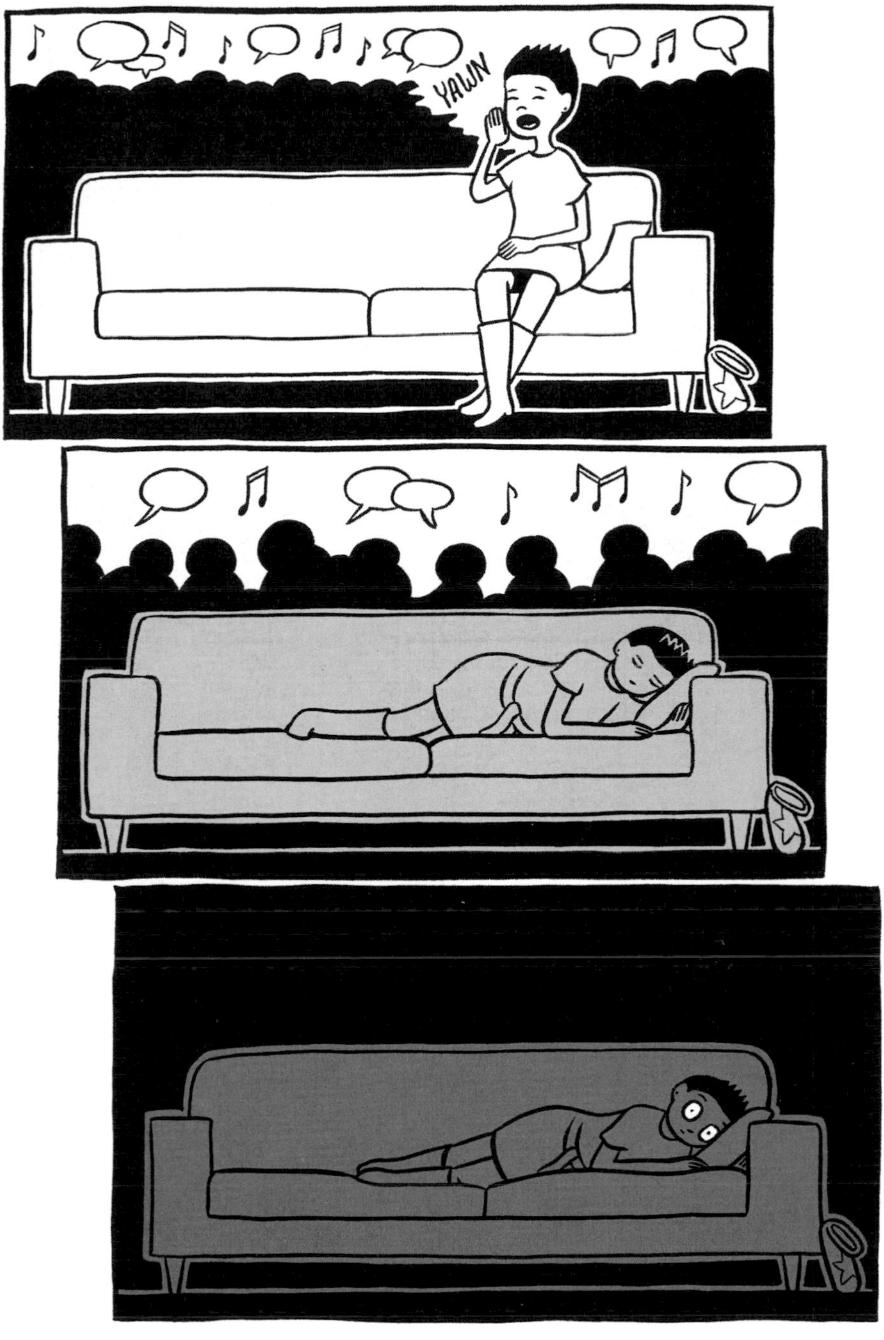
YAWN

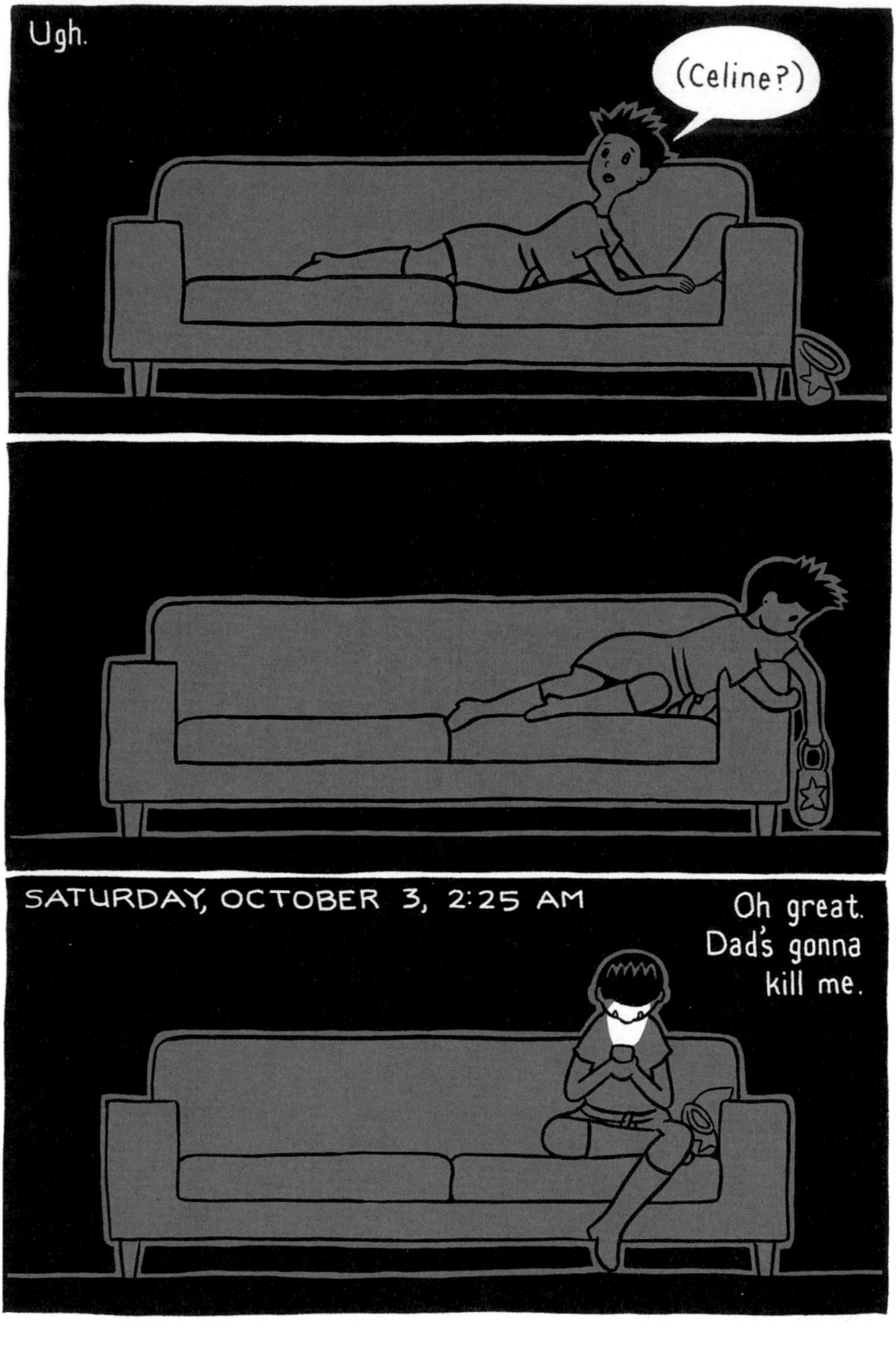
Ugh.
(Celine?)
SATURDAY, OCTOBER 3, 2:25 AM
Oh great. Dad's gonna kill me.

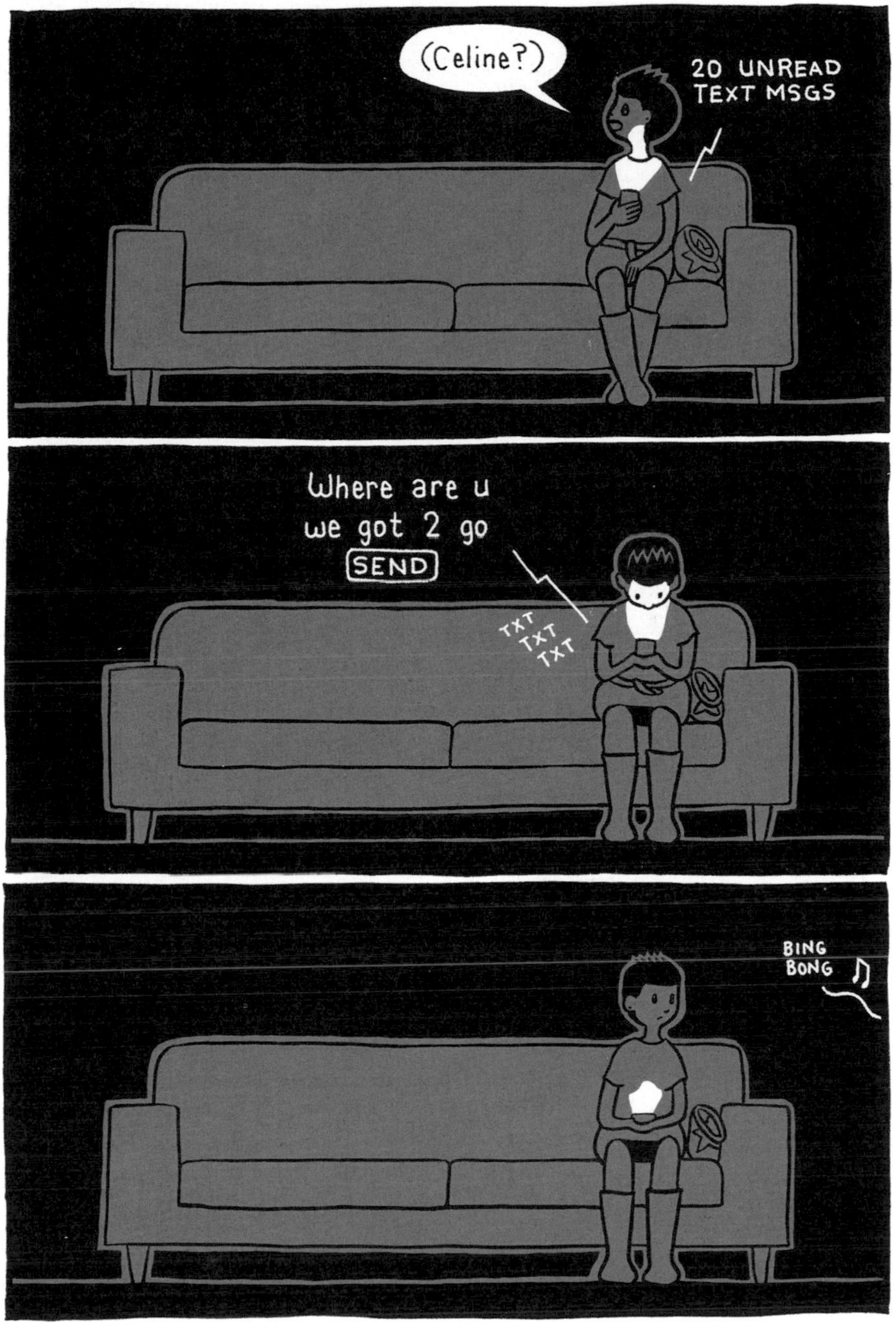
(Celine?)
20 UNREAD TEXT MSGS
Where are u
we got 2 go
SEND
TXT
TXT
TXT
BING
BONG

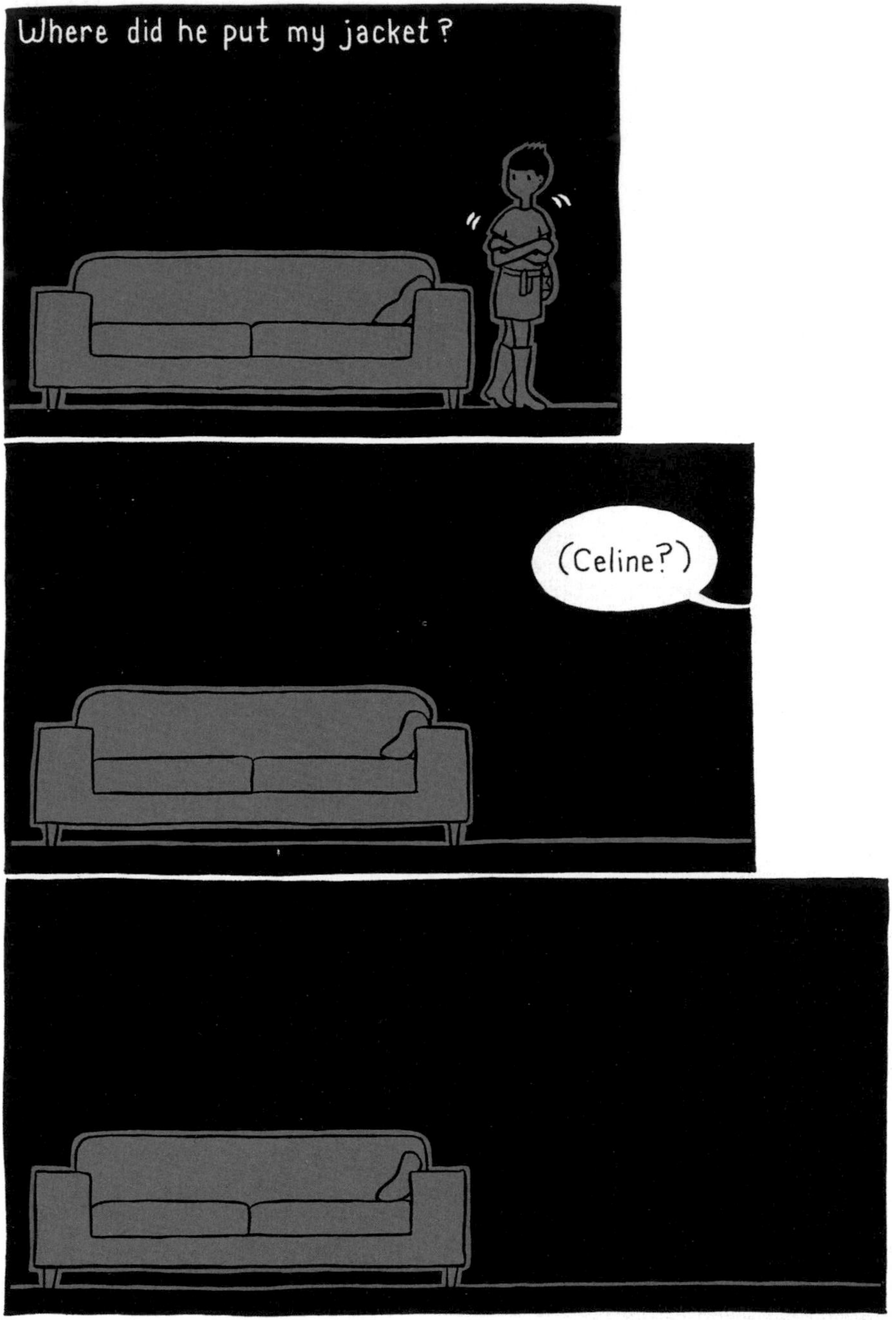
Where did he put my jacket?
(Celine?)

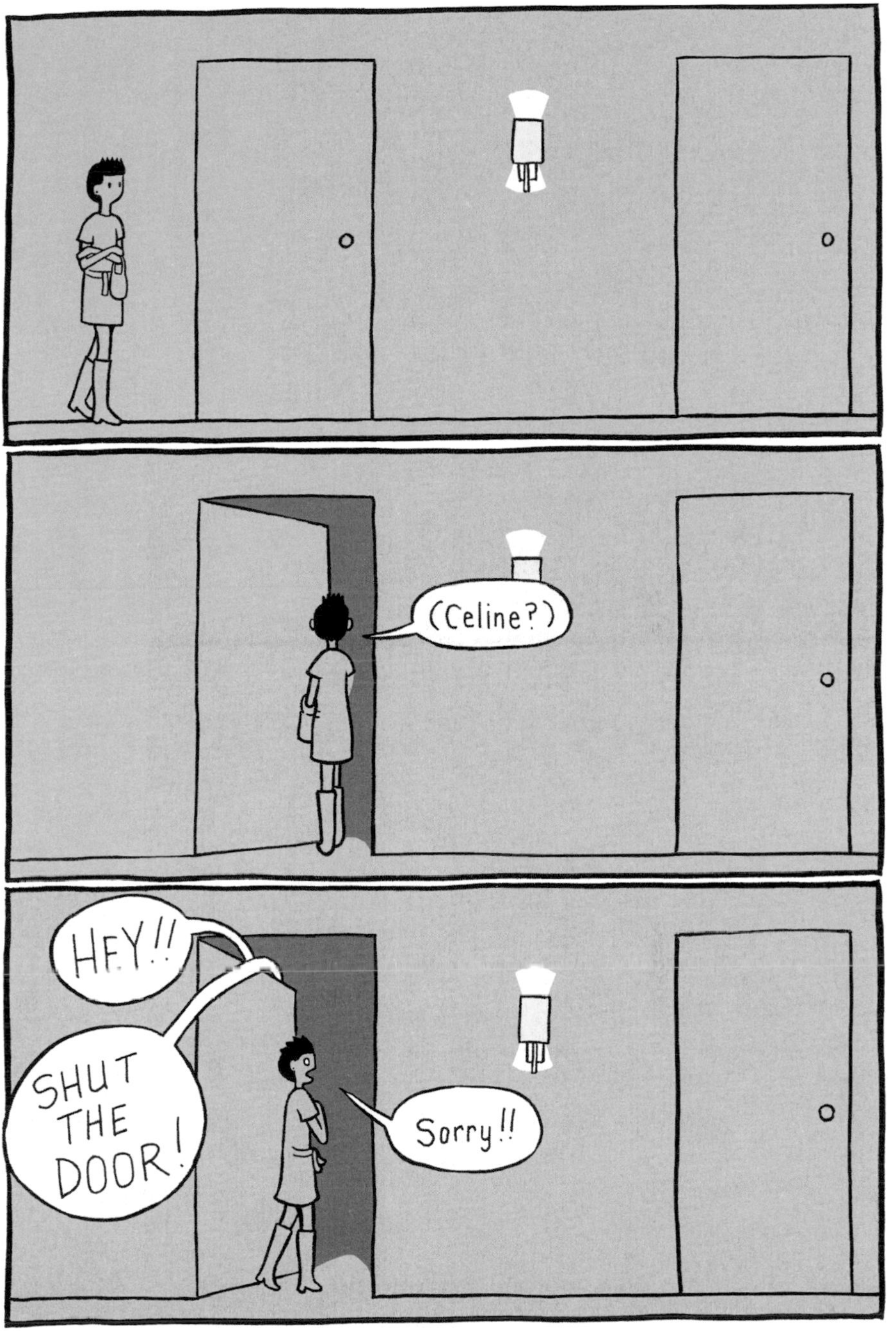
(Celine?)
HEY!!
SHUT THE DOOR!
Sorry!!

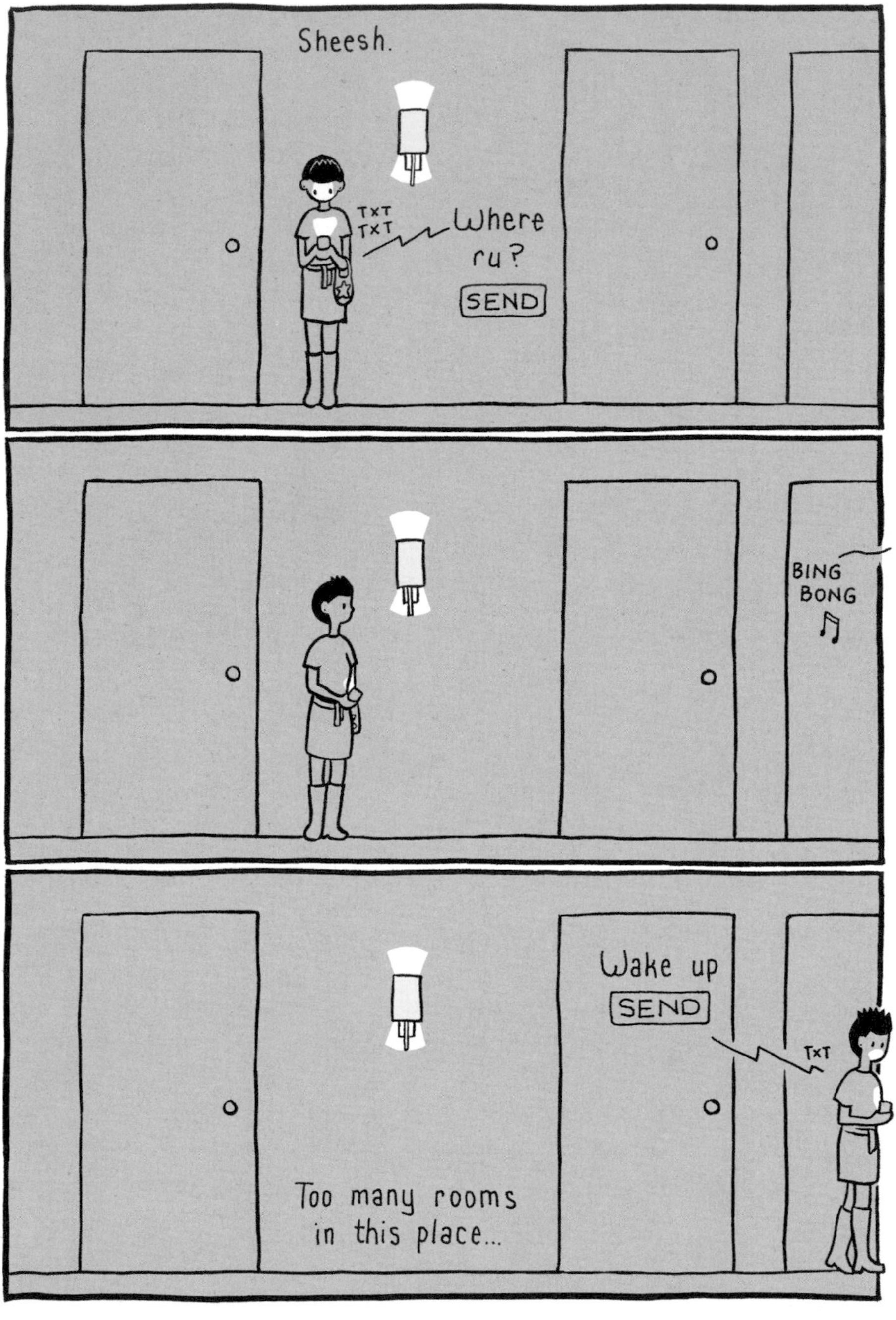
Sheesh.
TXT TXT
Where ru?
SEND
BING BONG
Wake up
SEND
TXT
Too many rooms in this place...

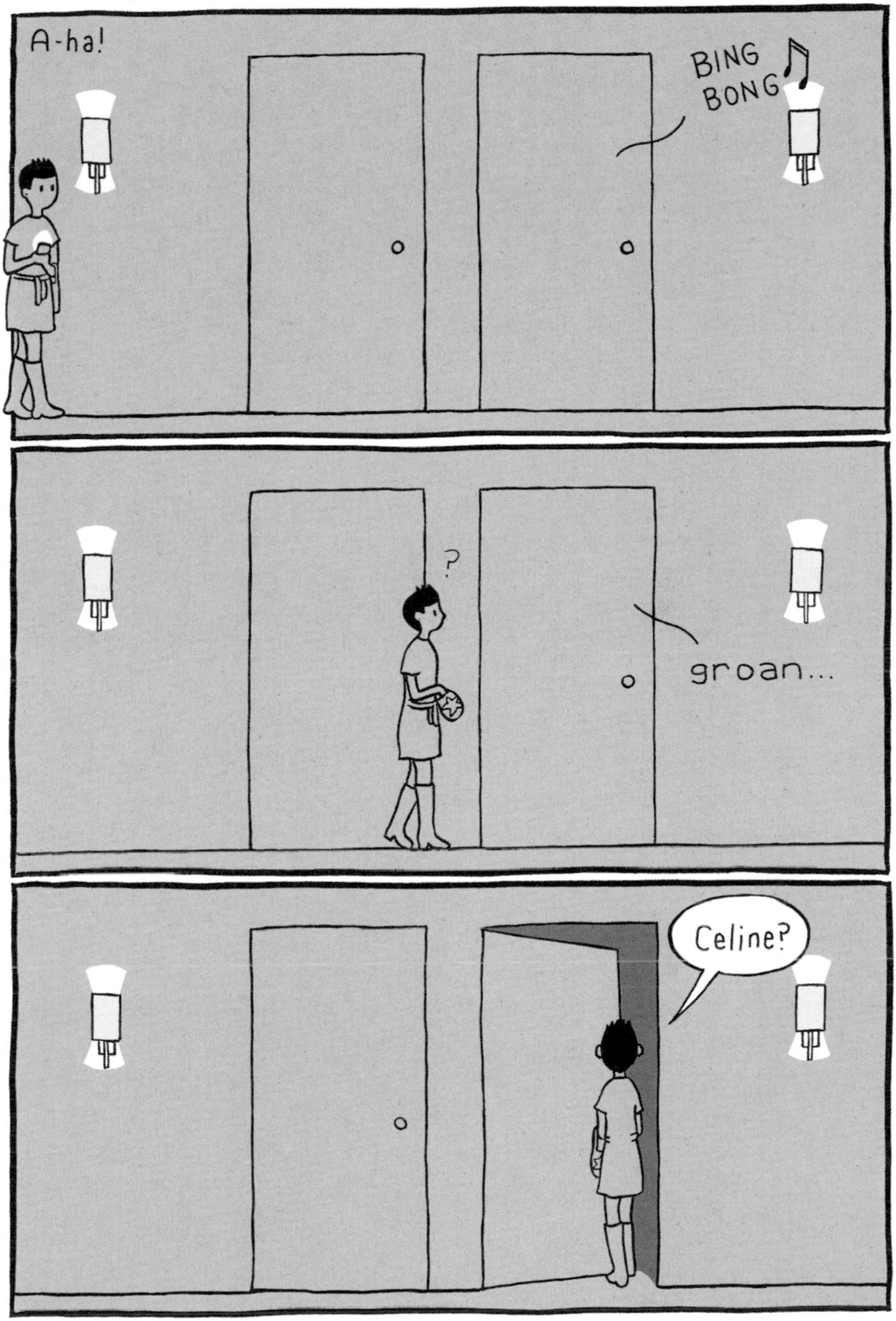
A-ha!
BING BONG
?
groan...
Celine?

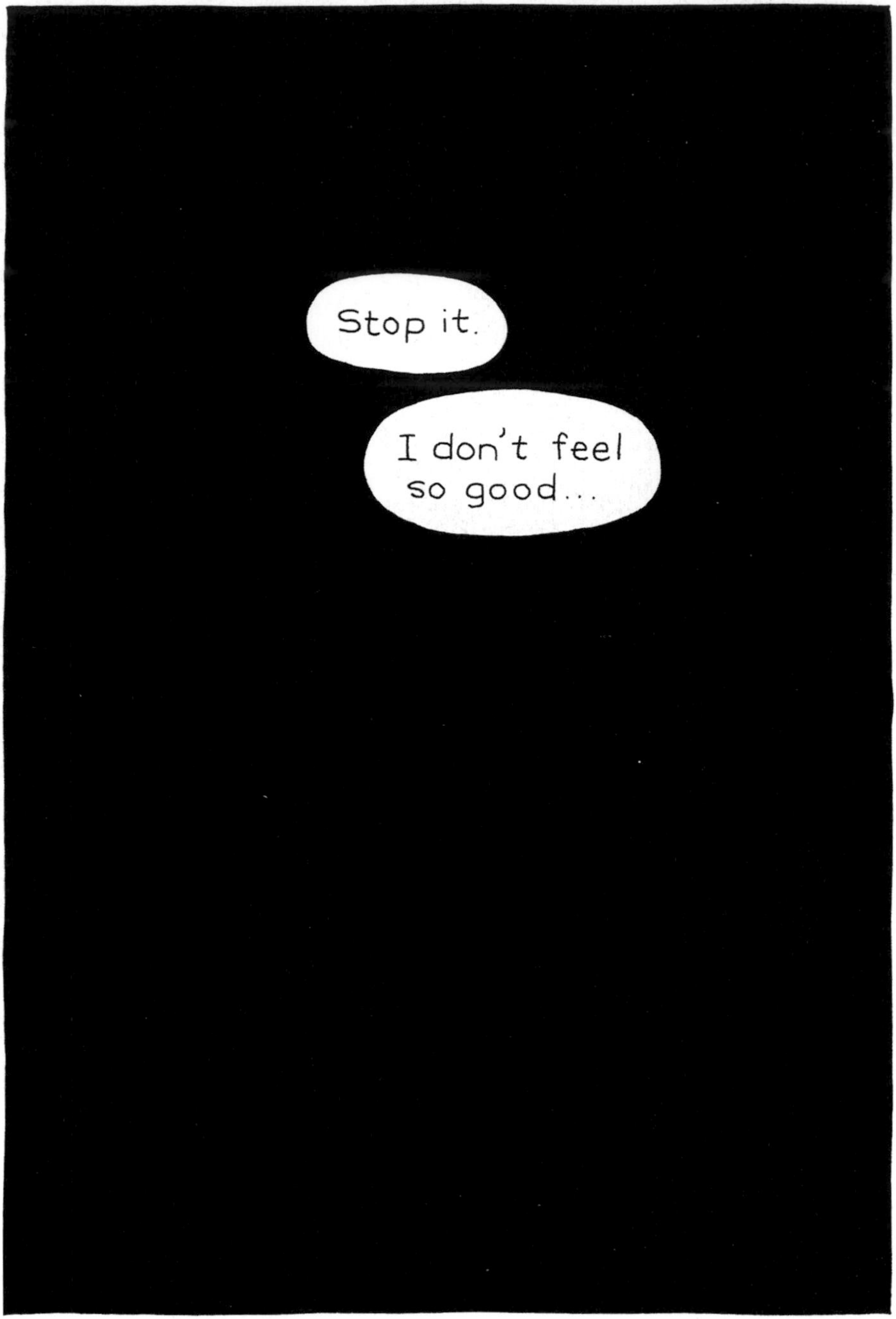
Stop it.
I don't feel so good...

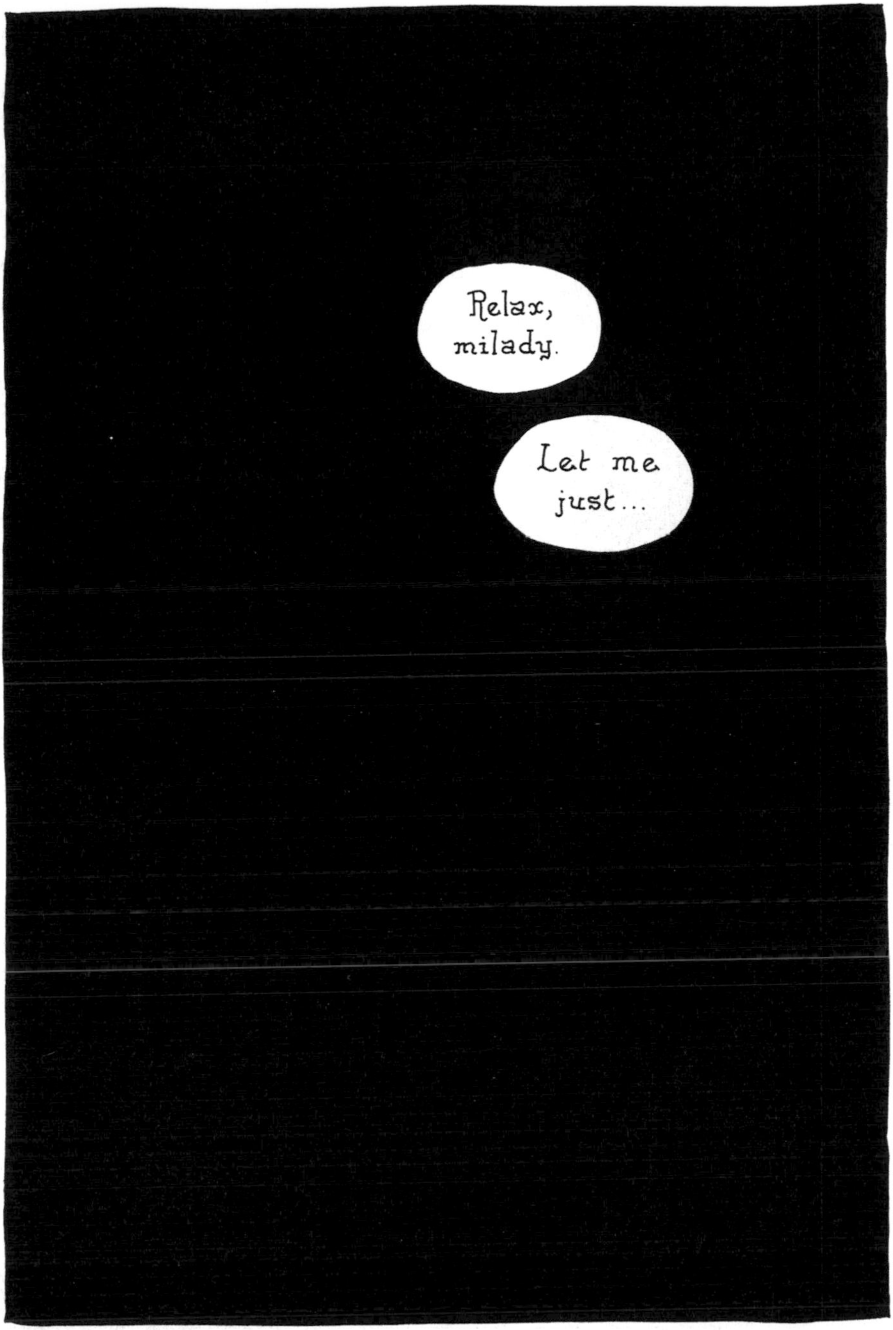
Relax, milady.
Let me just...

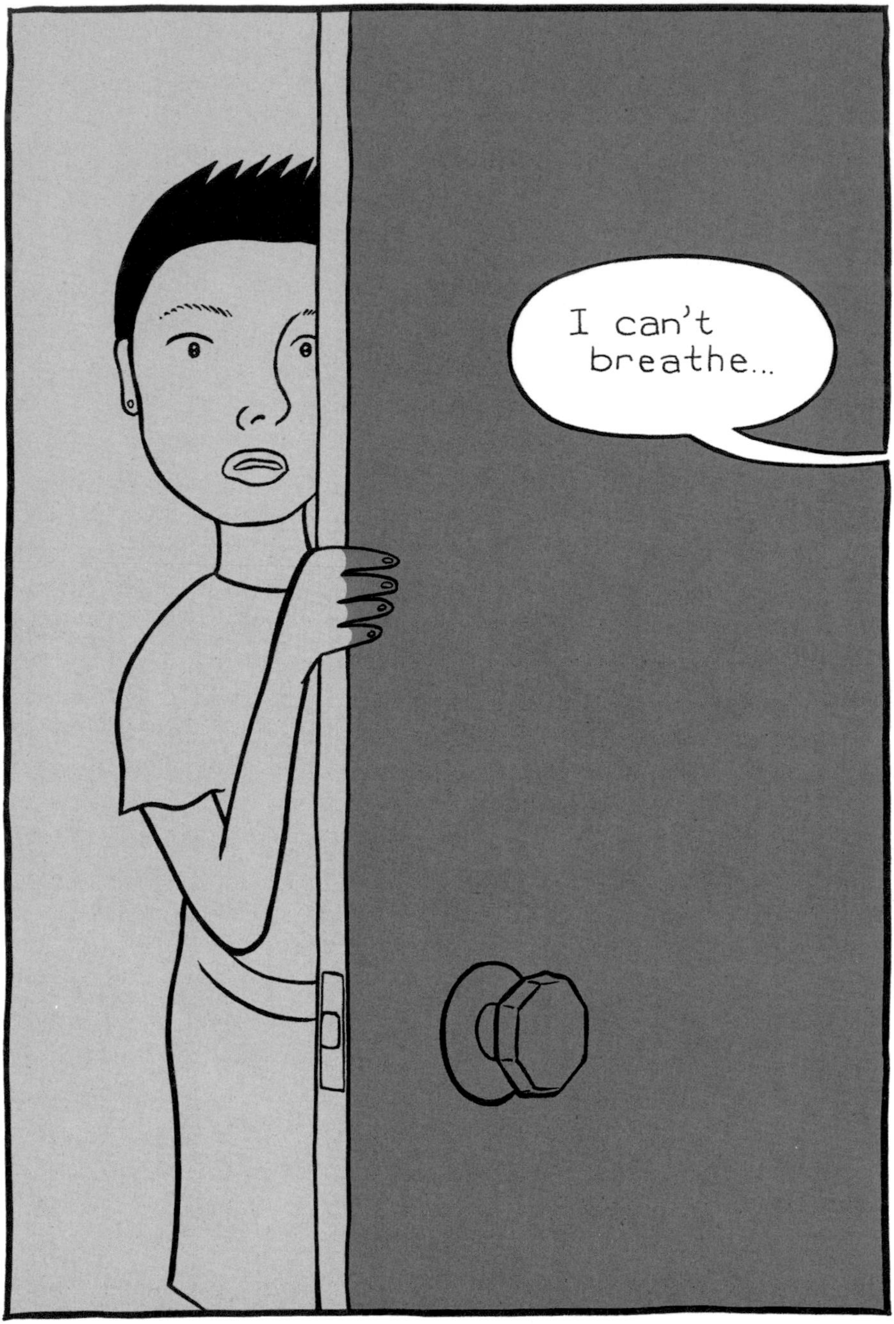
I can't breathe...

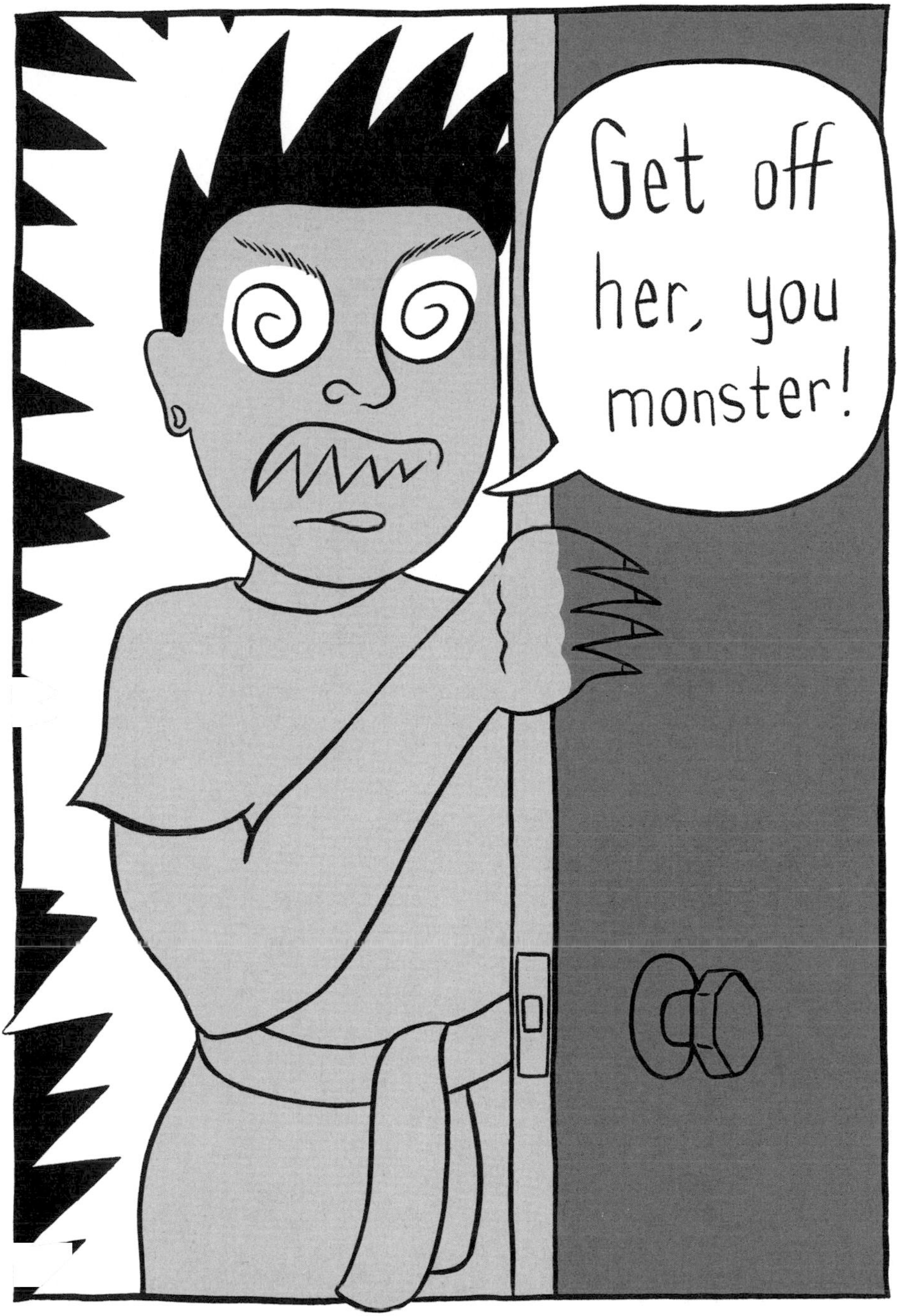
Get off her, you monster!

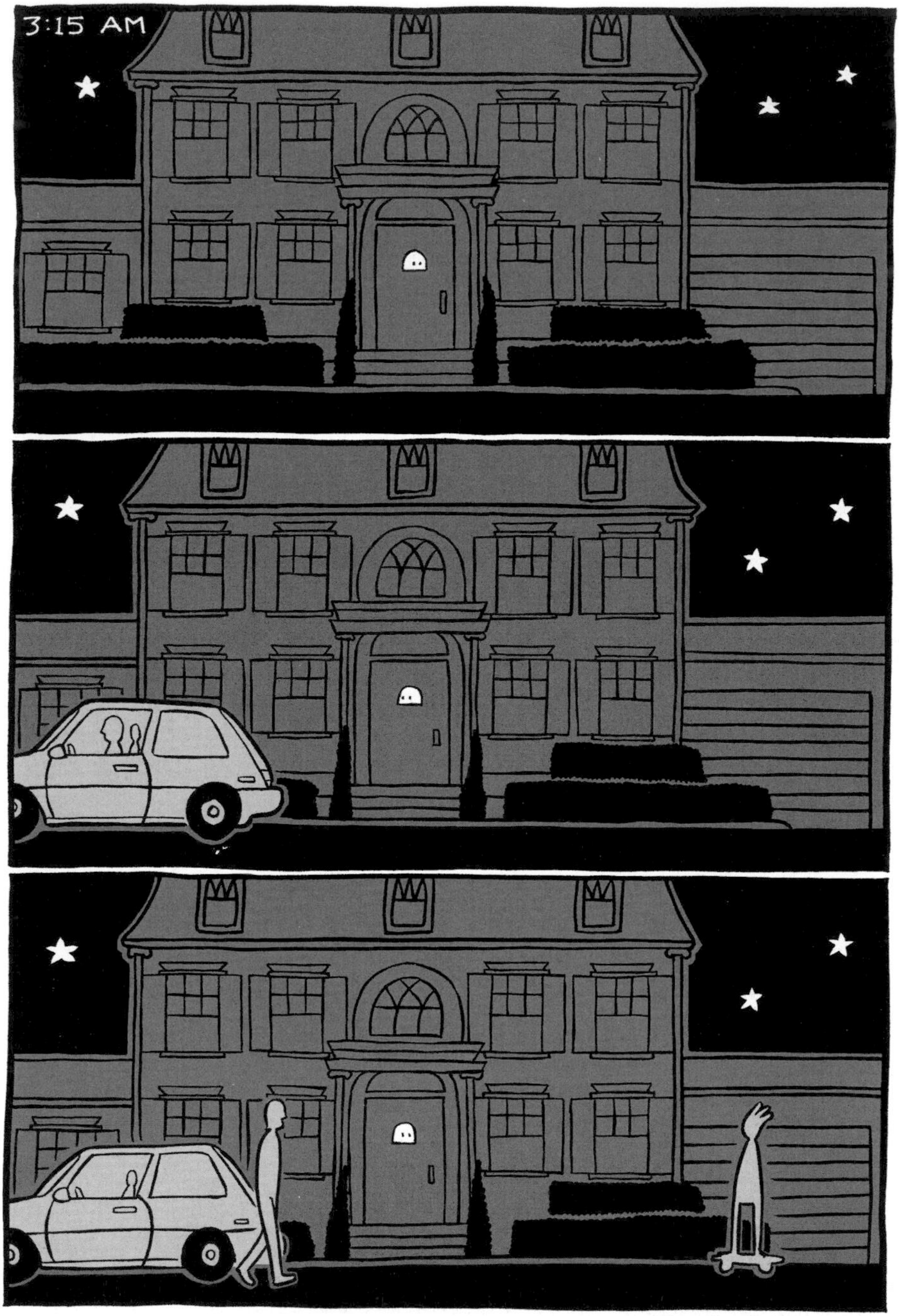
3:15 AM

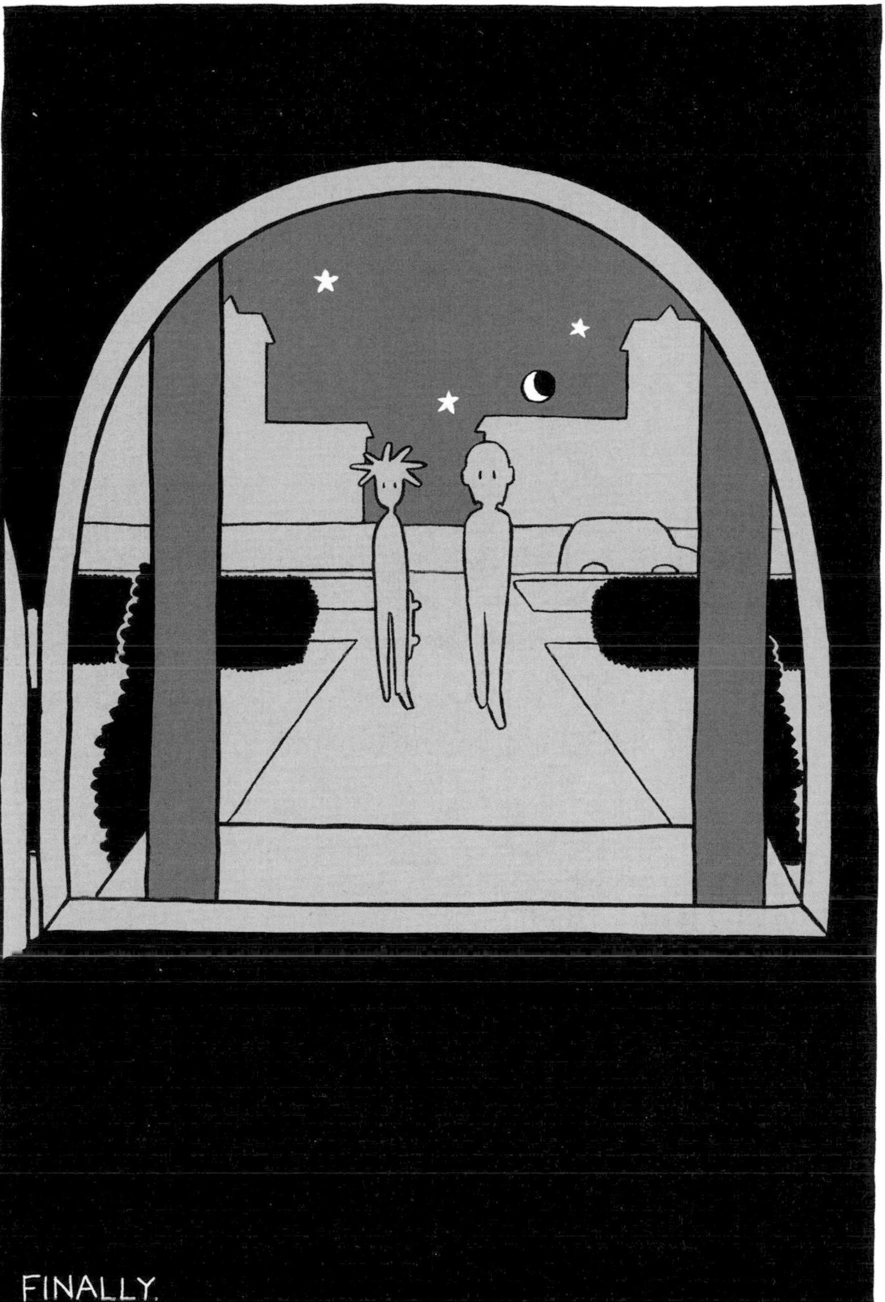
FINALLY.

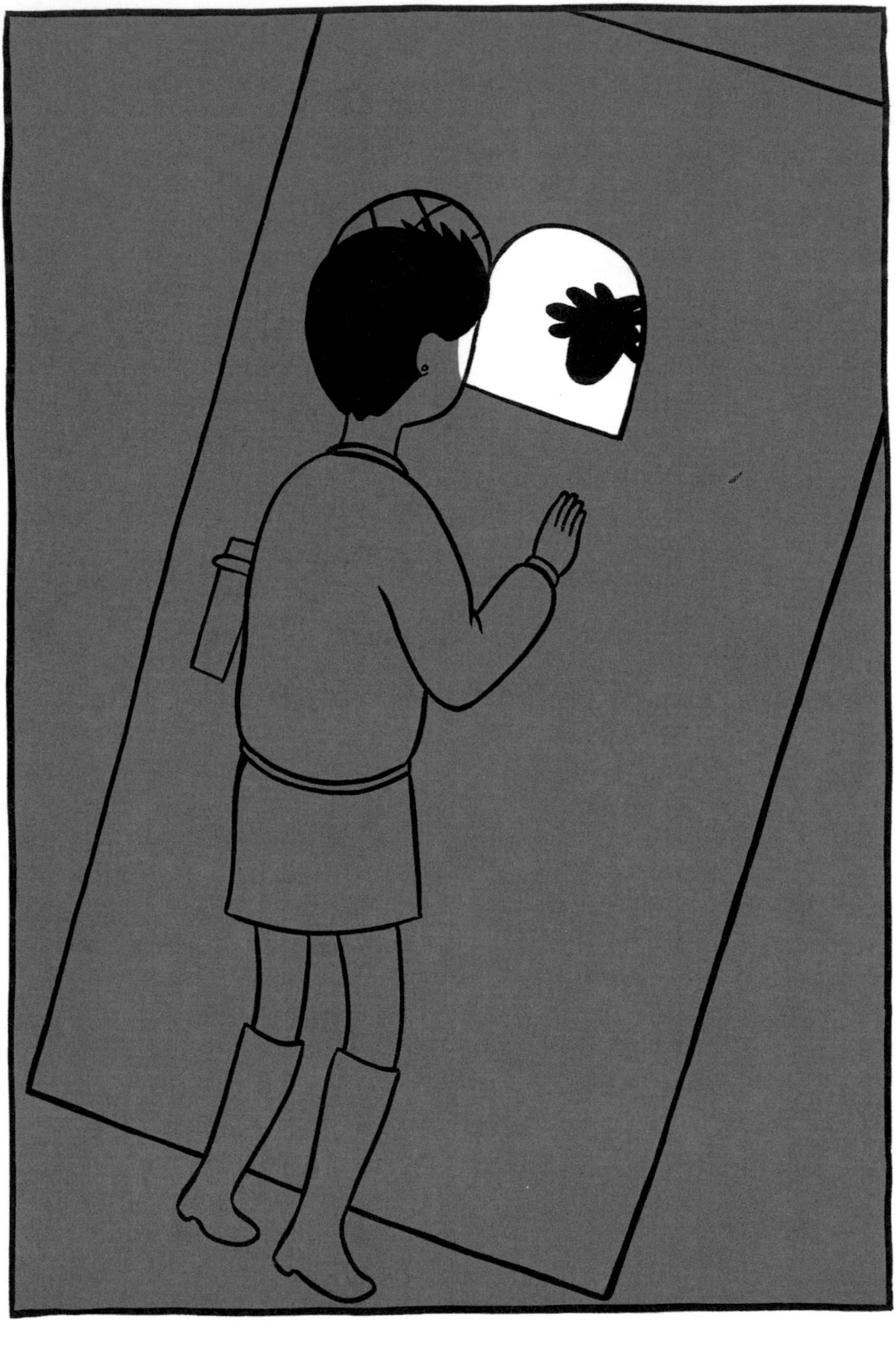

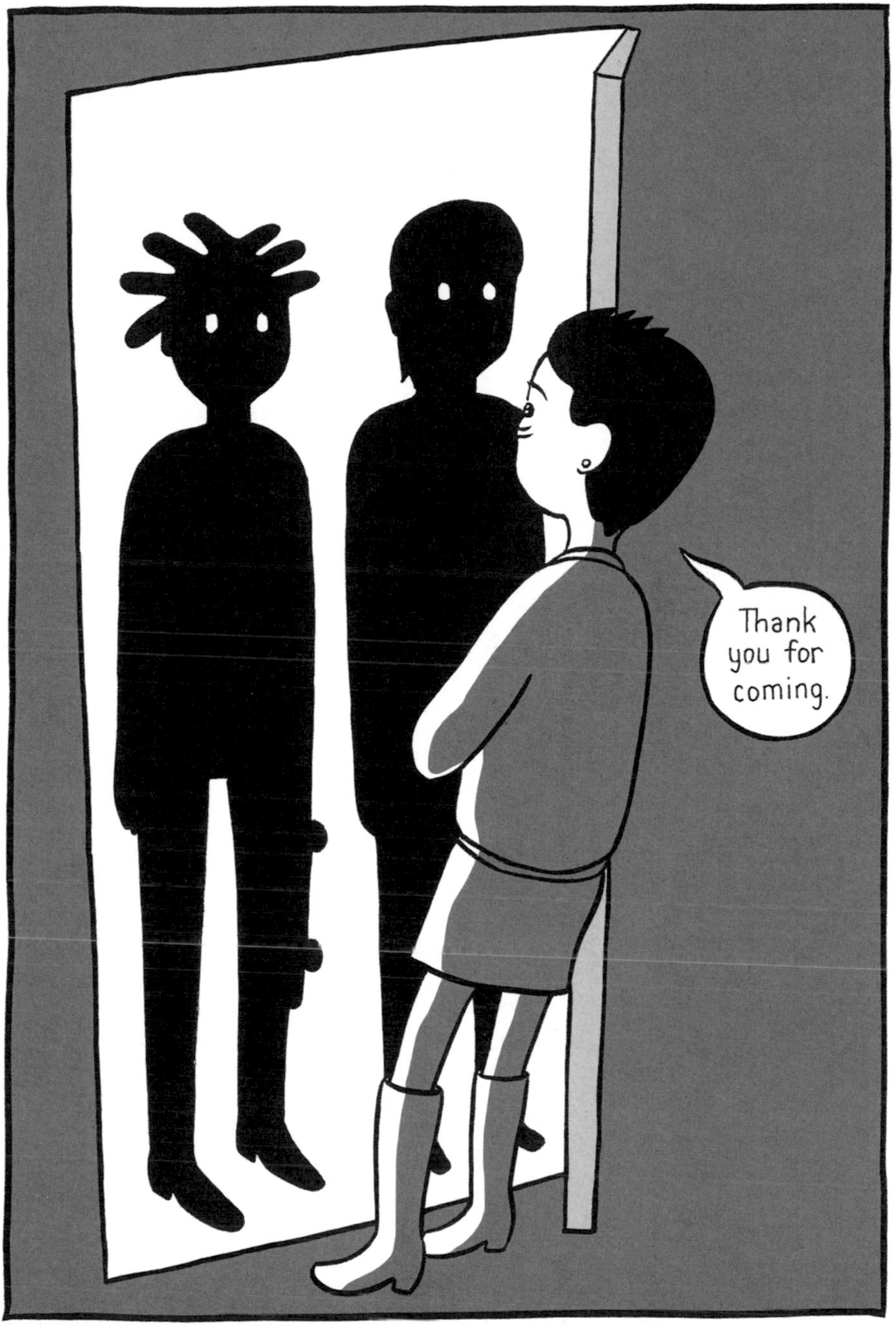
Thank you for coming.

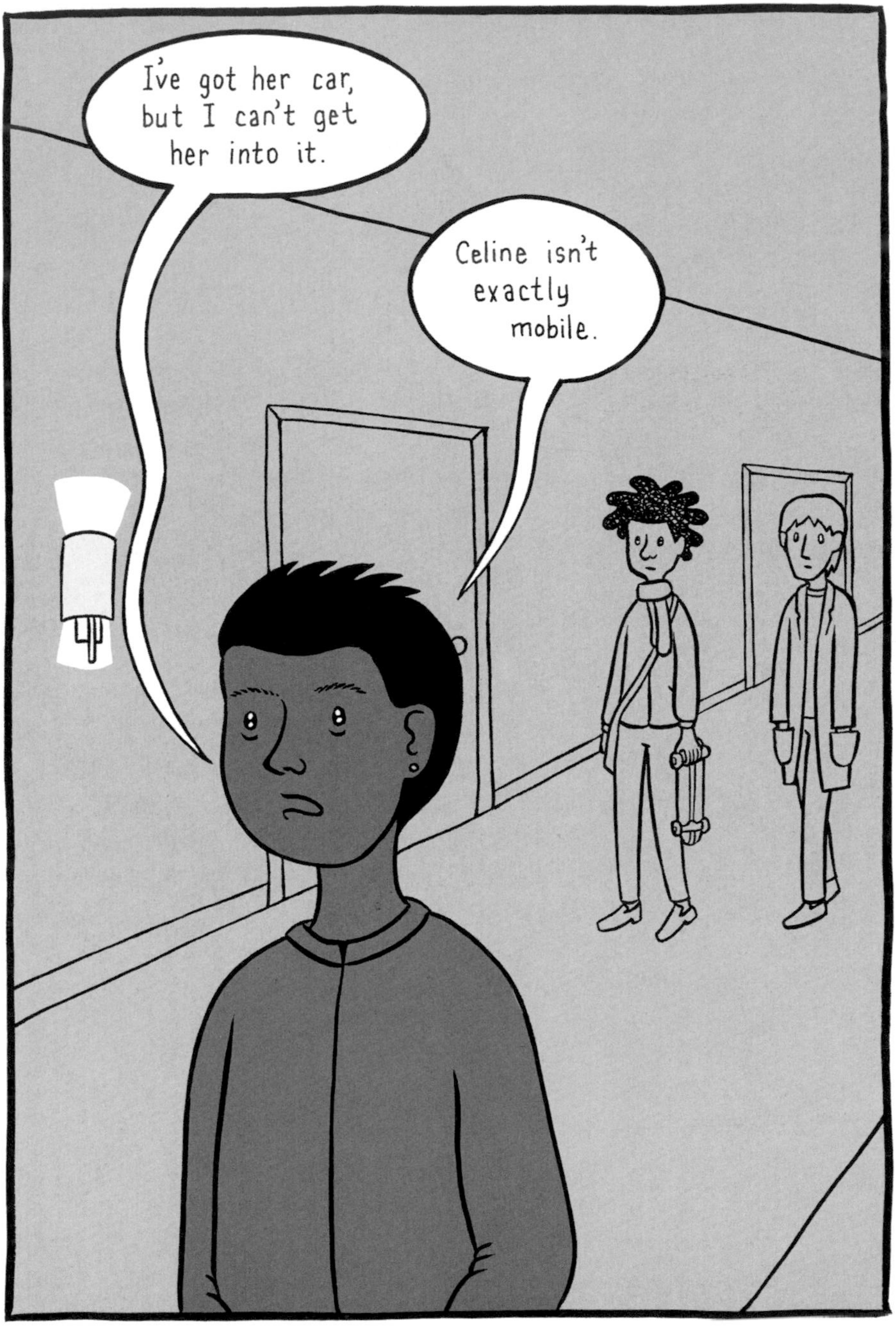
I've got her car, but I can't get her into it.
Celine isn't exactly mobile.

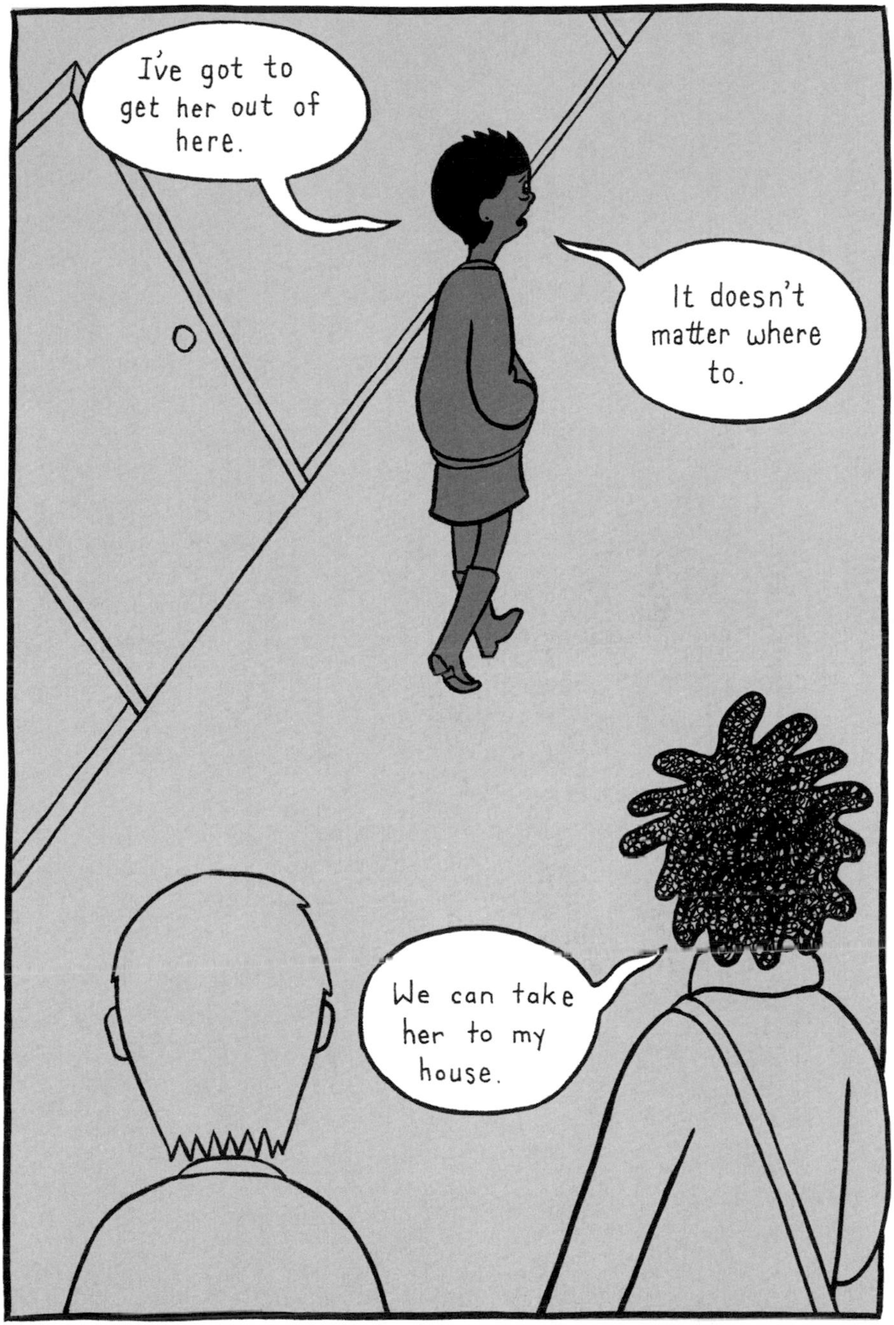
I've got to get her out of here.
It doesn't matter where to.
We can take her to my house.

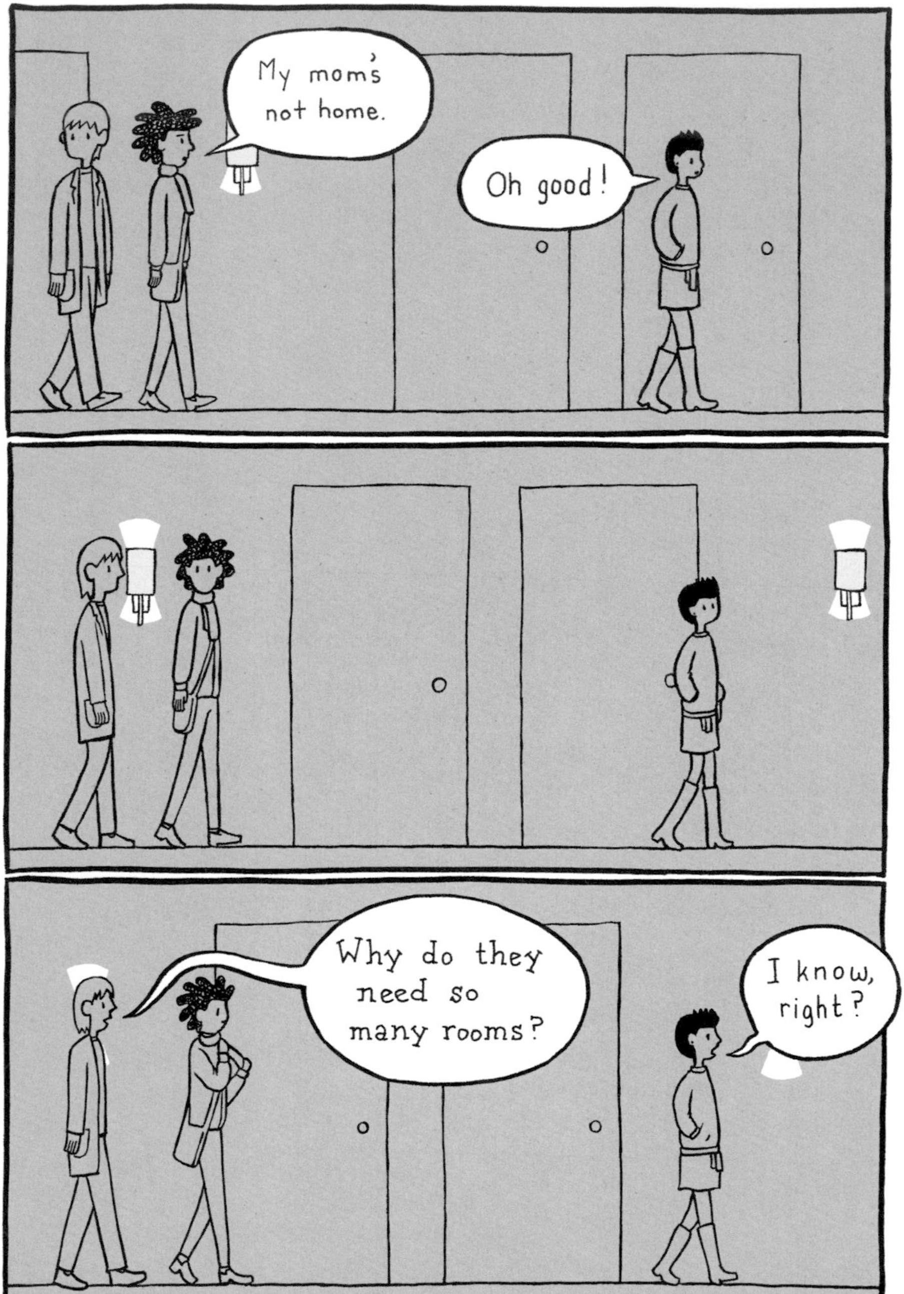
My mom's not home.
Oh good!
Why do they need so many rooms?
I know, right?

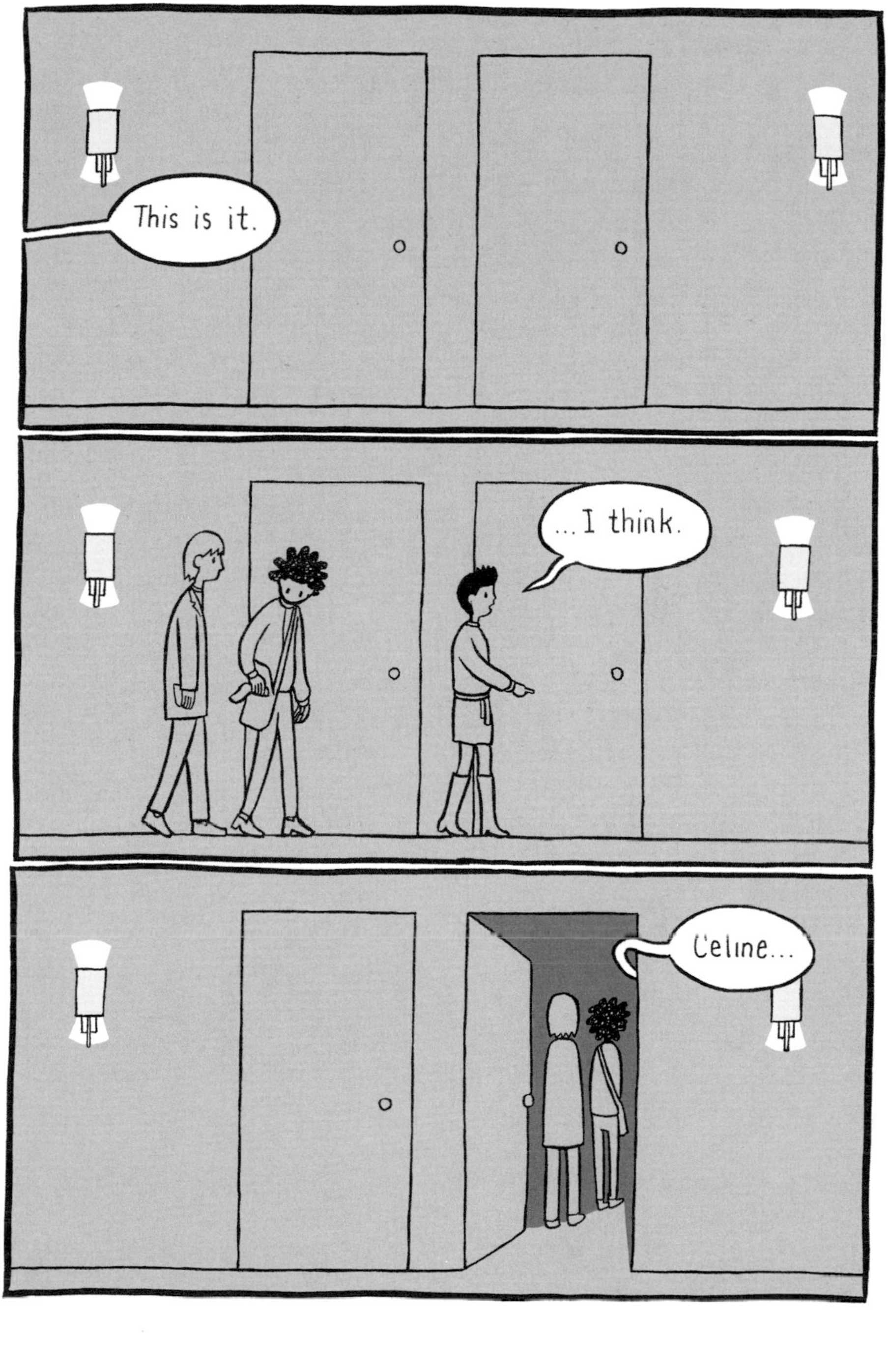
This is it.
...I think.
Celine...

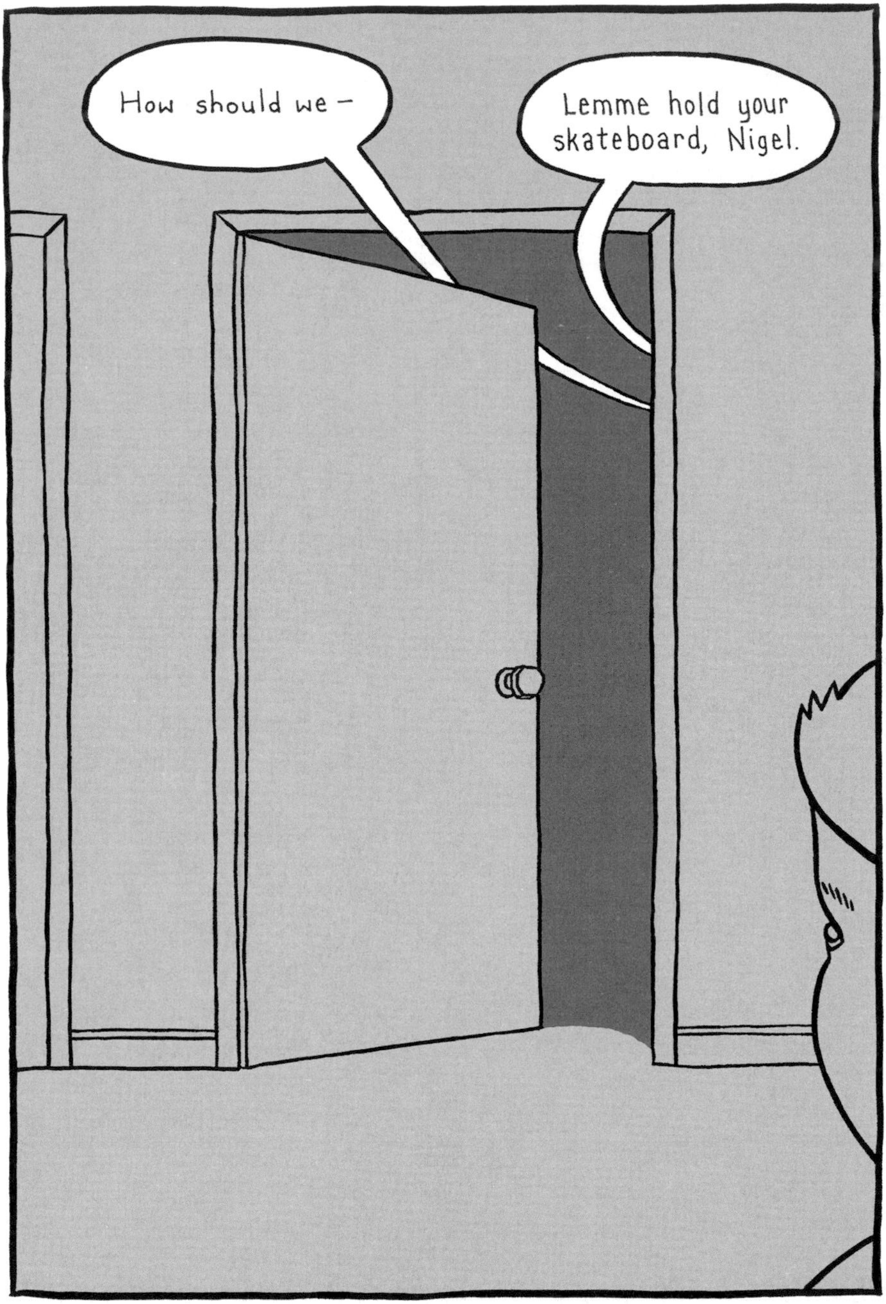
How should we-
Lemme hold your skateboard, Nigel.

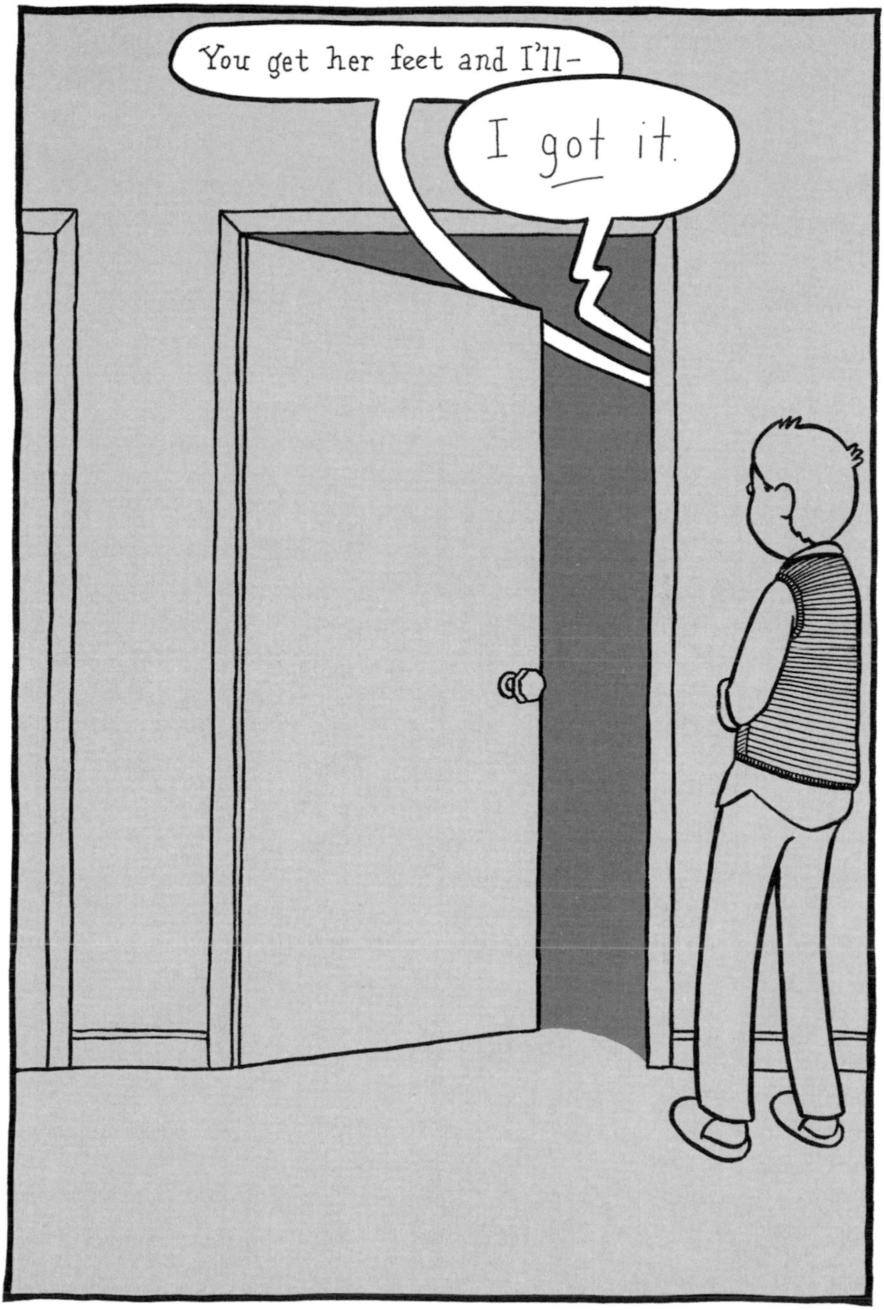
You get her feet and I'll-
I got it.

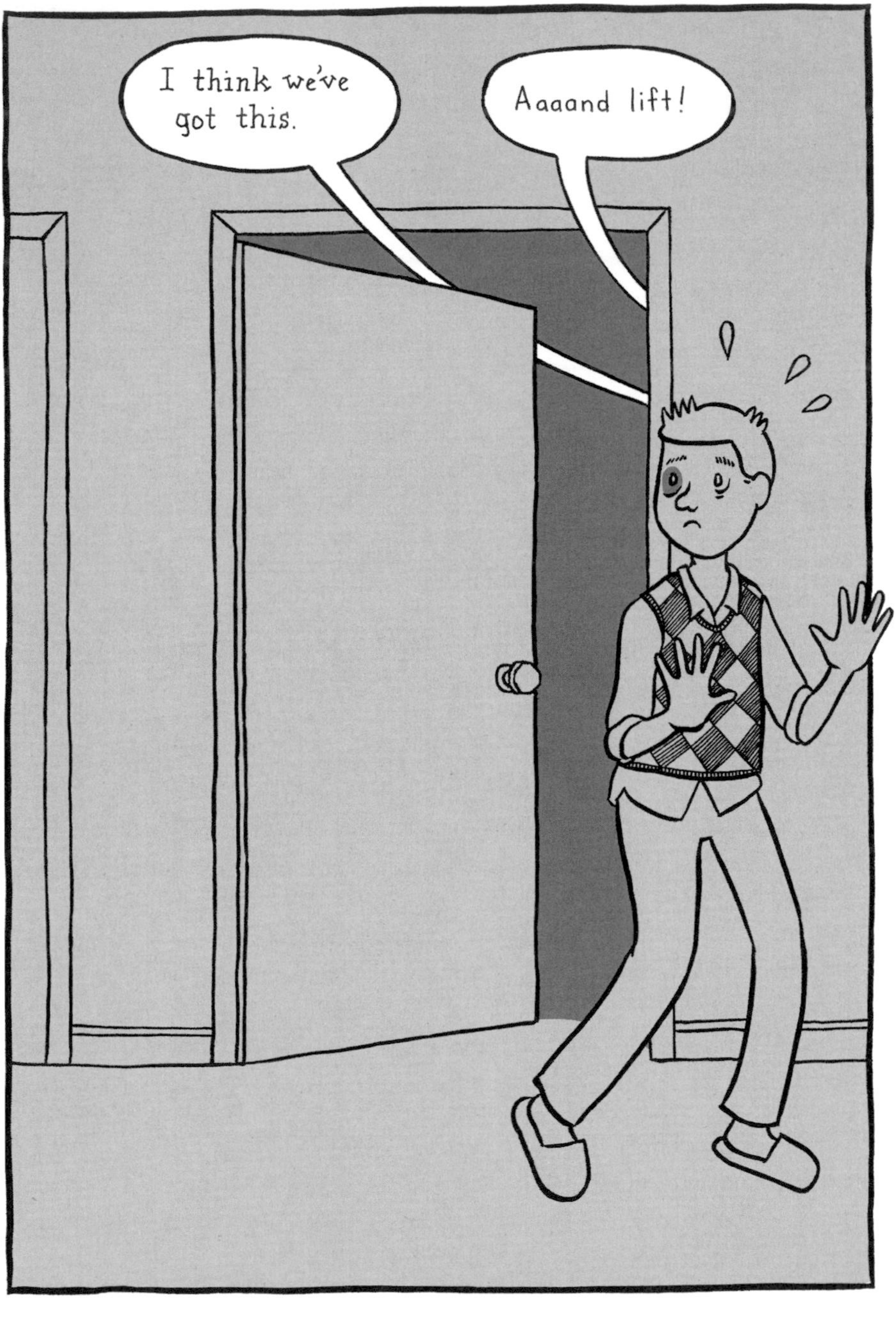
I think we've got this.
Aaaand lift!

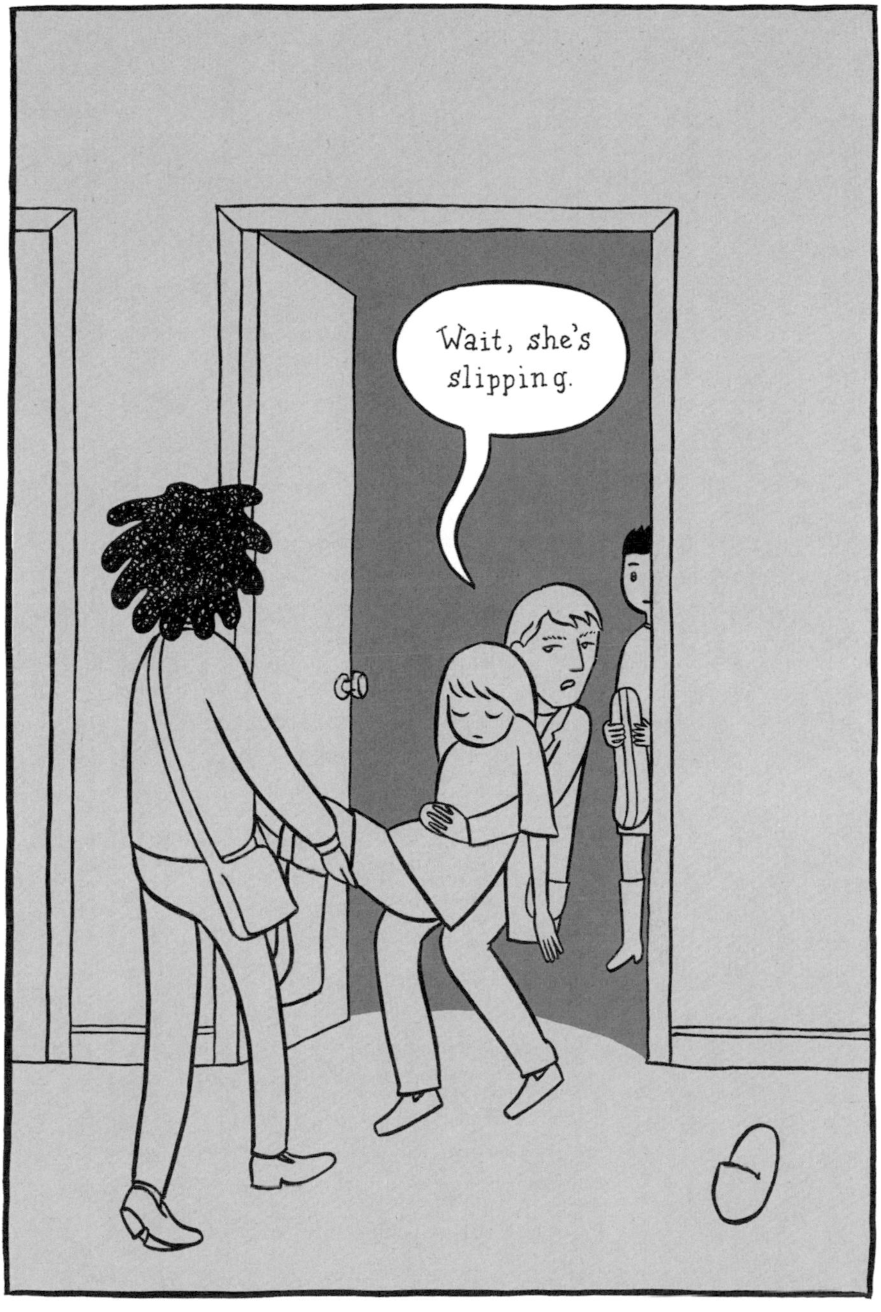
Wait, she's slipping.

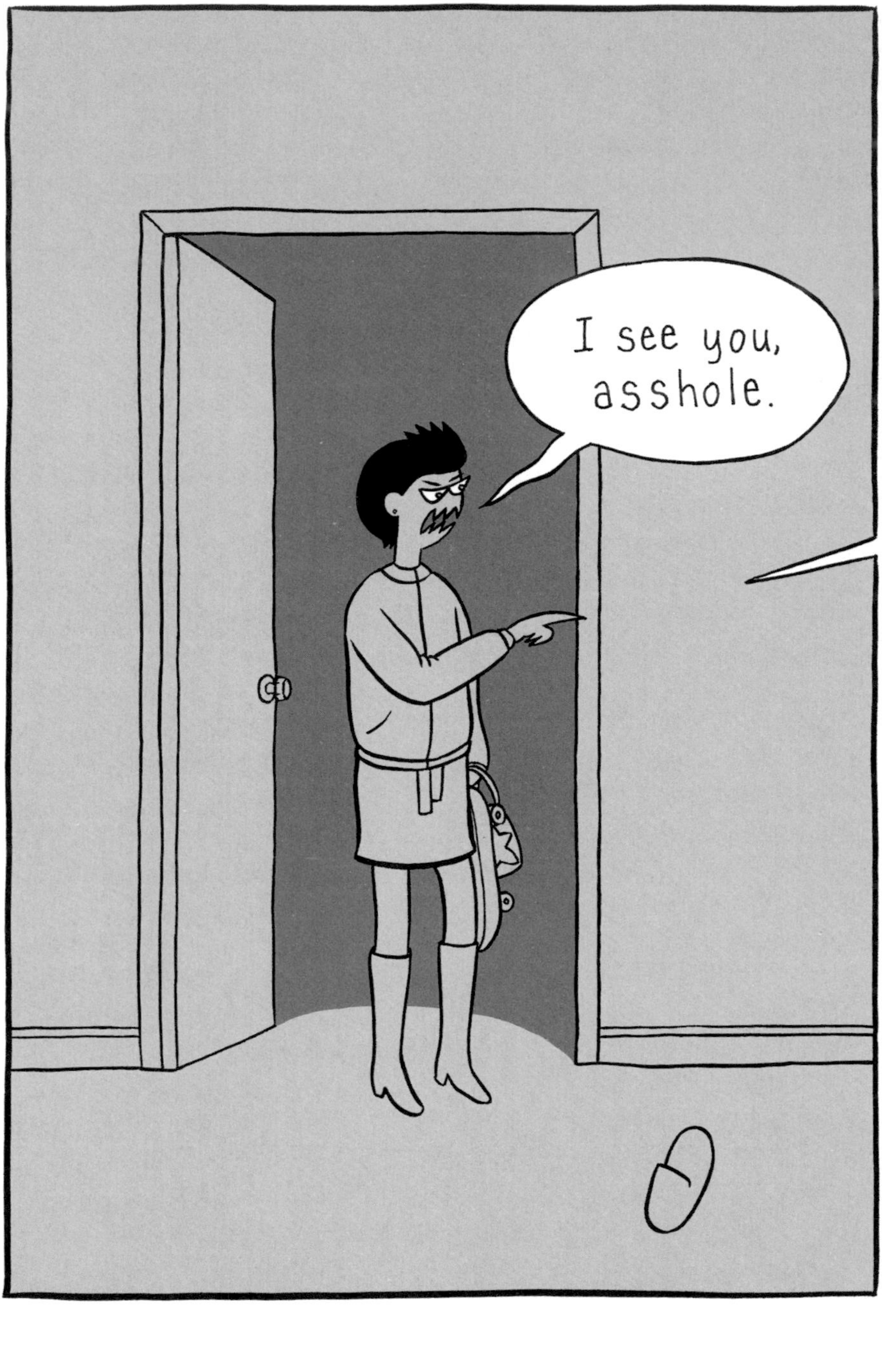
I see you, asshole.

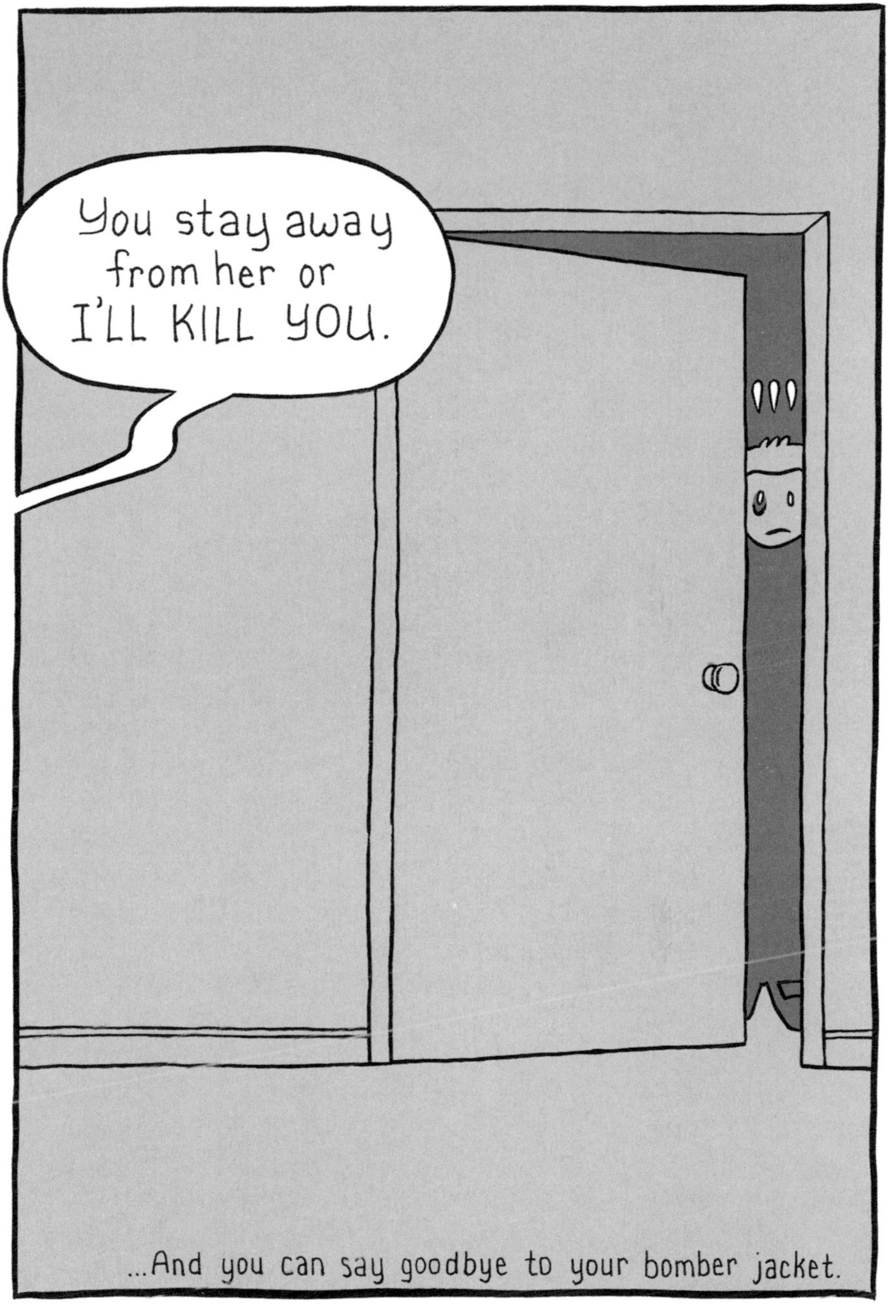
You stay away from her or I'LL KILL YOU.
...And you can say goodbye to your bomber jacket.

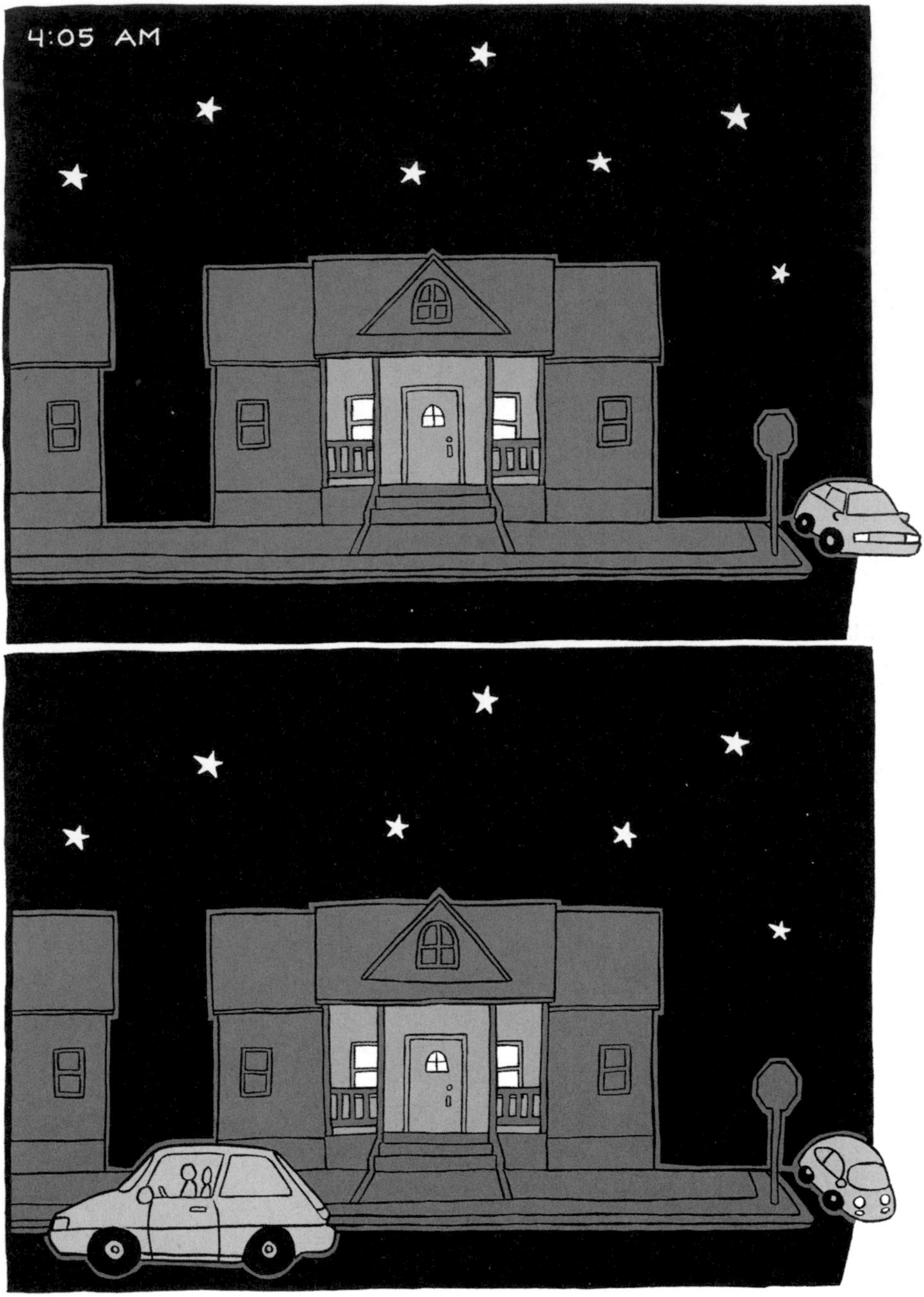
4:05 AM

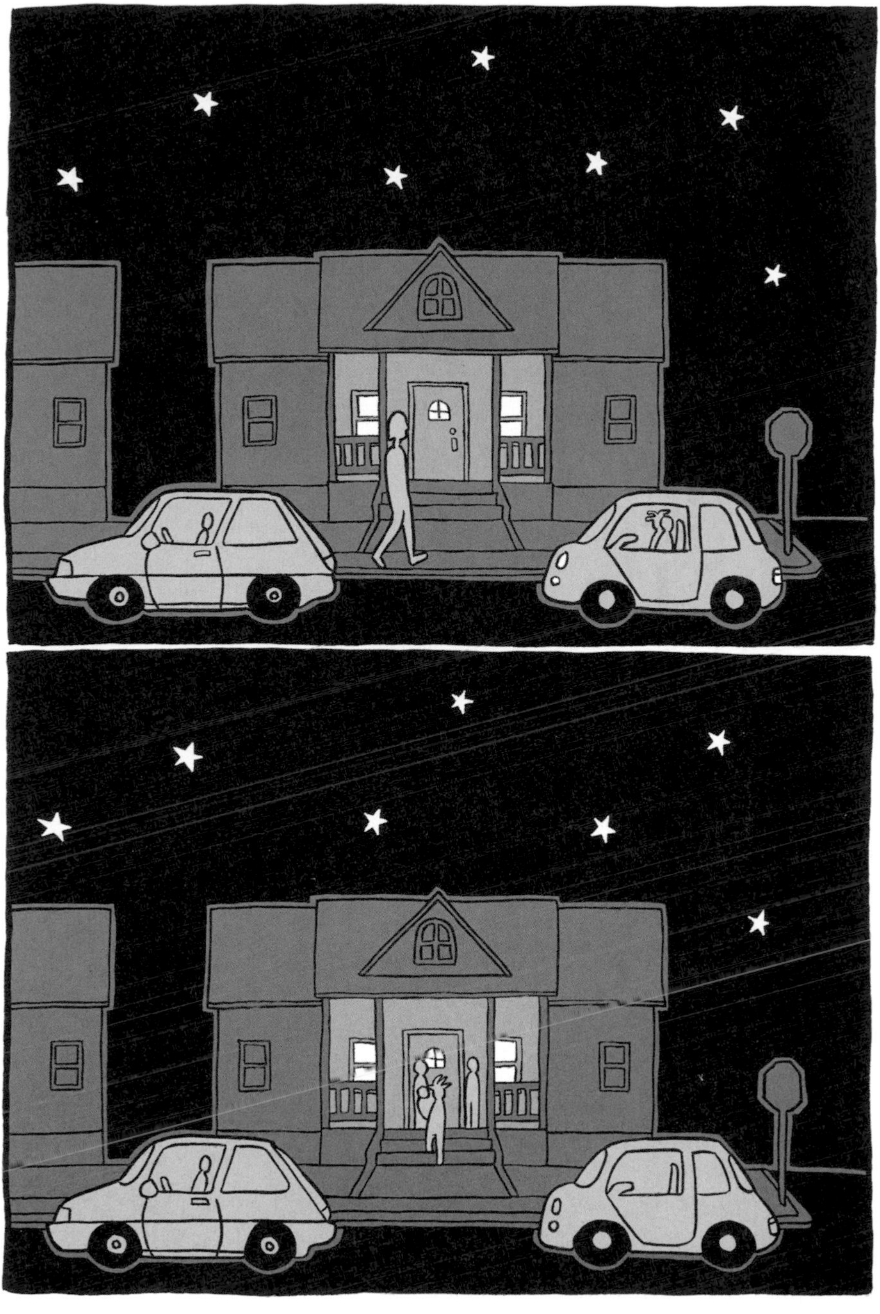

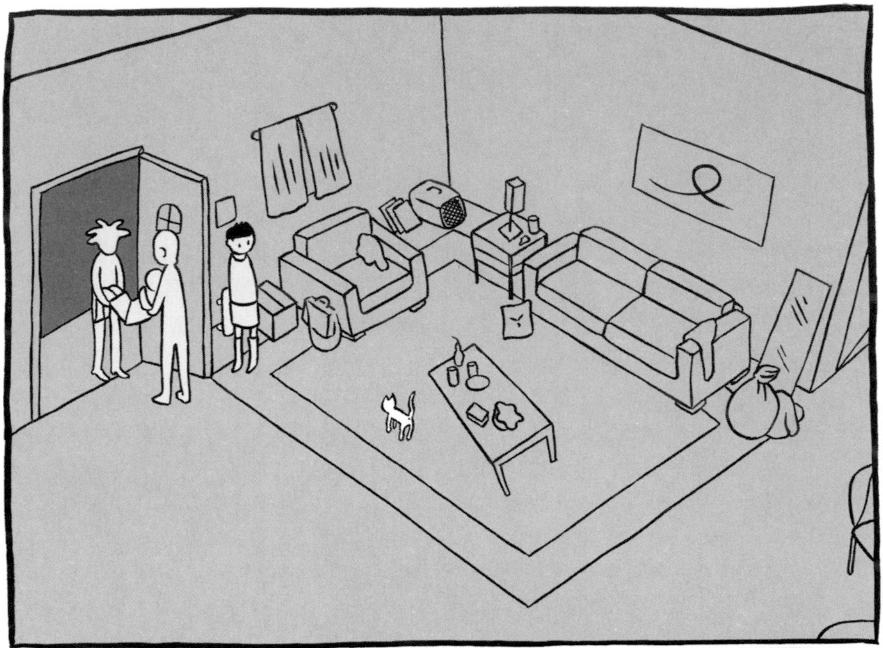

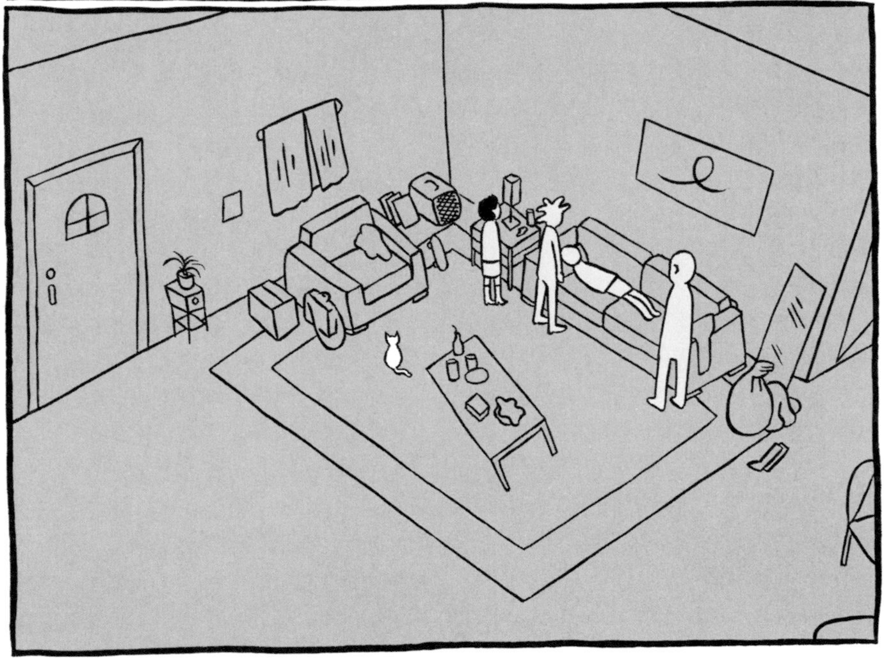

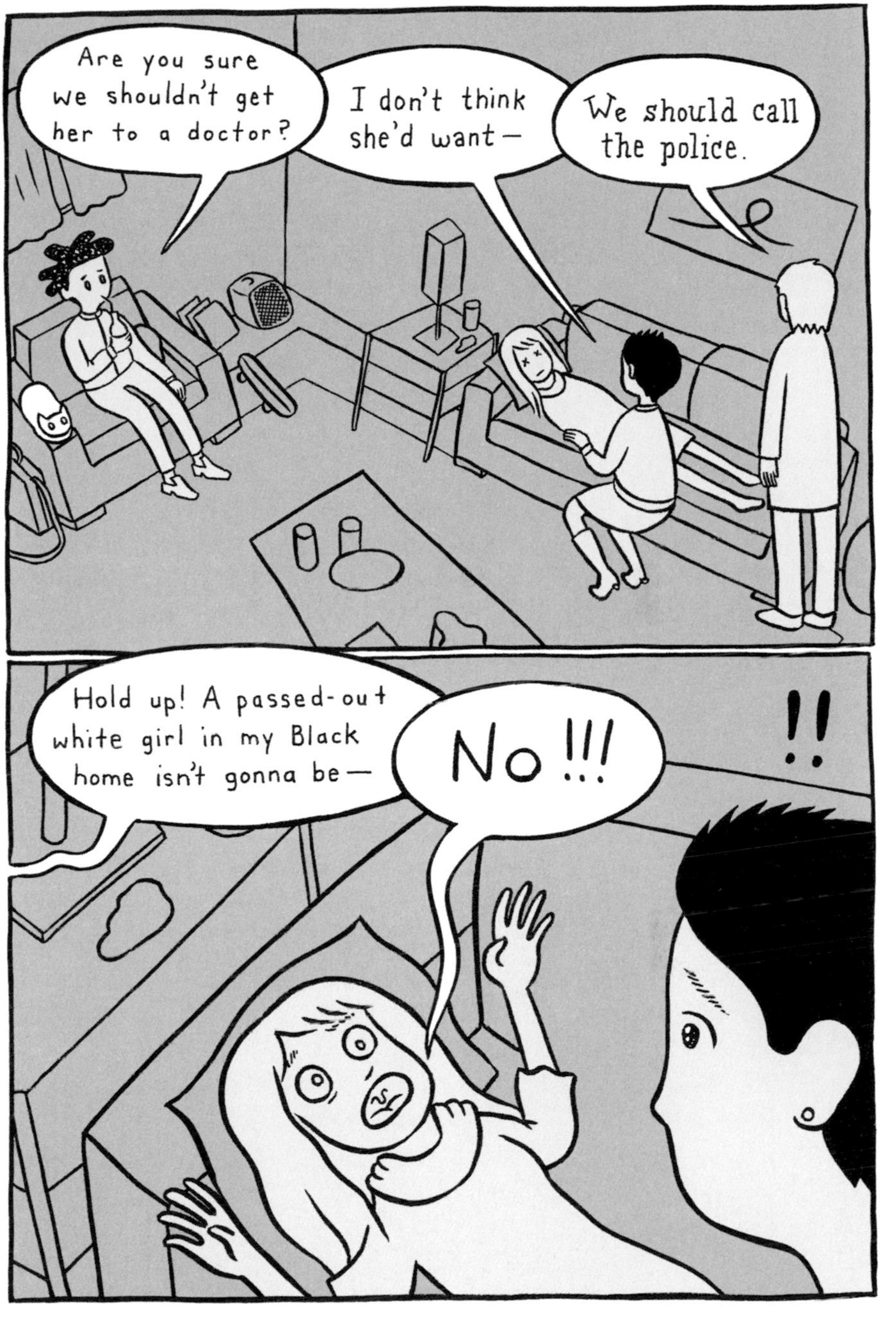
Are you sure we shouldn't get her to a doctor?
I don't think she'd want—
We should call the police.
Hold up! A passed-out white girl in my Black home isn't gonna be—
No!!!
!!

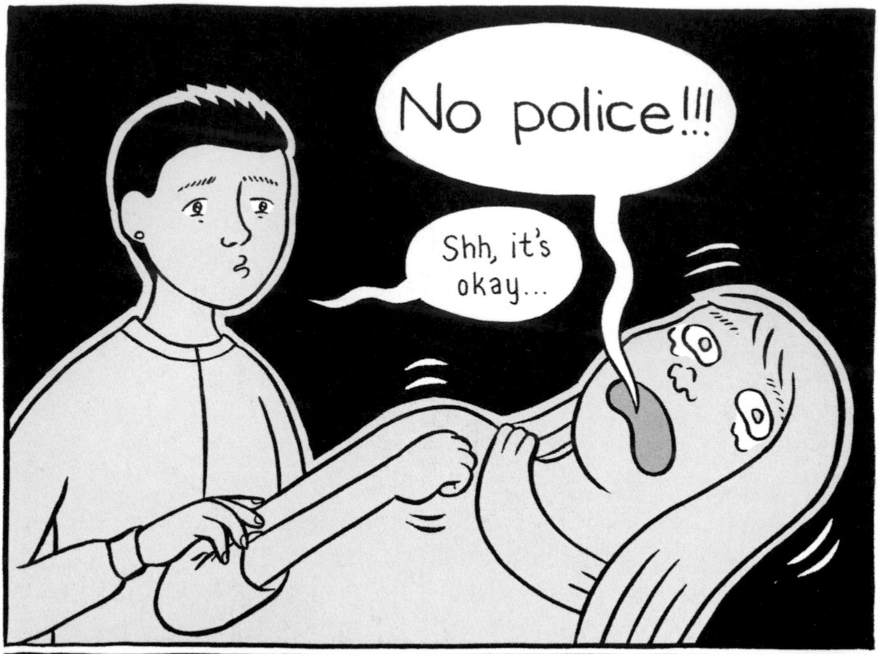
No police!!!
Shh, it's okay...

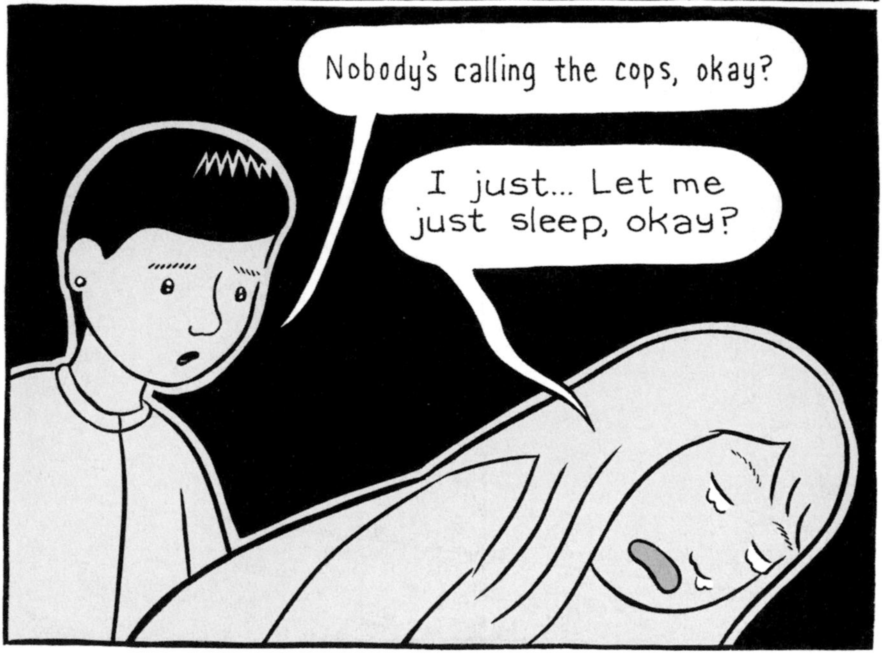
Nobody's calling the cops, okay?
I just... Let me just sleep, okay?

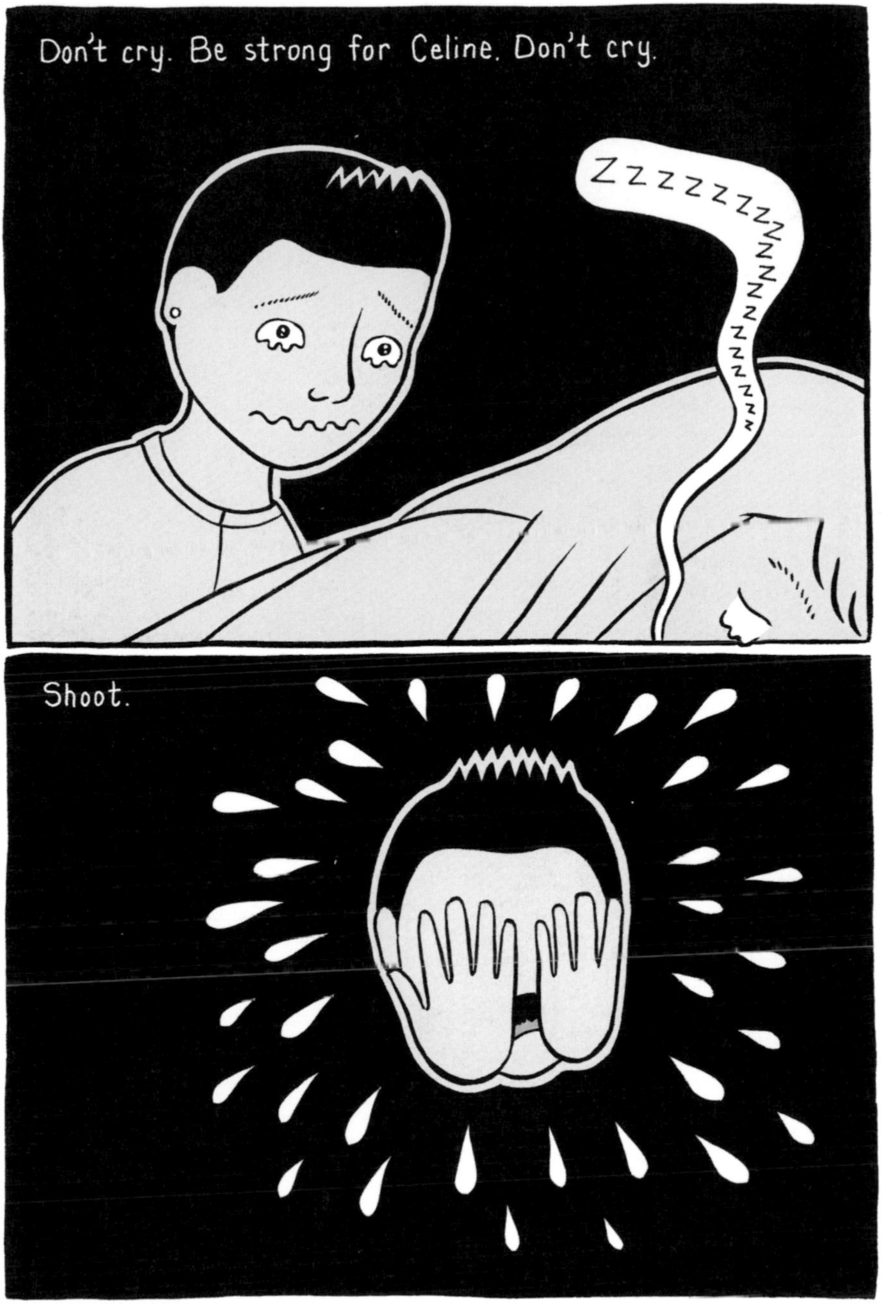
Don't cry. Be strong for Celine. Don't cry.
ZZZZZZZZZZZZZZZZZZ
Shoot.

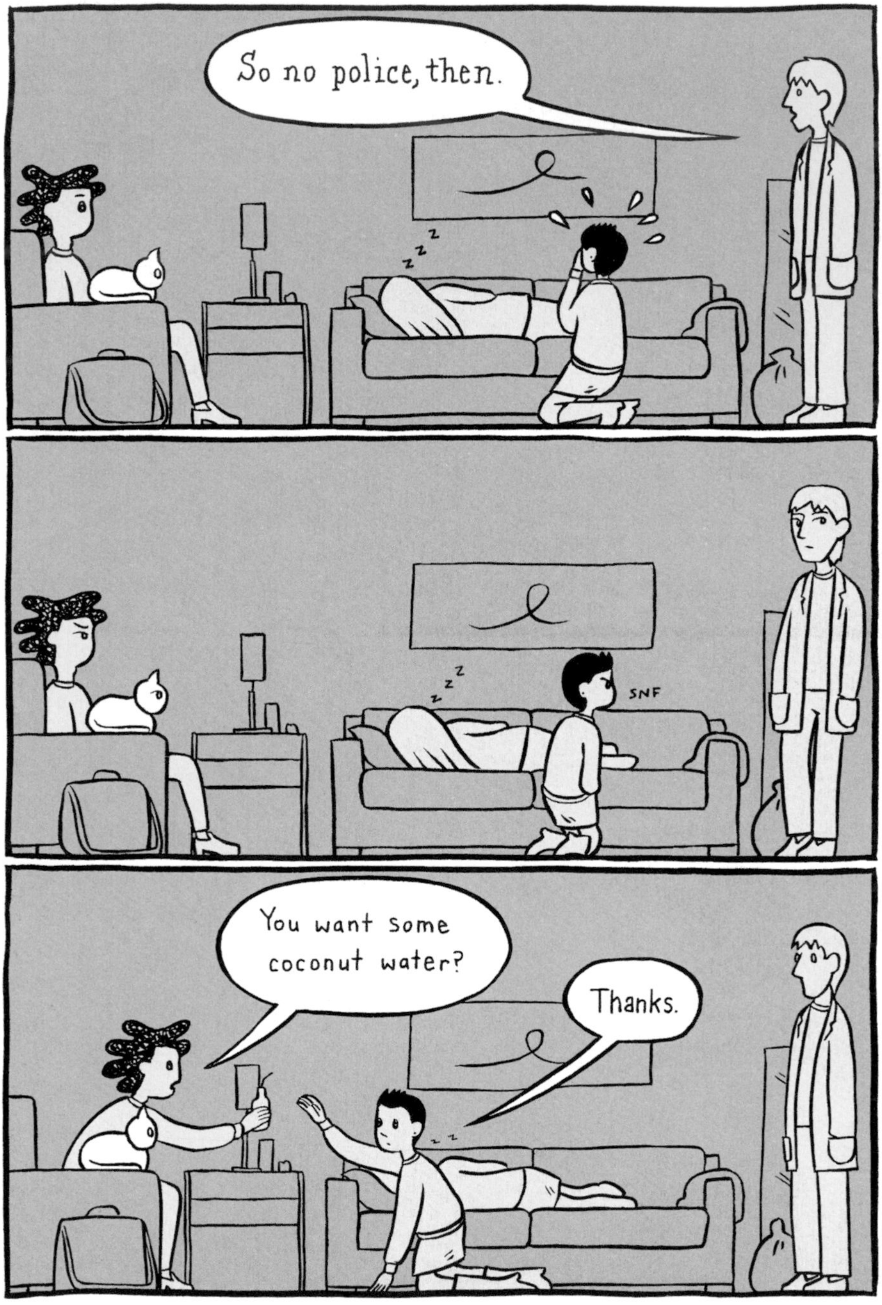
So no police, then.
z z z
z z z
SNF
You want some coconut water?
Thanks.
z z

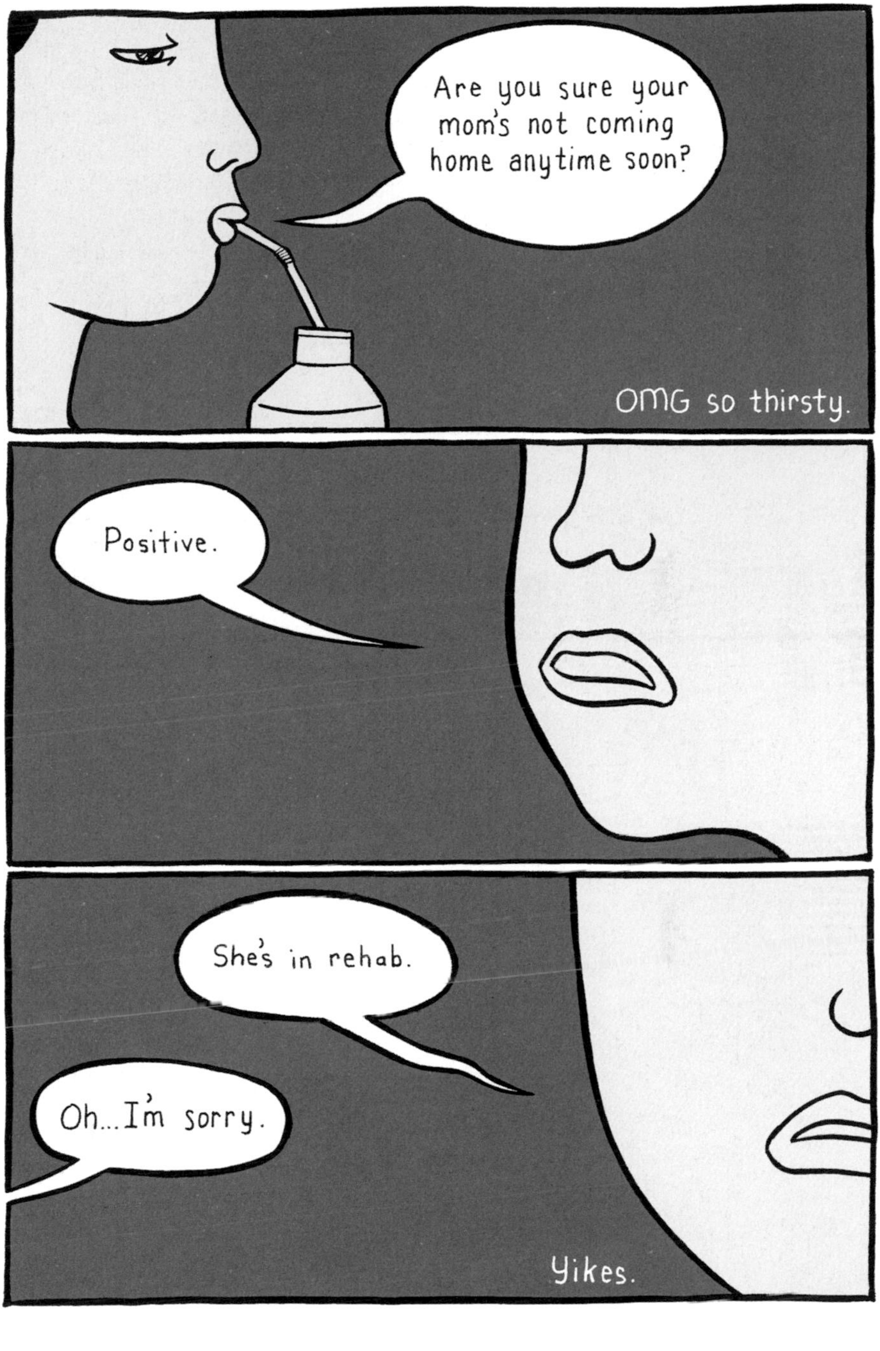
Are you sure your mom's not coming home anytime soon?
OMG so thirsty.
Positive.
She's in rehab.
Oh... I'm sorry.
Yikes.

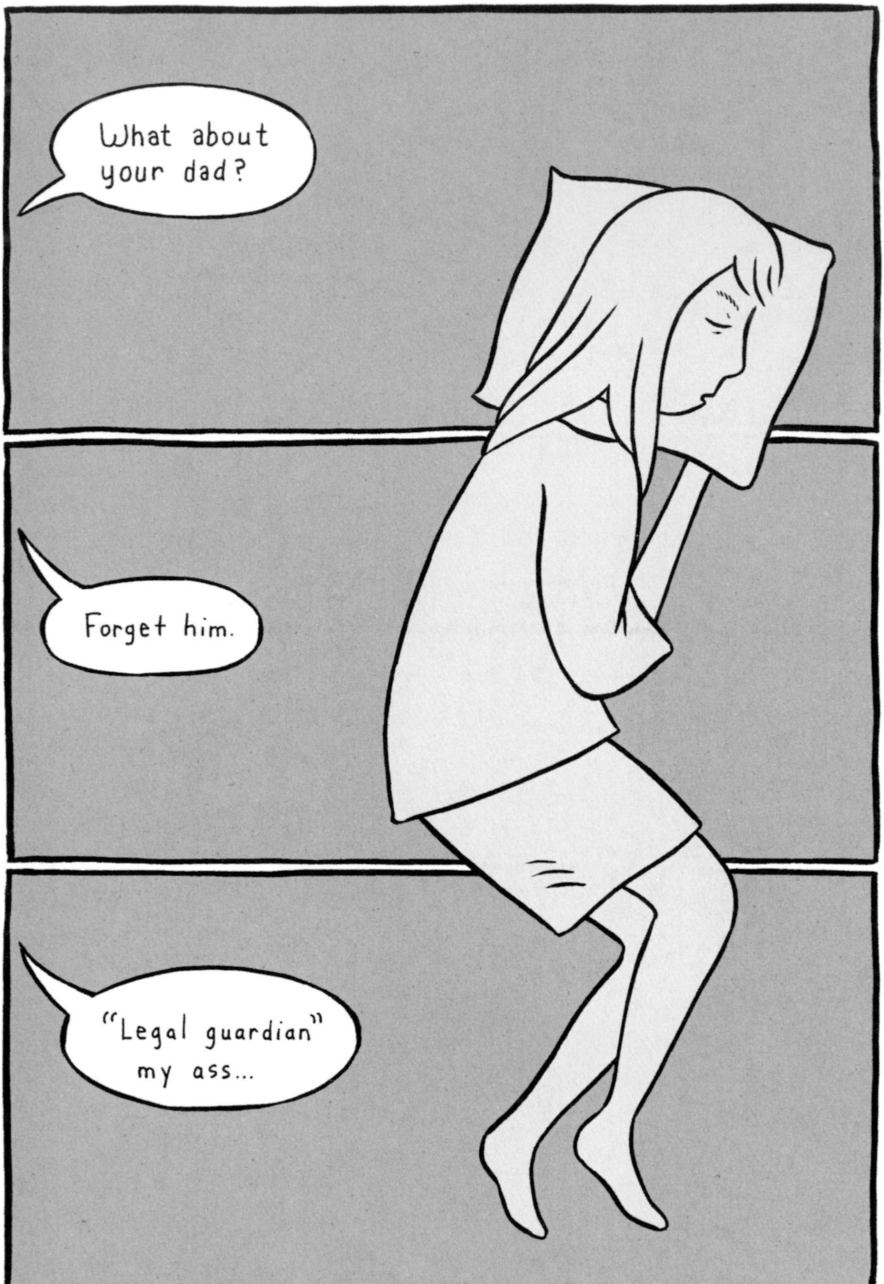
What about your dad?
Forget him.
"Legal guardian" my ass...

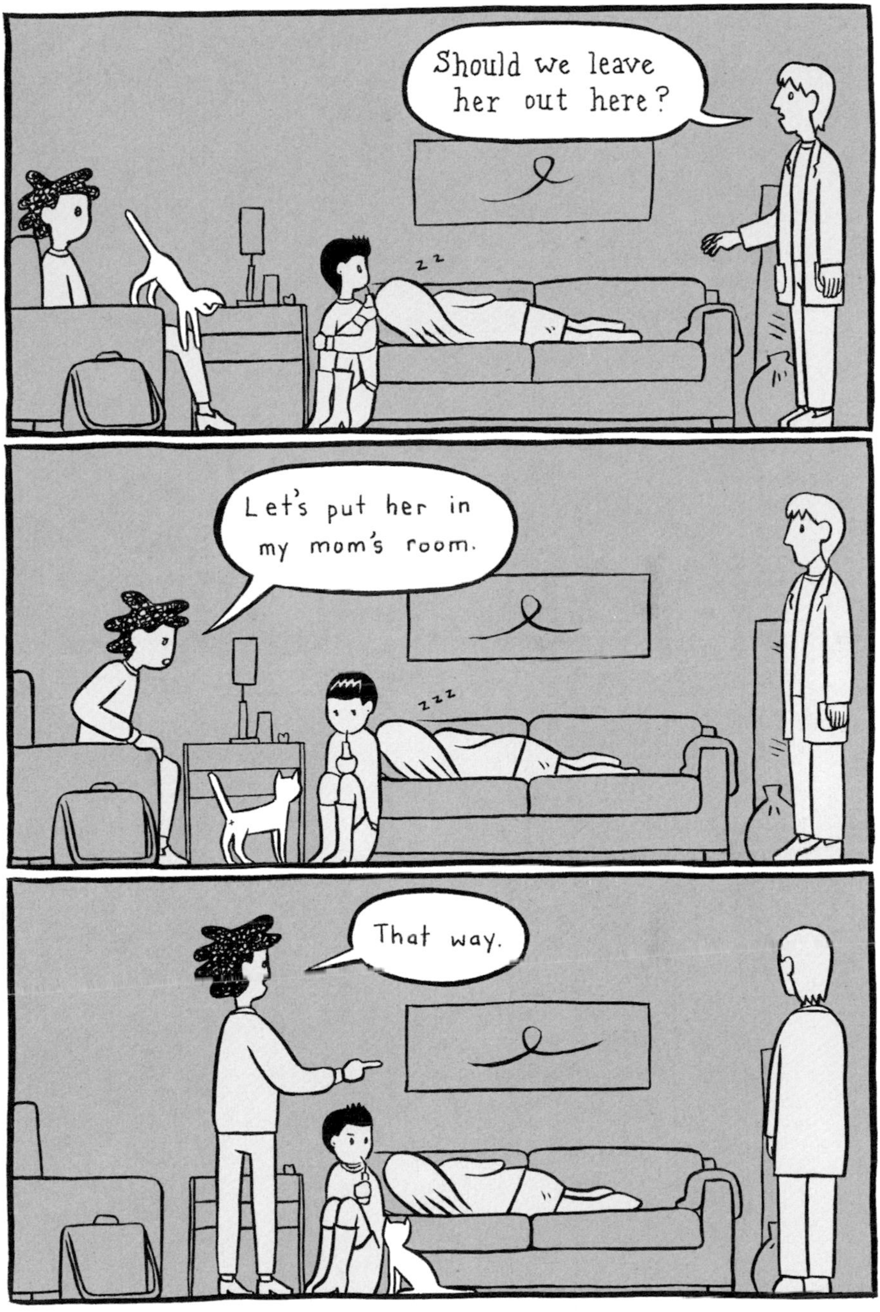
Should we leave her out here?
Let's put her in my mom's room.
That way.

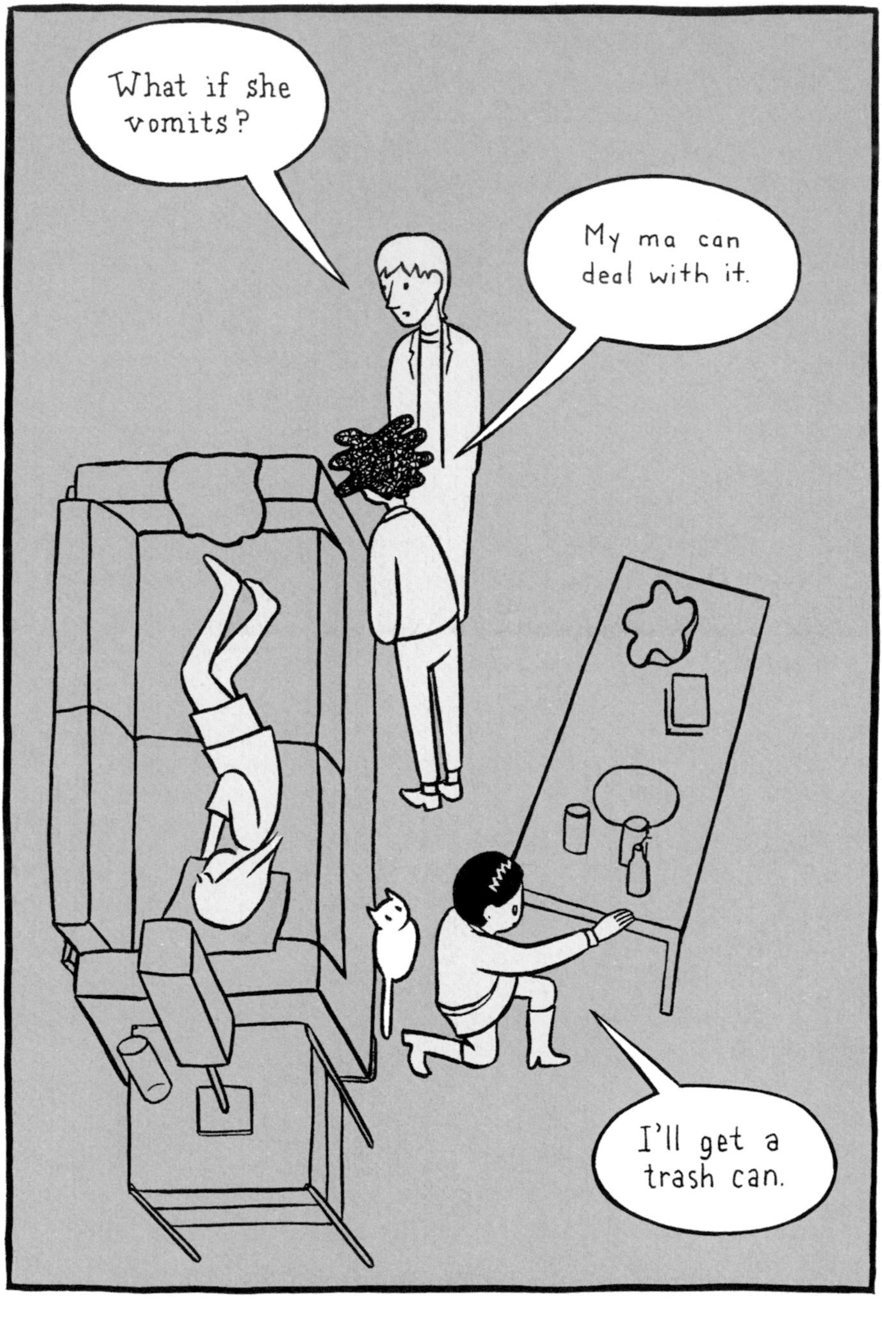
What if she vomits?
My ma can deal with it.
I'll get a trash can.

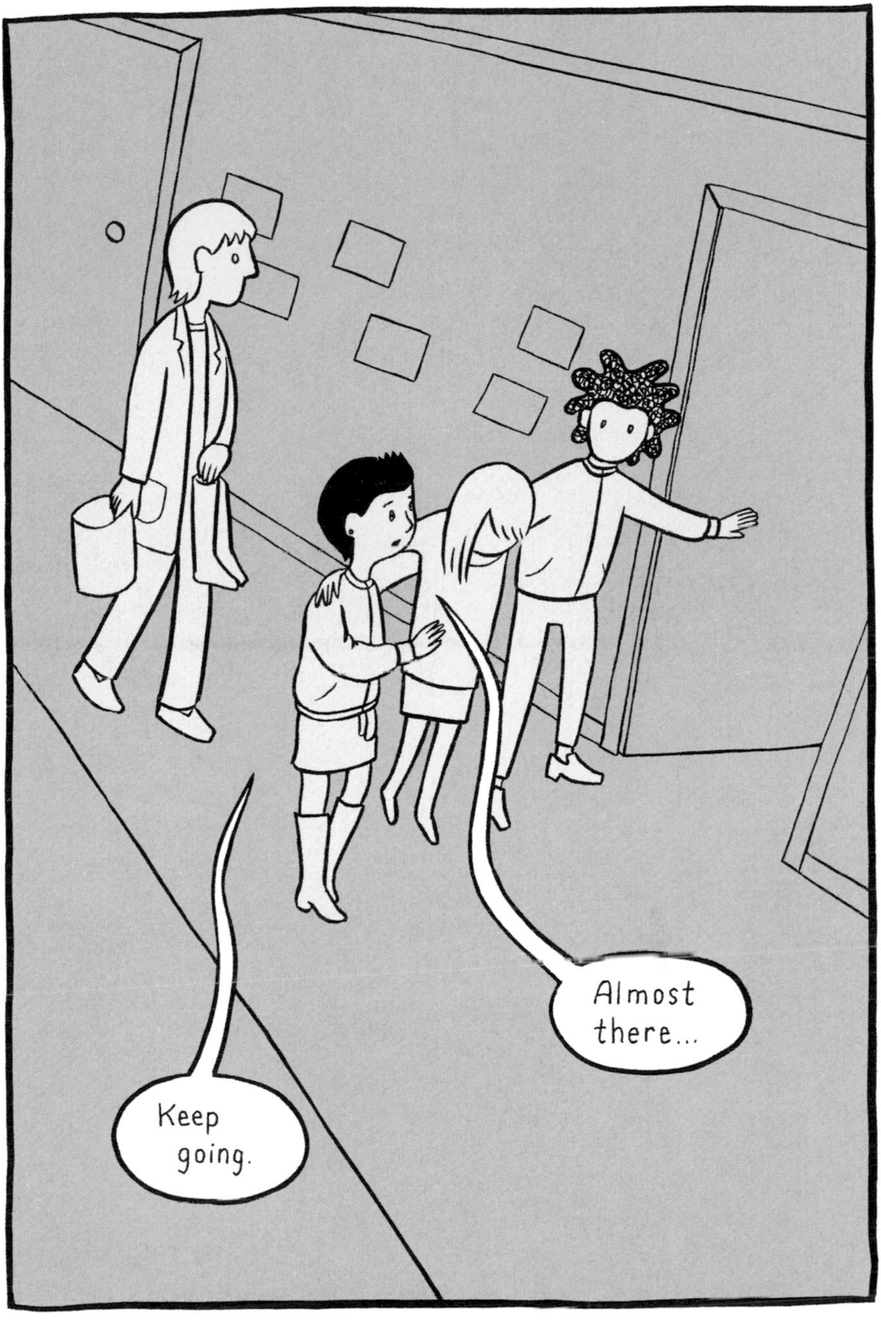
Almost there...
Keep going.

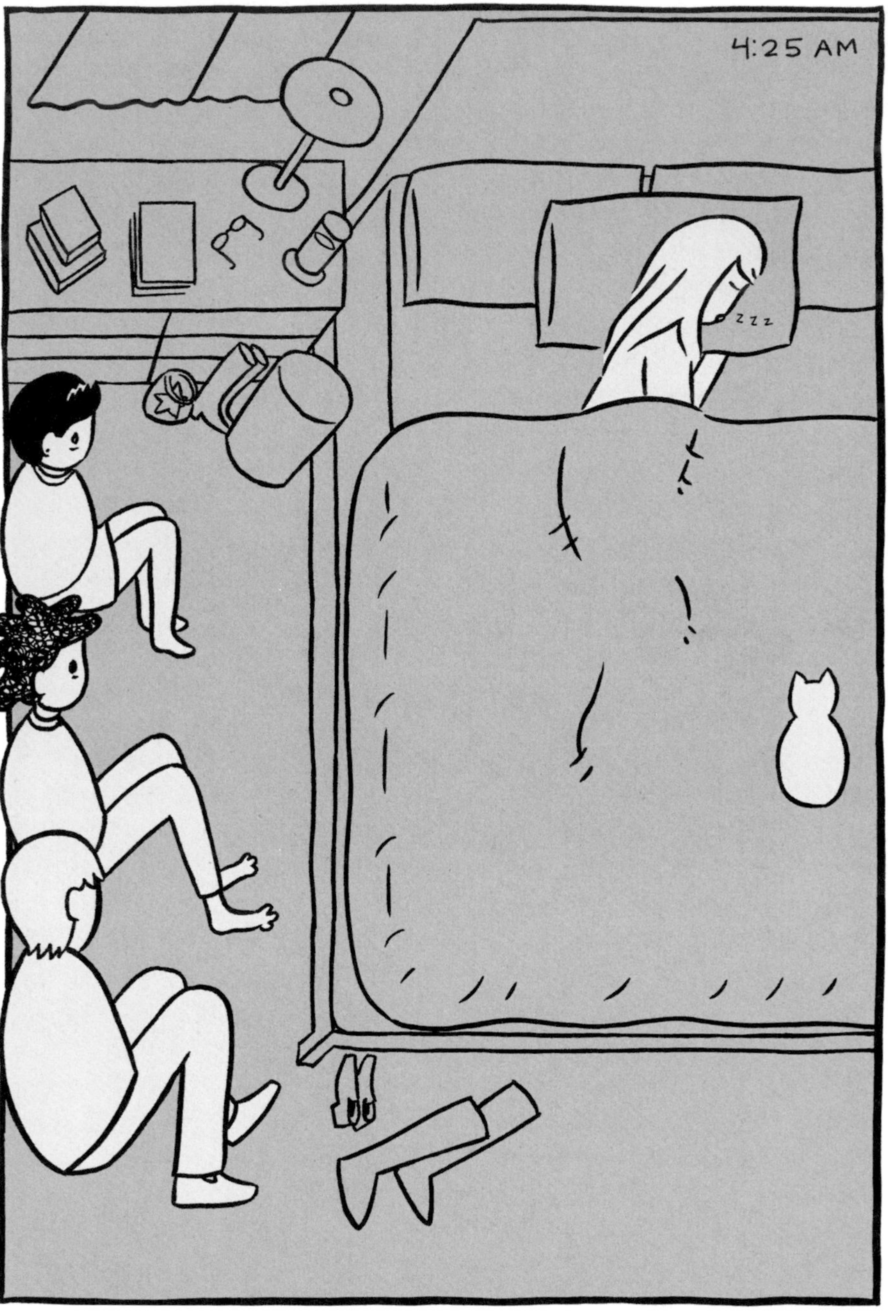
4:25 AM
zzz

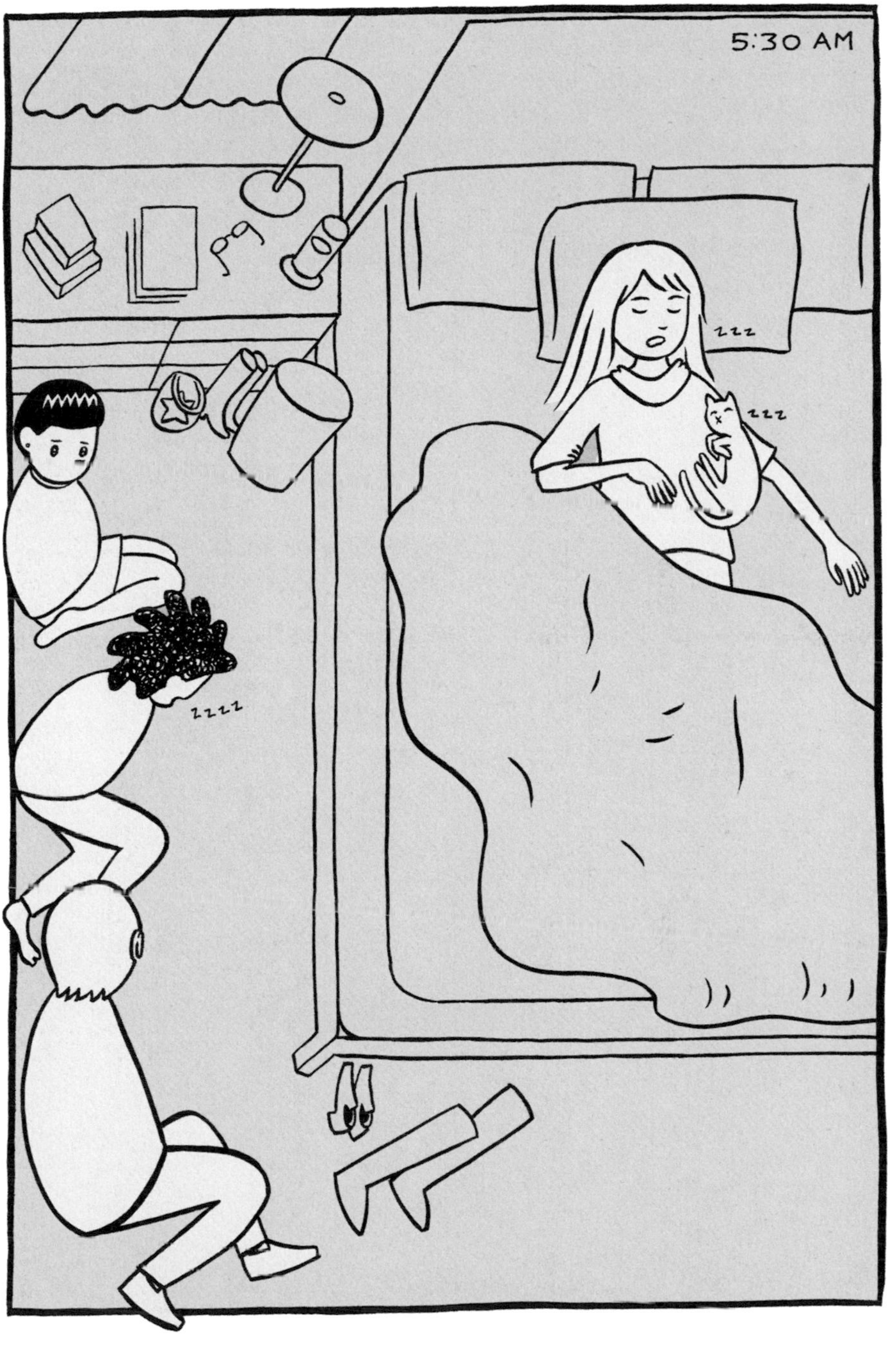
5:30 AM
zzz
zzz
zzzz

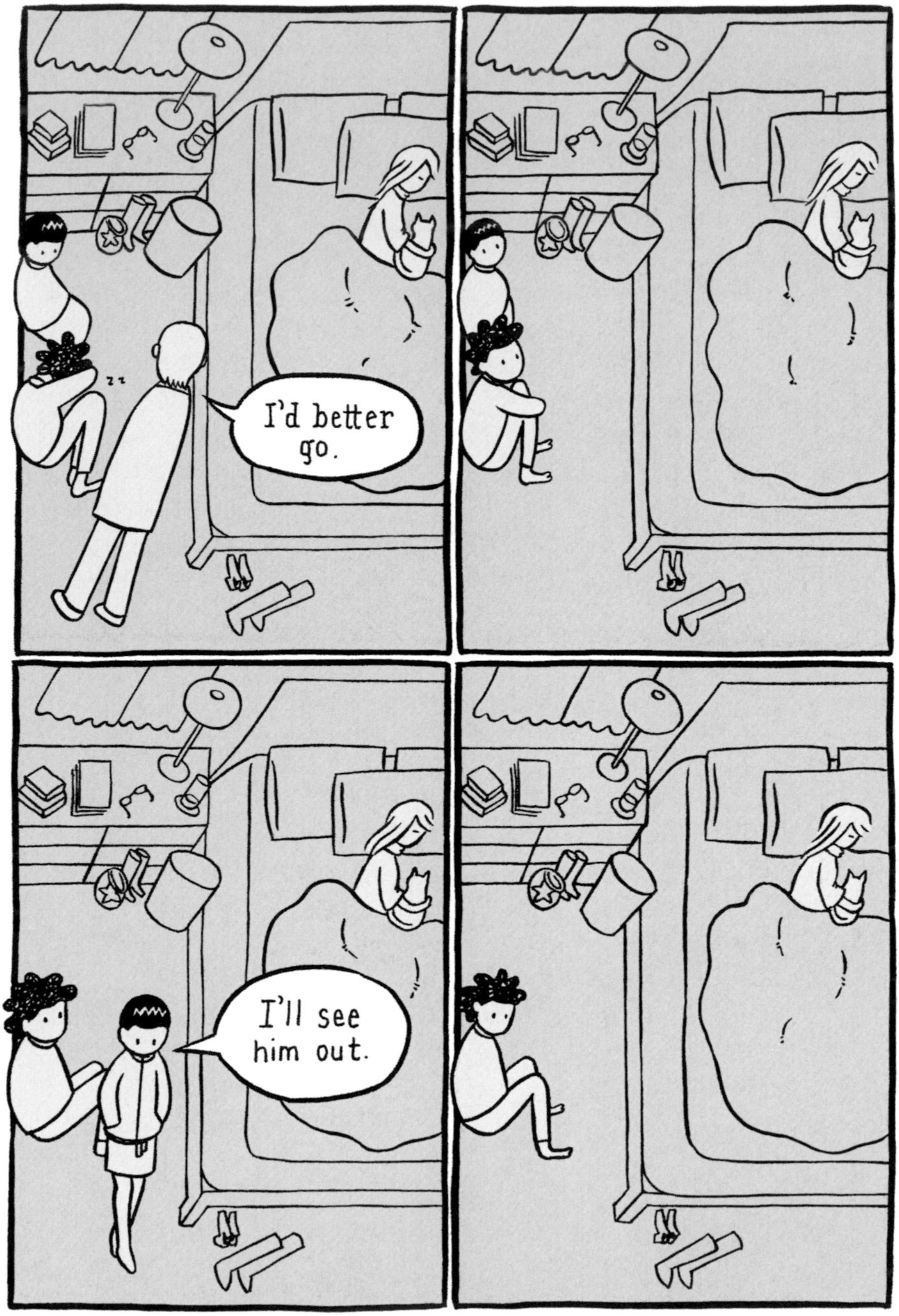
I'd better go.
I'll see him out.

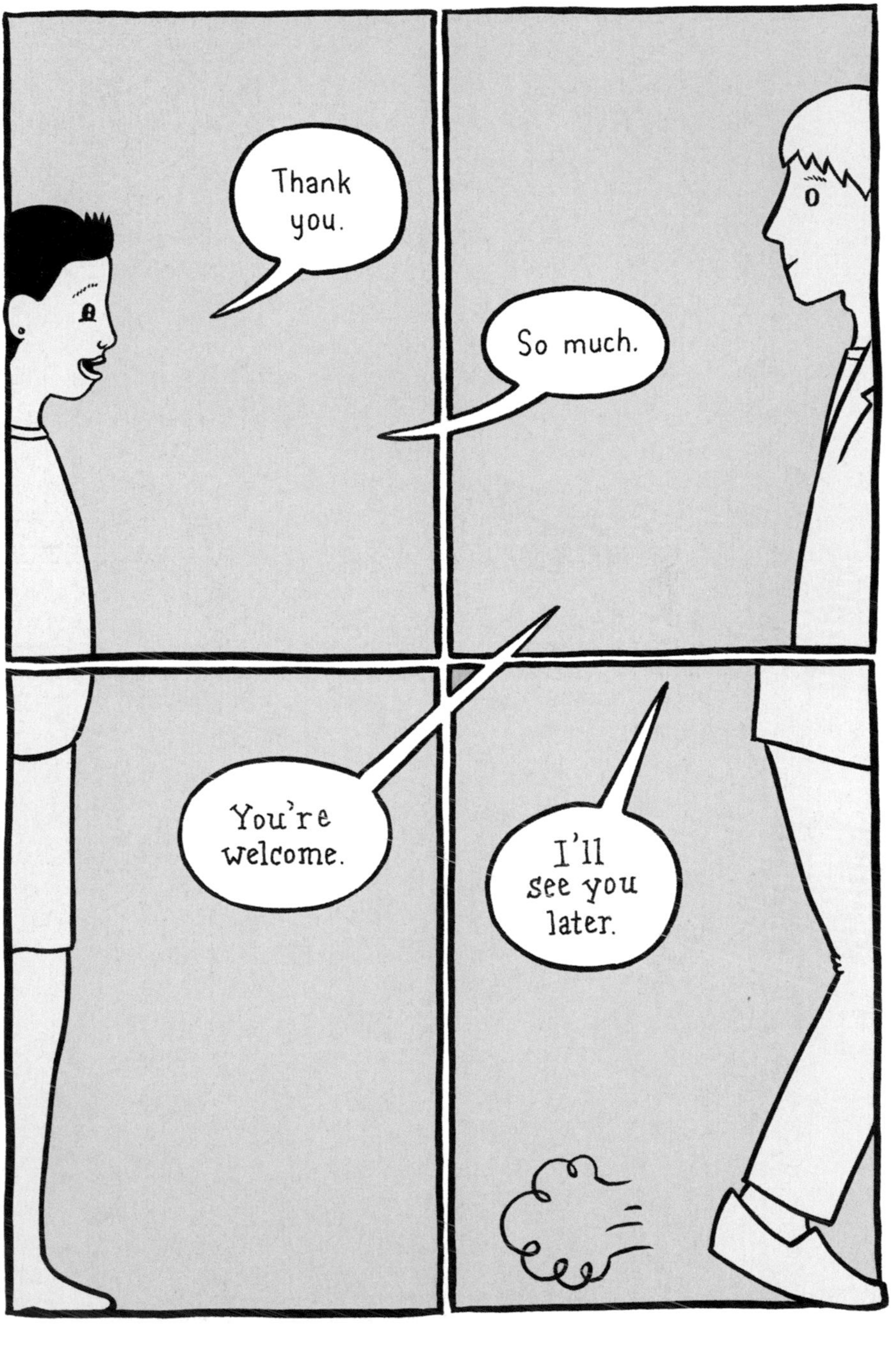
Thank you.
So much.
You're welcome.
I'll see you later.

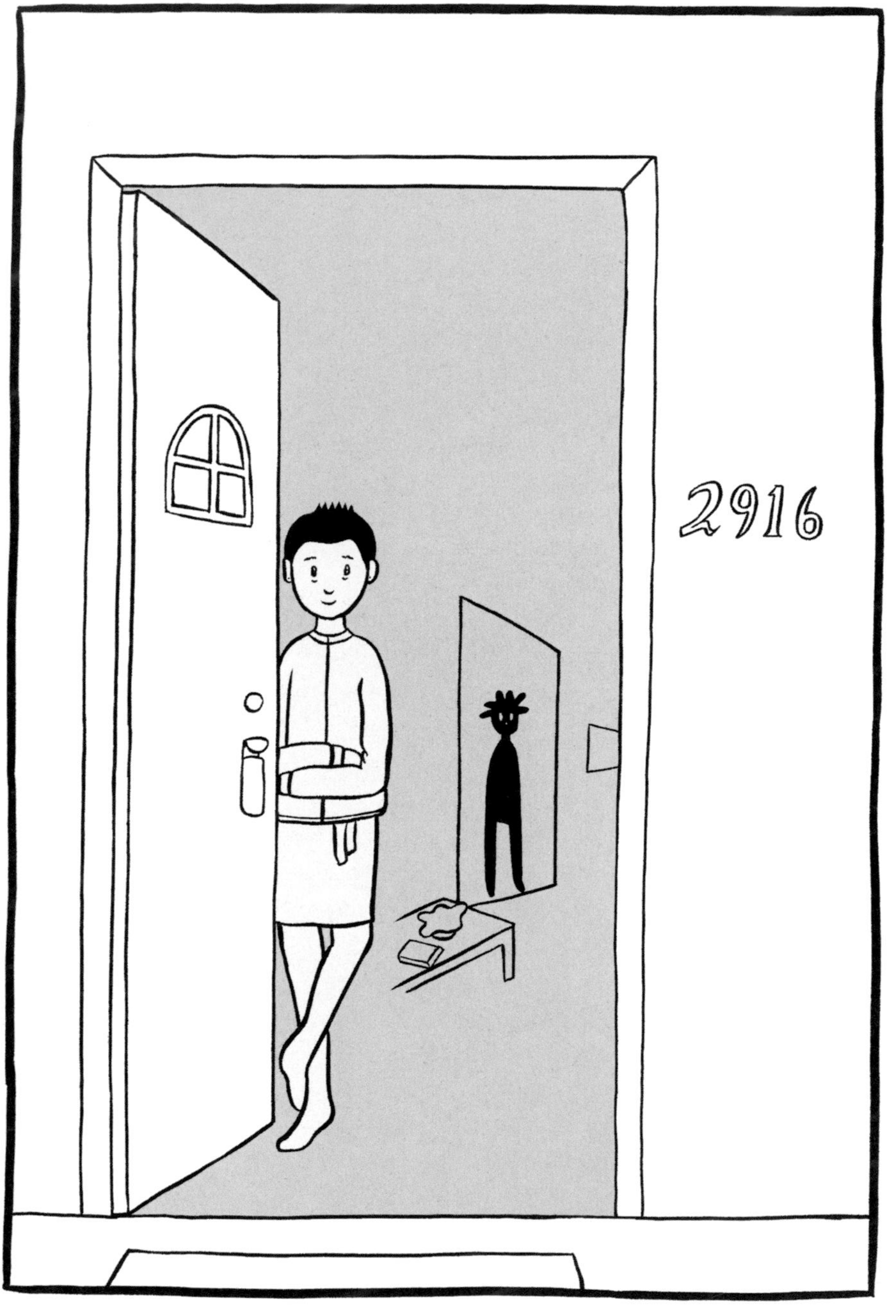
2916

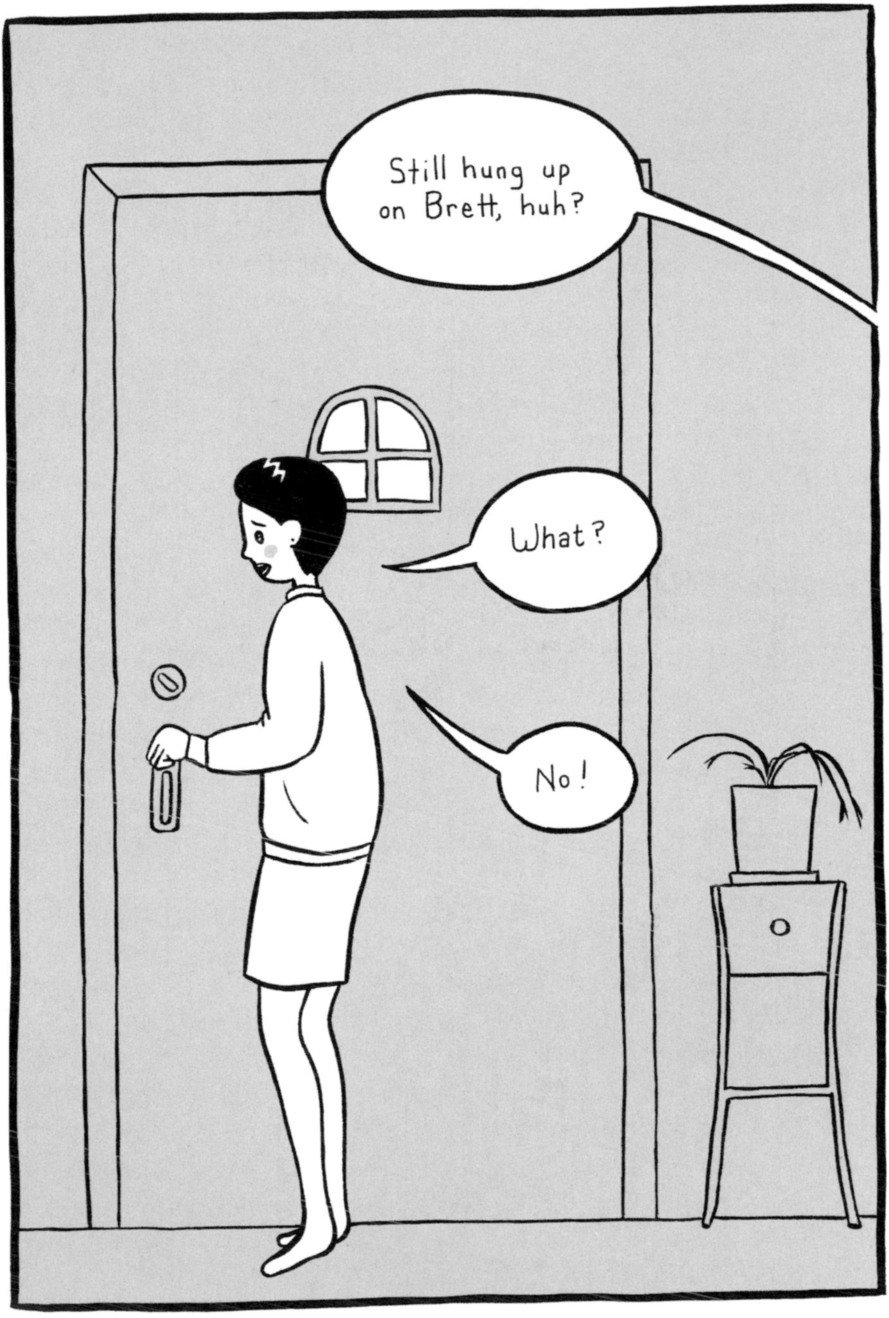
Still hung up on Brett, huh?
What?
No!

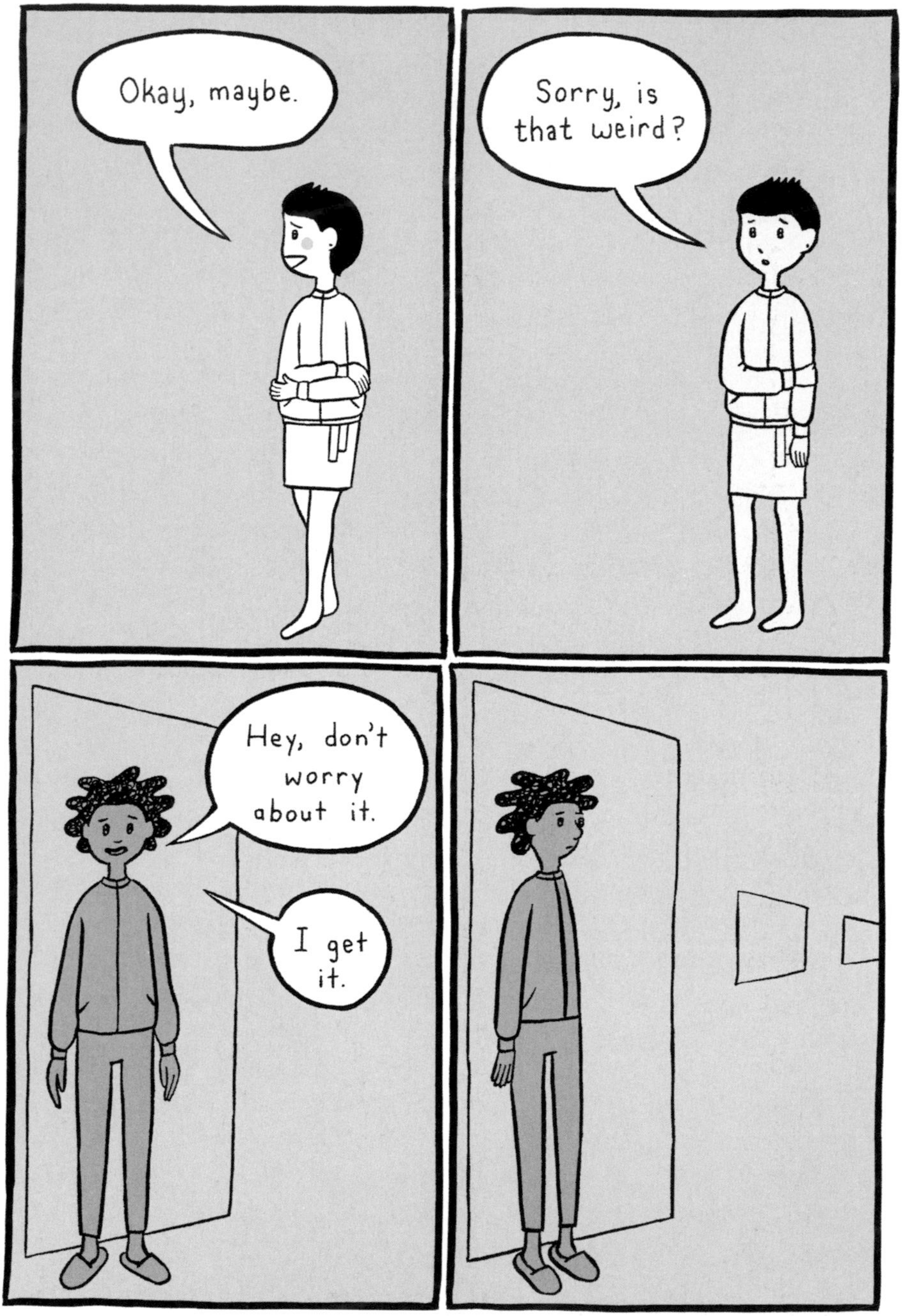
Okay, maybe.
Sorry, is that weird?
Hey, don't worry about it.
I get it.

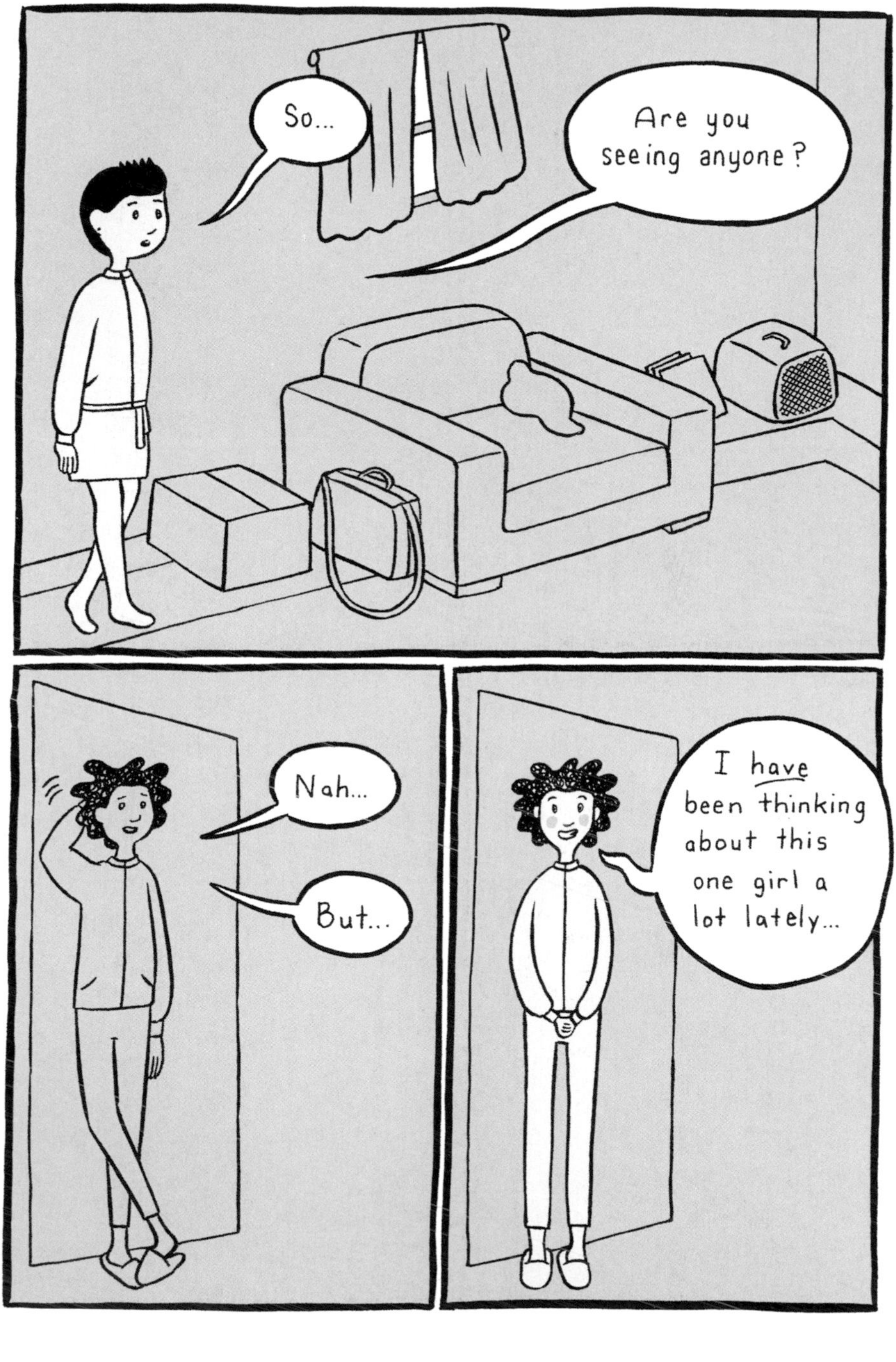
So...
Are you seeing anyone?
Nah...
But...
I have been thinking about this one girl a lot lately...

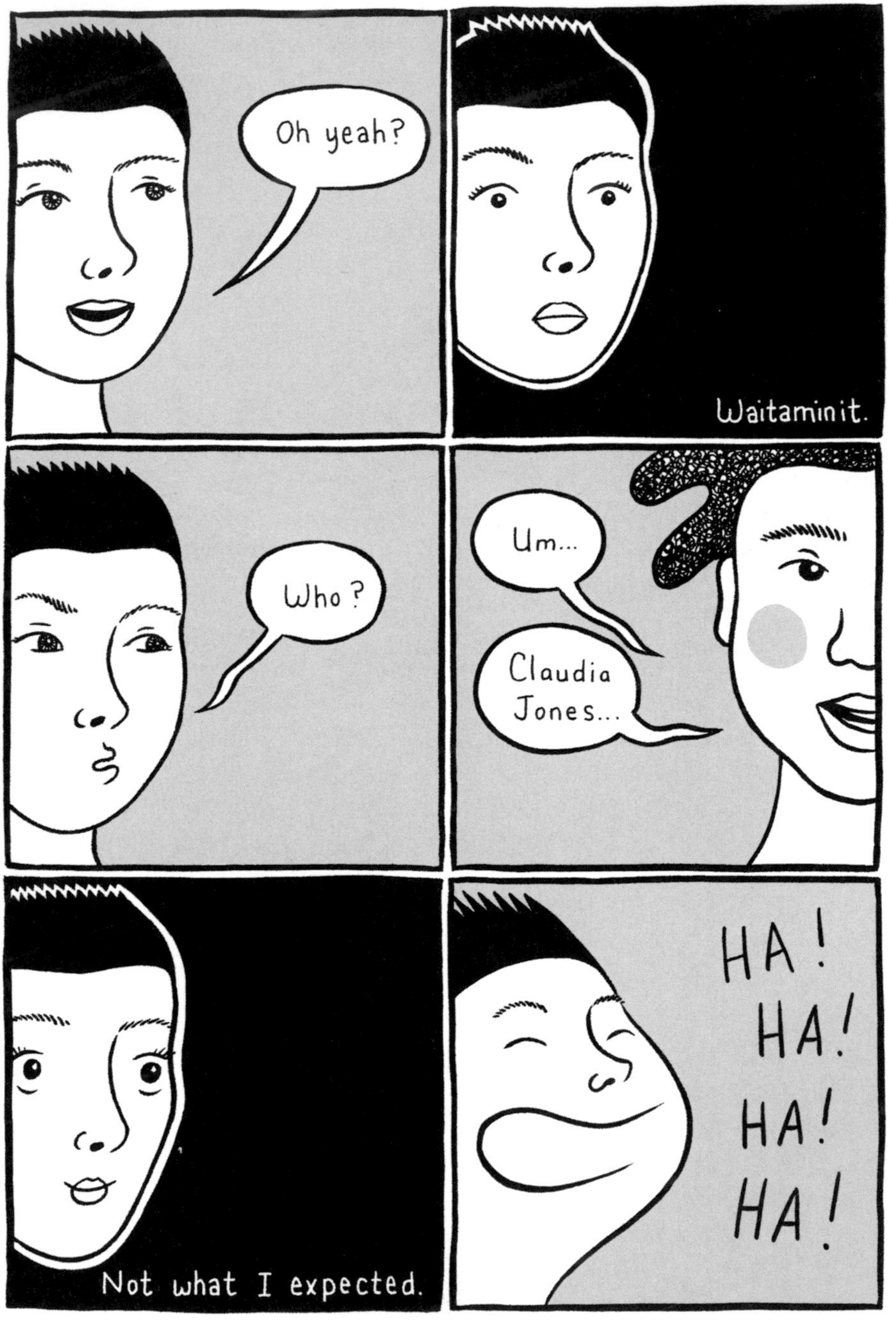
Oh yeah?
Waitaminit.
Who?
Um...
Claudia Jones...
Not what I expected.
HA! HA! HA! HA!

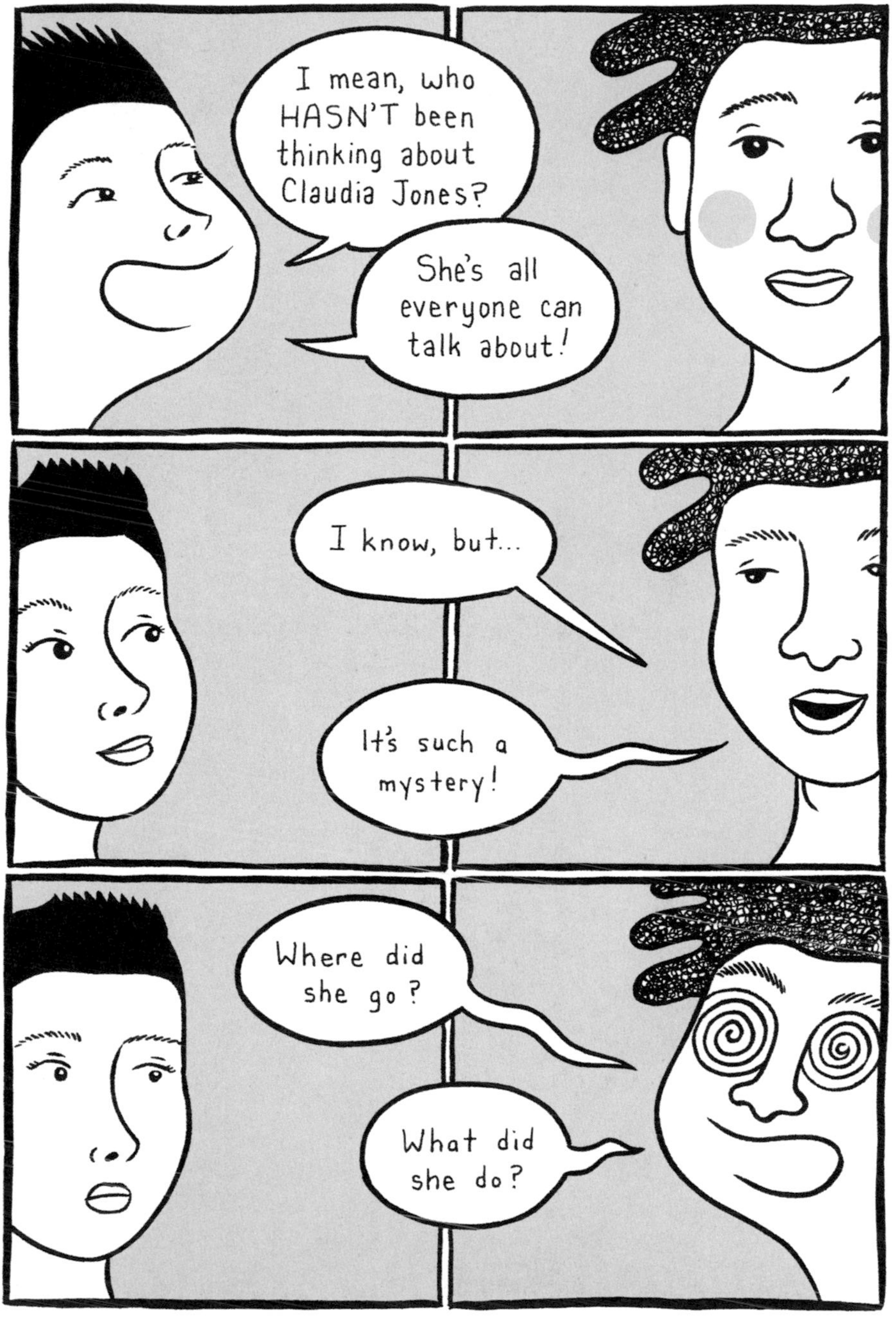
I mean, who HASN'T been thinking about Claudia Jones?
She's all everyone can talk about!
I know, but...
It's such a mystery!
Where did she go?
What did she do?

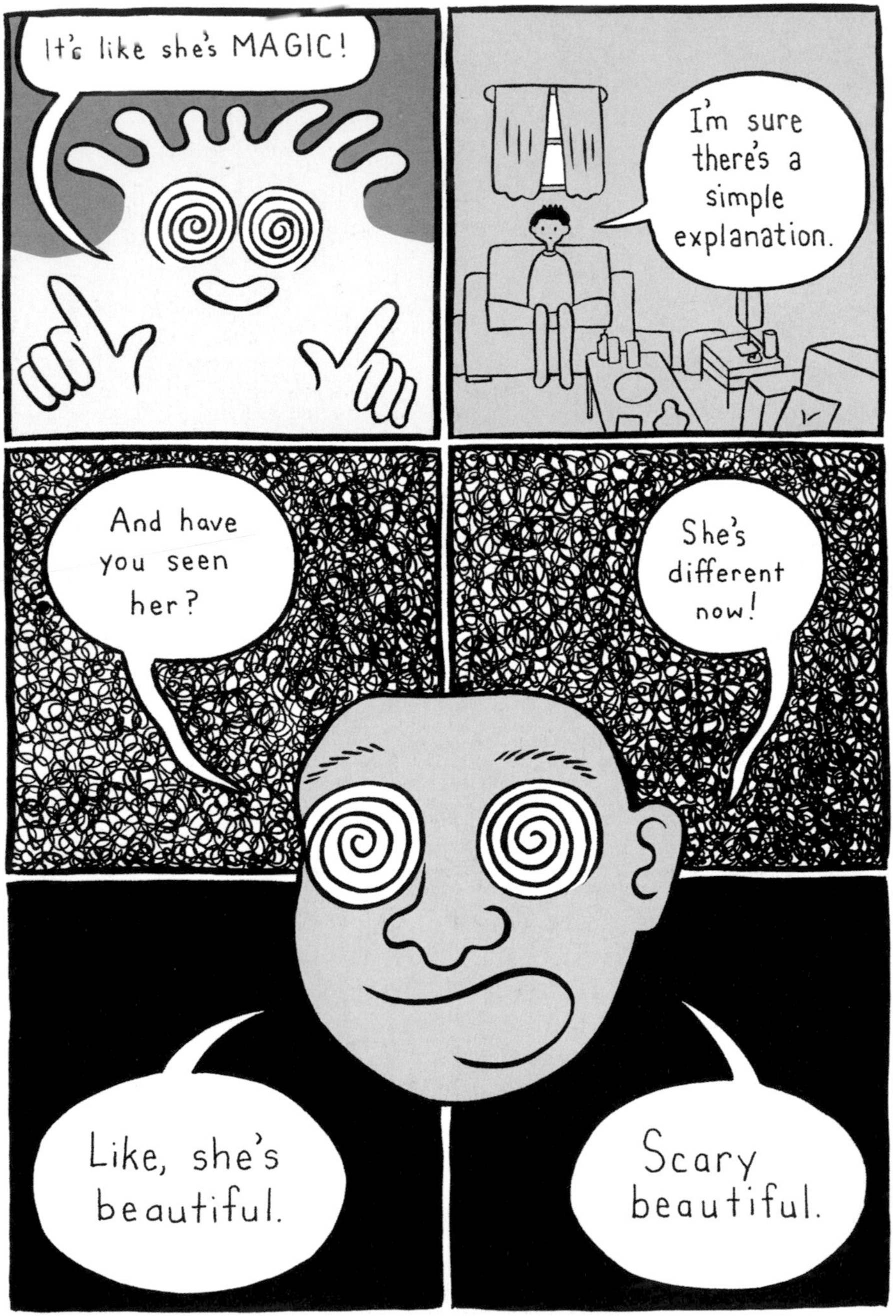
It's like she's MAGIC!
I'm sure there's a simple explanation.
And have you seen her?
She's different now!
Like, she's beautiful.
Scary beautiful.

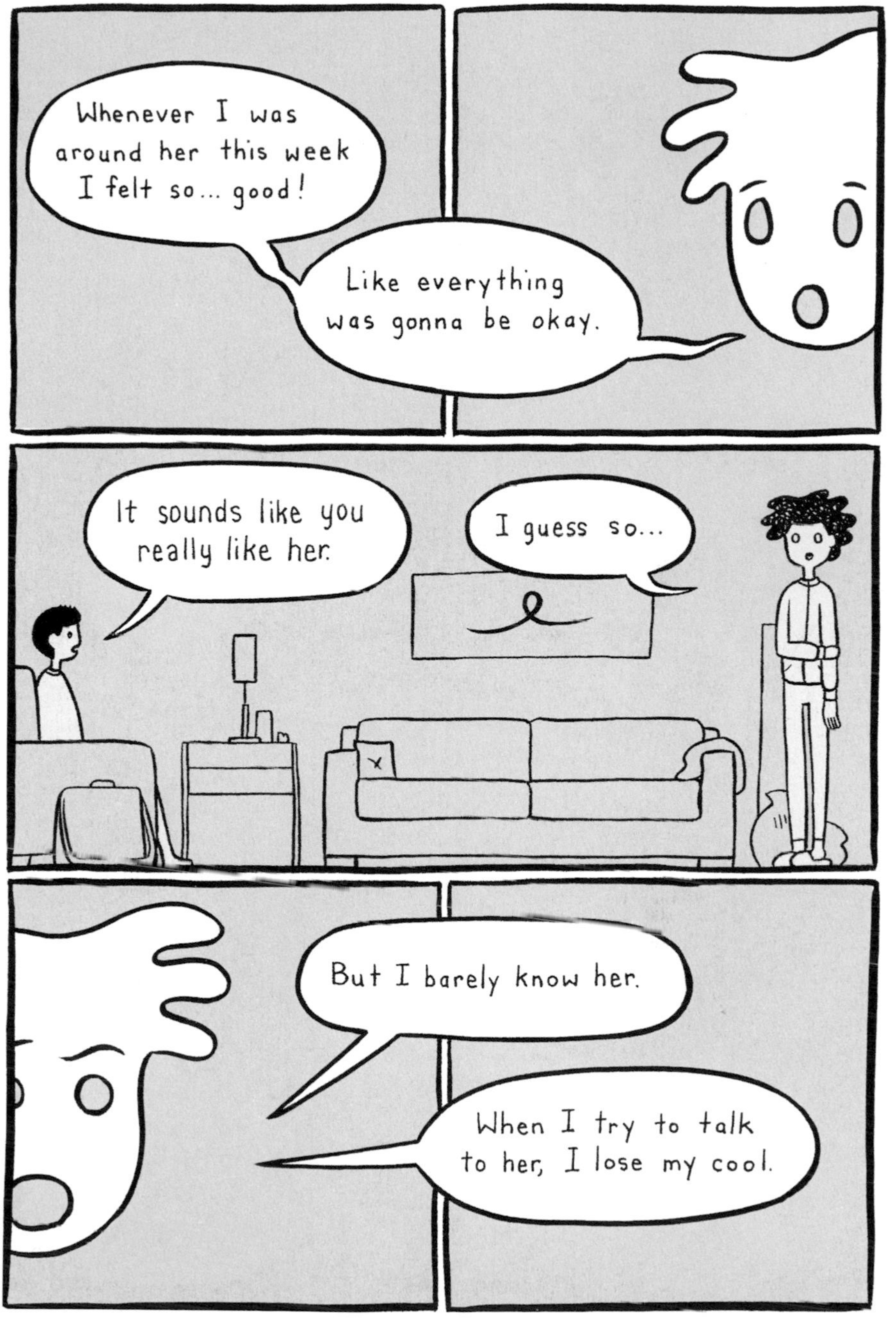
Whenever I was around her this week I felt so... good!
Like everything was gonna be okay.
It sounds like you really like her.
I guess so...
But I barely know her.
When I try to talk to her, I lose my cool.

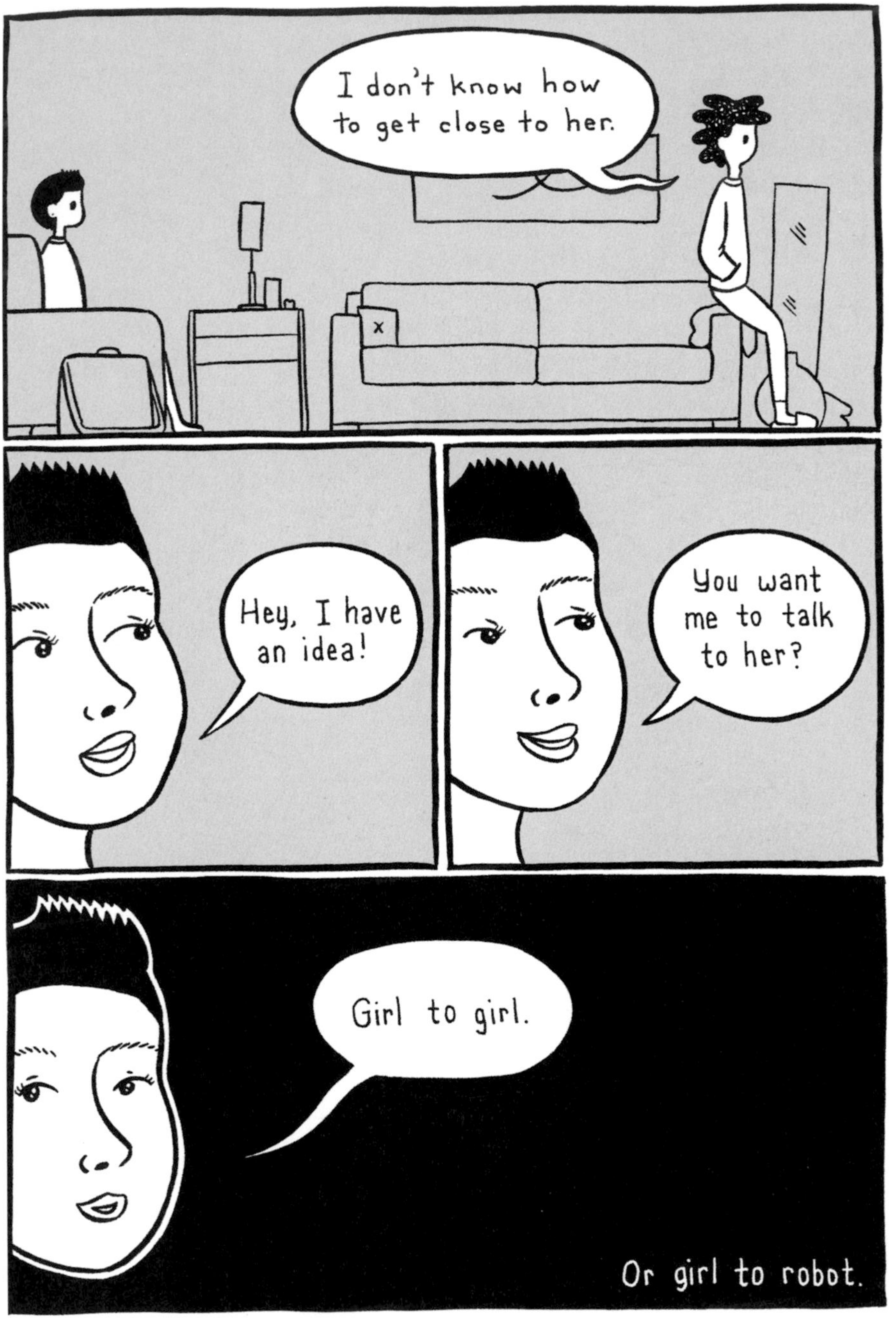
I don't know how to get close to her.
Hey, I have an idea!
You want me to talk to her?
Girl to girl.
Or girl to robot.

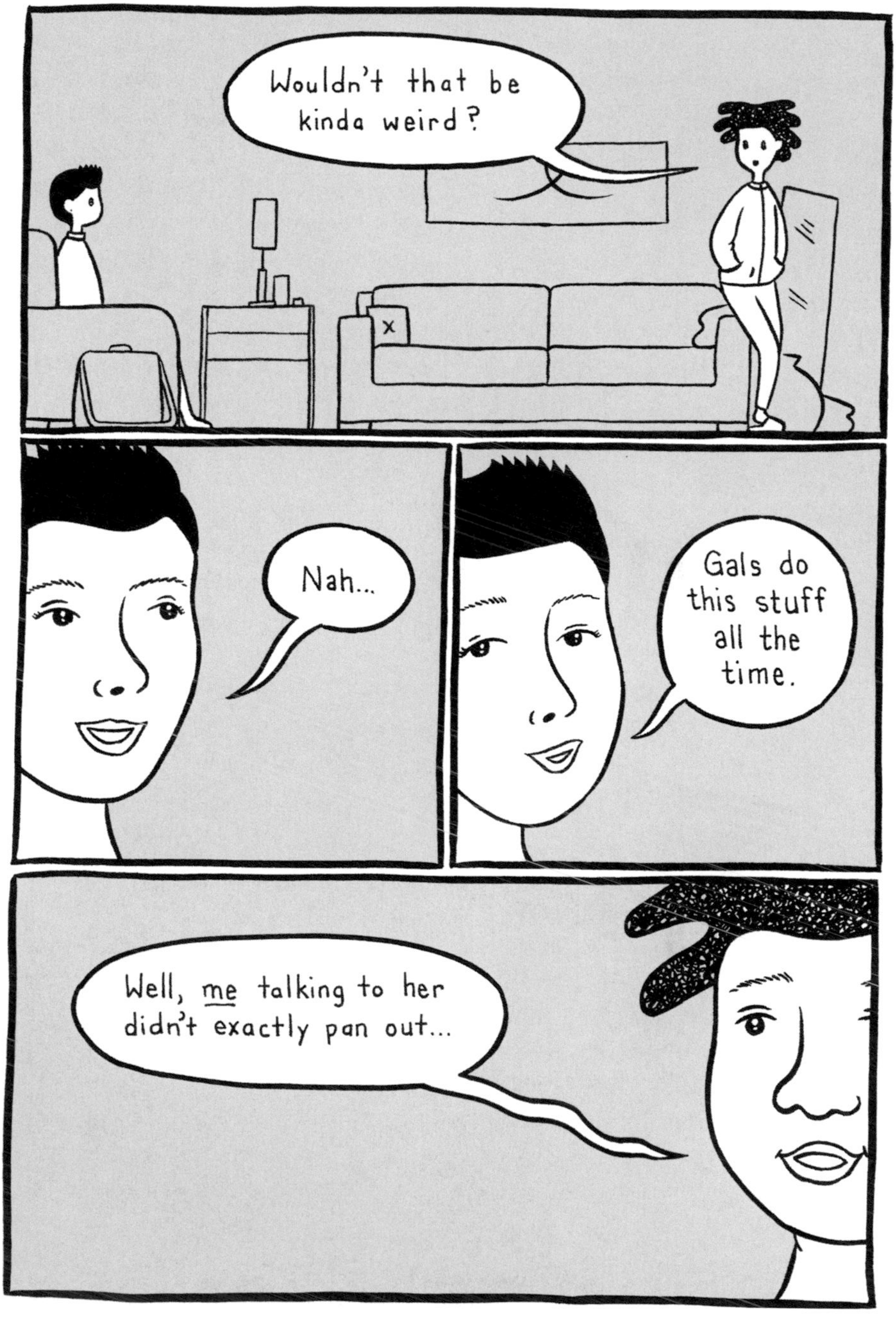
Wouldn't that be kinda weird?
Nah...
Gals do this stuff all the time.
Well, me talking to her didn't exactly pan out...

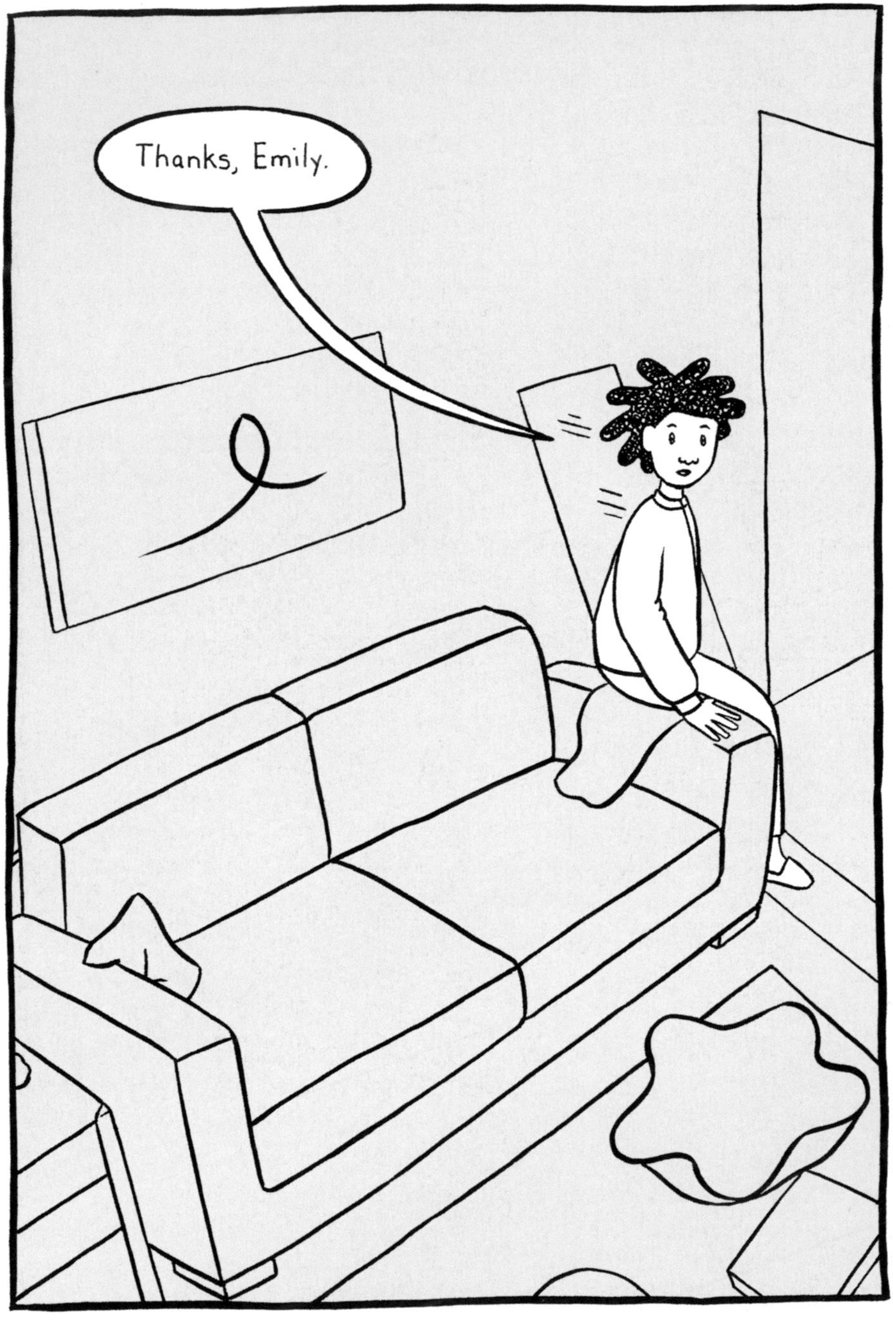
Thanks, Emily.

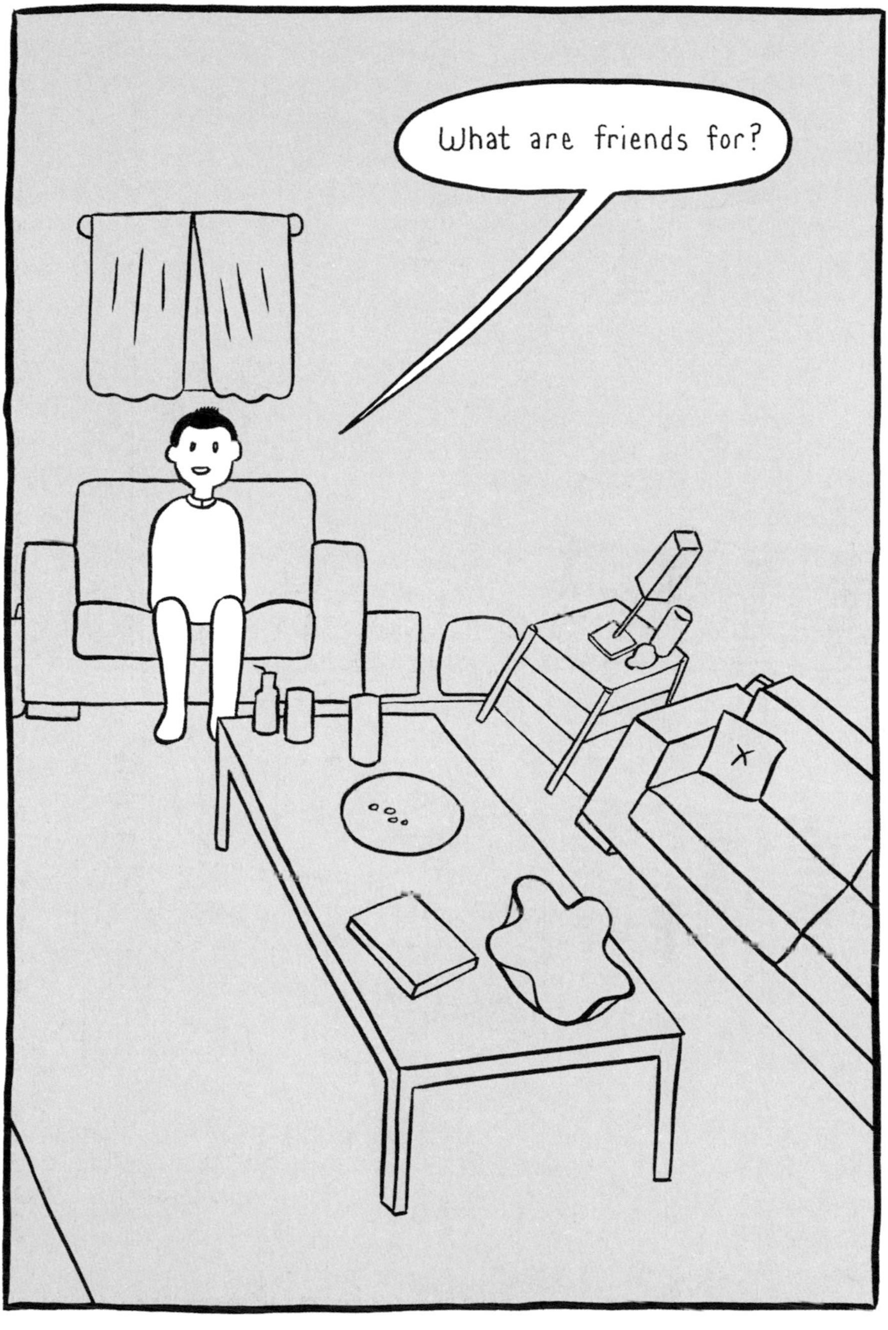
What are friends for?

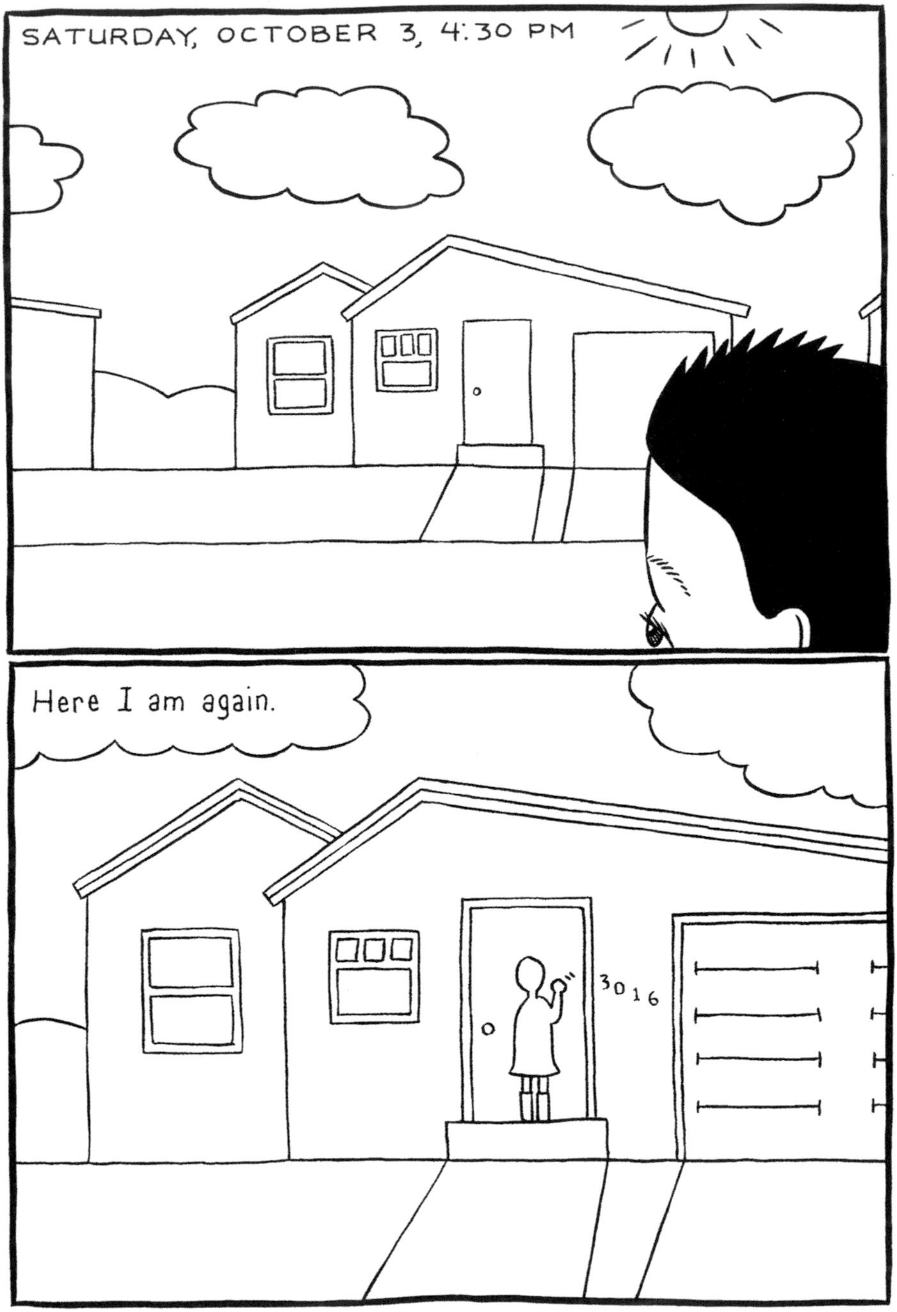
SATURDAY, OCTOBER 3, 4:30 PM
Here I am again.
3016

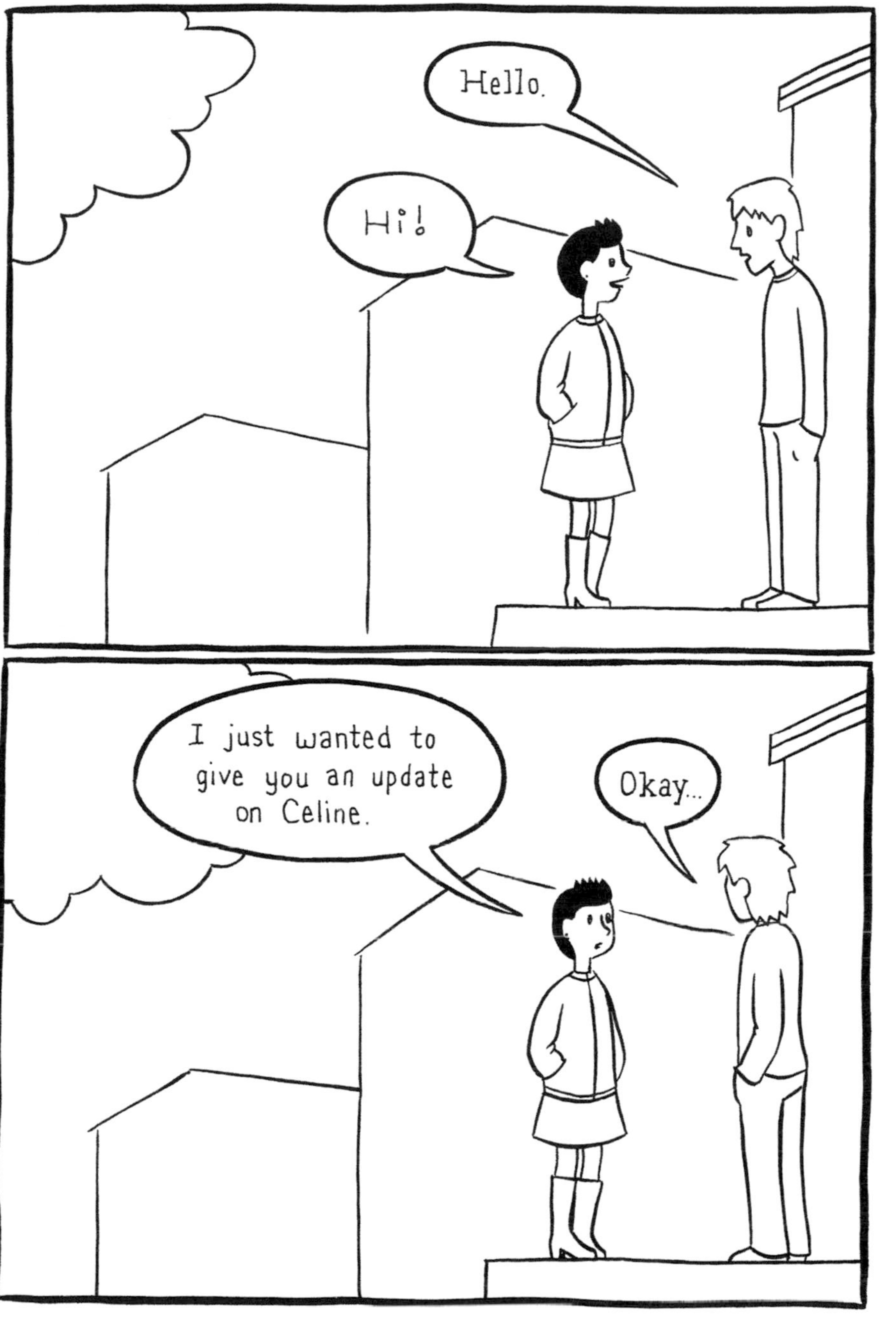
Hello.
Hi!
I just wanted to give you an update on Celine.
Okay...

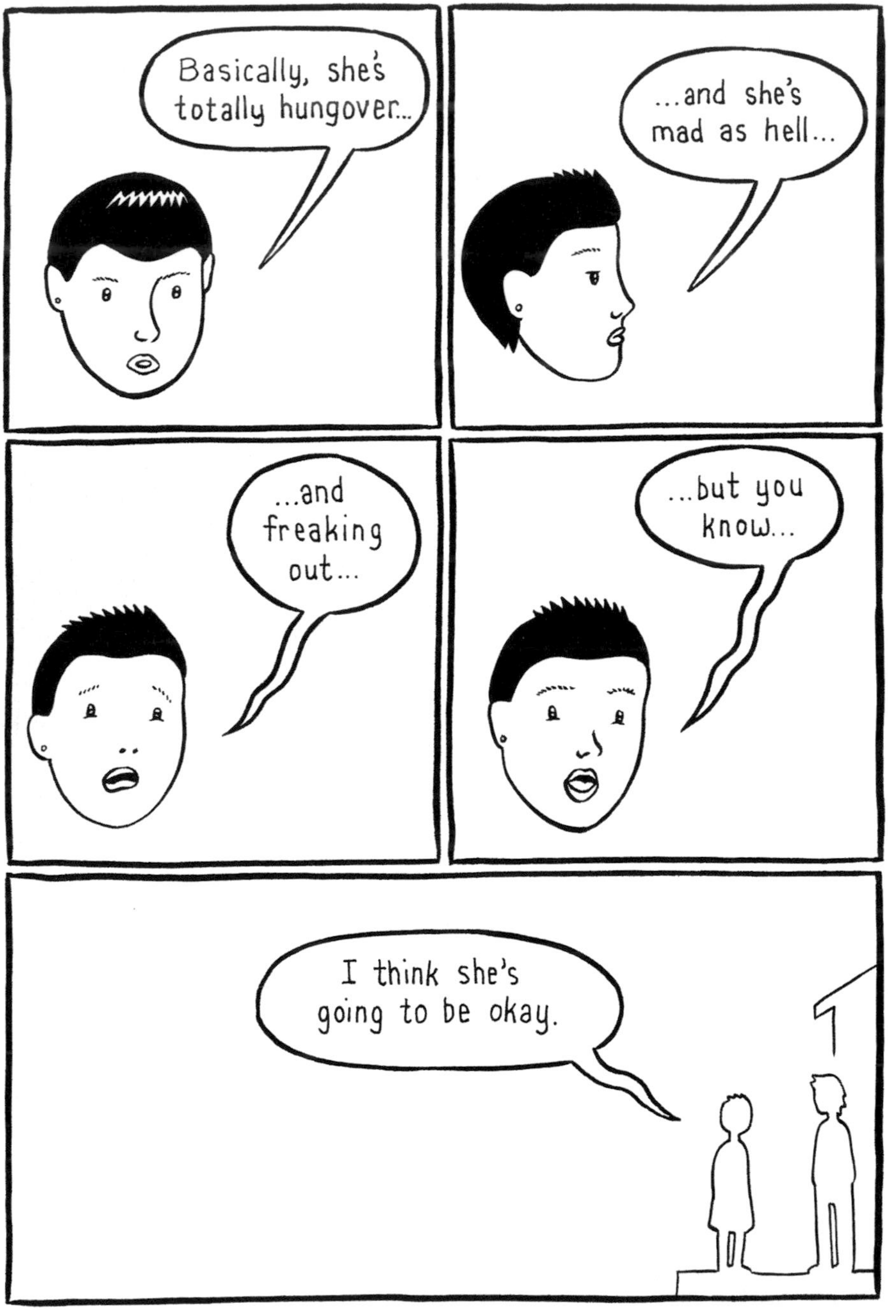
Basically, she's totally hungover...
...and she's mad as hell...
...and freaking out...
...but you know...
I think she's going to be okay.

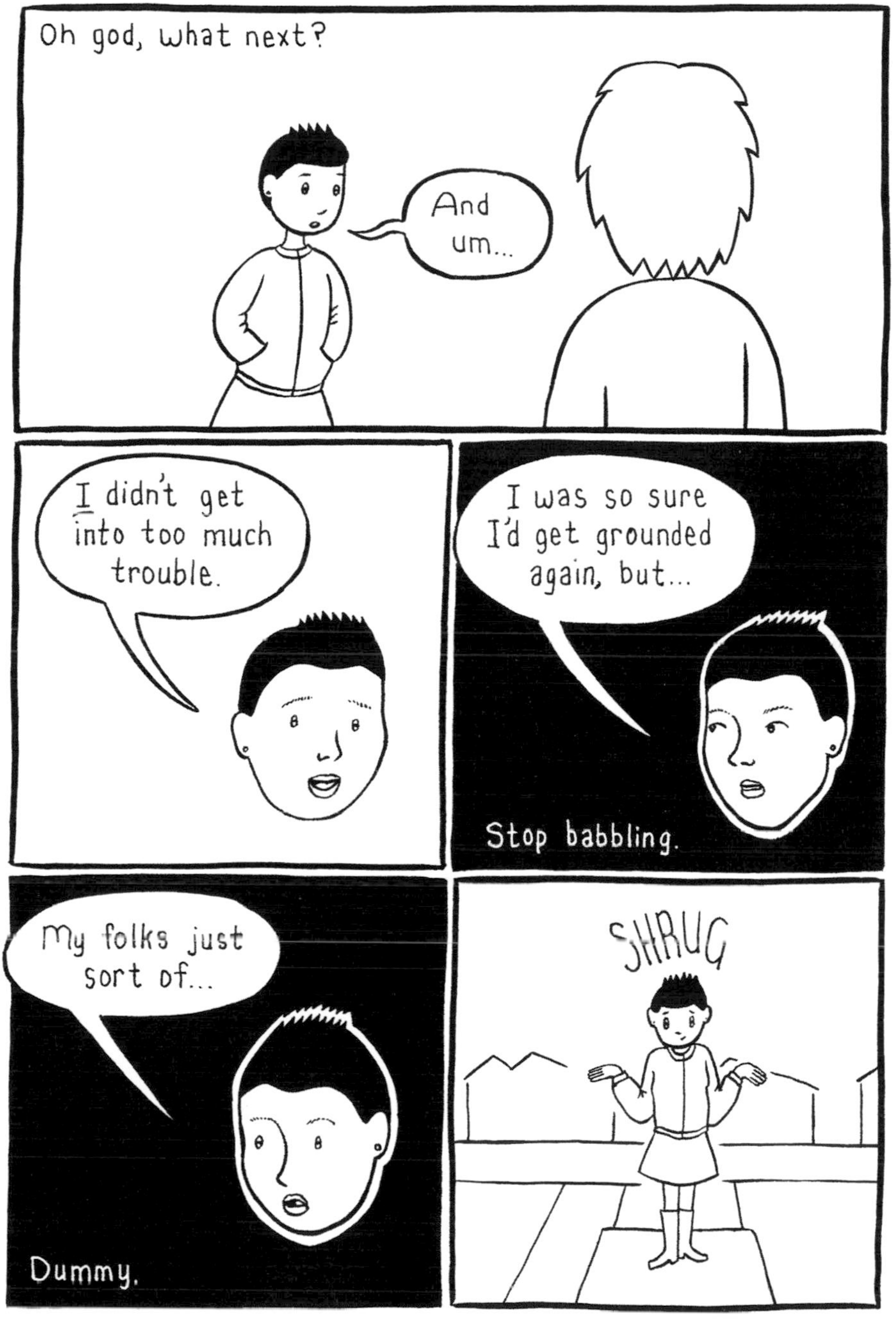
Oh god, what next?
And um...
I didn't get into too much trouble.
I was so sure I'd get grounded again, but...
Stop babbling.
My folks just sort of...
Dummy.
SHRUG

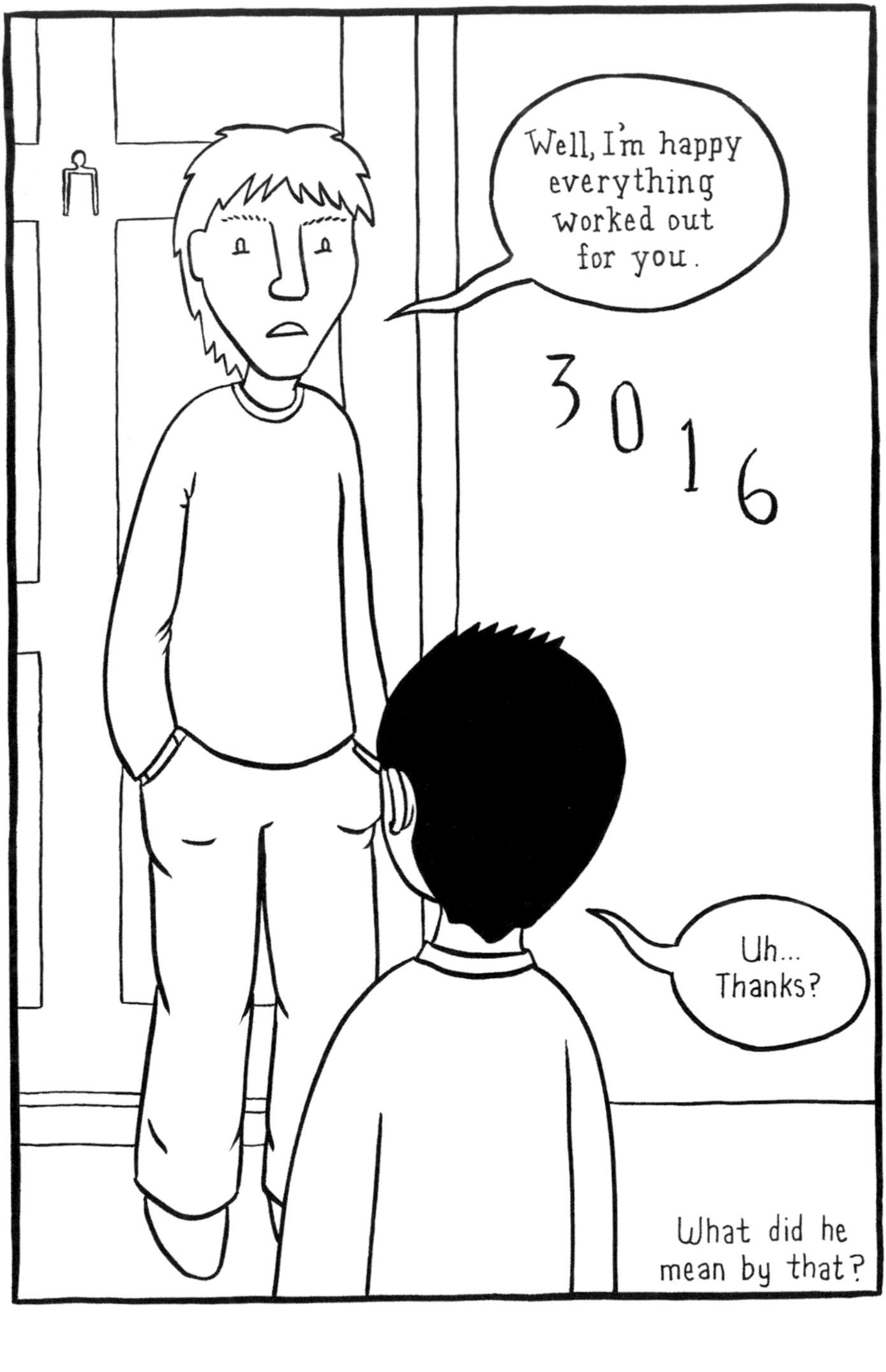
Well, I'm happy everything worked out for you.
3016
Uh... Thanks?
What did he mean by that?

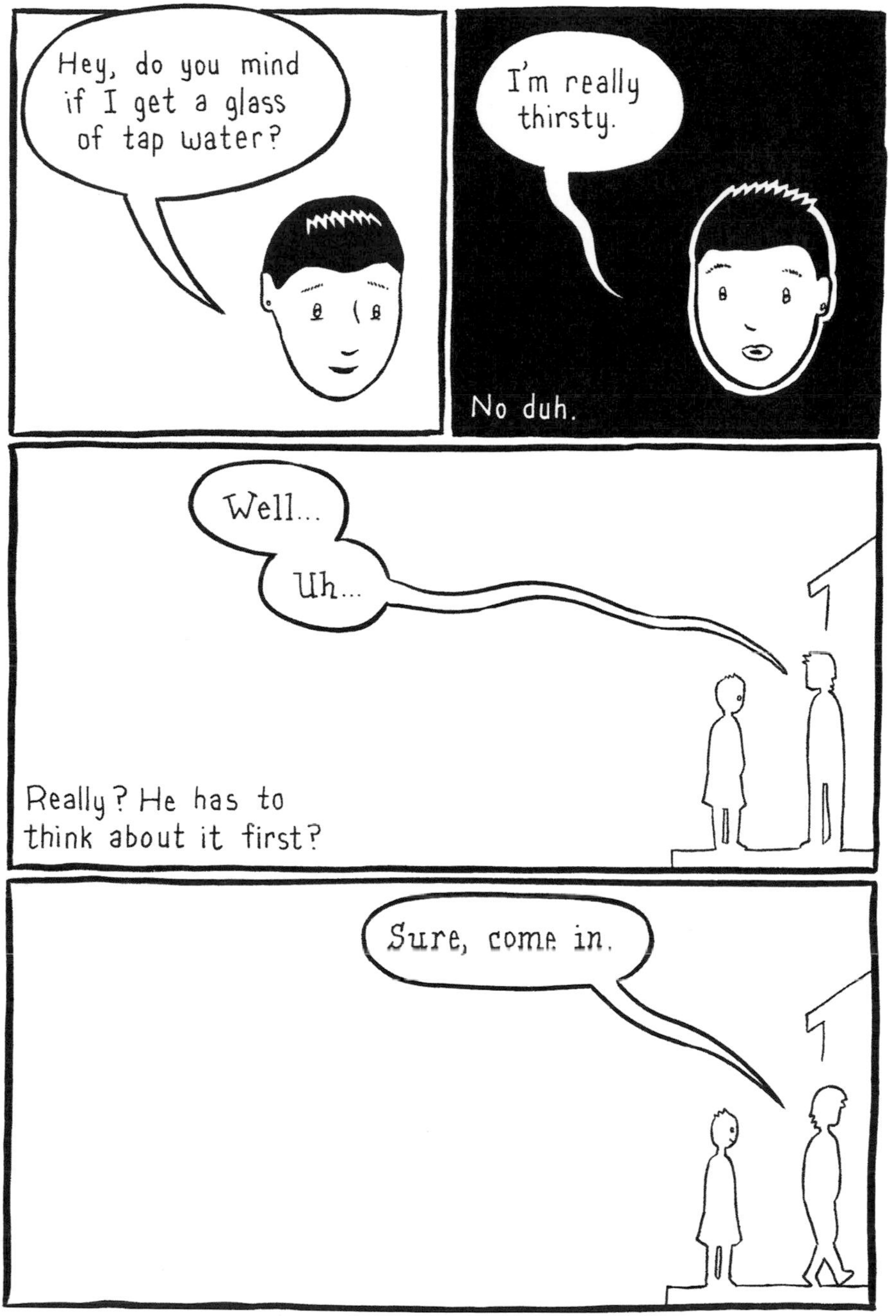
Hey, do you mind if I get a glass of tap water?
I'm really thirsty.
No duh.
Well...
Uh...
Really? He has to think about it first?
Sure, come in.

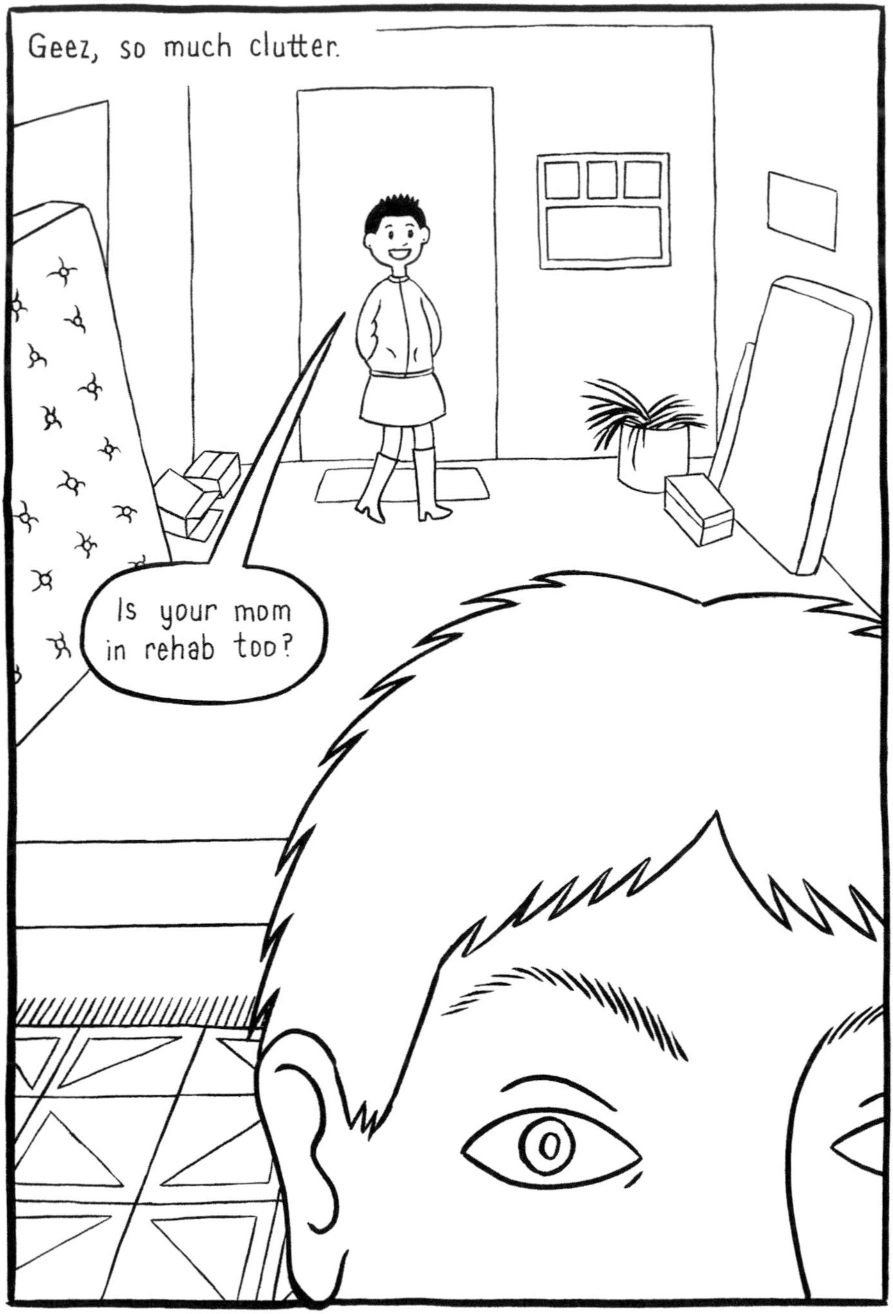
Geez, so much clutter.
Is your mom in rehab too?

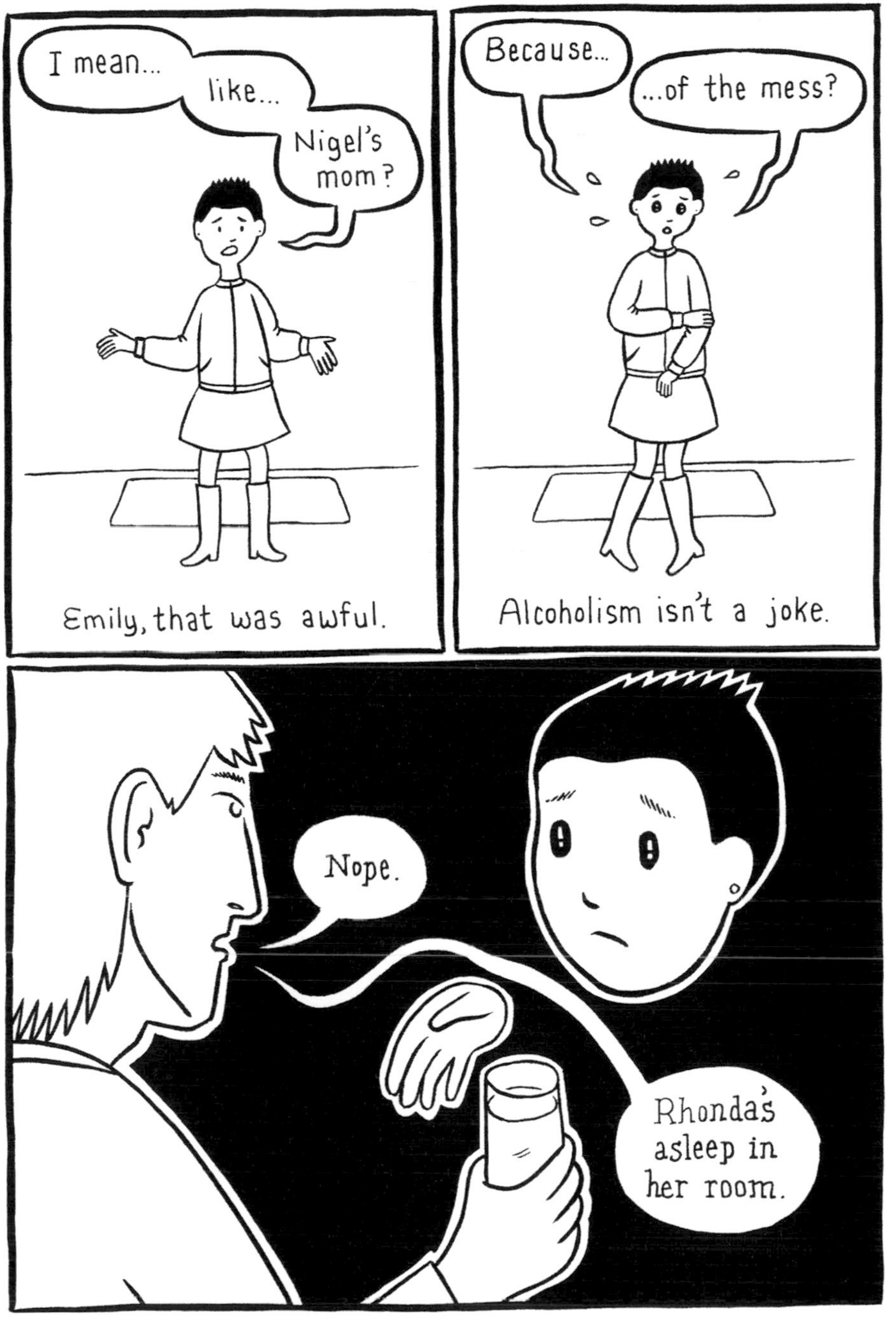
I mean...
like...
Nigel's mom?
Emily, that was awful.
Because...
...of the mess?
Alcoholism isn't a joke.
Nope.
Rhonda's asleep in her room.

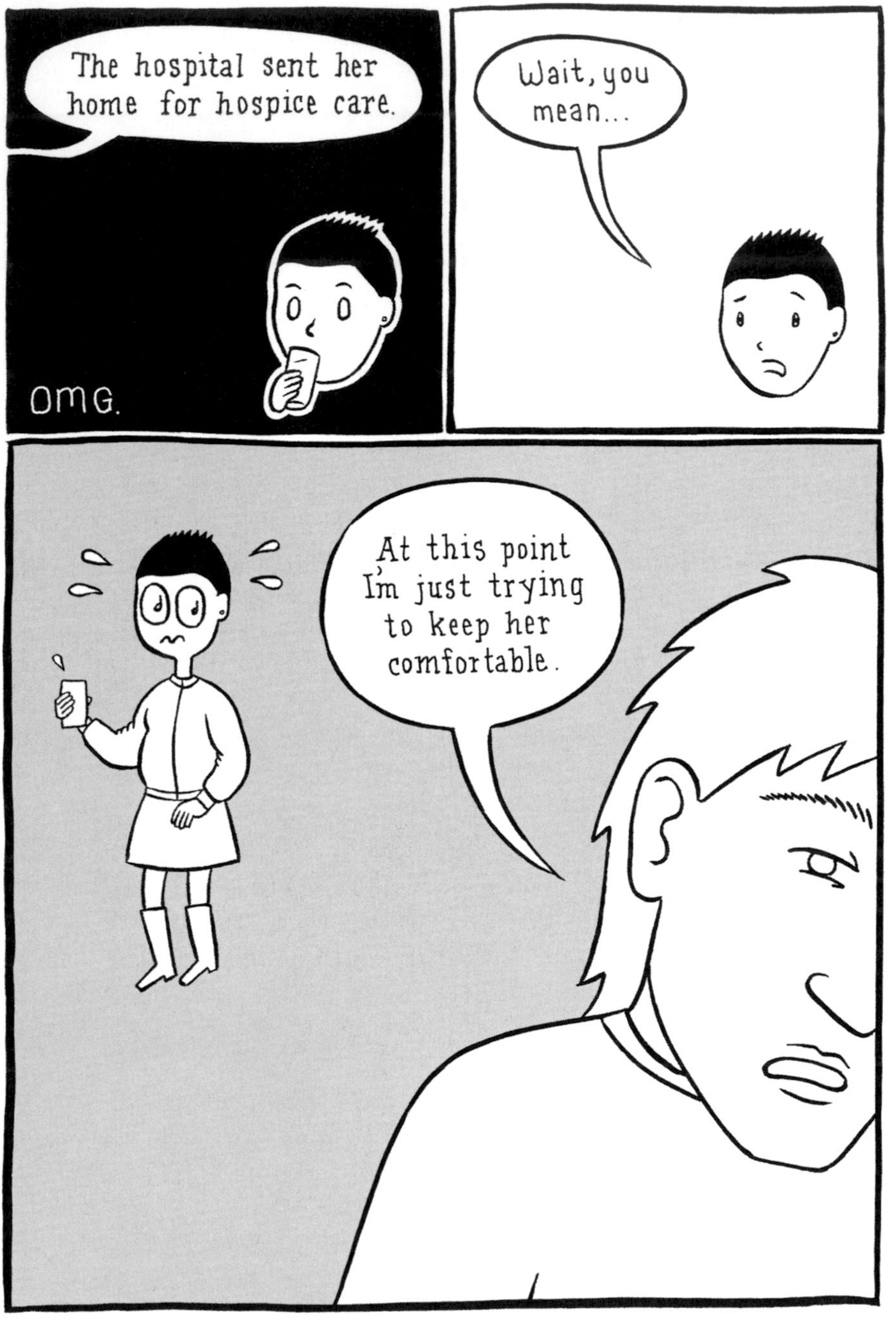
The hospital sent her home for hospice care.
OMG.
Wait, you mean...
At this point I'm just trying to keep her comfortable.

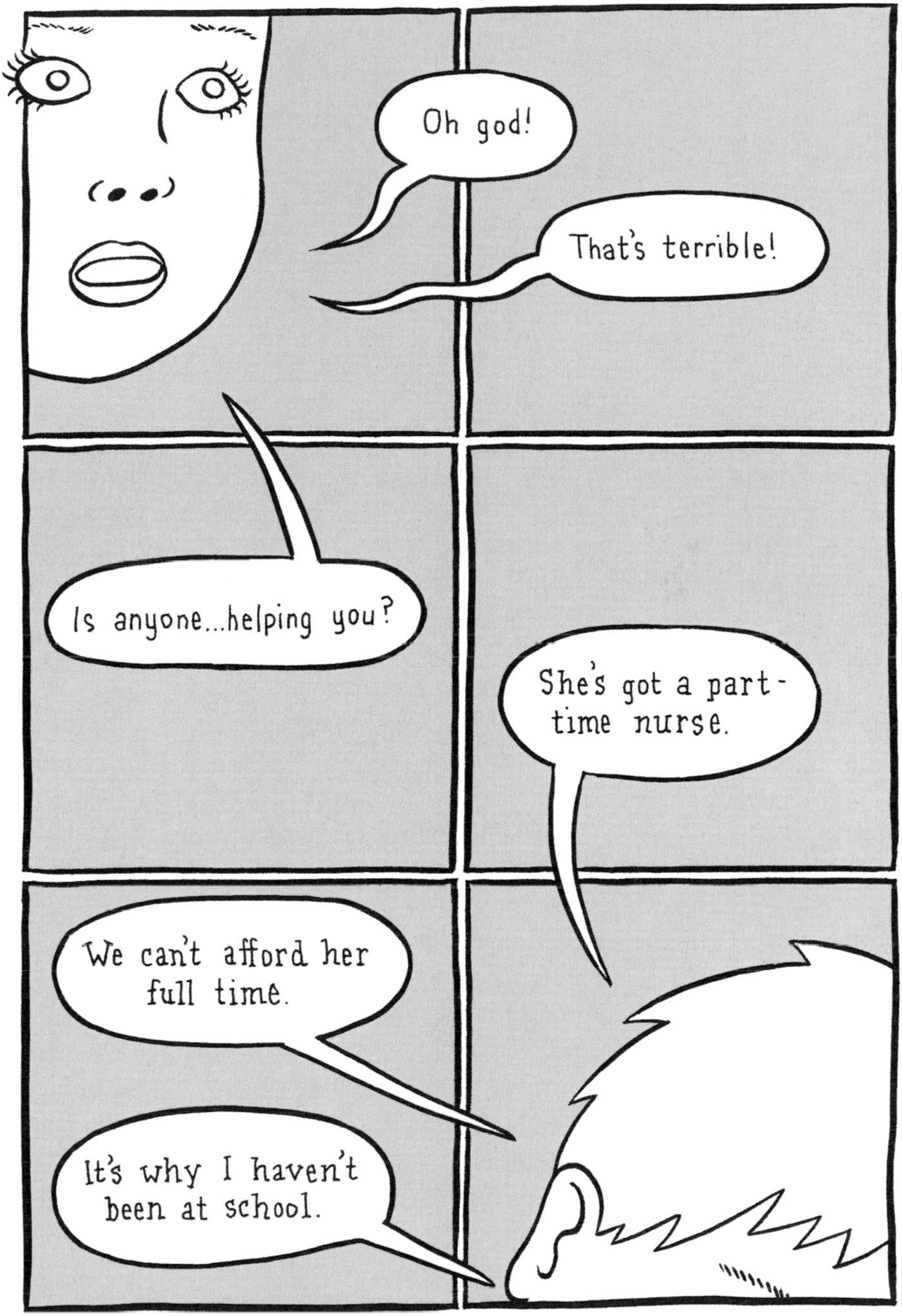
Oh god!
That's terrible!
Is anyone...helping you?
She's got a part-time nurse.
We can't afford her full time.
It's why I haven't been at school.

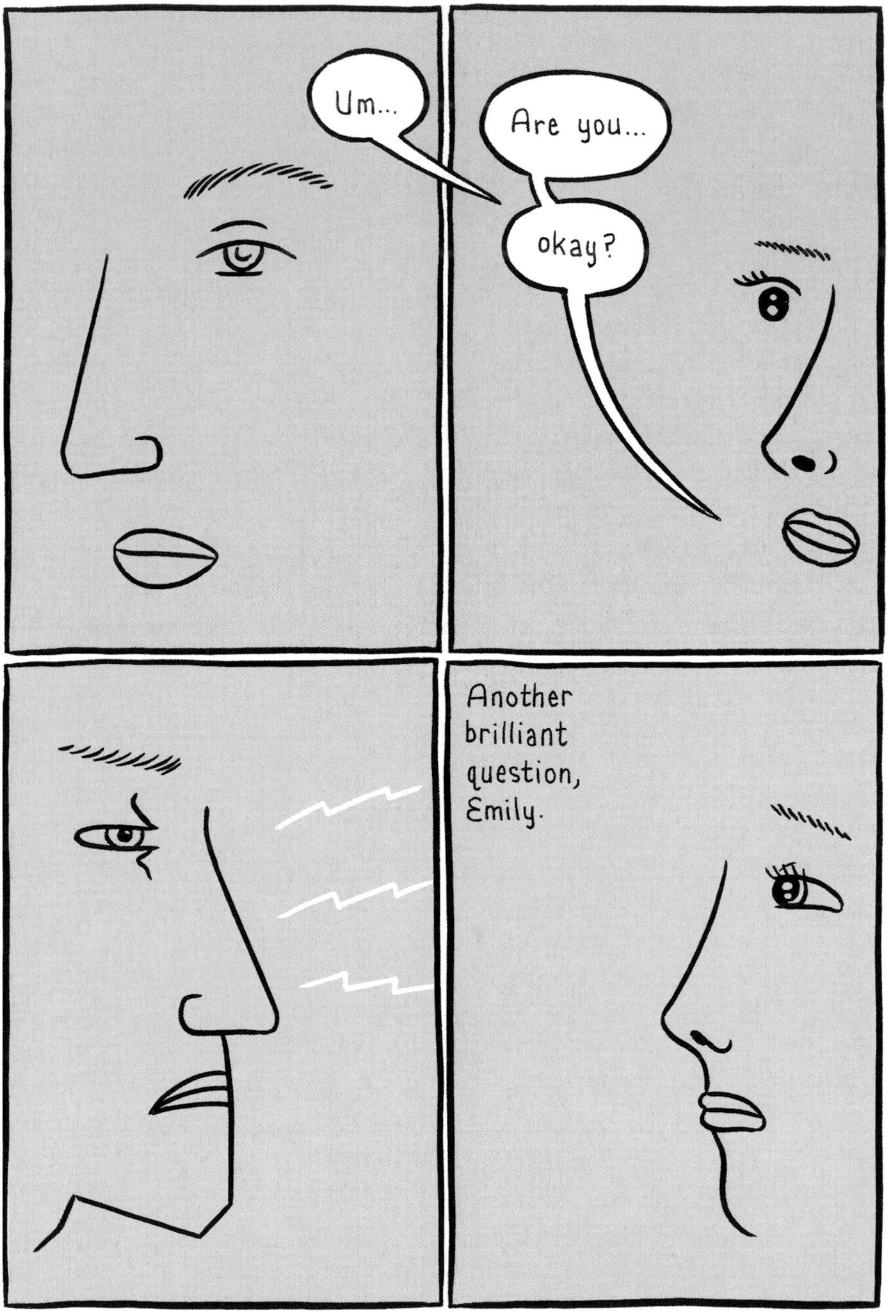
Um...
Are you...
okay?
Another brilliant question, Emily.

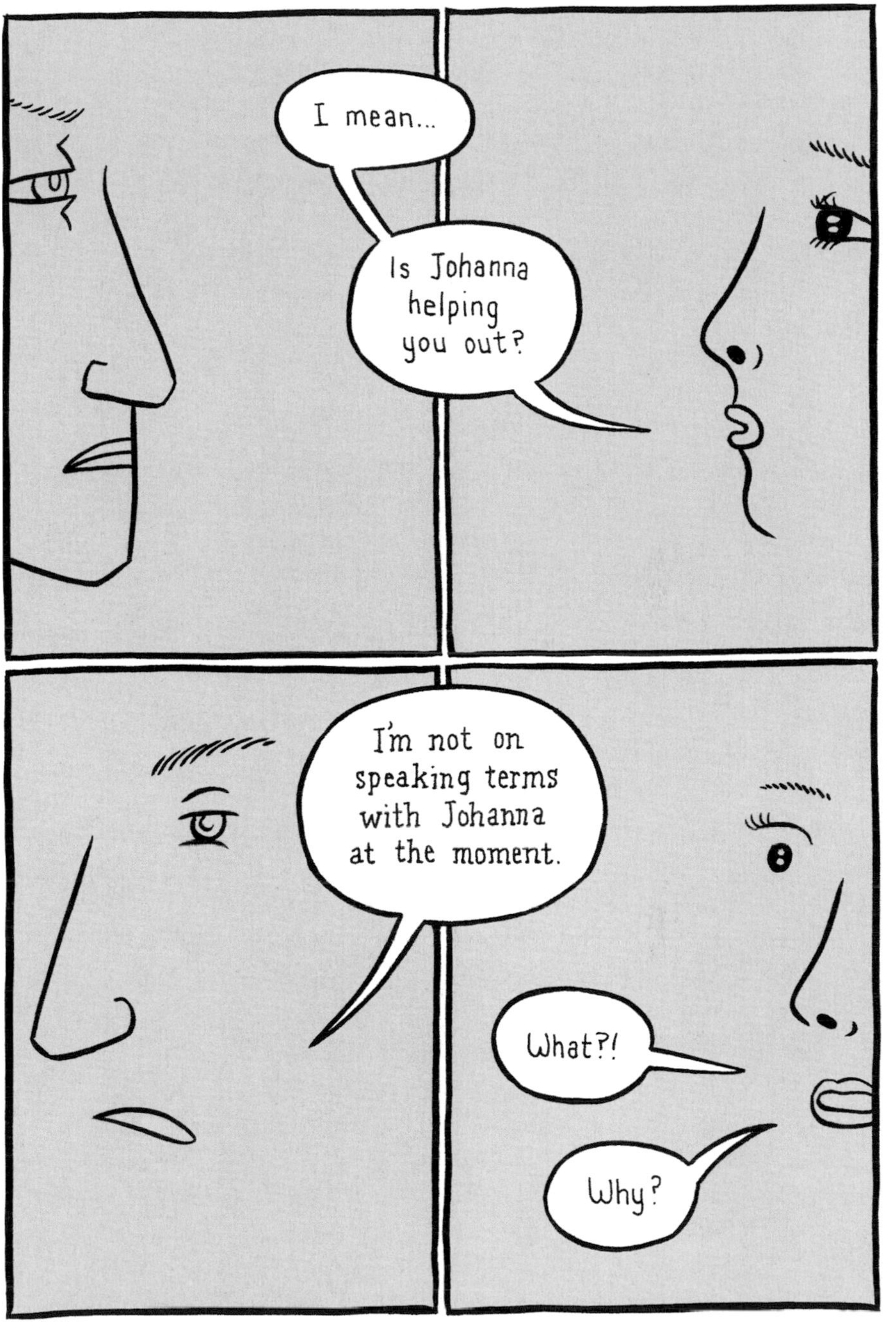
I mean...
Is Johanna helping you out?
I'm not on speaking terms with Johanna at the moment.
What?!
Why?

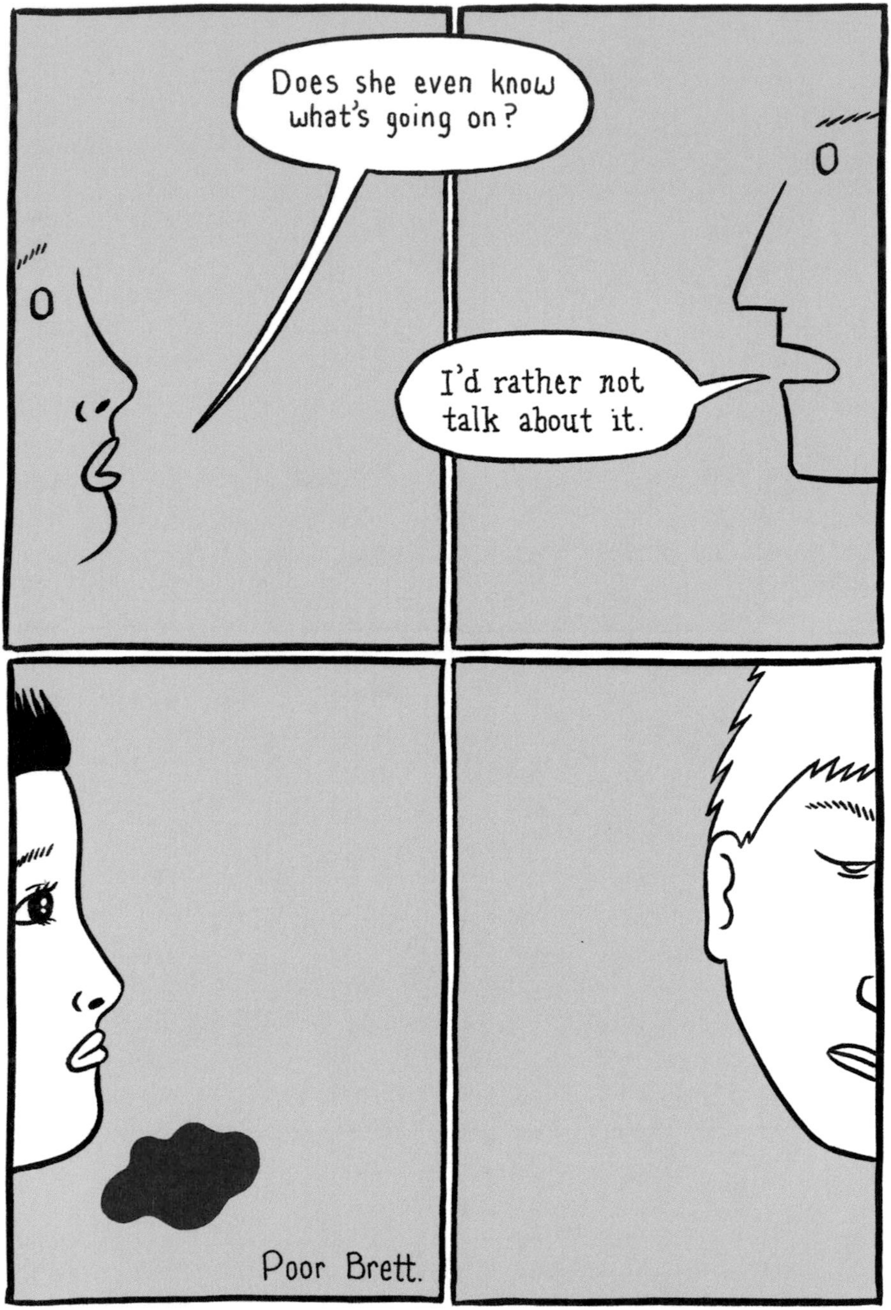
Does she even know what's going on?
I'd rather not talk about it.
Poor Brett.

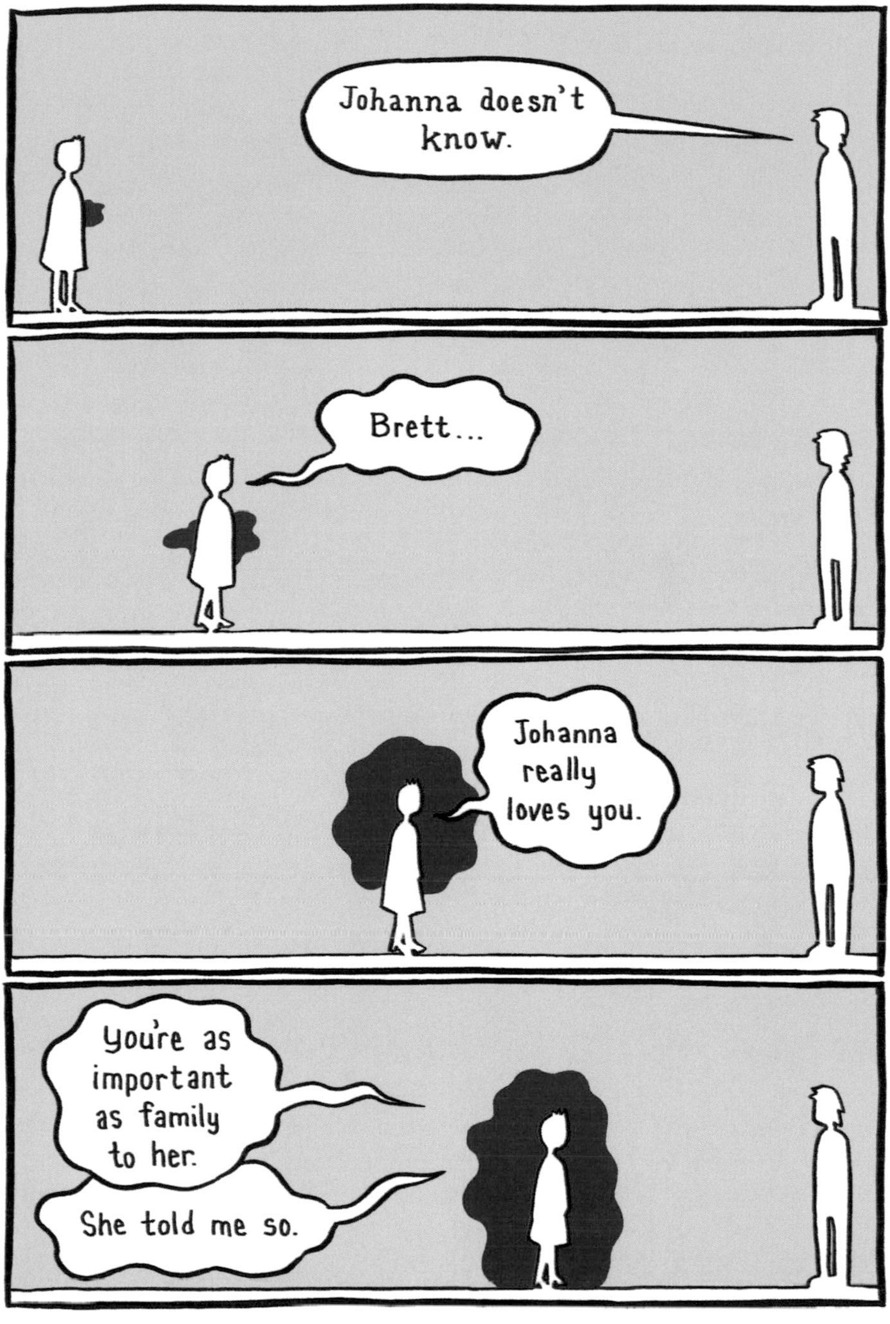
Johanna doesn't know.
Brett...
Johanna really loves you.
You're as important as family to her.
She told me so.

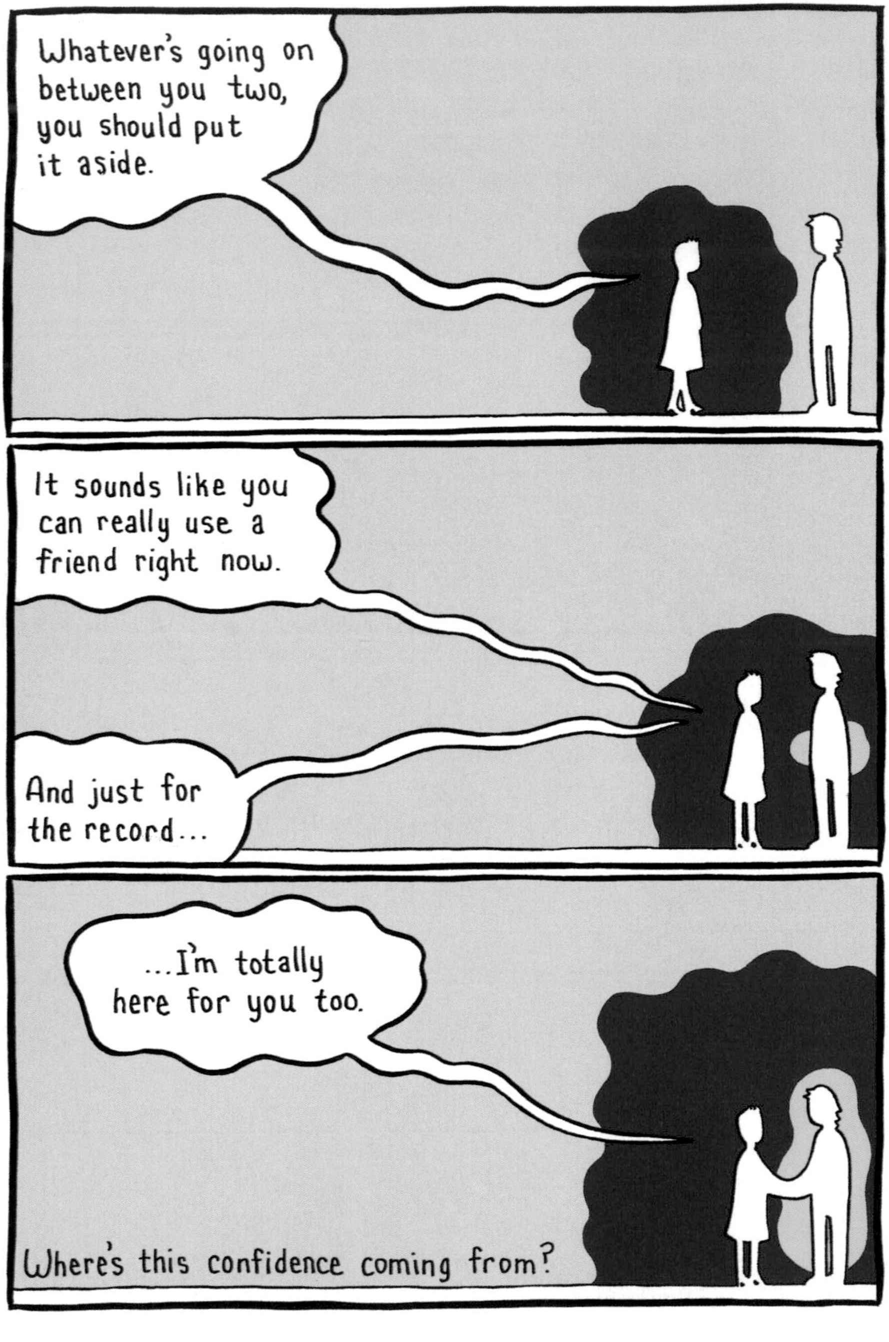
Whatever's going on between you two, you should put it aside.
It sounds like you can really use a friend right now.
And just for the record...
...I'm totally here for you too.
Where's this confidence coming from?

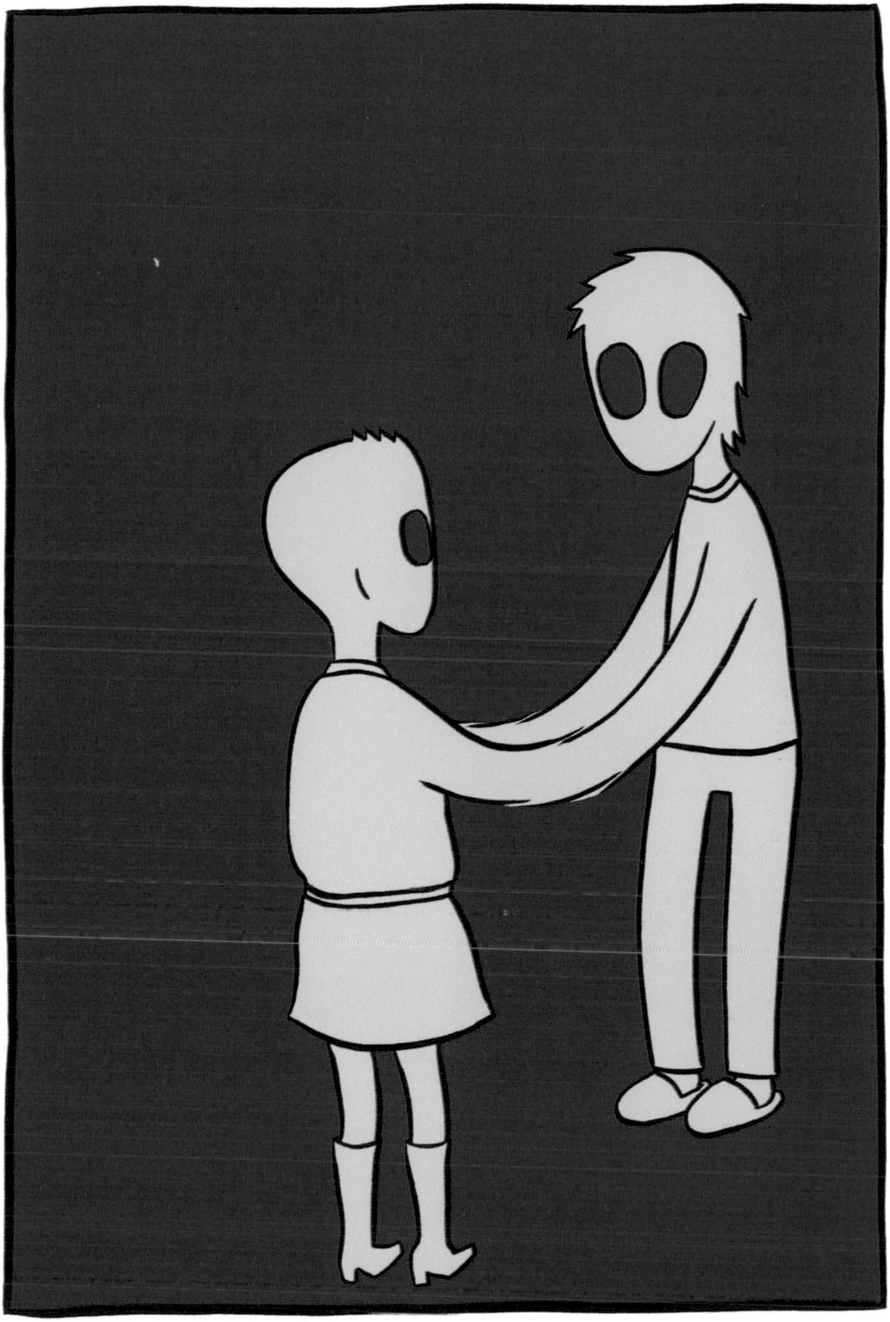

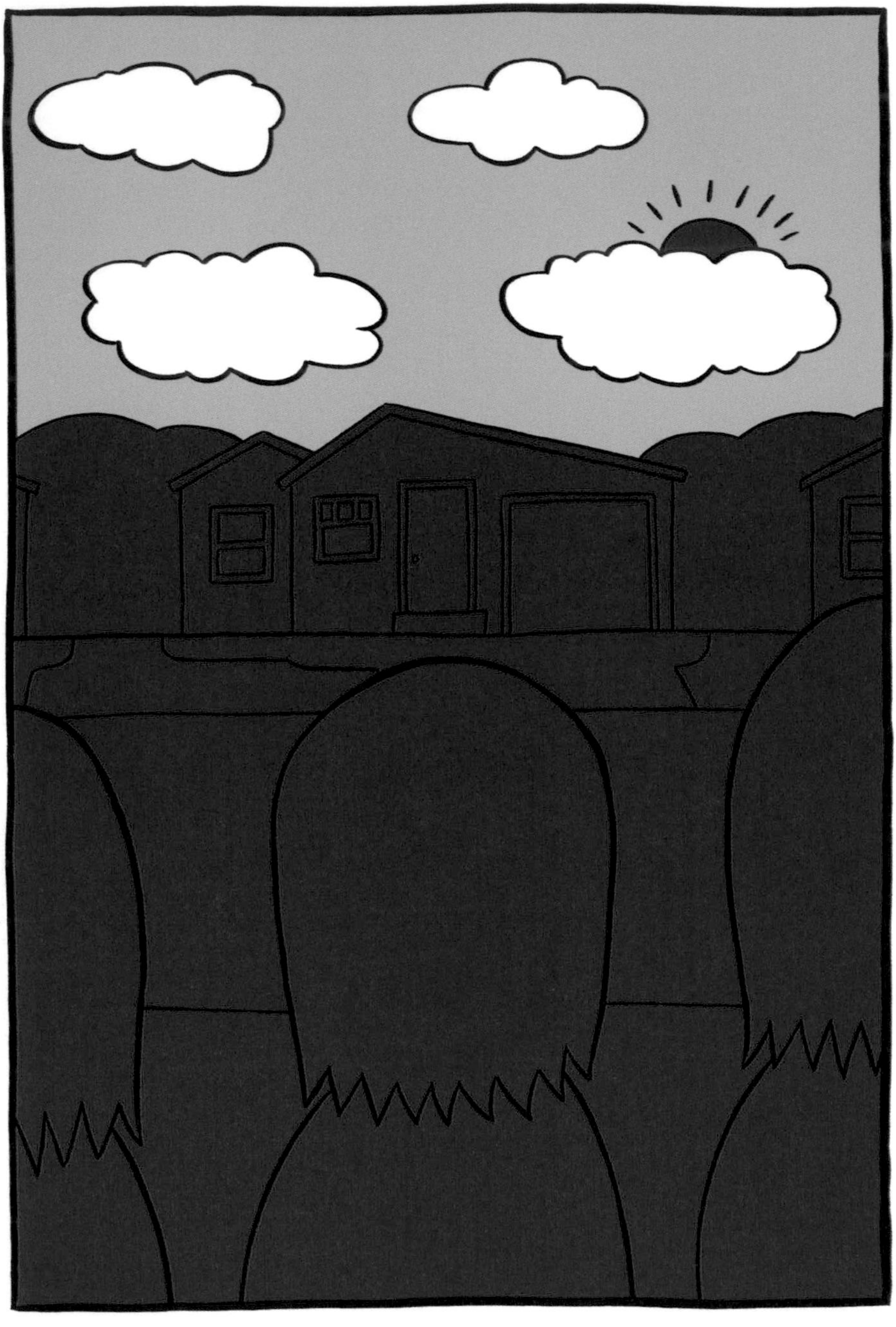

# PART FIVE

# Claudia Q. Jones

MONDAY, OCTOBER 5, 11:30 AM

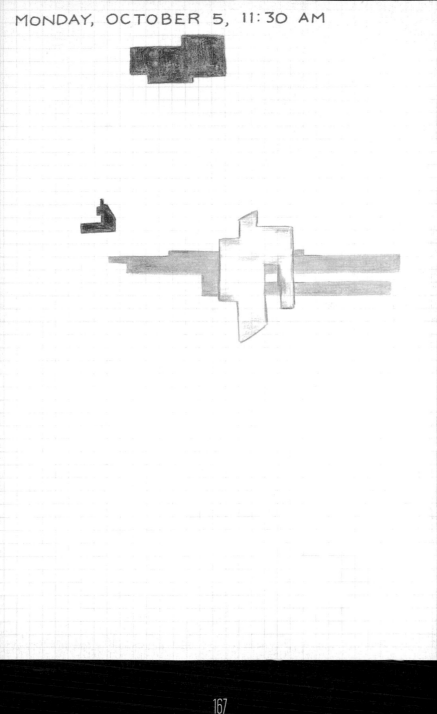

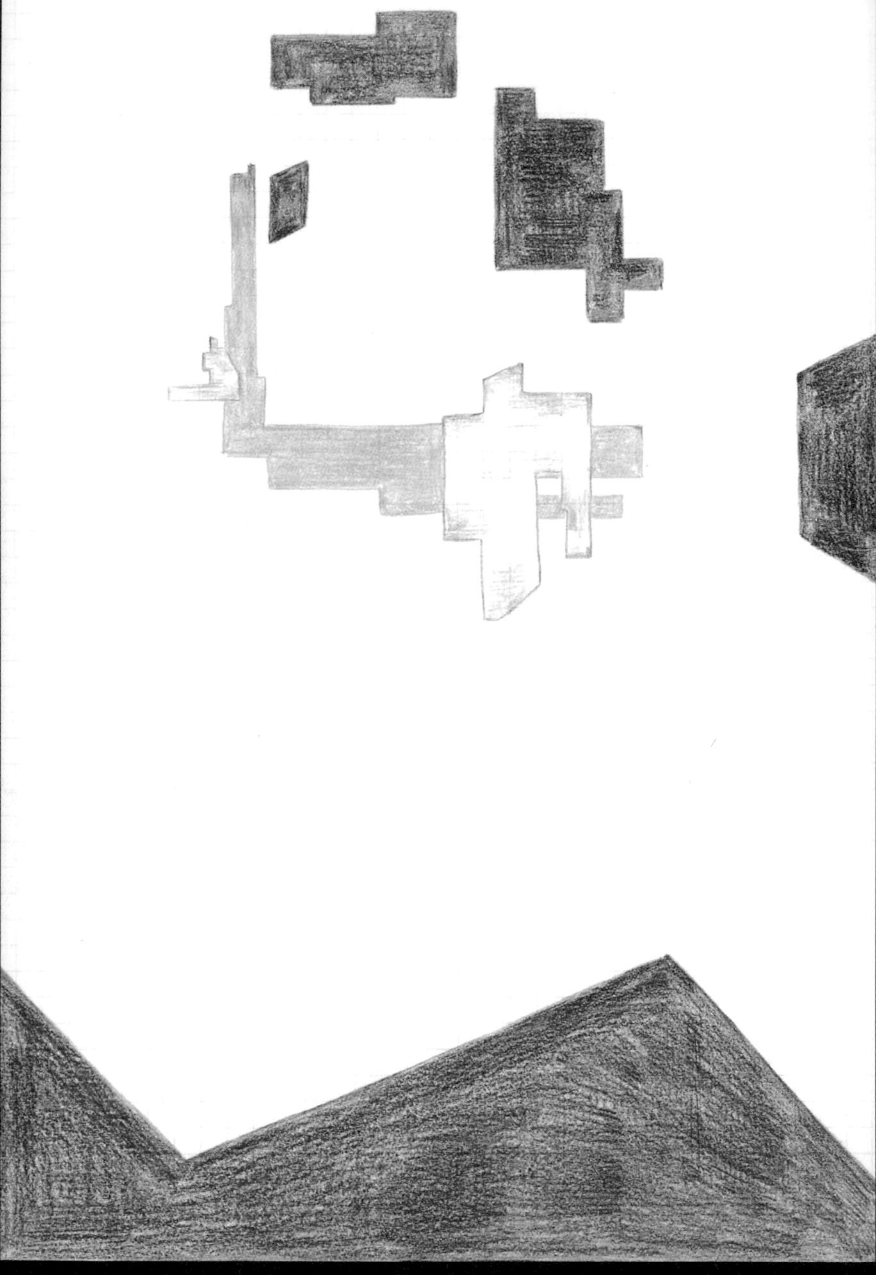

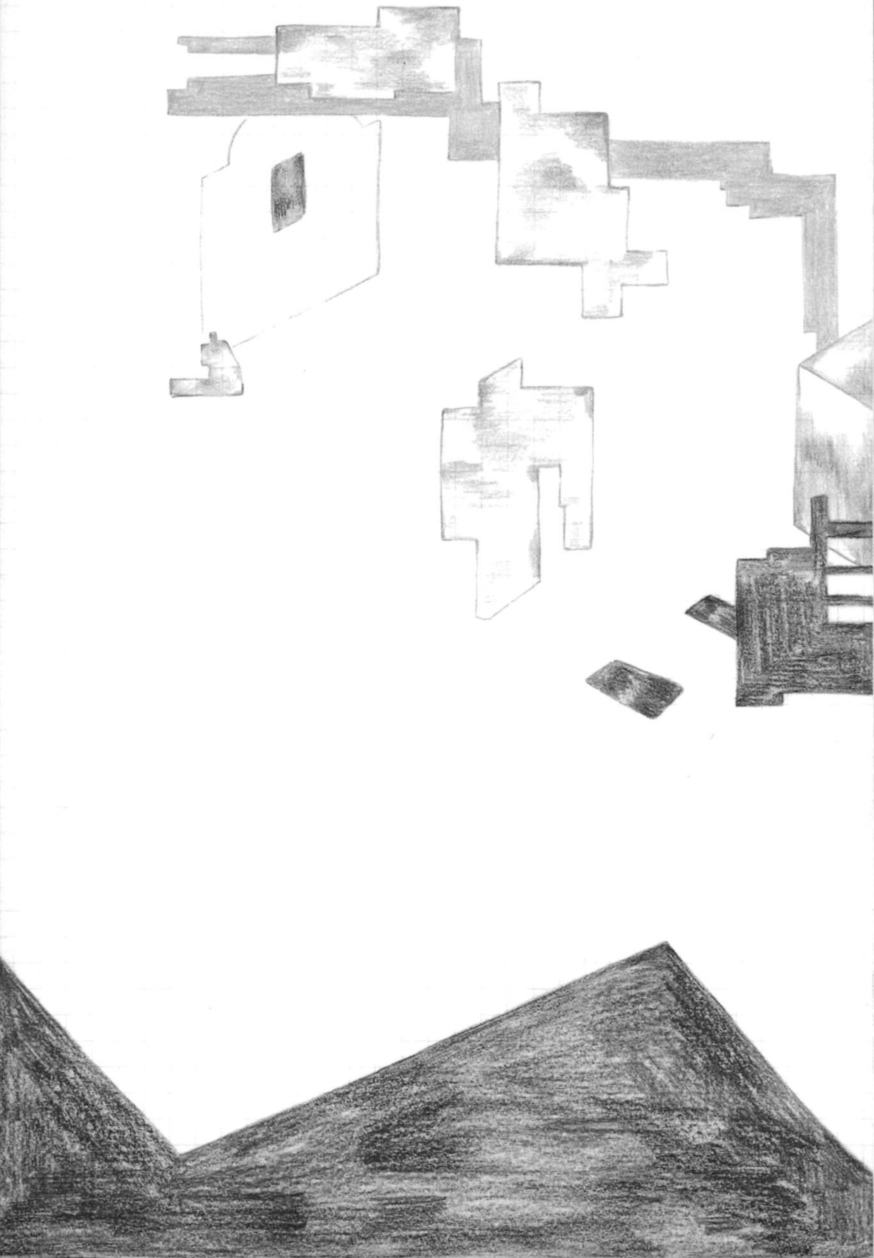

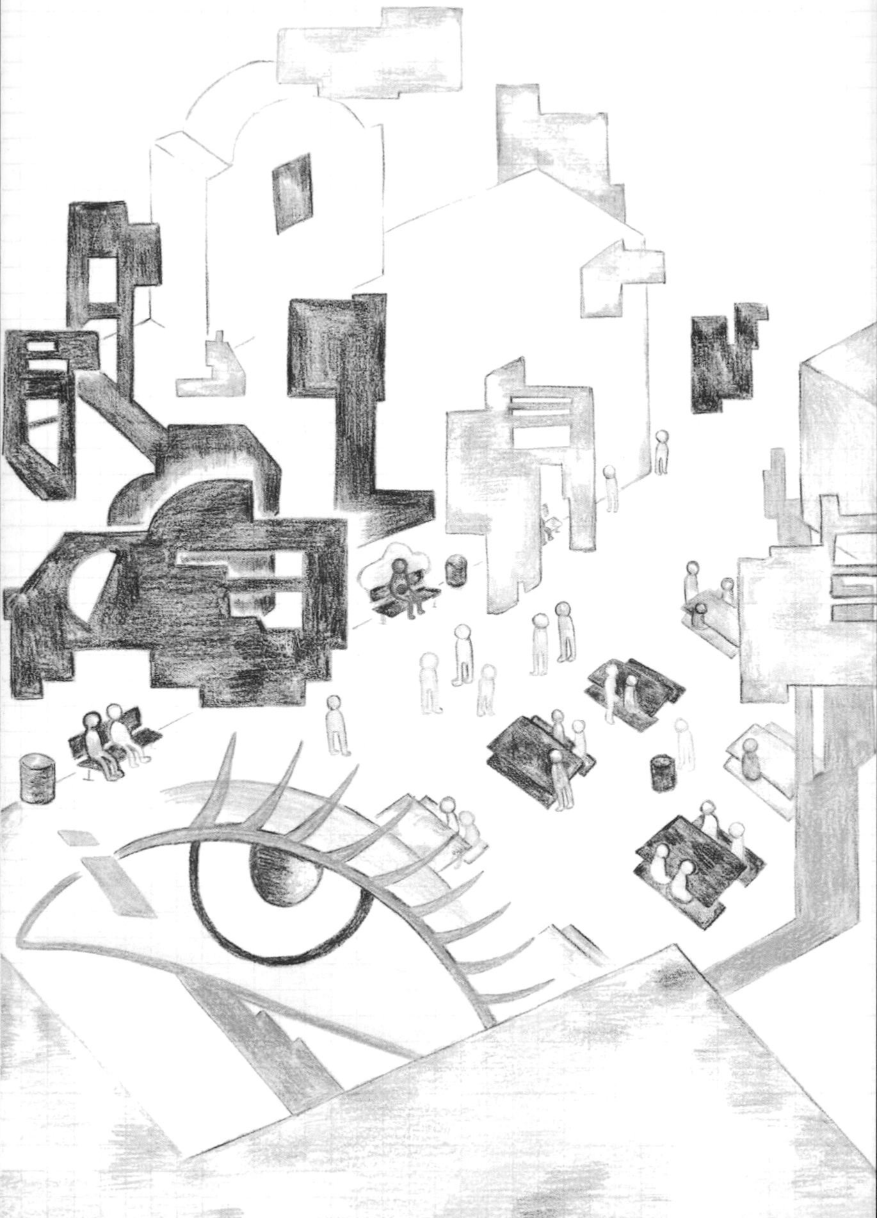

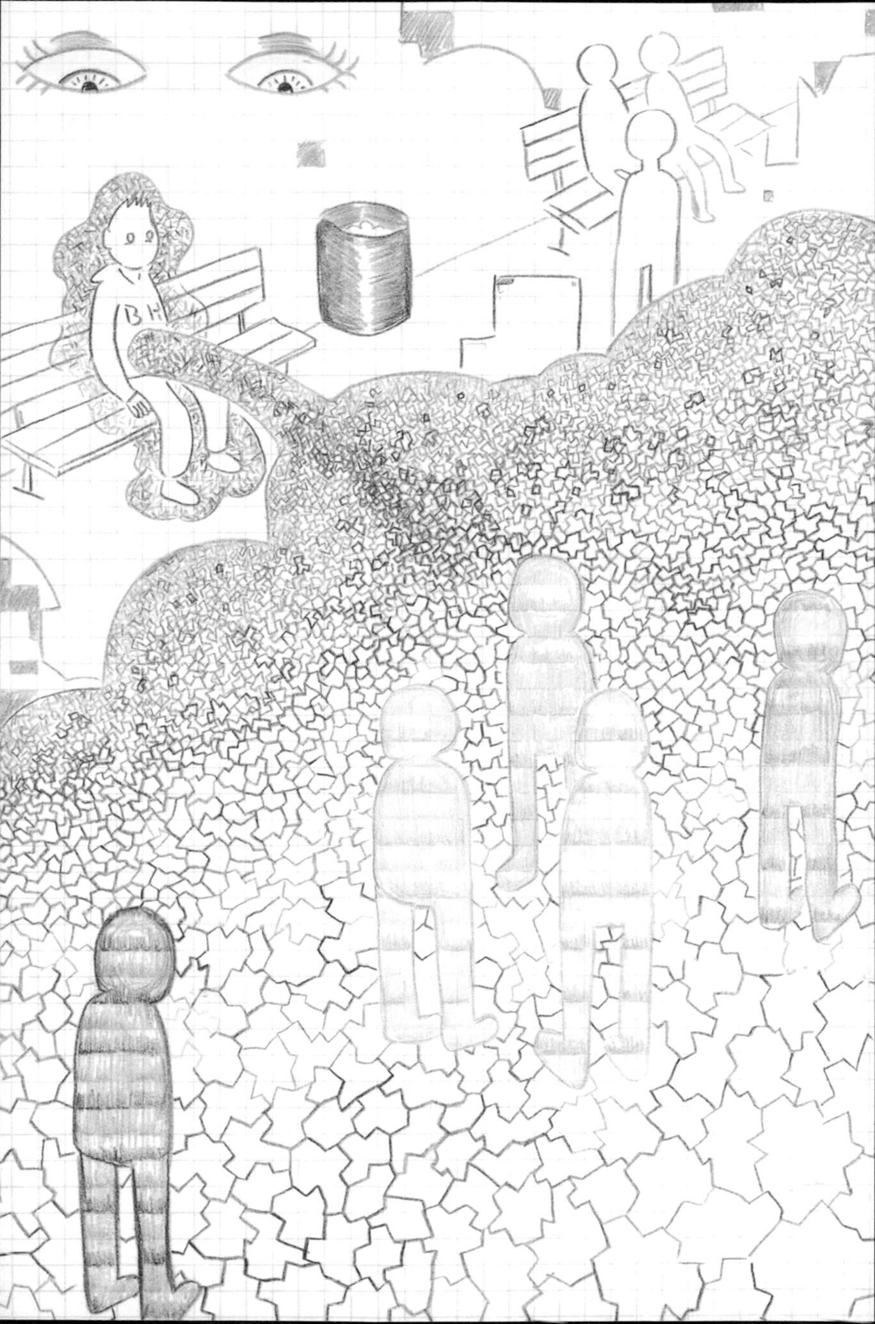
BH

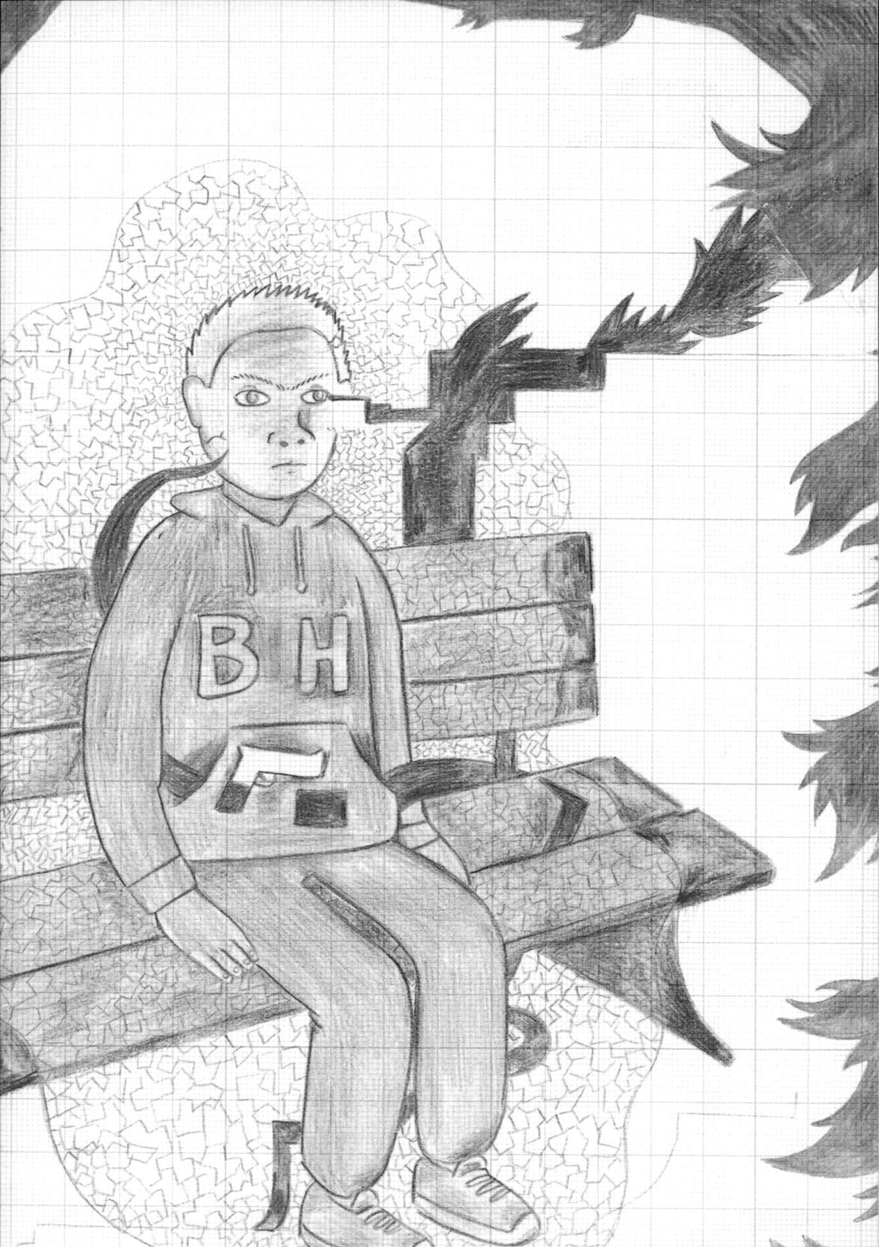
B H

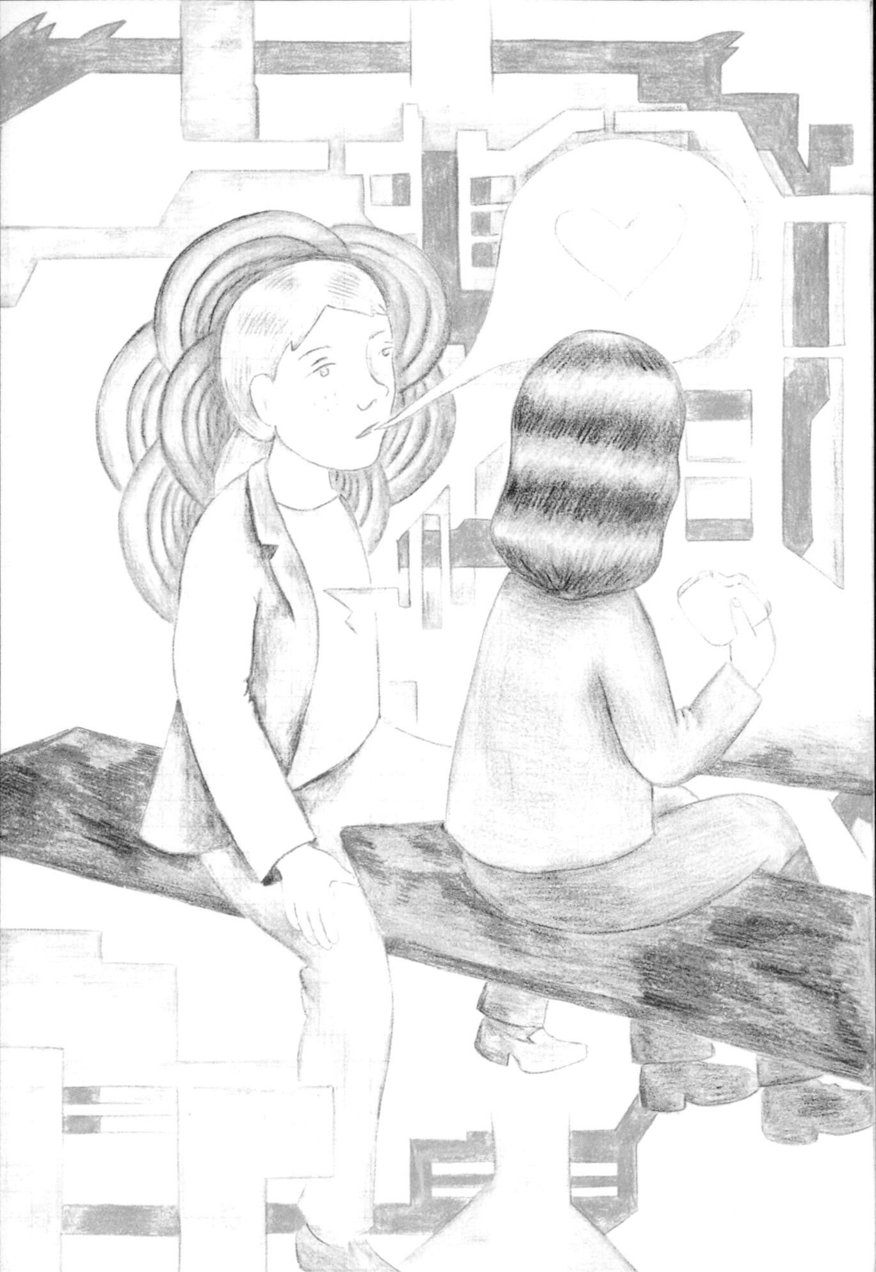

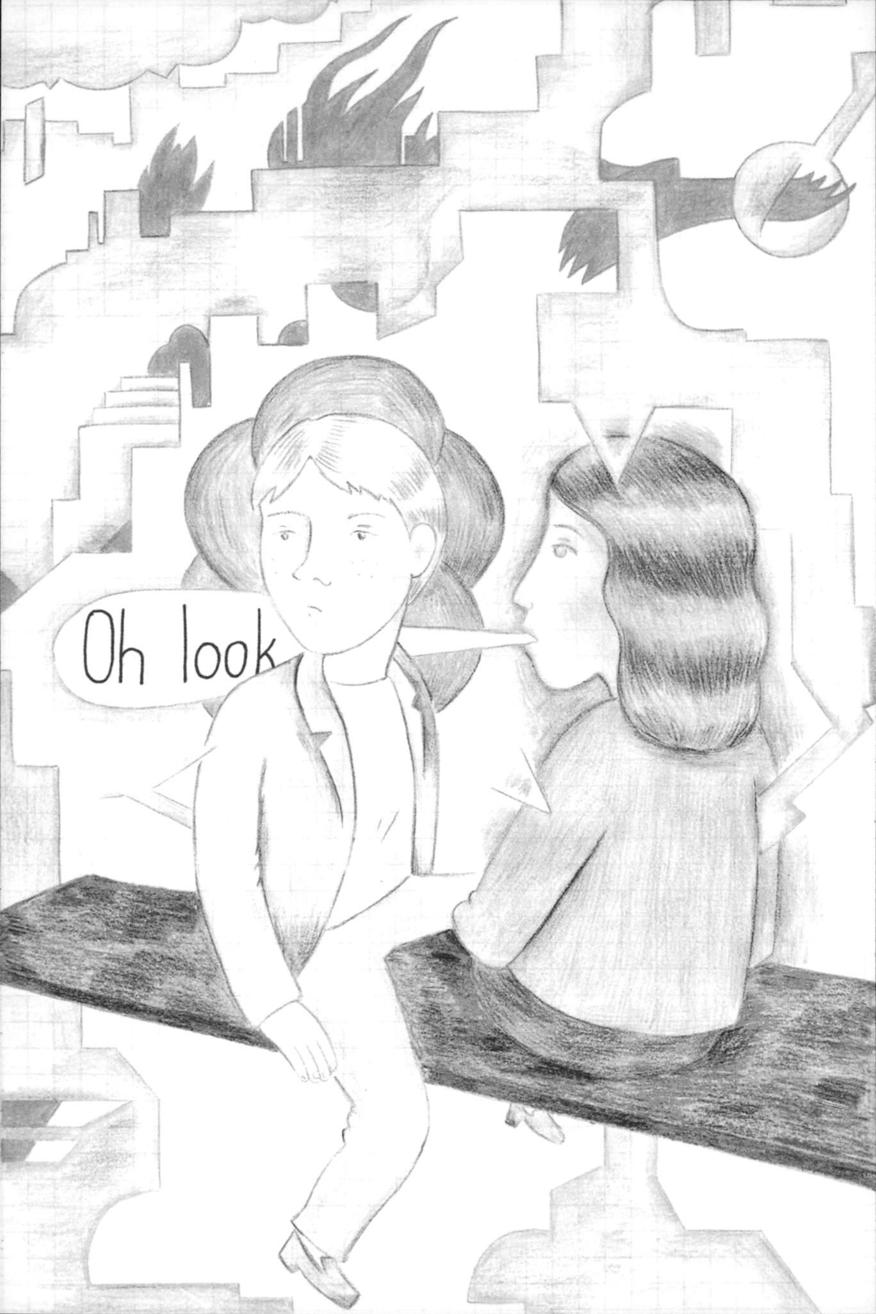
Oh look

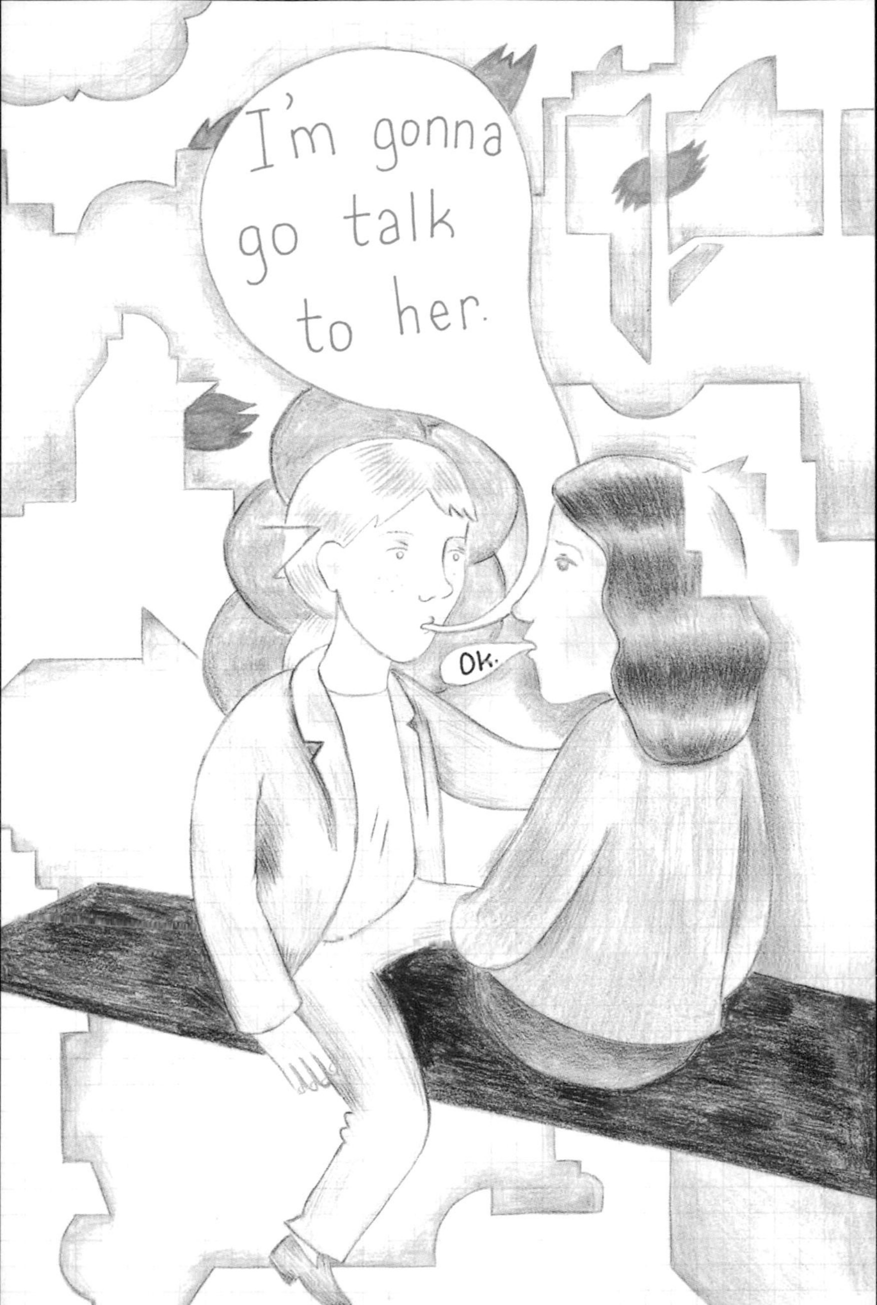
I'm gonna go talk to her.
OK.

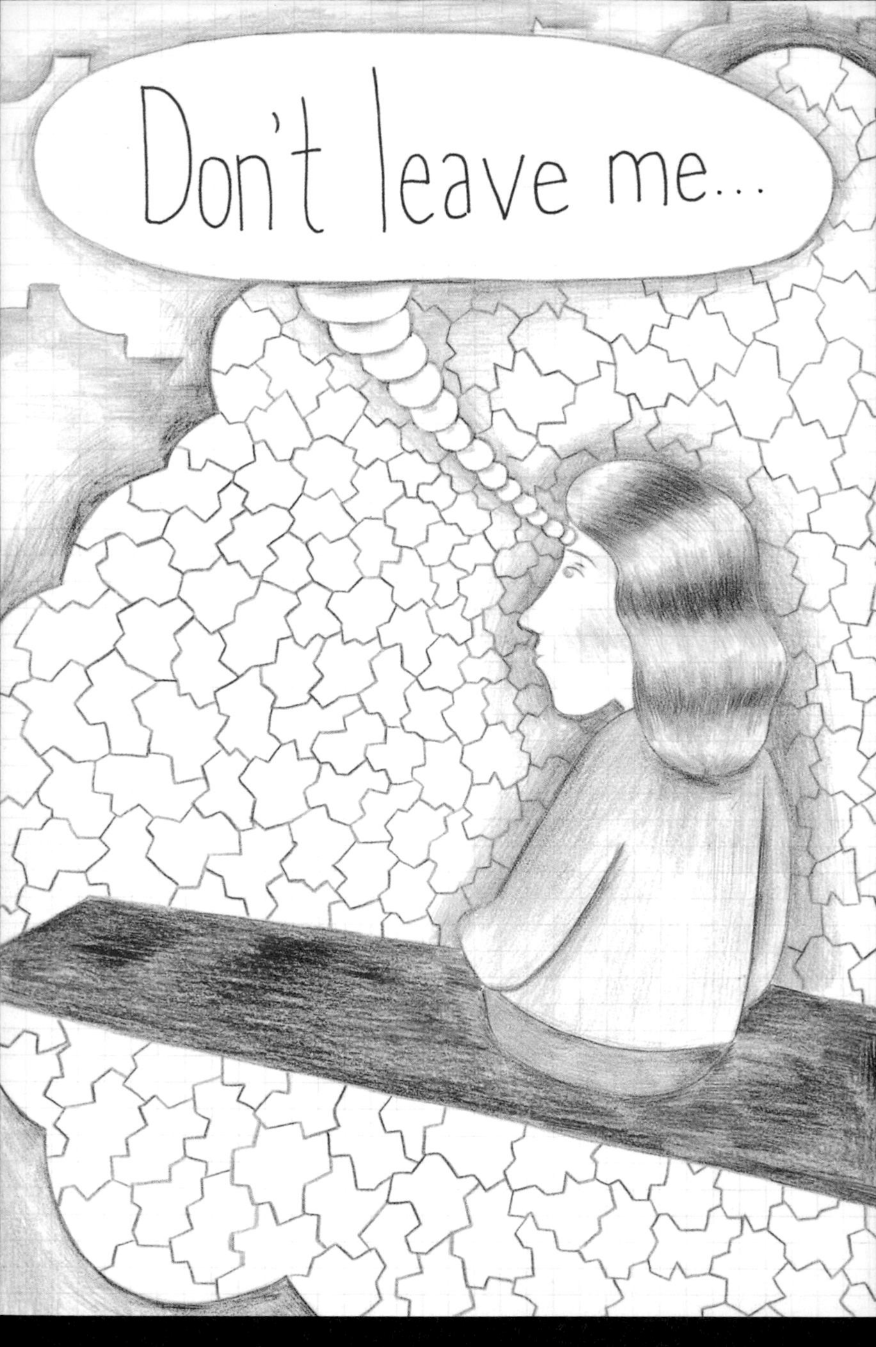
Don't leave me...

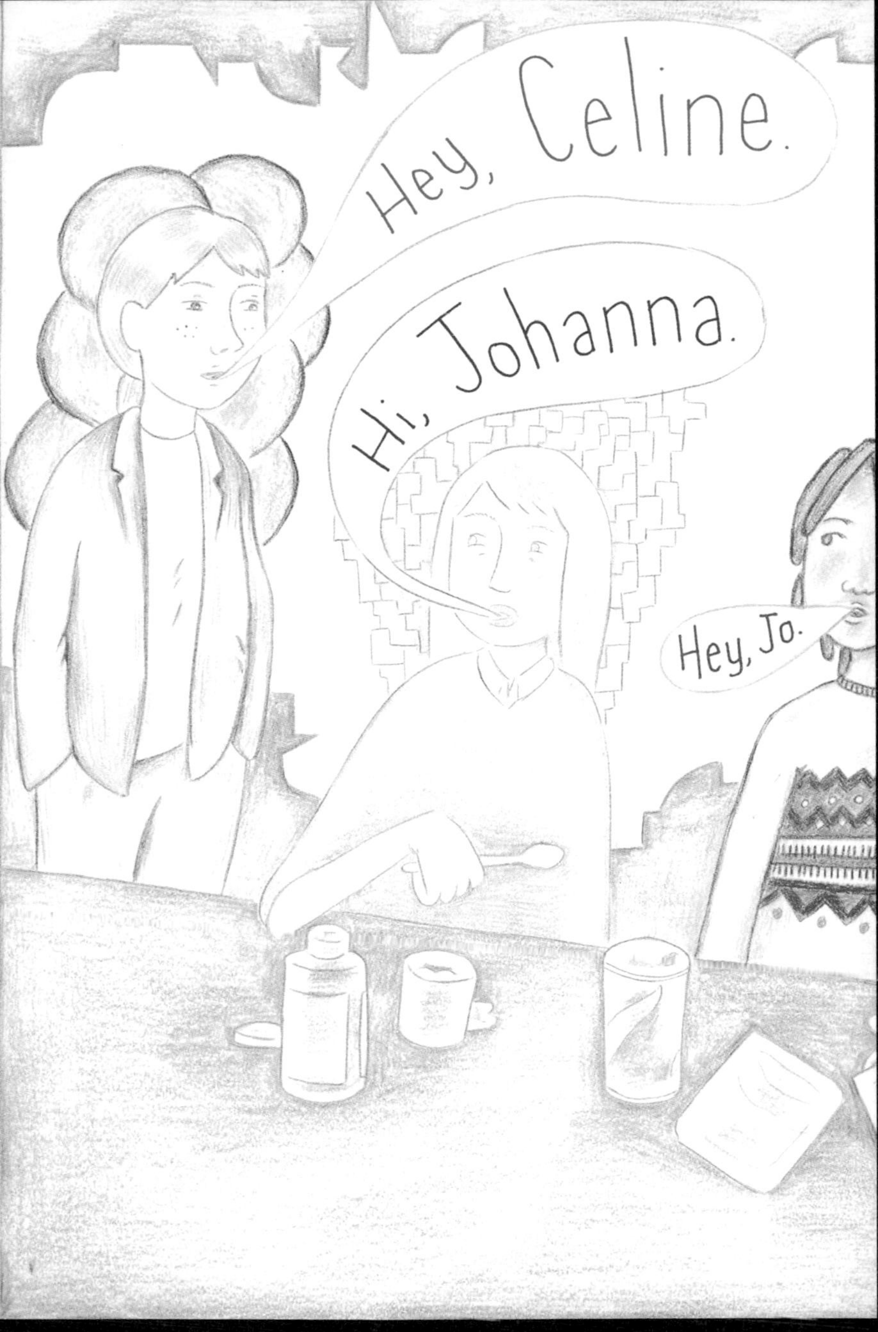
Hey, Celine.
Hi, Johanna.
Hey, Jo.

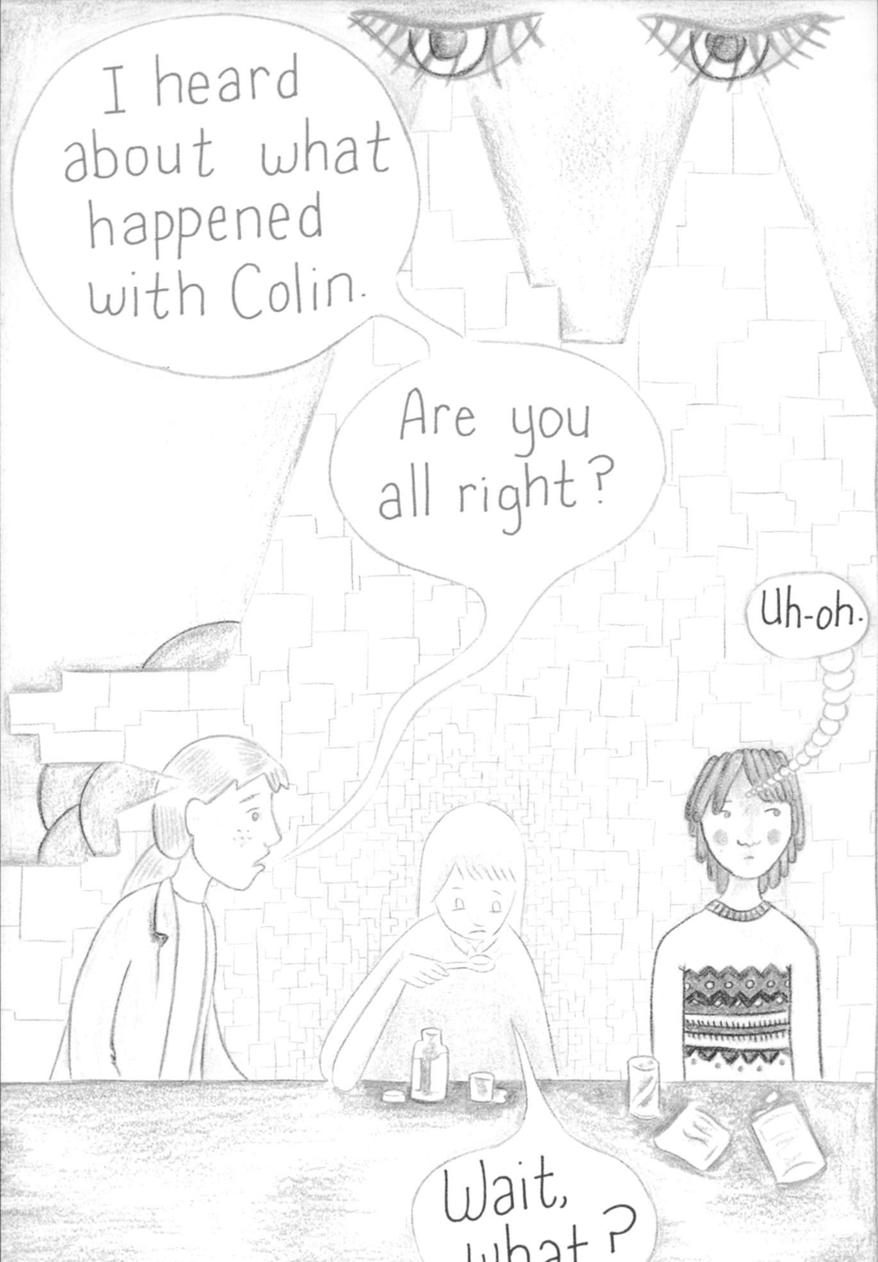
I heard about what happened with Colin.
Are you all right?
Uh-oh.
Wait, what?

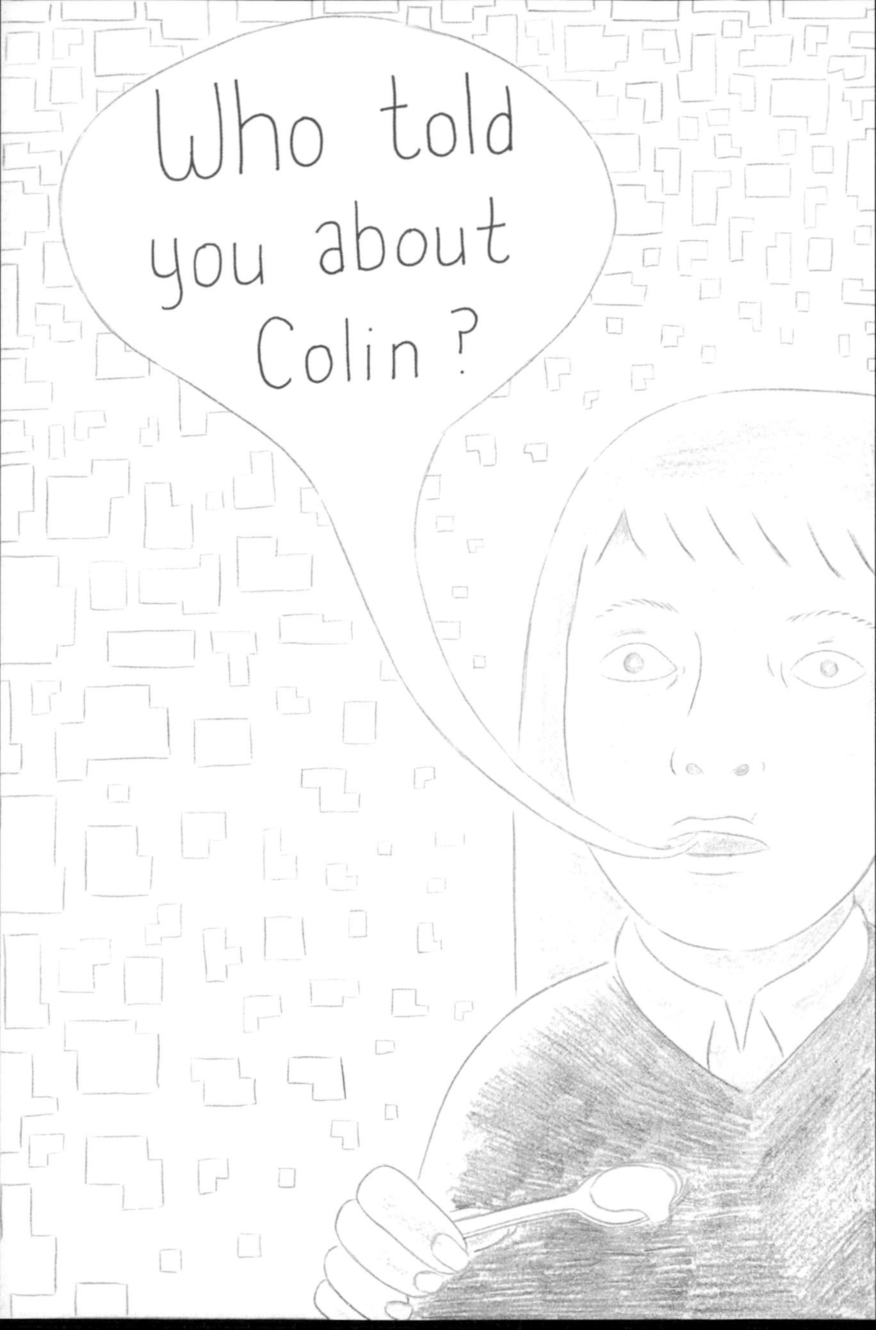
Who told you about Colin?

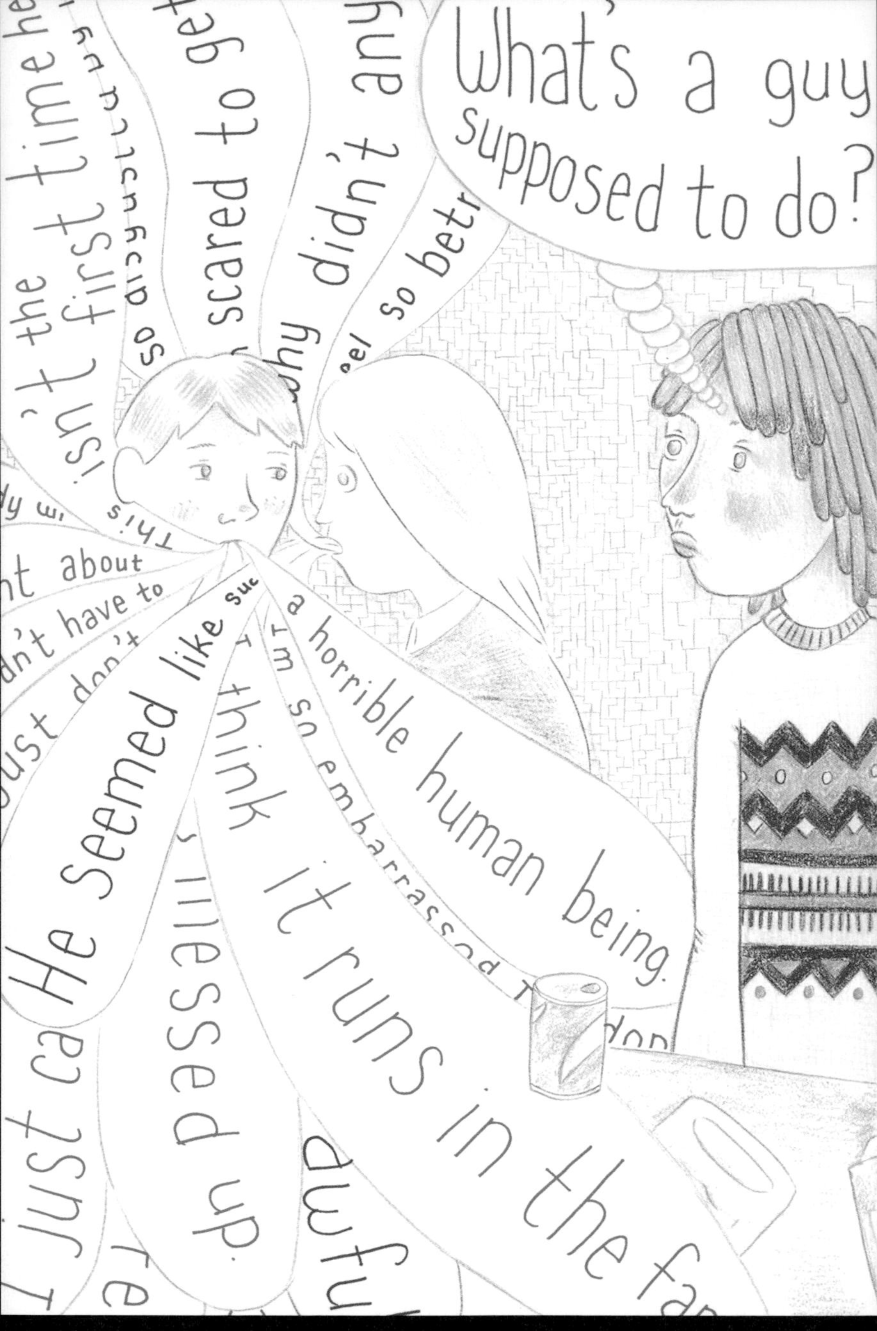
What's a guy supposed to do?
isn't the first time he
so scared to get
why didn't any
so betr
nt about
dn't have to
just don't
He seemed like
a horrible human being.
I'm so embarrassed
I think it runs in the fa
I just ca

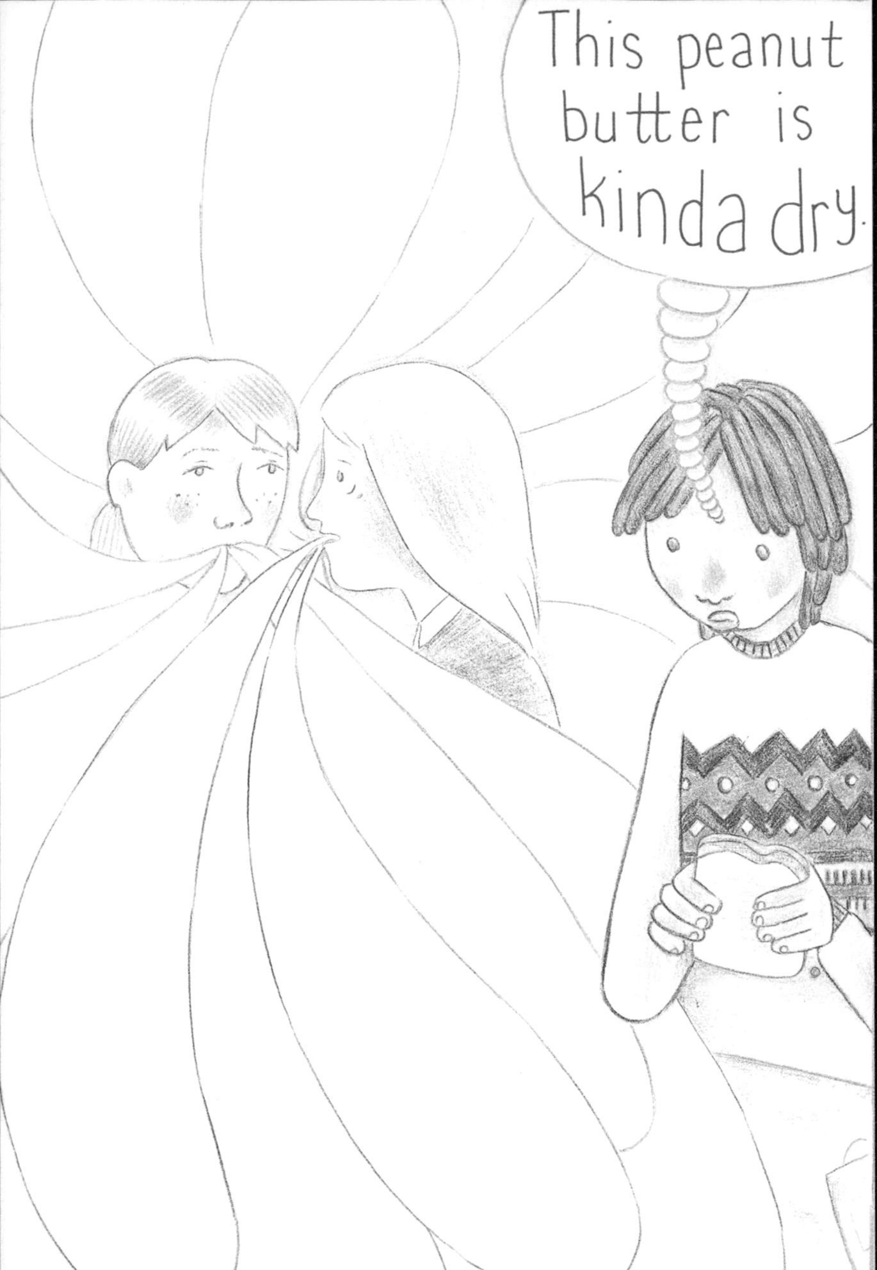
This peanut butter is kinda dry.

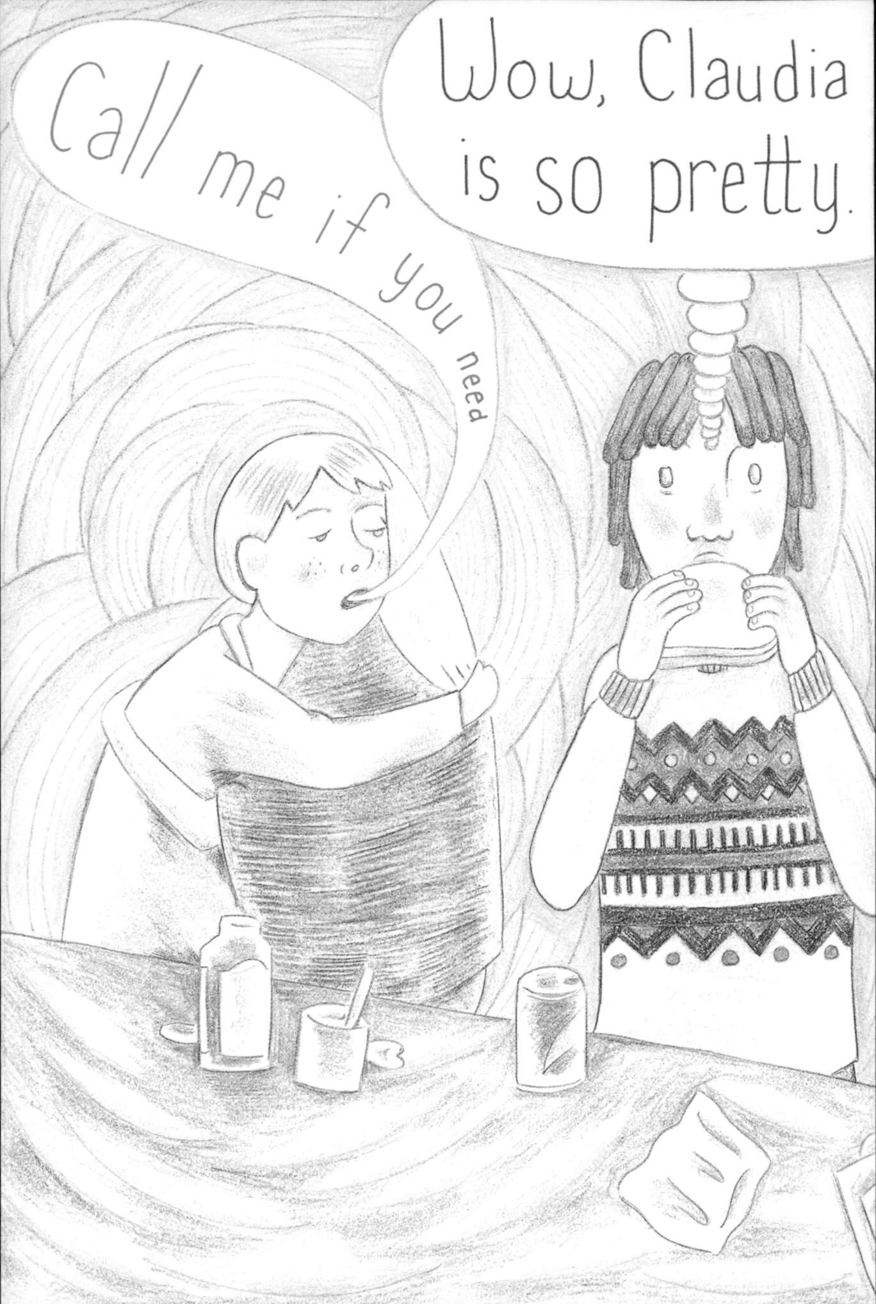
Call me if you need
Wow, Claudia is so pretty.

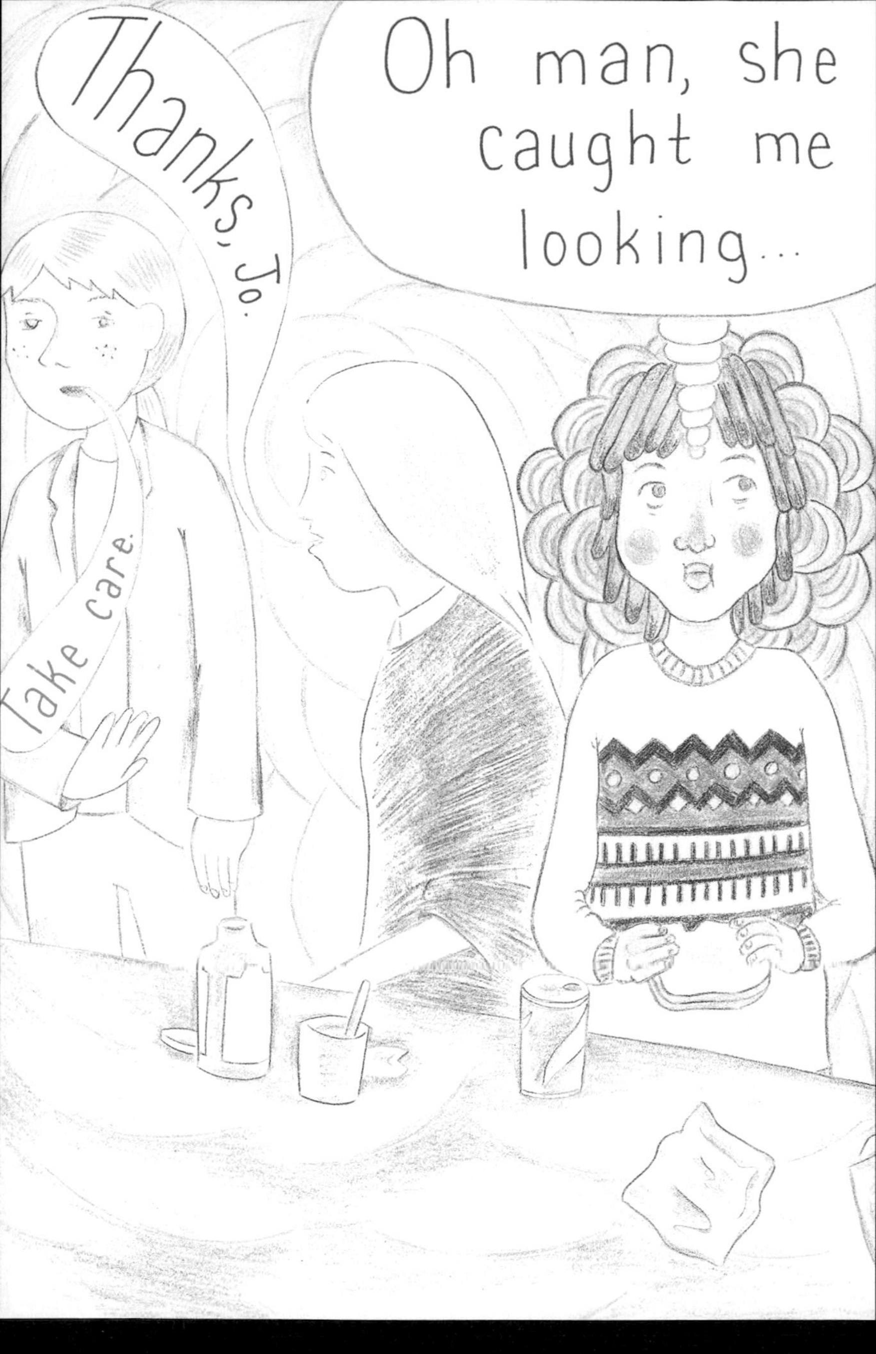
Thanks, Jo.
Oh man, she caught me looking...
Take care.

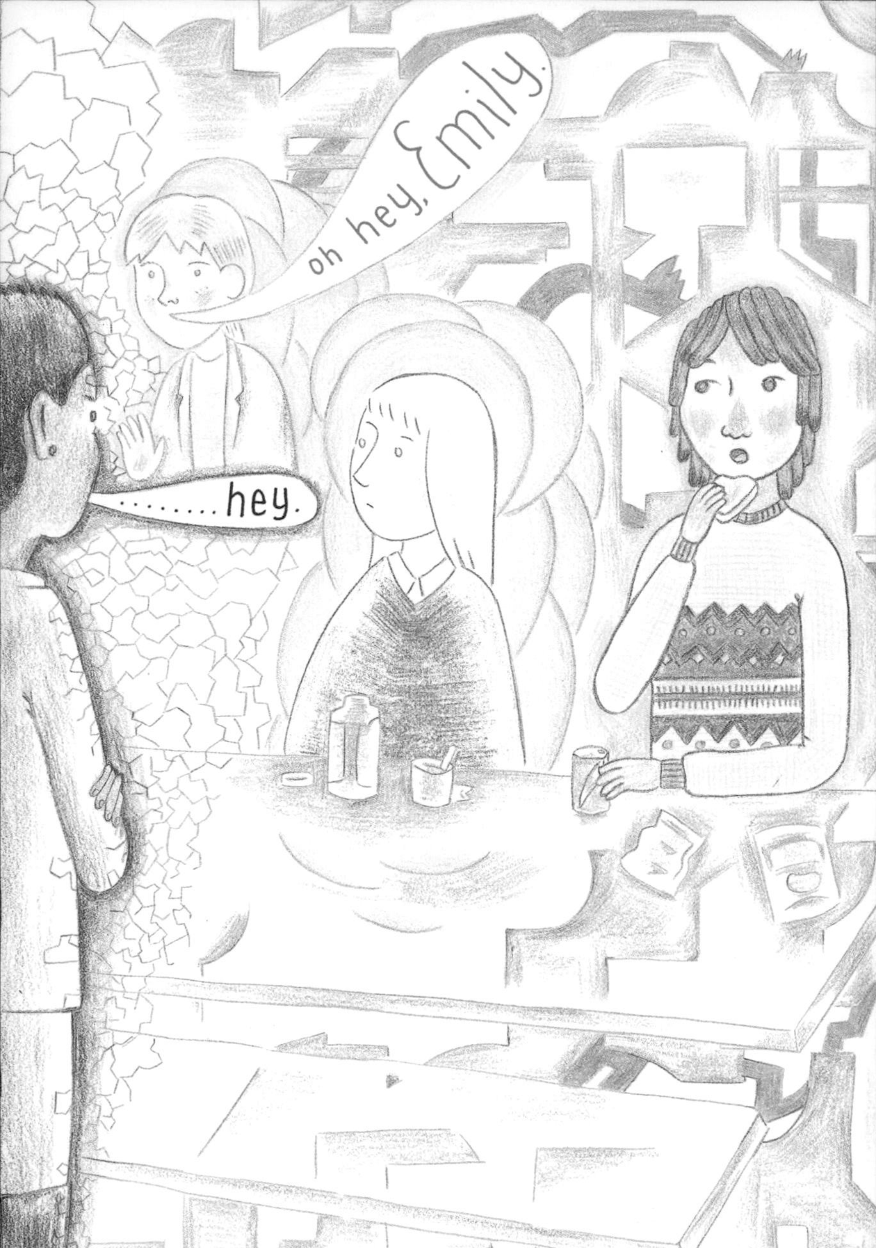
oh hey, Emily.
.........hey.

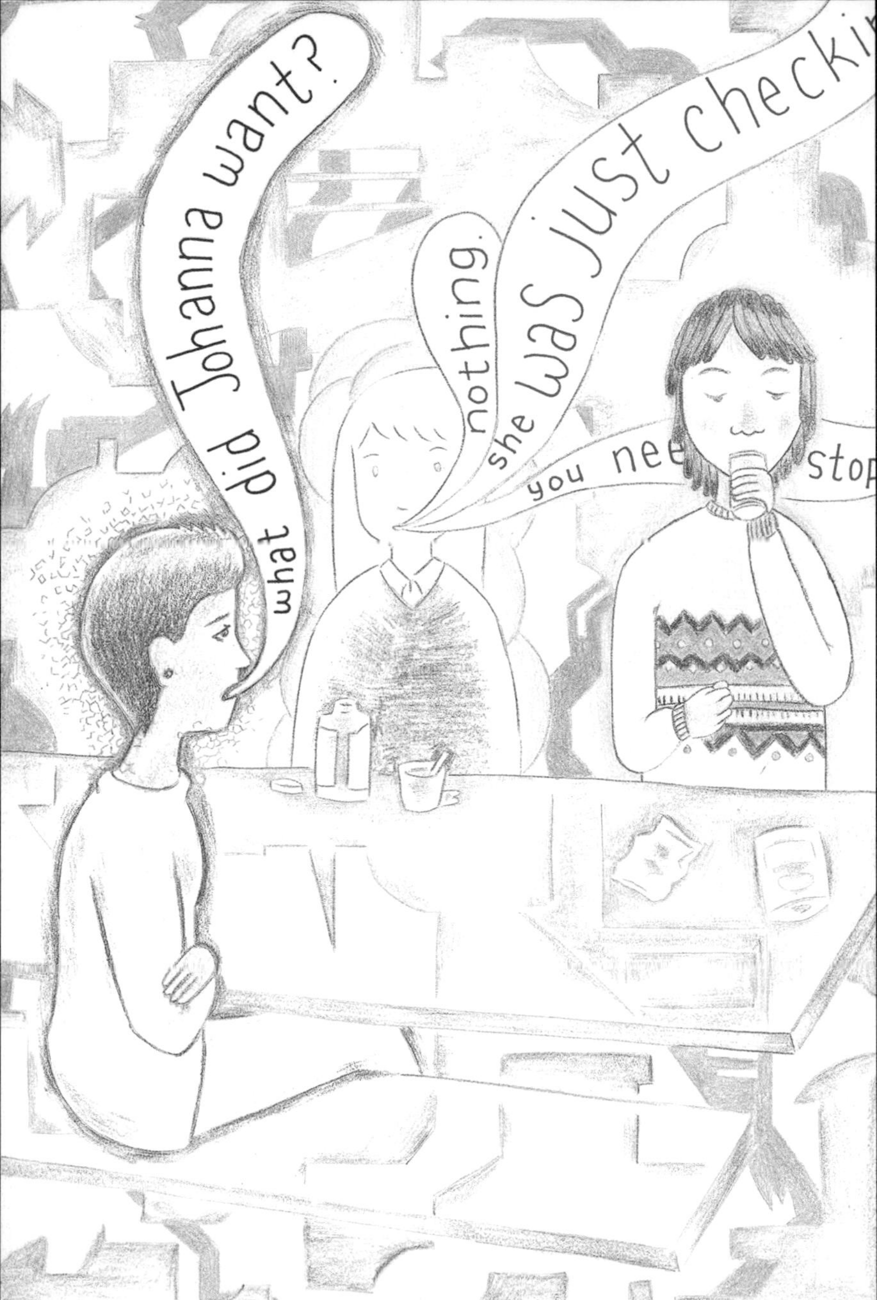
what did Johanna want?
nothing. she WAS just checki
you nee stop

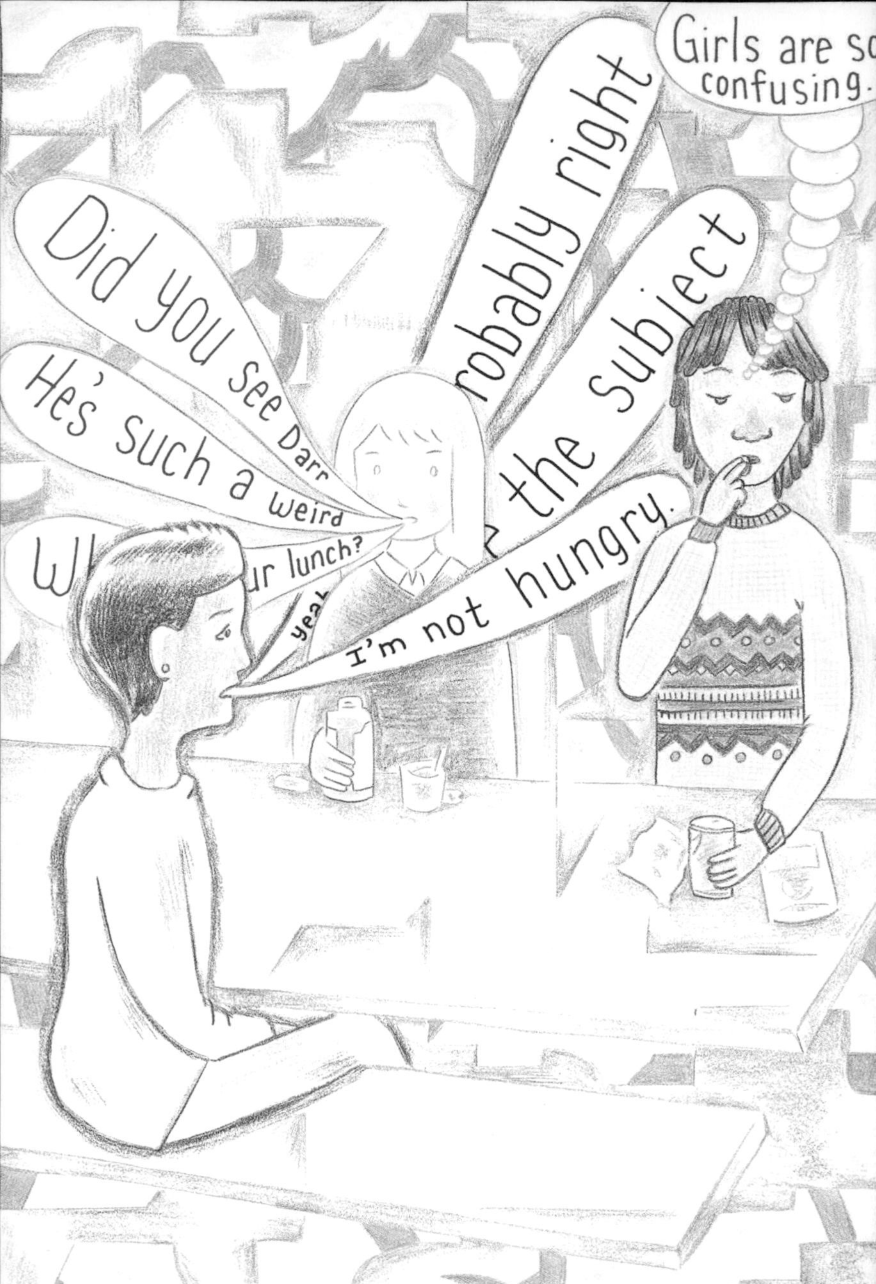
Girls are so
confusing.
Did you see Darr
He's such a weird
ur lunch?
robably right
the subject
I'm not hungry.

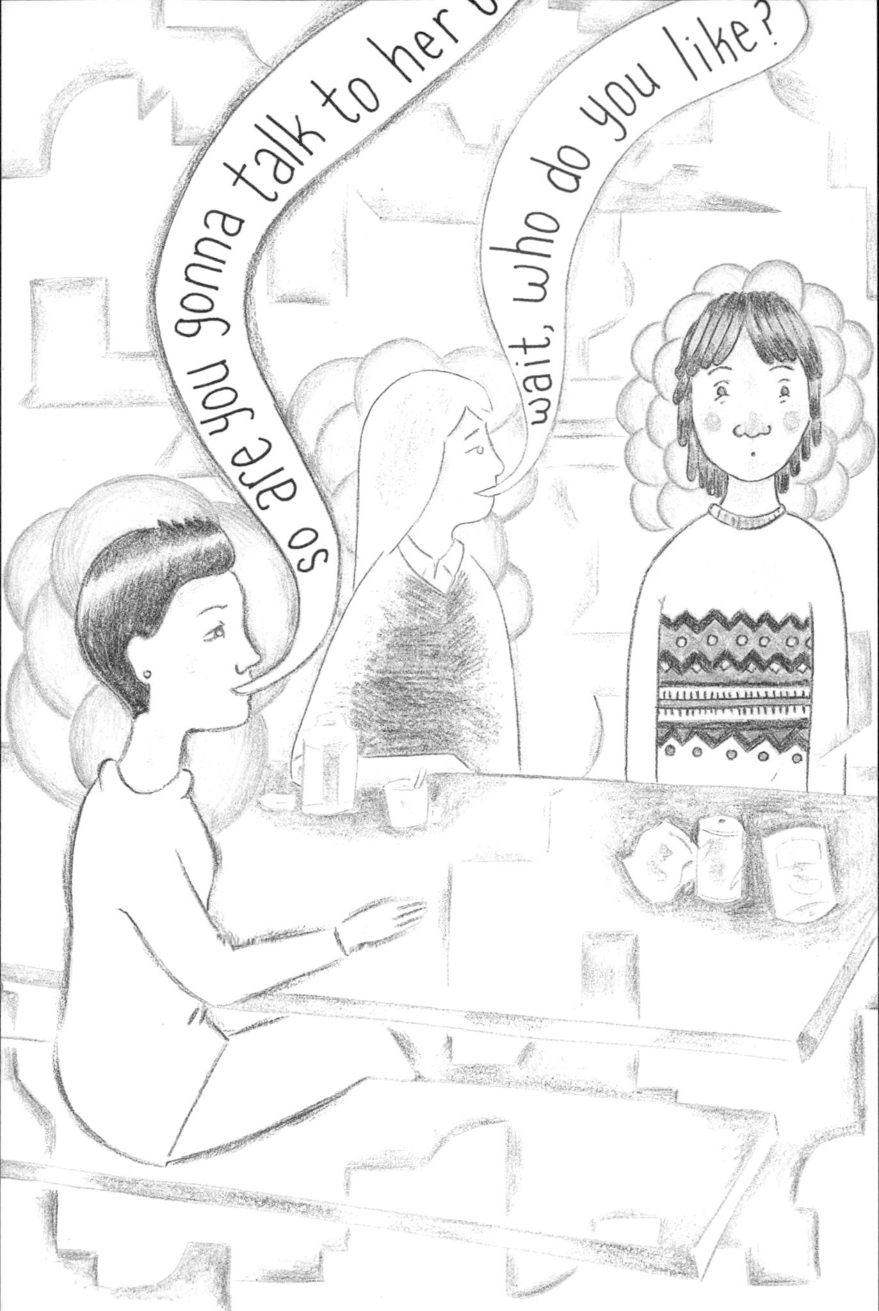
so are you gonna talk to her
wait, who do you like?

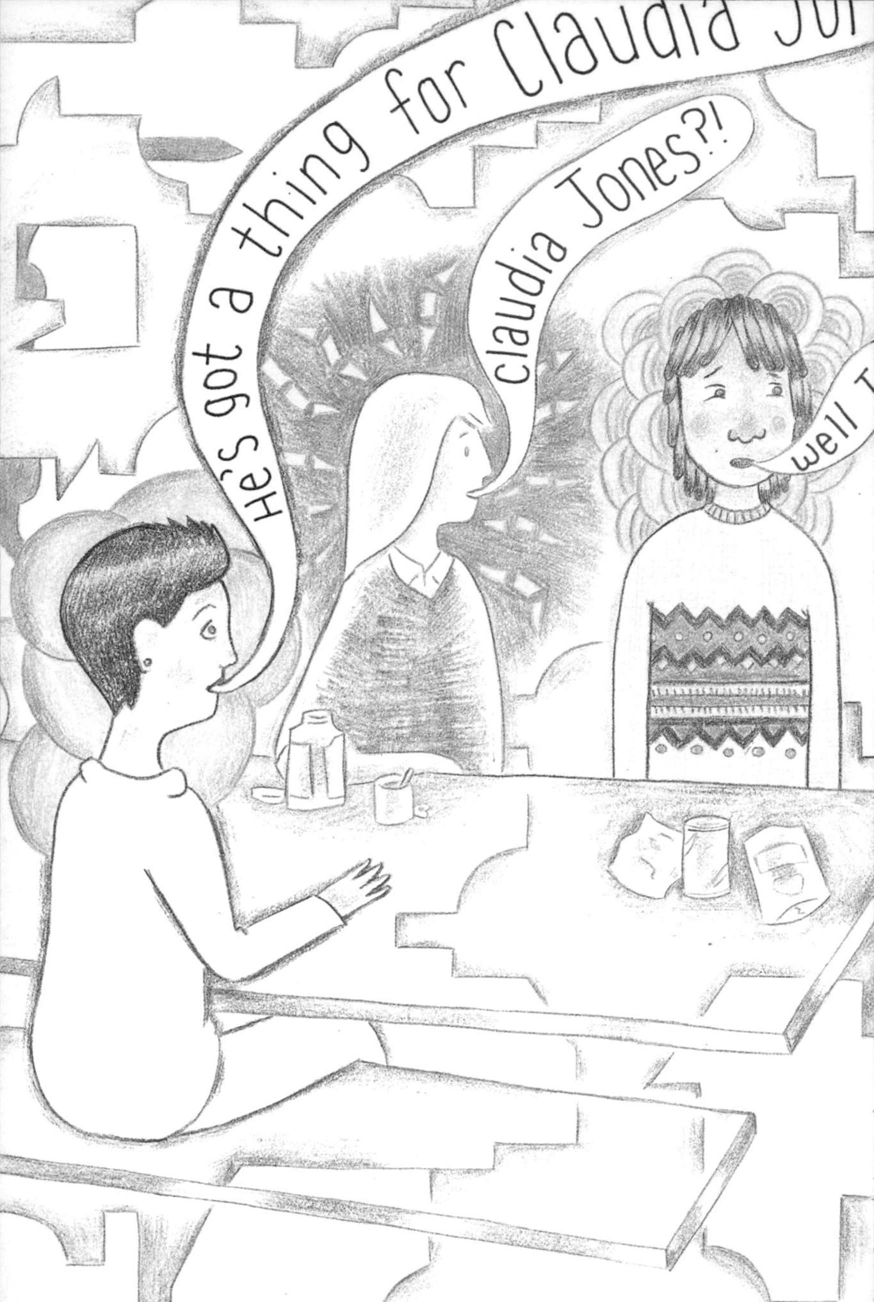
He's got a thing for Claudia Jo
Claudia Jones?!
well I

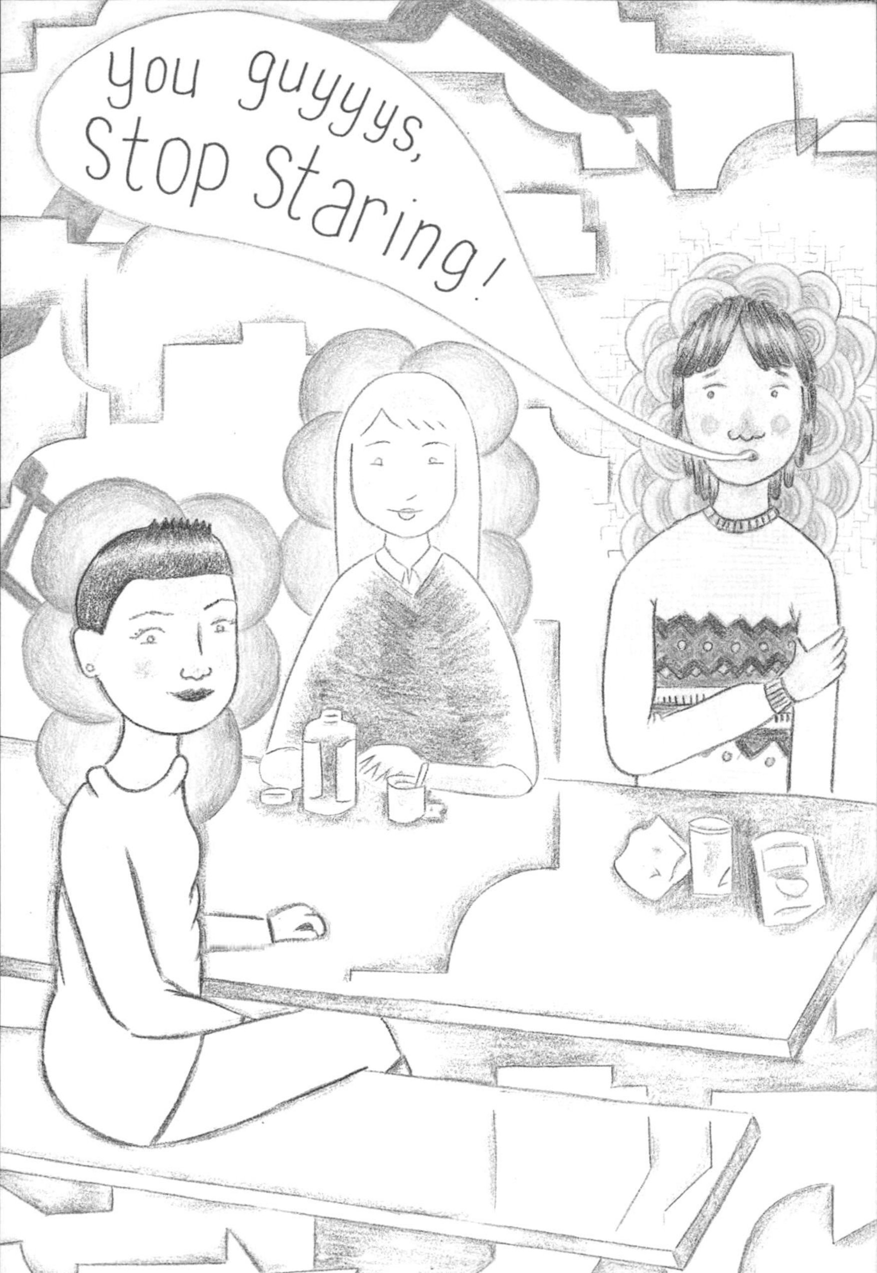
you guyyys, Stop Staring!

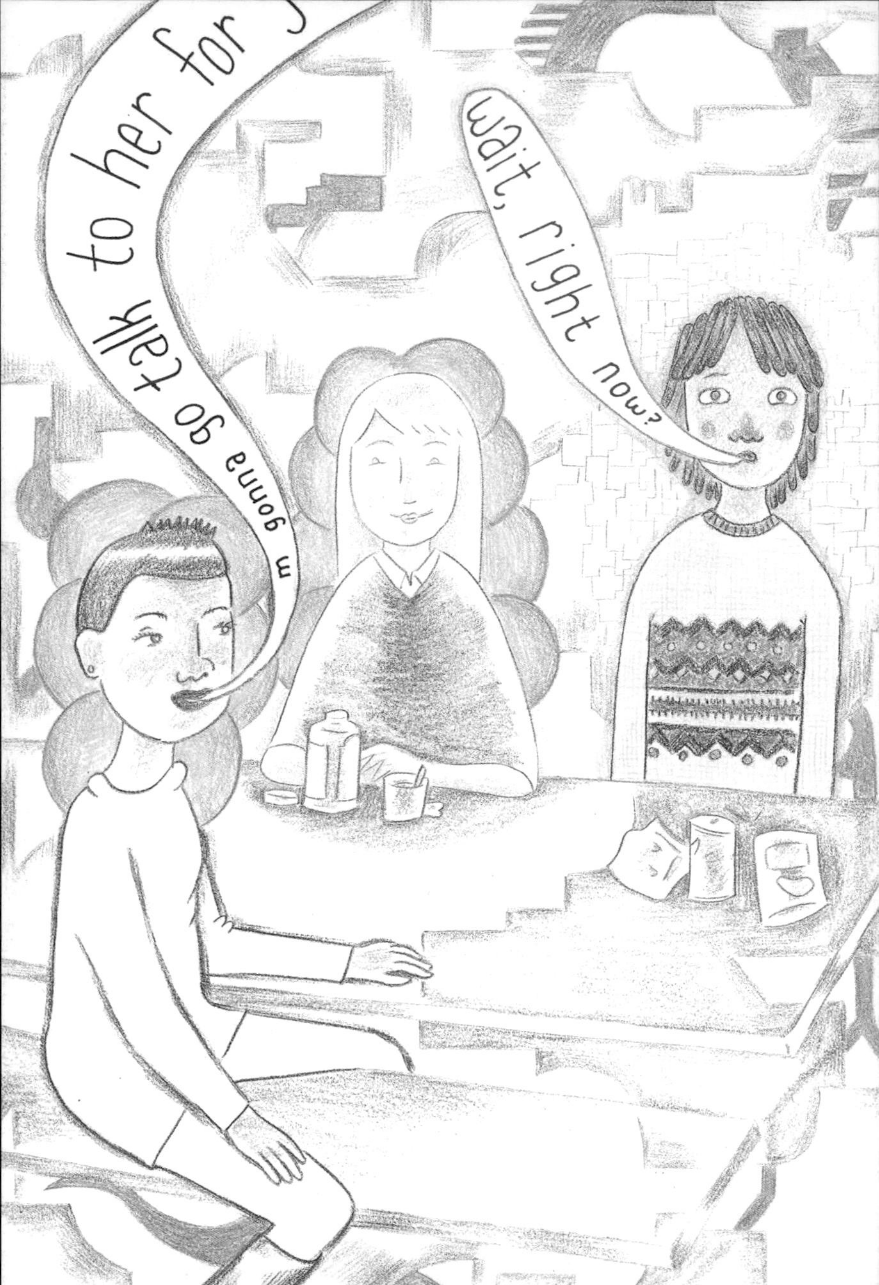
m gonna go talk to her for
wait, right now?

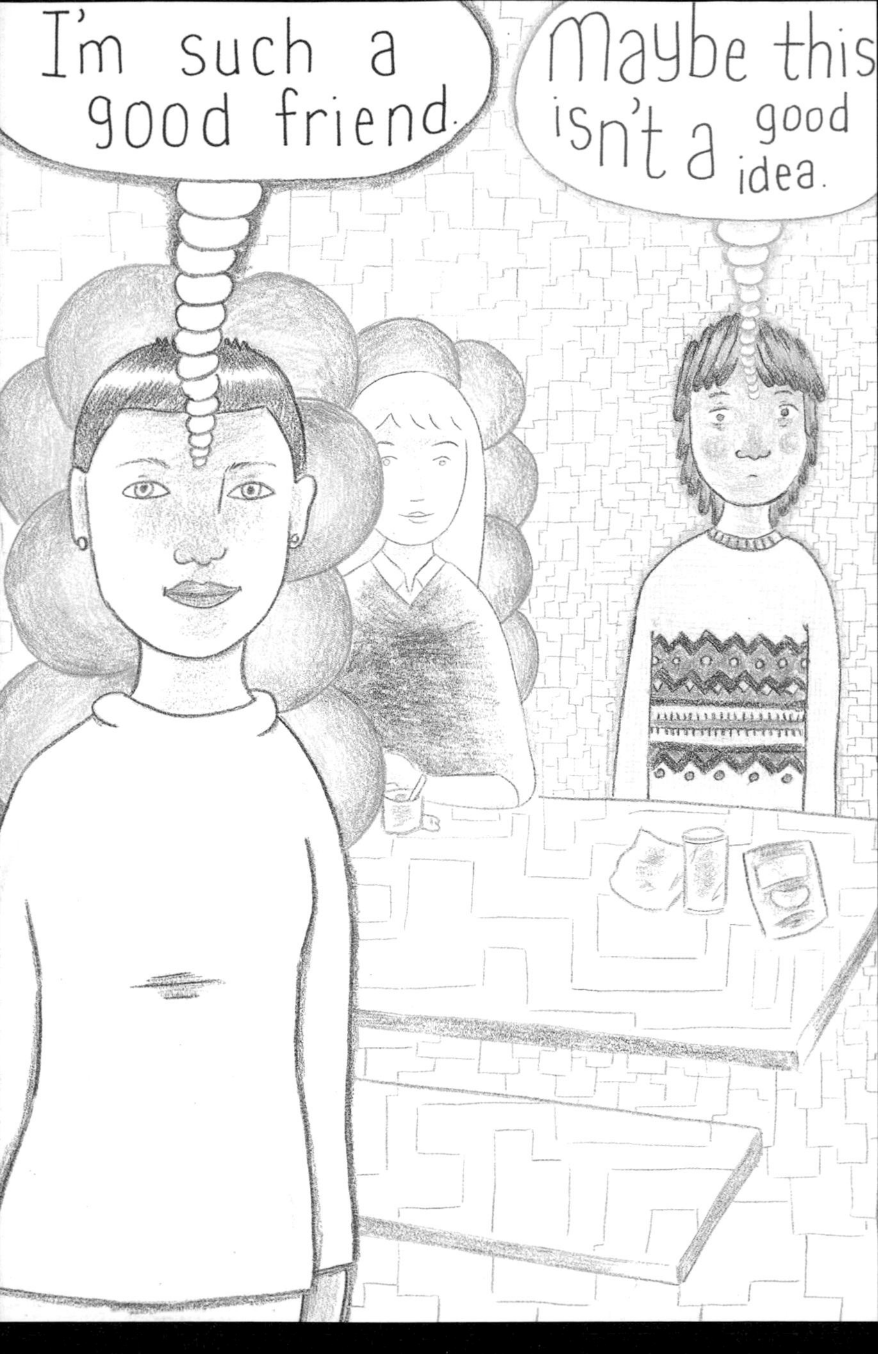
I'm such a good friend.
Maybe this isn't a good idea.

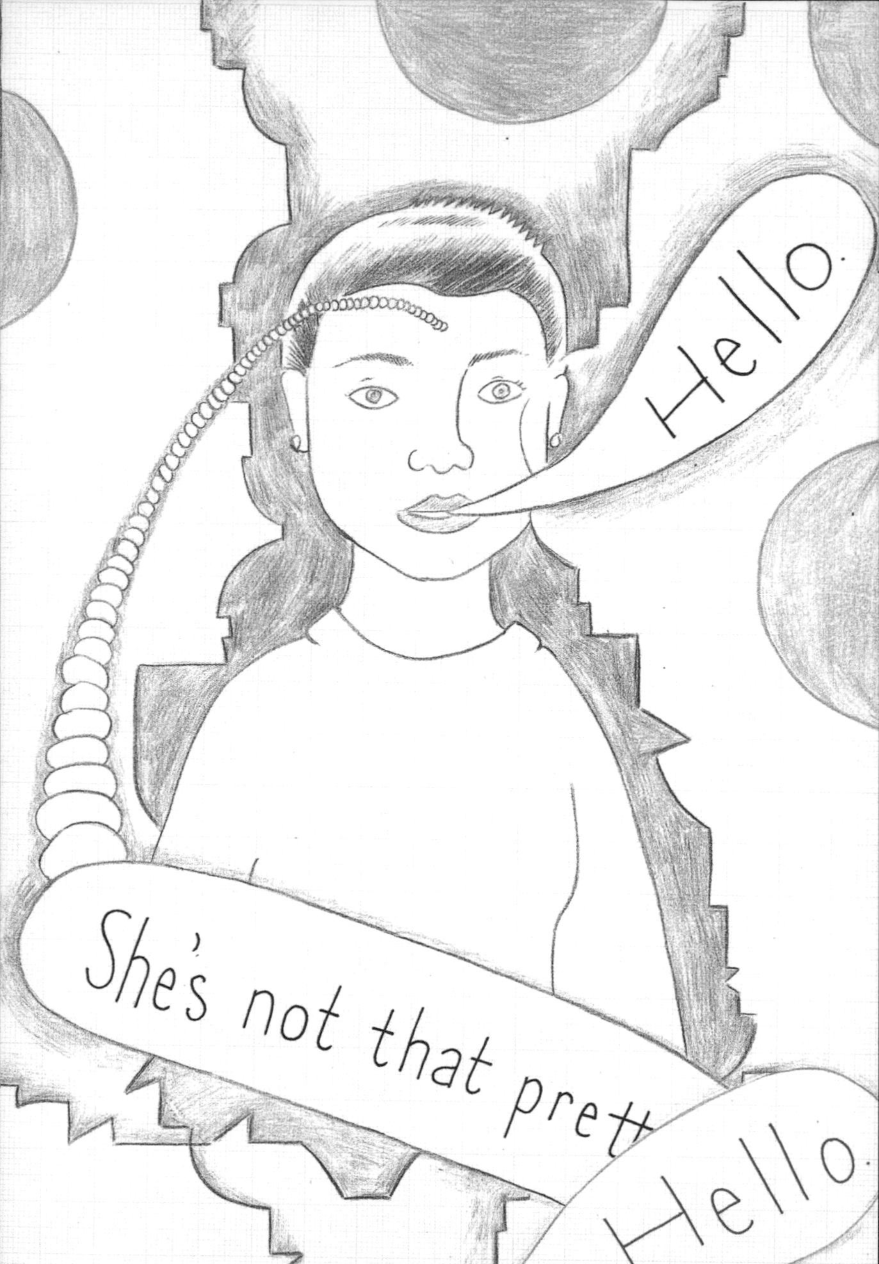
Hello.
She's not that prett
Hello.

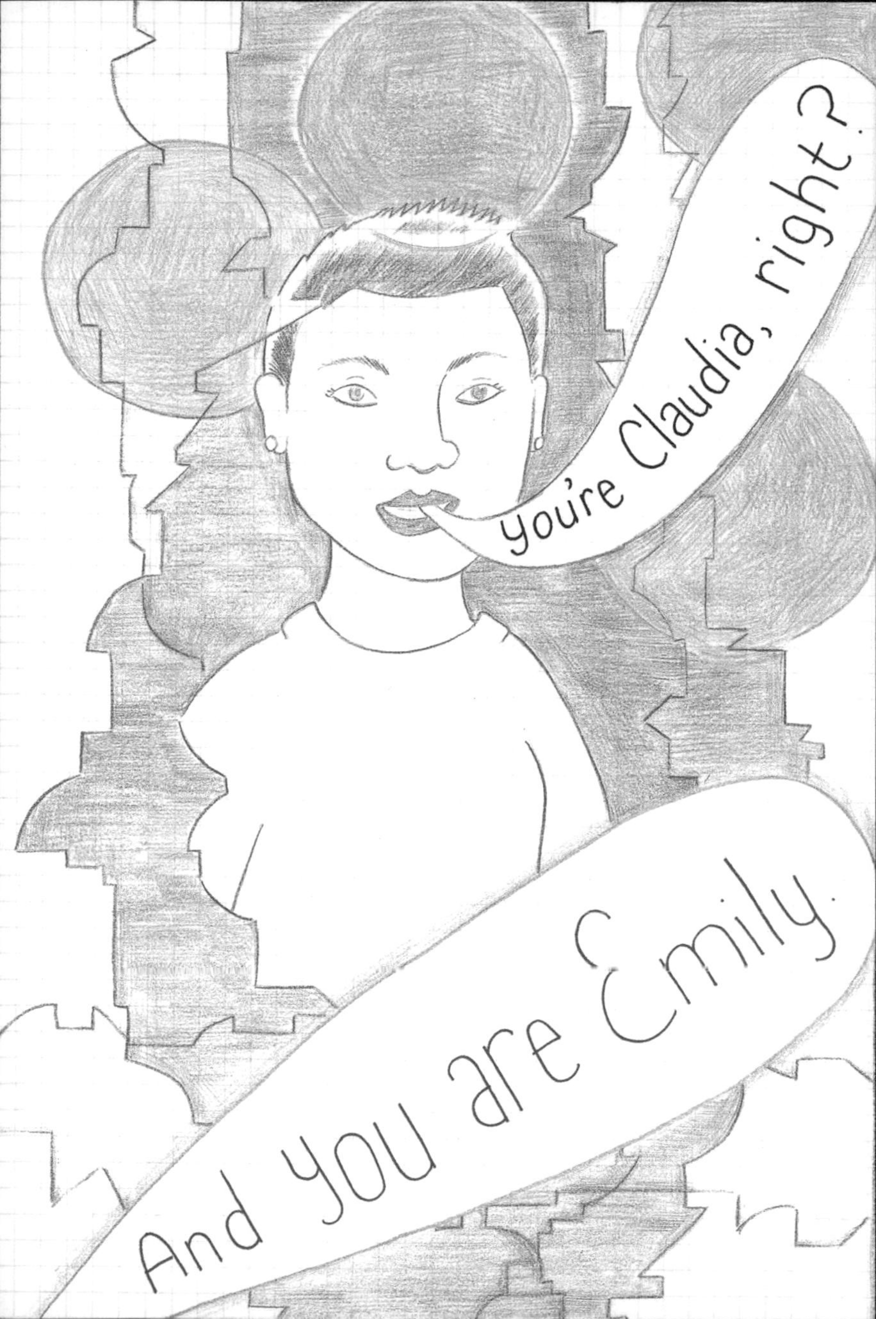
You're Claudia, right?
And you are Emily.

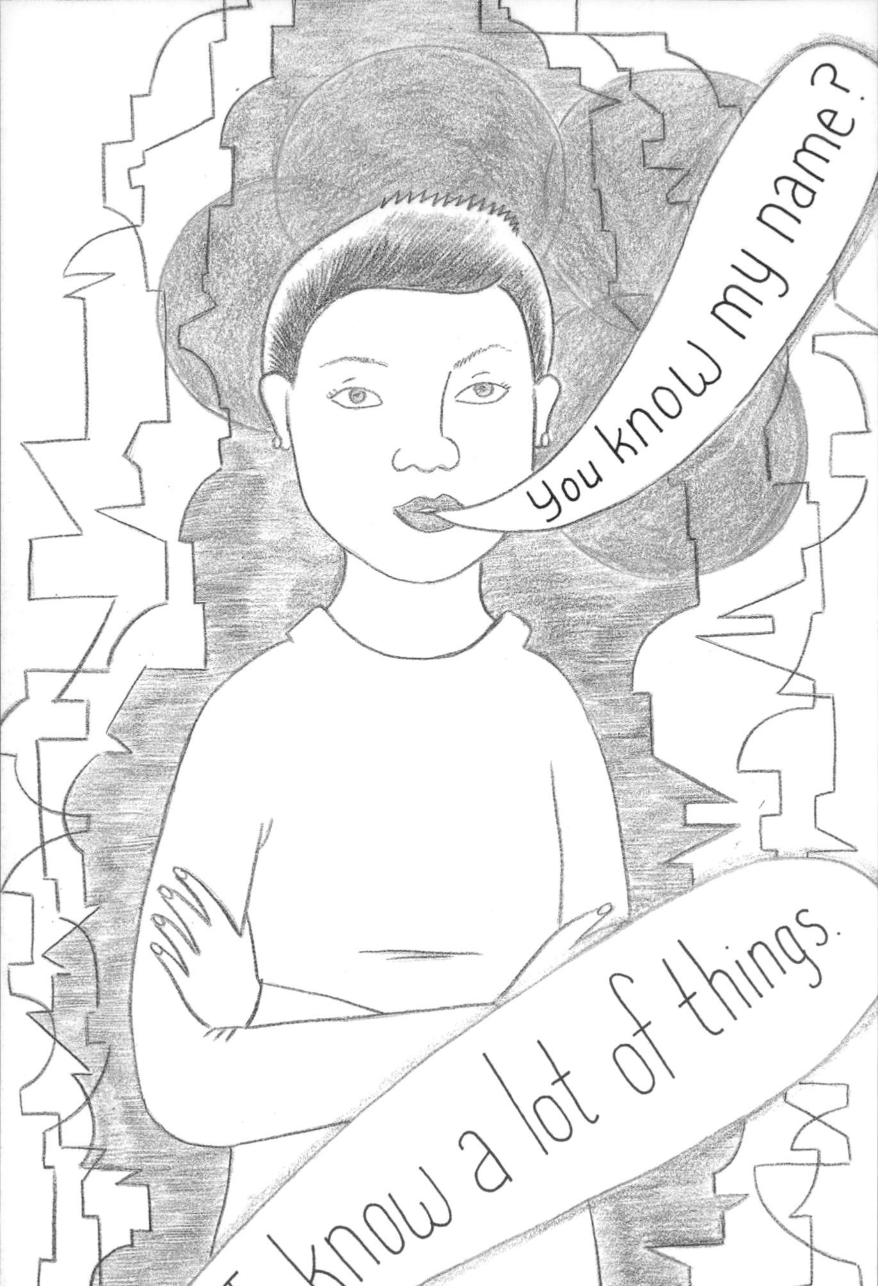
You know my name?
I know a lot of things.

such as........
you
avoid
your good
friends, the lovers,
despite your forgiving
nature.
Wait, what?
who
?

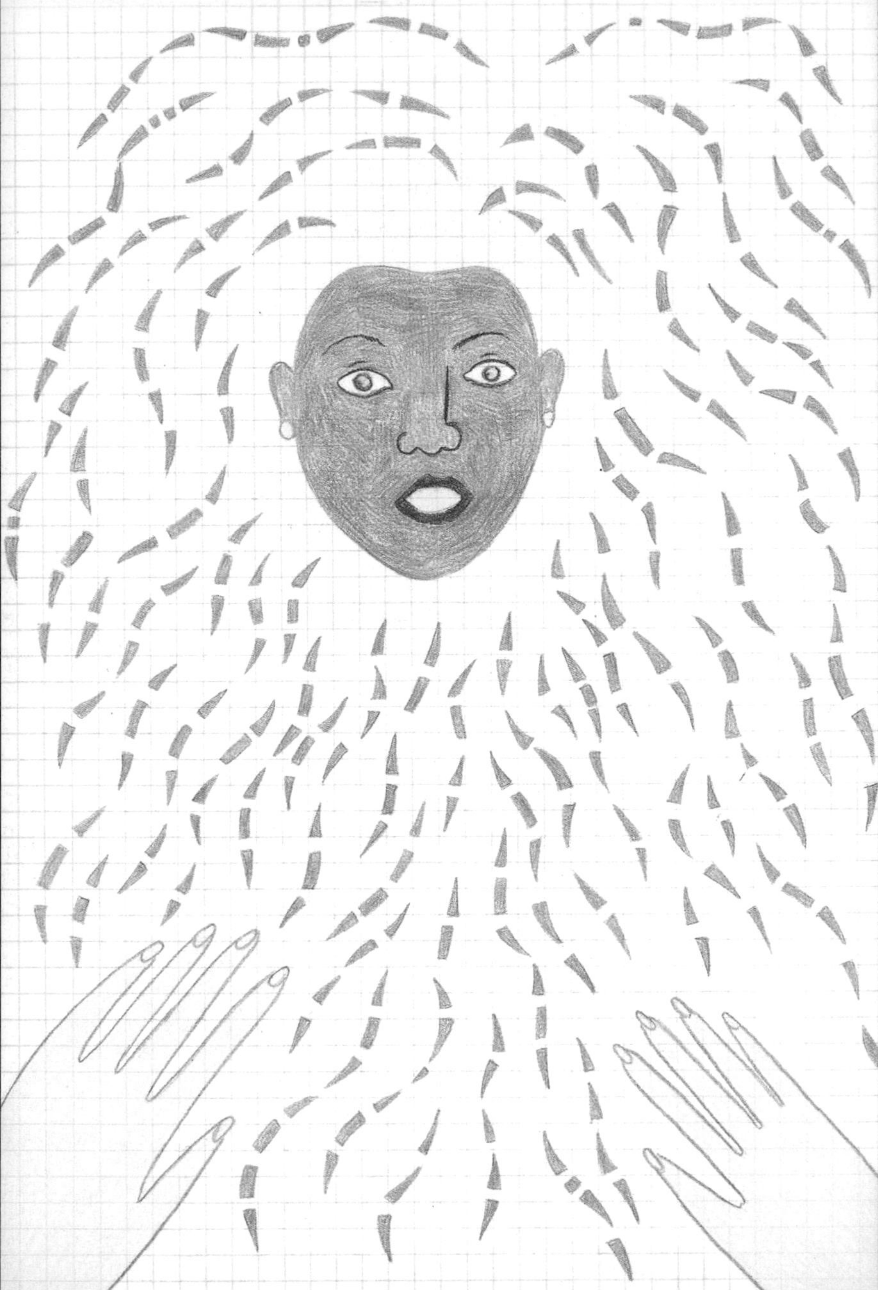

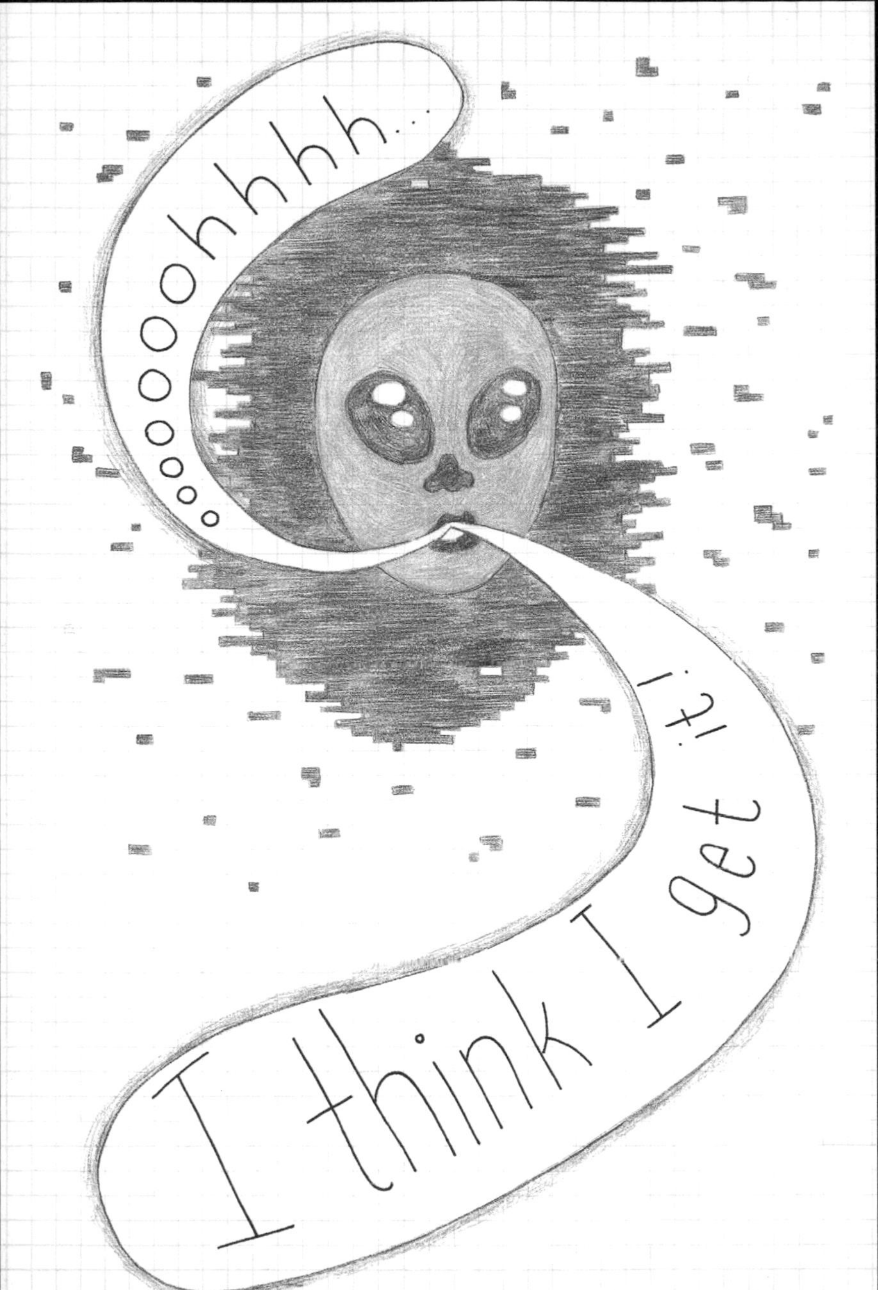

oooooooohhhh...
I think I get it!

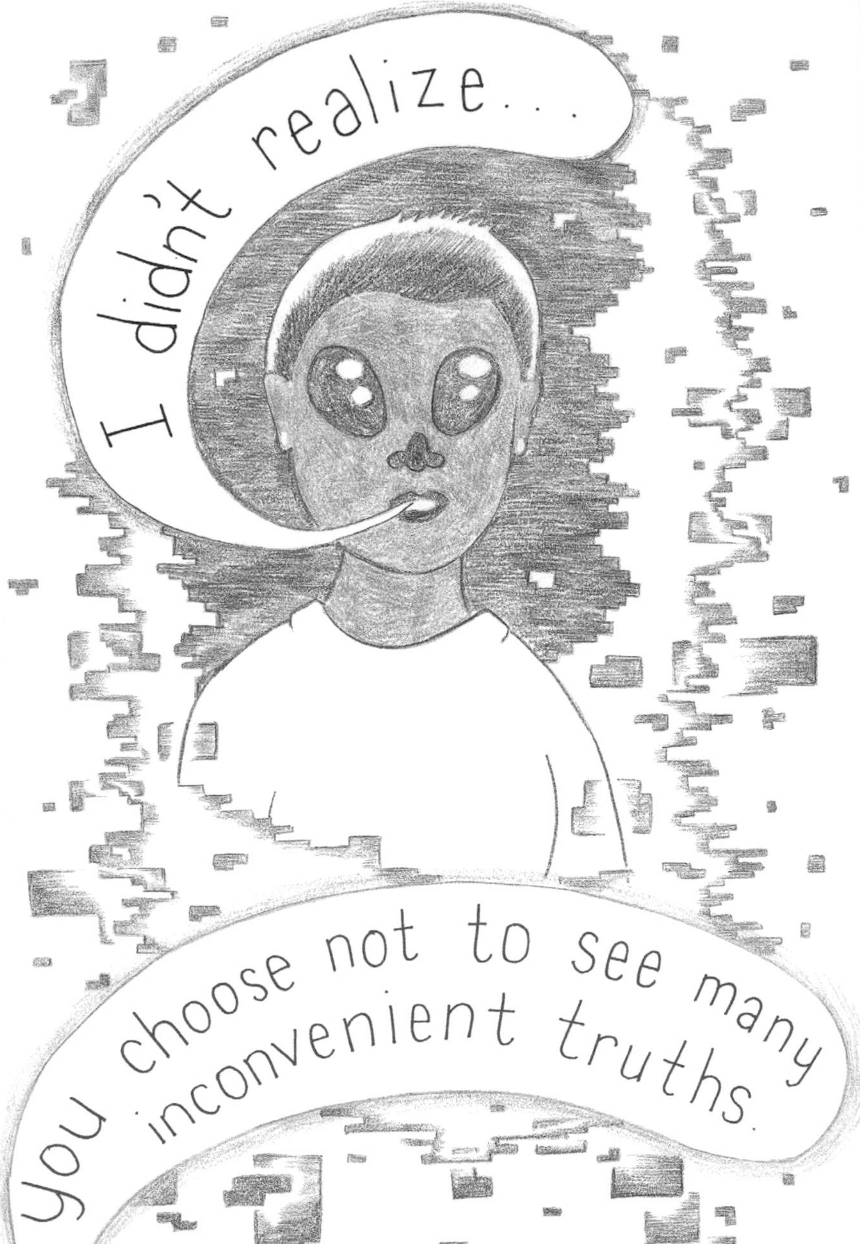
I didn't realize...
you choose not to see many inconvenient truths.

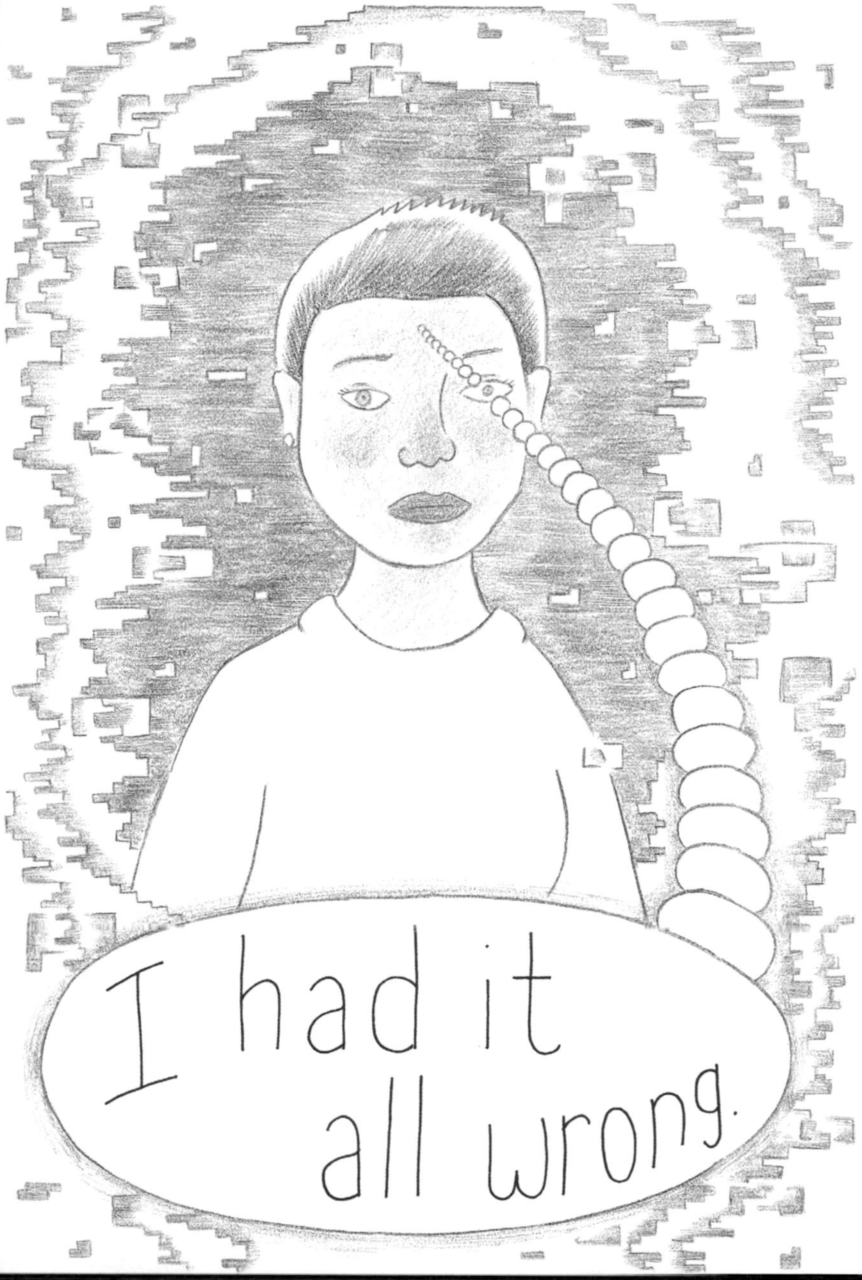
I had it all wrong.

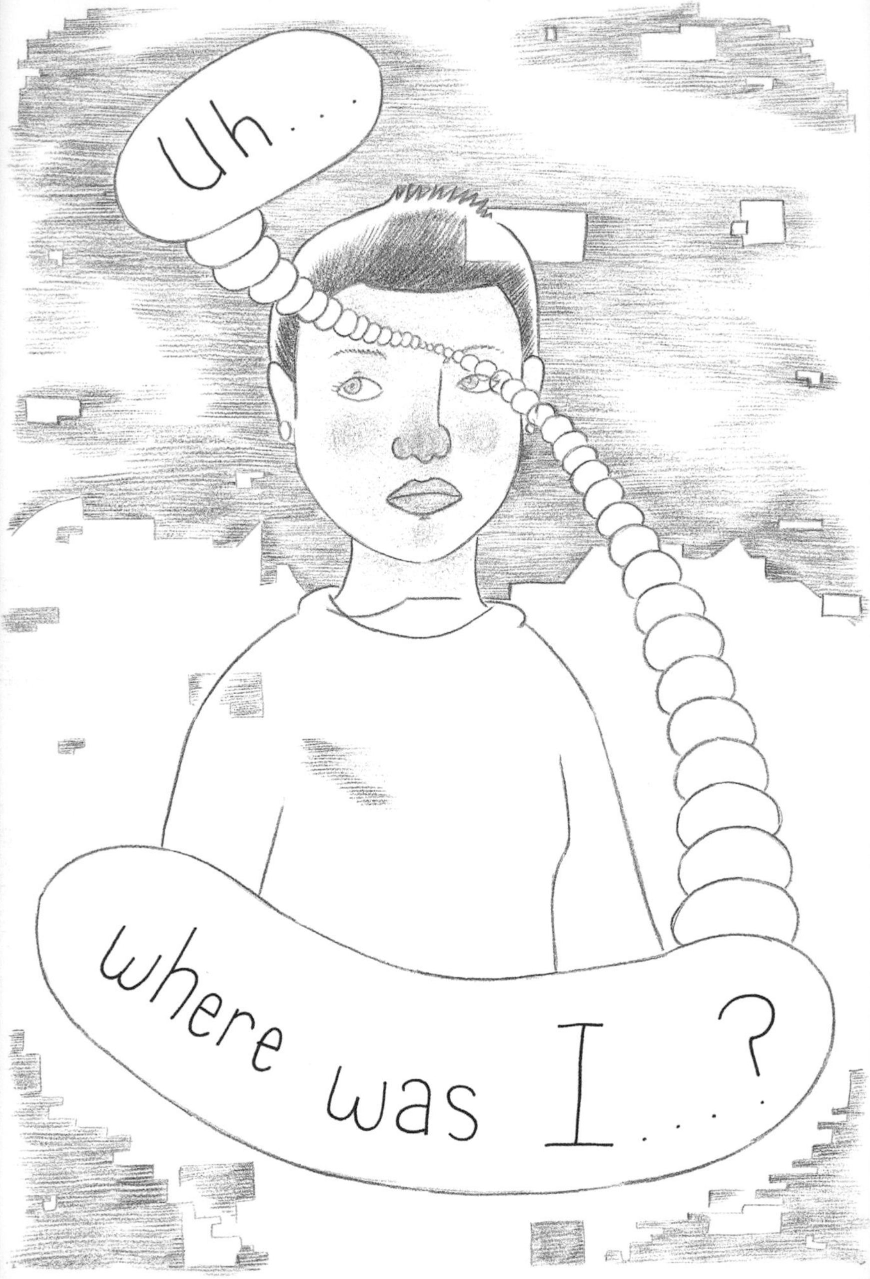
Uh...
where was I...?

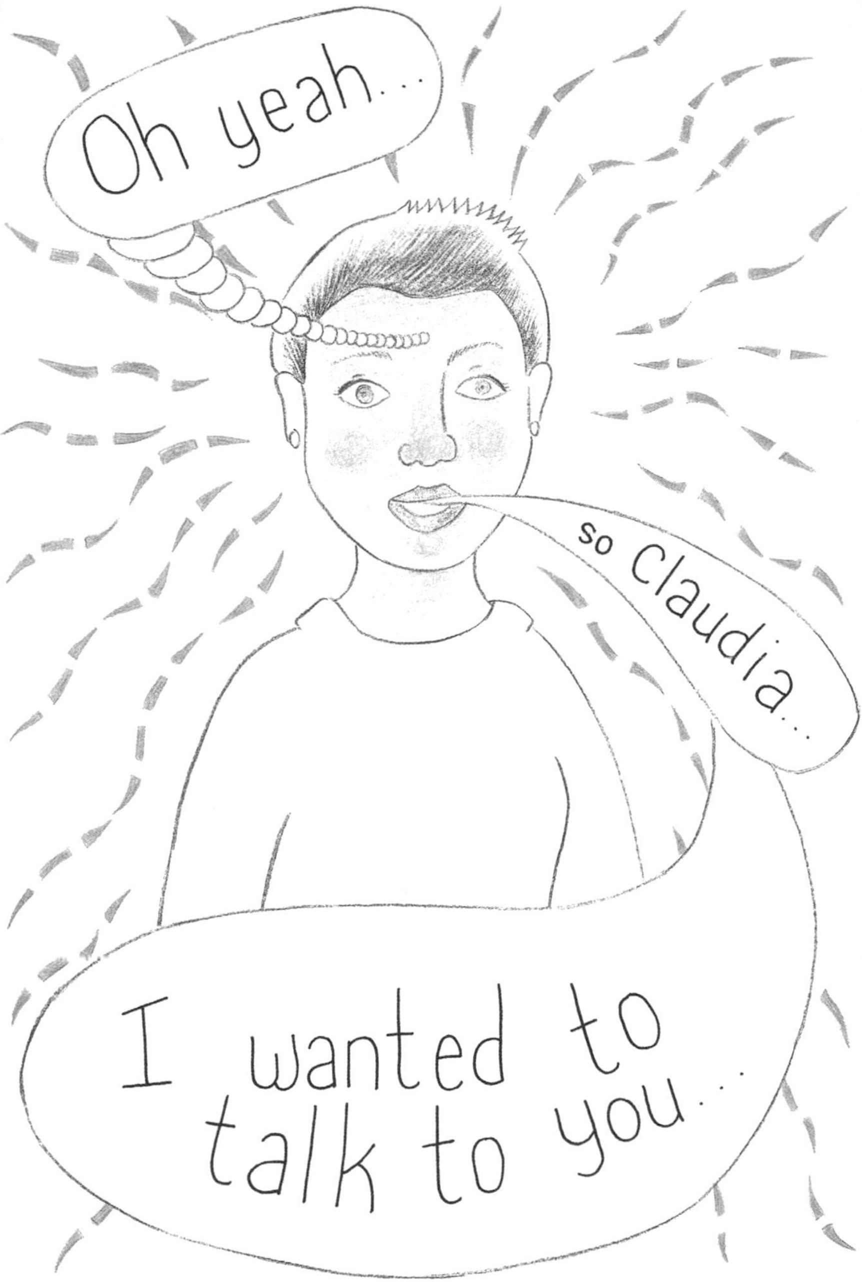
Oh yeah...
so Claudia...
I wanted to talk to you...

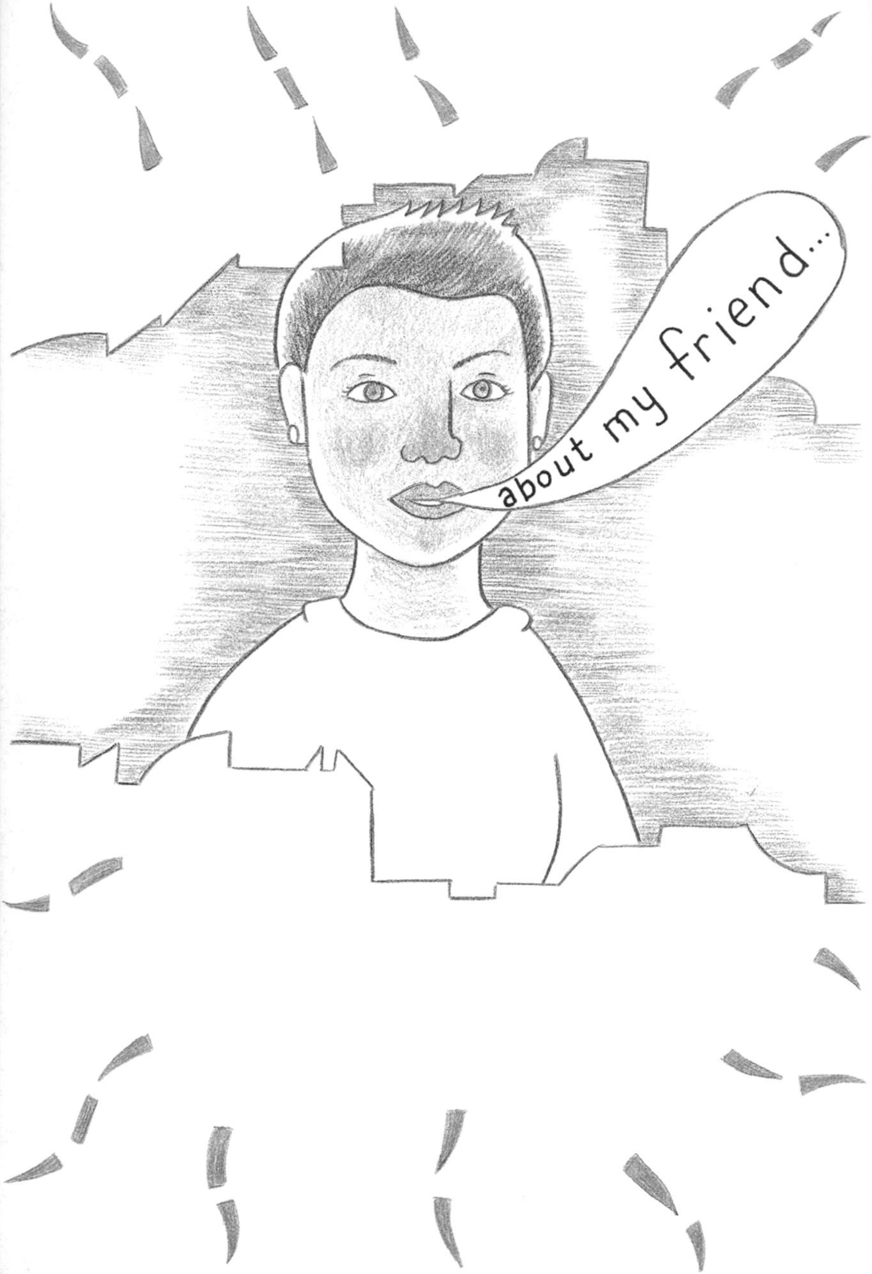
about my friend...

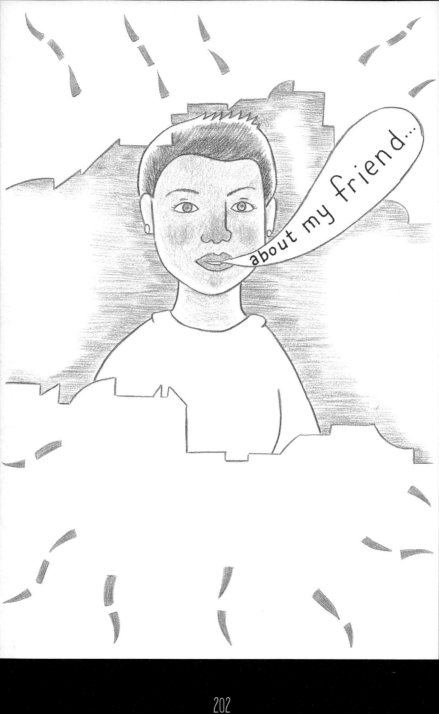

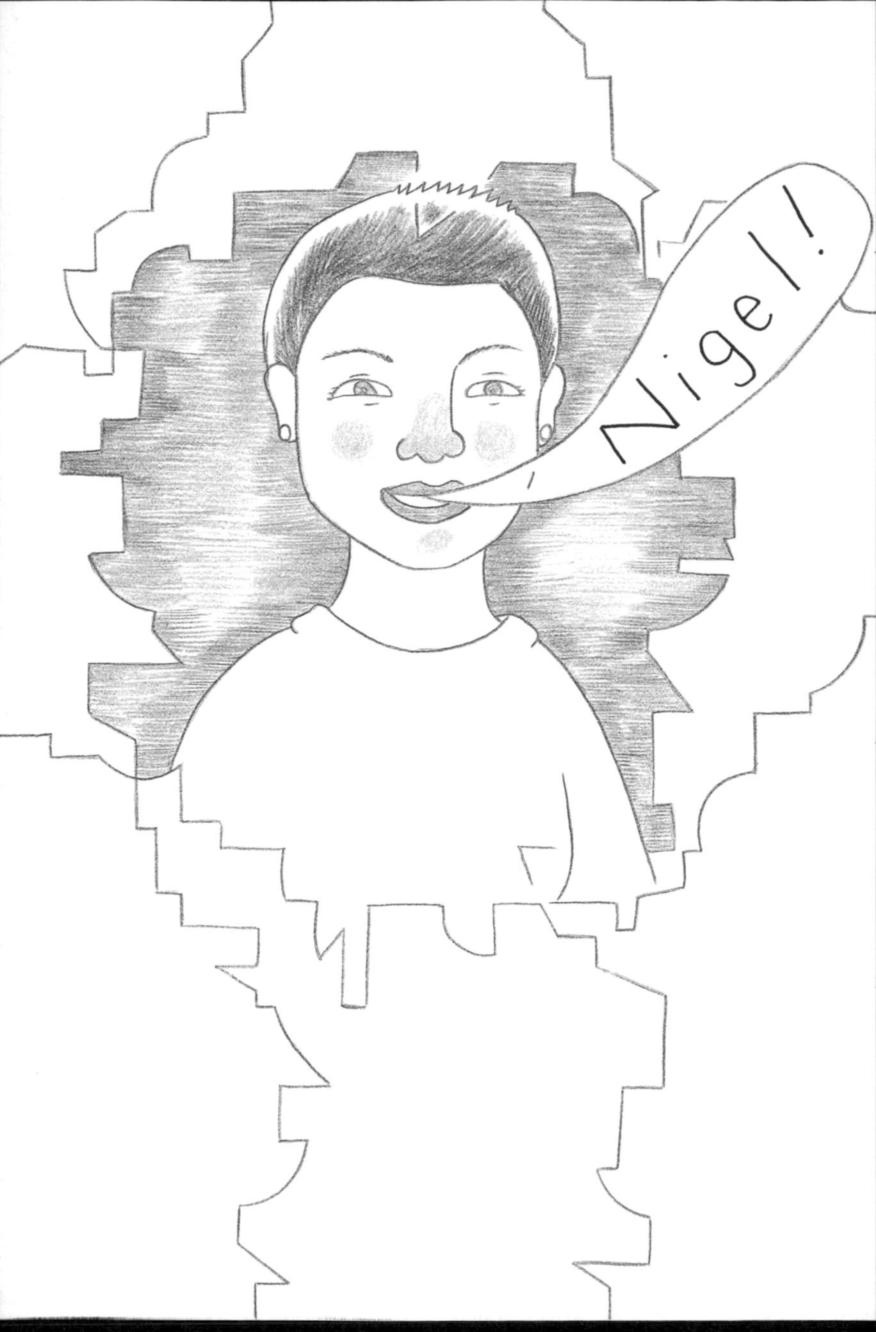
Nigel!

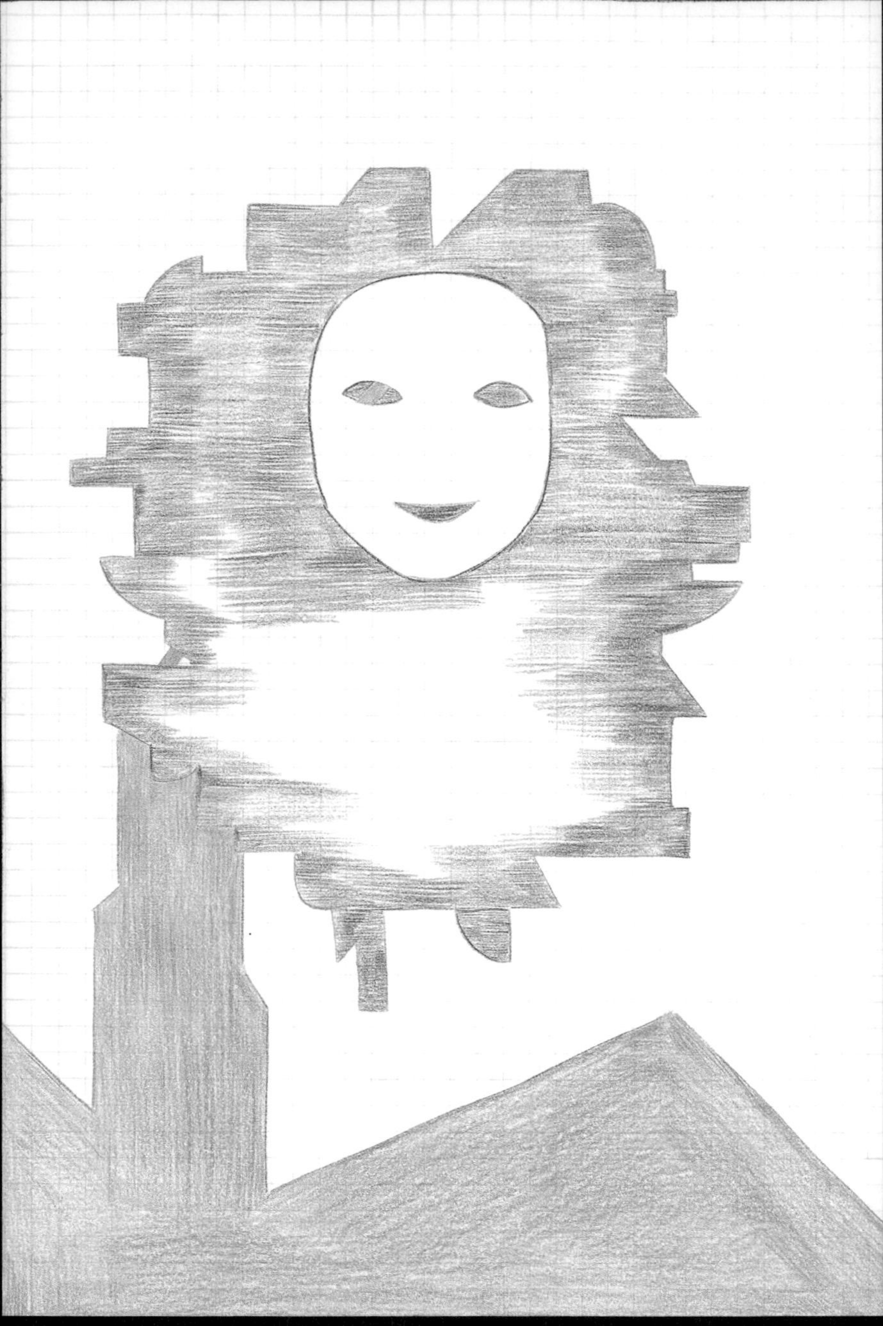

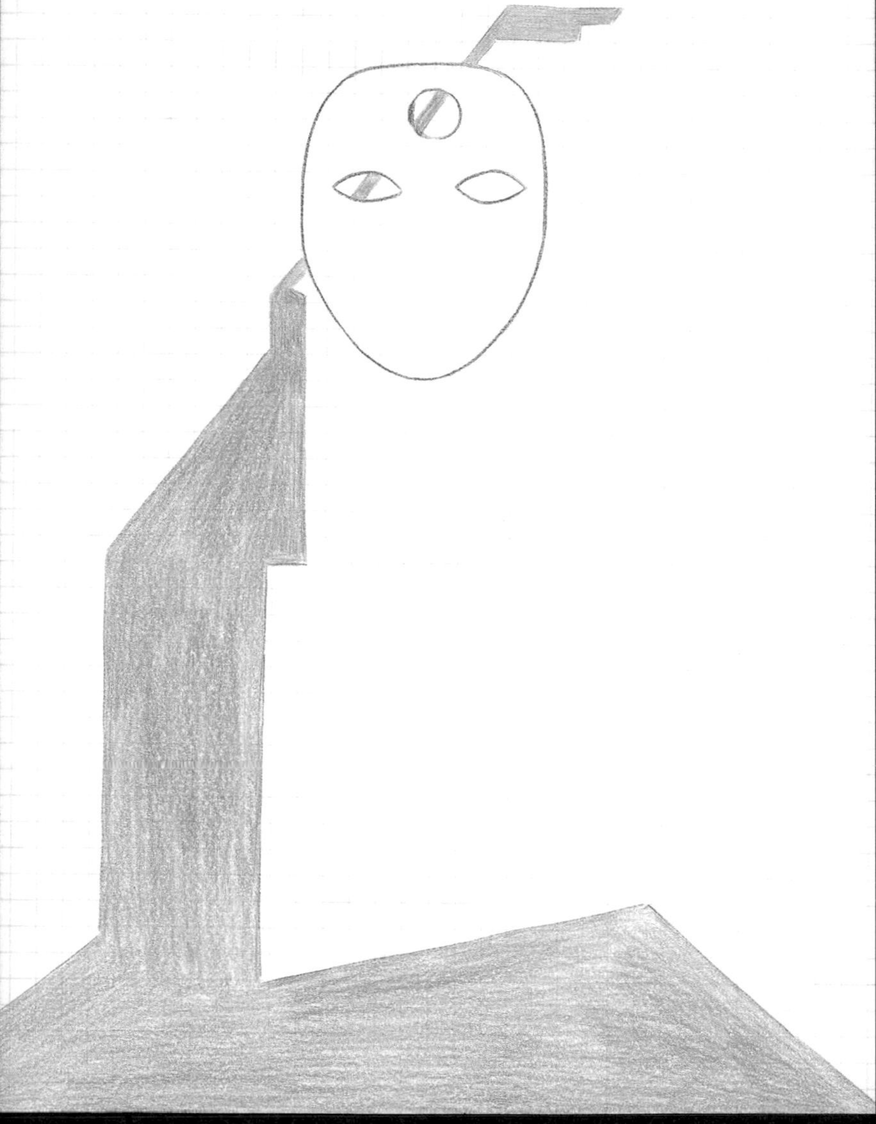

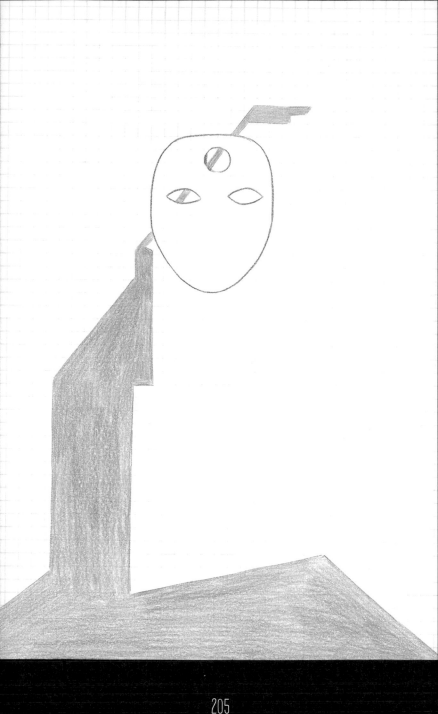

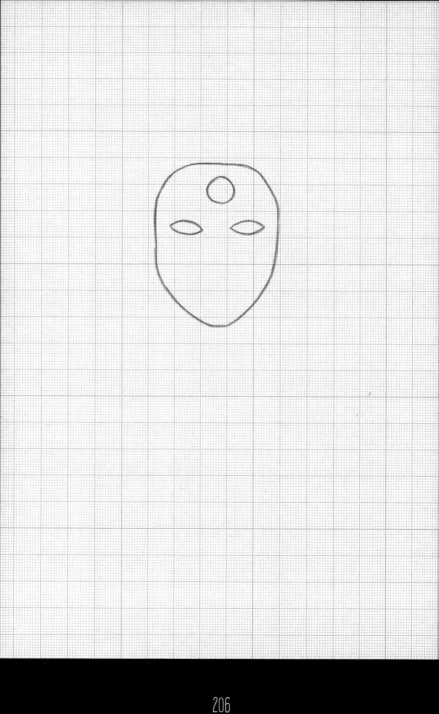

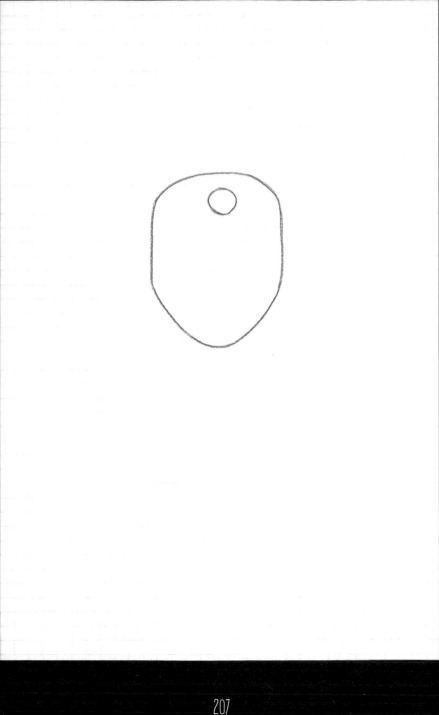

# PART SIX

Nigel Q. Jones

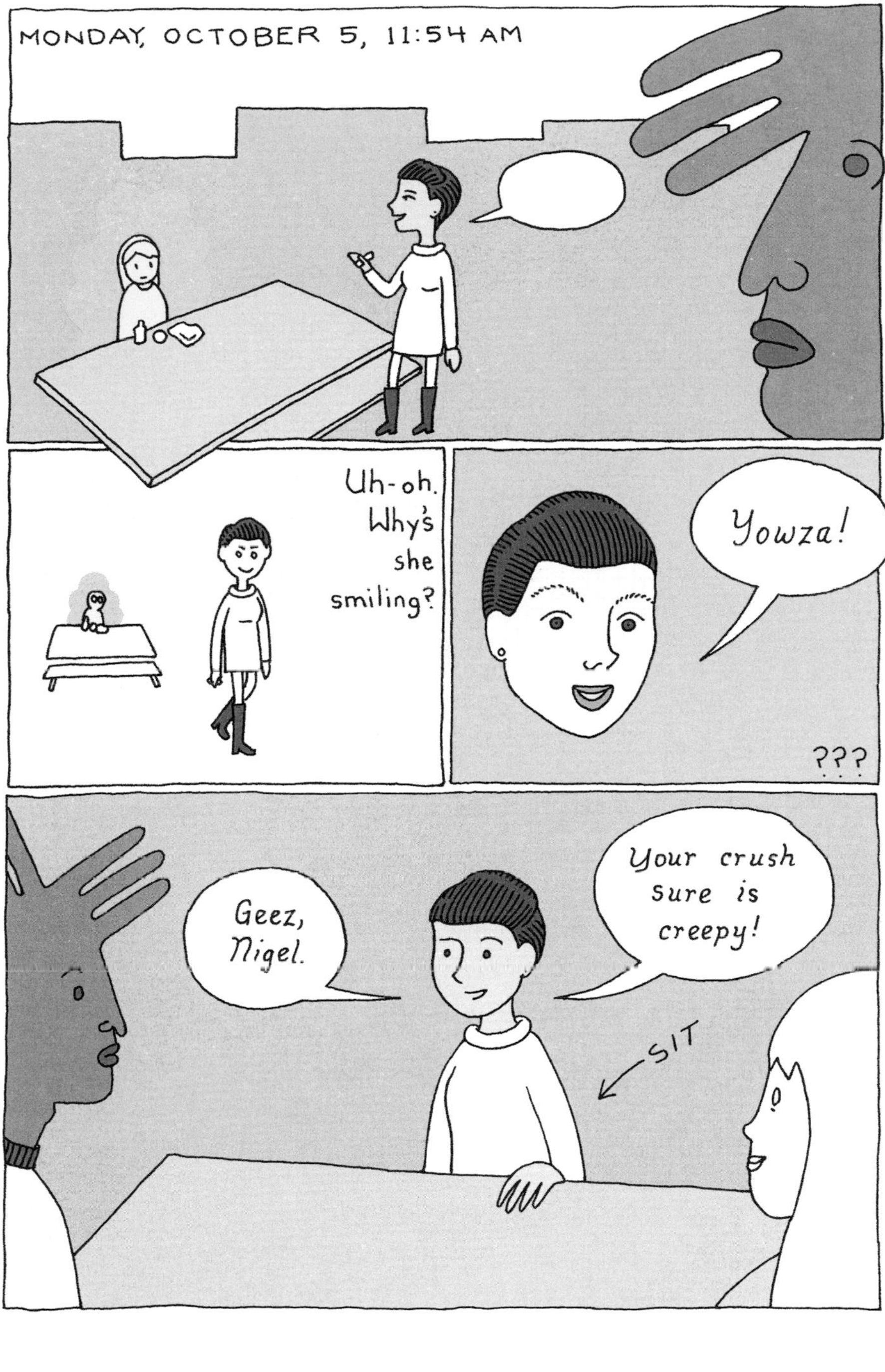
MONDAY, OCTOBER 5, 11:54 AM
Uh-oh. Why's she smiling?
Yowza!
???
Geez, Nigel.
Your crush sure is creepy!
SIT

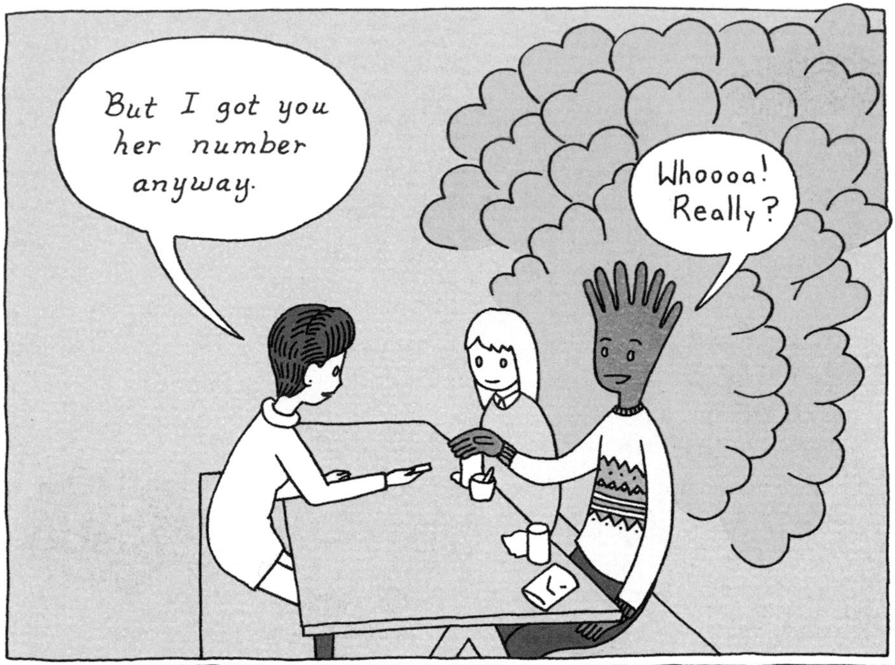
But I got you her number anyway.
Whoooa! Really?

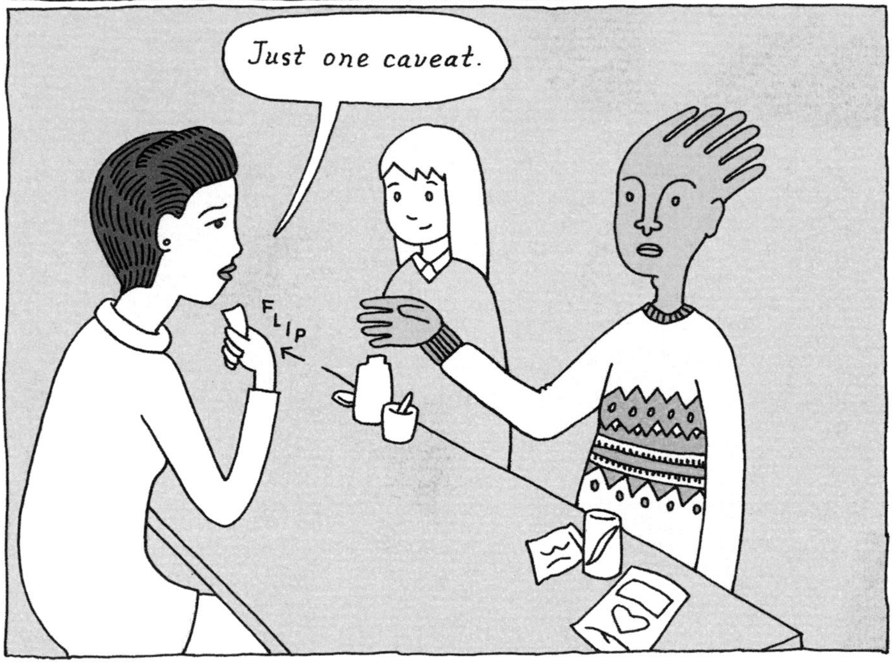
Just one caveat.
FLIP

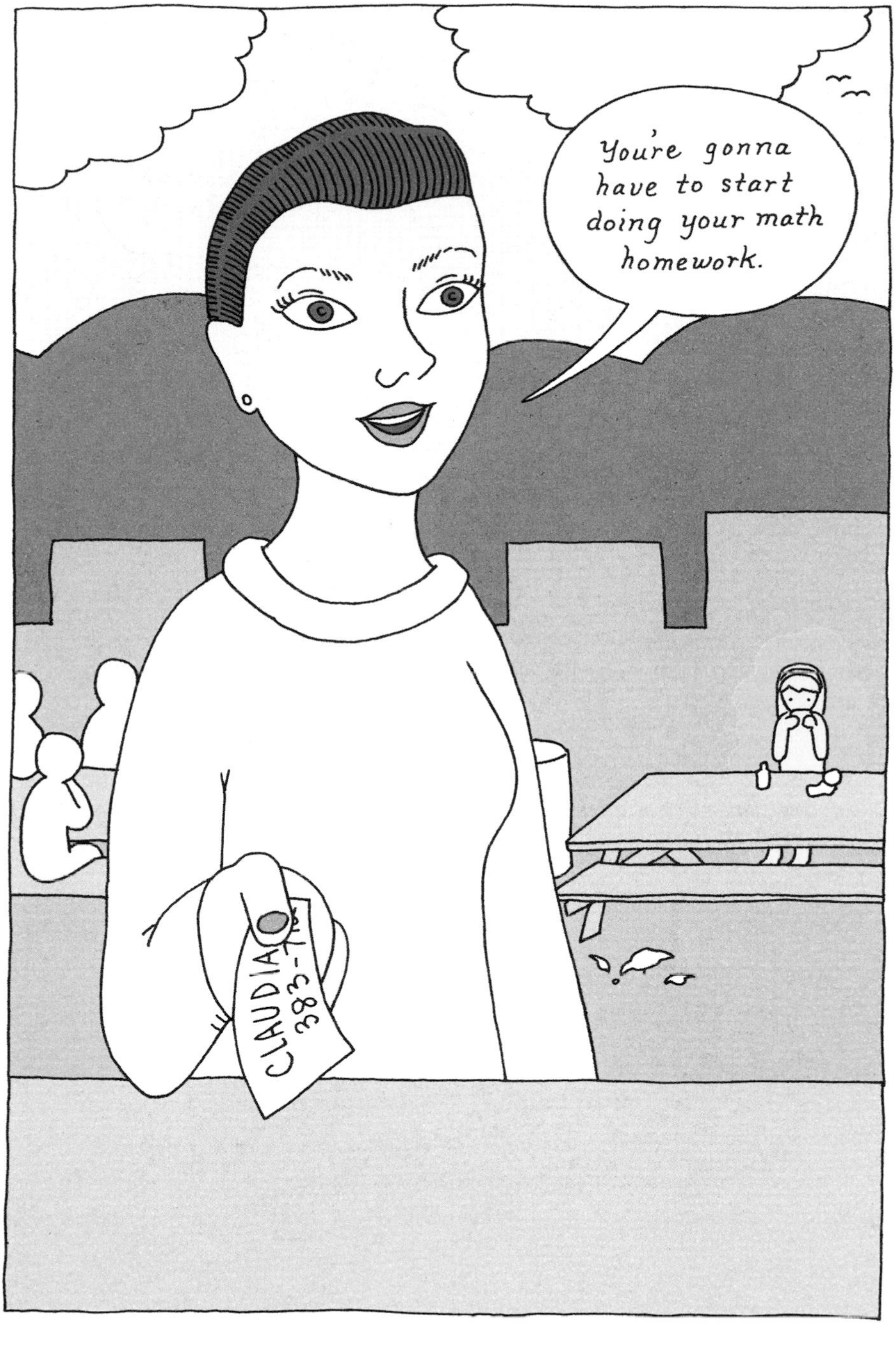
You're gonna have to start doing your math homework.
CLAUDIA
383-

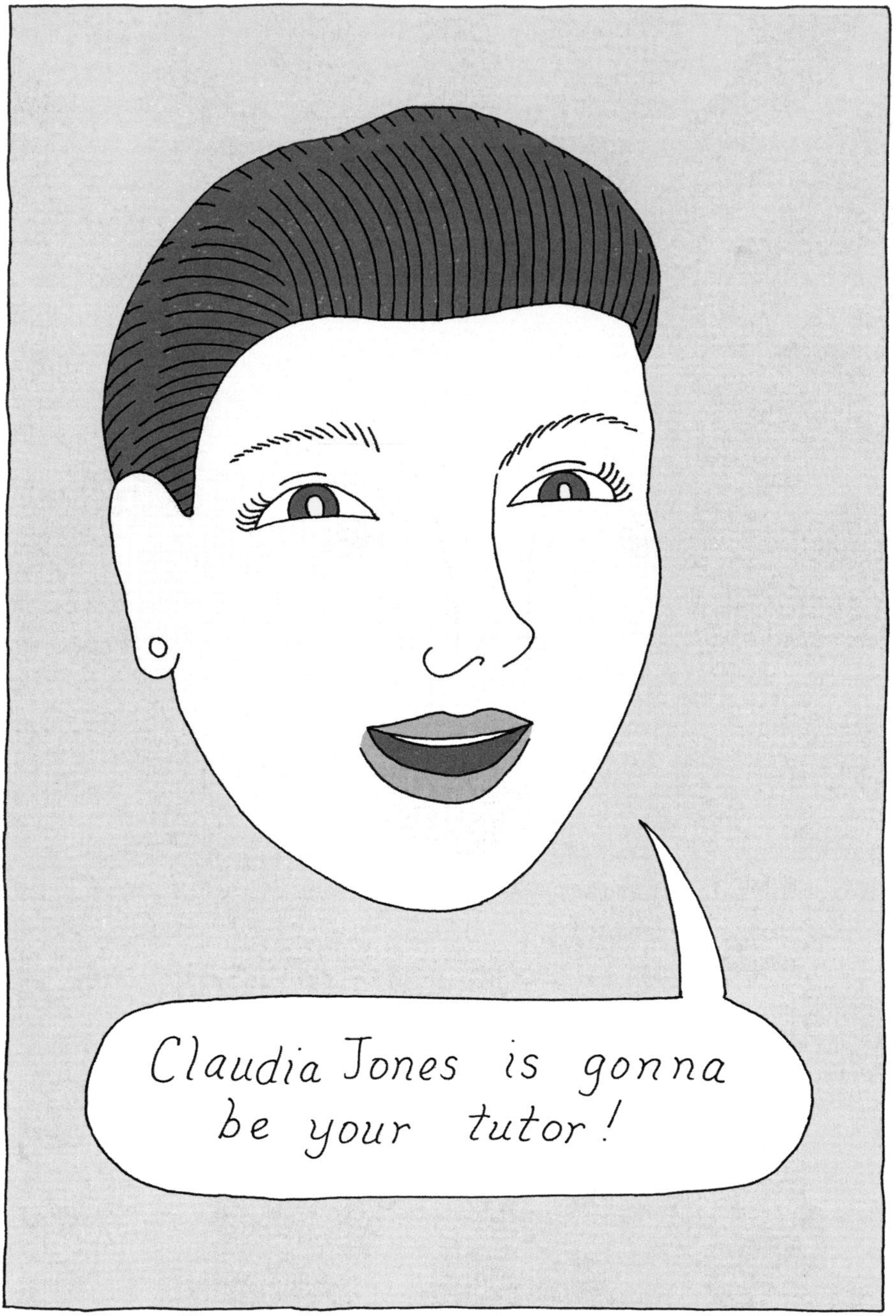
Claudia Jones is gonna be your tutor!

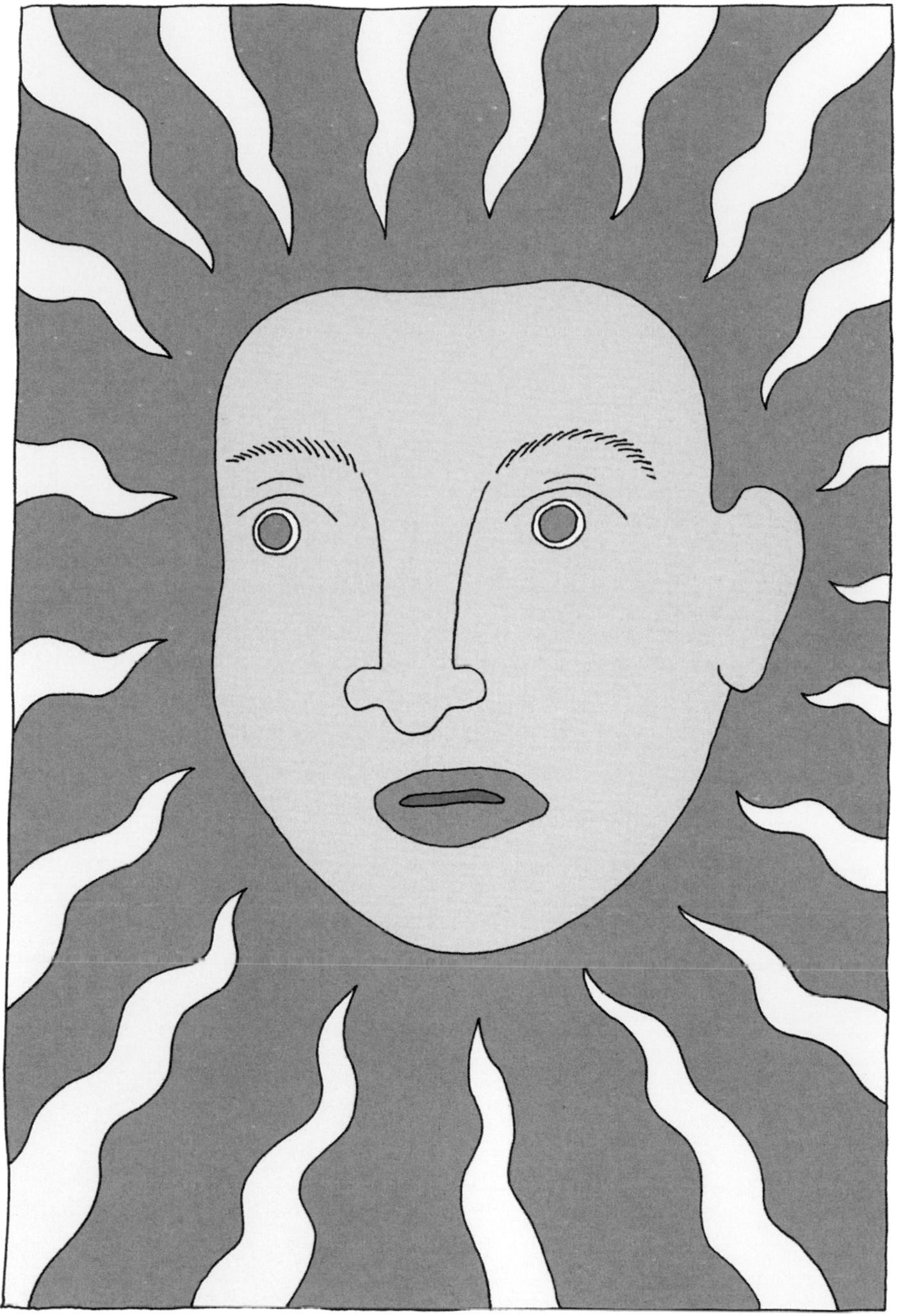

TO BE
CONTINUED...

# ACKNOWLEDGMENTS

A big double-thanks to everyone I thanked in book one. (You know who you are.) Thanks also to my Patreon subscribers, who have helped keep me afloat. Extra-special thanks to Gary, my muse, my partner in love, and accomplice in animal rescue.

# ABOUT THE AUTHOR

MariNaomi is the award-winning author and illustrator of four comics memoirs and the Life on Earth graphic novel trilogy. She's also the creator of the Cartoonists of Color and Queer Cartoonists databases, cohost of the *Ask Bi Grlz* podcast, and the caretaker of a menagerie of cats and dogs. Visit her at MariNaomi.com.